Robin Hood
FORBIDDEN LEGEND

AIRSHIP 27 PRODUCTIONS

Robin Hood: Forbidden Legend
© 2014 I.A. Watson

An Airship 27 Production
www.airship27.com
www.airship27hangar.com

Interior llustrations © 2014 Rob Davis
Cover Painting © 2014 Jesus Rodriguez

Editor: Ron Fortier
Associate Editor: Gordon Dymowski
Production and design by Rob Davis.

ISBN-13: 978-0692317754 (Airship 27)
ISBN-10: 0692317759

Printed in the United States of America

10 9 8 7 6 5 4 3 2 1

Robin Hood
Forbidden Legend
by I.a. watson

Contents:

Dedication:

This volume is dedicated to Rob and Ron, those merry men who have brought forth this series of Robin Hood adventures, and to the outlaw pulp creators who happily kibitzed on the name and content of this work: Bill Cunningham, Bobby Nash, Roman Leary, Robert Kennedy, Peter Miller, Mark Halegua, Ralph L. Angelo, James Palmer, Van Allen Plexico, and a cast of, well, several; laughing swashbuckling rogues the lot of them.

*W*hen the law no longer serves justice, justice must be an outlaw.

By winter of 1191 King Richard the Lionheart was eighteen months gone from England on crusade. Those noble counsellors he'd left to administer his kingdom had squabbled then warred with each other while Richard's younger brother and heir, Prince John "Lackland", fanned the conflict. Armed barons and rich office-holders took advantage of the times to do whatsoever they pleased.

Yet there was resistance. Men without rights or liberty whispered that in deep Sherwood Forest a company of free outlaws robbed from the rich and gave to the poor, mocking the powerful and bringing hope to the powerless. The cruel Sheriff of Nottingham was unable to catch them. Mighty Prince John had nightmares about them. Secret stories were told of these men, and wheresoever these outlaw tales were spoken rebellion flourished.

It was forbidden to speak of Robin Hood, yet everyone knew his name.

Prologue: Tales of Robin Hood

"**P**lease, milord!" the wandering entertainer cried, "'Tis naught but a bit of fun!" He clutched his cheek where the Norman lord's leather gauntlet had struck him.

Sir Guillot Ingram, Lord of Alfreton, glared at the rag-tag collection of performers in the marketplace, and at his own serfs and tenants who'd gathered for the mummers play. "*Fun?* Not if I read aright who you vagabonds are portraying." He pointed his finger at the fallen troupe-master. "You're dressed in green leaves with a bow. You're playing Robin i' the Hood, aren't you?"

"No, master, I swear it"

"You are. And that big fellow in the sheepskin's meant to be the giant they call Little John. The tonsured fellow plays the fat monk they call Friar Tuck. And the red-haired strumpet's being the girl Maid Marion. You're performing one of those scurrilous Robin Hood plays!"

"It's no harm," the plump fellow in the stained monk's habit pleaded. "Just a lark. Something to cheer folks up."

Sir Guillot's face reddened. "My villeins do not need to be happy. They need to be productive. They need to obey."

"We're not pretending to be Robin Hood and his merry men," the young ringleader on the ground insisted. "I swear it."

Sir Guillot gestured to some of the soldiers accompanying his treasure-cart. The master of Alfreton was due to render his knight's fee to his over-lord today so his tribute wagon was heavily guarded. He'd scarcely set foot from his fortress when he'd discovered this unauthorised revel outside Alfreton's moot-hall.

He pointed to the mummers. "Clap them in chains!" he commanded his soldiers.

But then the lad with the bow had a shaft aimed right at Sir Guillot. "Stand just where you are," he commanded. "I'm really not *pretending* to be Robin Hood!"

"W-what?" gasped the knight. "What's this?"

"John, Tuck, Scarlet, disarm the guards. Nobody else move or there'll be a new lord of Alfreton come tomorrow."

Fifty guards accompanied the treasure-wagons. They looked on helplessly as the vagabond players passed amongst them confiscating weapons. When the sergeant-at-arms looked like he might give fight the outlaw named Scarlet downed him with a savage head-butt.

Sir Guillot finally worked out what was happening. "You… you are Robin Hood!"

"He really is," Maid Marion admitted. "Apparently nothing can be done about it."

Little John whistled. More bandits broke from cover. Much the Miller's Son, David of Doncaster, Gilbert Whitehand, the poacher Arthur a Bland, and the pinder George a Green hastened up to remove the wagon.

Sir Guillot tried to keep one eye on the cart that contained a year's worth of squeezing his serfs for all they had and another on the grinning bowman who held him hostage. "You can't just steal that!" he objected.

Robin Hood disagreed. "We can. That is our Sherwood bad landlord tax. We hear everything in Sherwood. *You've* been a bad landlord. We know how you treat the people you're lord over. And now you've qualified for our personal attention."

The people of Alfreton watched in amazement as a mummer's play was performed that was much better than anything they'd expected when the rag-tag players had shuffled into the village.

"Tuck, what do you think Sir Guillot Ingram's due to render for his bad behaviour?" Hood asked.

The friar shrugged. "Well, Rob, there's quite a number of things he's got to regret. A good number of floggings, a few maids he's done wrong by, and enough other deeds to be a general blight and a miserable sinner. I'd say twenty lashes in the stocks will help him treat his folks better in future."

"Wait!" the knight objected. "You can't do that! I'm the lord of this manor! I'll have the Sheriff of Nottingham on you!"

"Maybe twenty-five lashes," Little John suggested.

Sir Guillot's disarmed guards looked on helplessly as their master was dragged to the pillory. The villagers of Alfreton watched with mounting delight that they tried hard to conceal.

"There'll be some goods heading back to you in a few days time," Marion whispered confidentially to the headwoman. "See that your lord knows nothing about them – when he's able to sit on his seat of office again."

"He's right that the Sheriff will hunt you down," the village elder warned.

"Hunting us is hard. Catching us is harder," the lady of Sherwood replied. "So far."

Richard the Lionheart sat in a plush chair that might have been a throne and watched the Sicilian sunset. Messina, though damaged by recent war, was beautiful.[1]

A discreet cough warned him of the approach of Walter de Coutances, Archbishop of Rouen. The administrator sweated heavily in the unaccustomed heat, mopping his brow with his ermine sleeve. He proffered a thick parchment scroll to the king.

The Lionheart gestured for the career administrator to take a stool beside him. "It's done?" Richard asked.

"It is done," Coutances promised. He laid the document on a salver beside his monarch. "Do you want to hear all the points?"

"What do you think?" The monarch's disdain for the trivia of rulership was plain in his growl.

"The brief summary, then. In exchange for you and your armies getting on your ships and sailing on to the Crusade, King Tancred grants you pretty much everything you wanted. Your sister Joan gets 20,000 ounces of gold as compensation for the inheritance Tancred cheated her of when her husband died. When your cousin and heir Arthur of Brittany comes of age, Tancred will supply one of his daughters as bride.[2] And he'll pay you another 20,000 now as advance dowry - as long as you leave quickly."

Richard snorted. The usurper King of Sicily had changed his attitude after the Lionheart had captured and ravaged Messina. Richard's crusader forces, travelling to the Levant at the Pope's call for a third crusade, had quickly shown themselves more organised, effective, and brutal than any-

---

1   Tancred of Lecce seized power in Sicily, imprisoned the widow of the former king and confiscated her inheritance. Unfortunately this Queen Joan was the Lionheart's sister and he took exception to it. Richard, en route to his crusade, conquered Messina, released his sister, and forced Tancred to pay her 20,000 ounces of gold – around $25 million in modern money - as compensation.

2   Arthur of Brittany was the son of Geoffrey, Richard's late brother. Because Geoffrey had been older than John, his child preceded John in line for the throne of England. When Richard I was on his deathbed in 1199 he was concerned that Arthur, then only twelve years old, was too much under the influence of the King of France. He therefore named Prince John his heir in preference to his nephew. At the age of 15 Arthur fought against John in Normandy but was captured by John's barons. He was imprisoned at the Château de Falaise and then at Rouen. The following year, 1203, he vanished from history. It was commonly supposed the John had murdered the boy. The *Margam Annals* claims, "After King John had captured Arthur and kept him alive in prison for some time, at length, in the castle of Rouen, after dinner on the Thursday before Easter, when he was drunk and possessed by the devil, he slew him with his own hand, and tying a heavy stone to the body cast it into the Seine."

thing the locals had ever seen.

"What about Philip?" the king asked.

Philip II was King of France, the Lionheart's great rival and occasional enemy. The two men had taken the crusader vow together and had set off to the Holy Land in each other's company. Neither dared leave the other behind to take advantage of a royal absence. Philip and his French knights were also on the island.

"Philip is finally willing to absolve you of your vow to marry his sister Alys," Walter de Coutances reported.

"I should think so, after his plots with Tancred to see me dead," Richard snarled. "That betrothal was arranged by my father when I was an infant. *And* my father got my supposed bride with child."

"Dowager Queen Eleanor has a different girl in mind for you," Coutances understood. The Lionheart was much influenced by his mother's advice.

"So I gather. Anyhow, Tancred's given in, Philip's ready to sail on to Acre, and we can all get on now, yes?"

"I suppose that's the very short summary," Richard's administrator admitted.

The Lionheart relented and smiled a little. "You've done well for me, Walter – again. And you know what that means."

"Another set of insoluble problems somewhere else?"

"I'm afraid so."

"What and where, majesty?"

Richard sighed. "Do you remember in the last crusade, the deeds of a knight called Sir Richard at the Lee?"

Coutances was well informed. "He stood alone against a Saracen horde, saved some holy relic? An old ally of your father's. Good reputation as a fighter and as a man. He must be ancient now."

"Yes. His oldest son's amongst my young paladins out there, eager for Paynim blood. It's his youngest daughter and son where the problems start."

"How so, majesty?"

Richard gestured to a packet of courier papers newly-arrived from England. There were two score of reports and letters in different hands. Each told tales and made complaints about one or more of the other correspondents.

"My slack-jawed brother John decided to seduce Sir Richard's daughter. Presumably to upset the old man, or to make a statement to the barons about his power, or maybe just sheer pigheaded lust. She turned him down. Hard."

Coutances brows rose. "Brave girl."

"Very. So John got vindictive as John does. He went after her family. The boy Adam Fitzwarren got provoked into a duel-brawl with one of John's favourites and accidentally killed him. My brother had his newly-installed Sheriff of Nottingham imprison the lad and try to fine Sir Richard Fitzwarren into oblivion. And to blackmail the girl into John's bed after all. Malicious, nasty stuff."

"The Fitzwarrens are great in reputation but not in fortune or power," Walter of Coutances judged. "Some good family ties, perhaps, but..."

The Lionheart held up a hand to cut his advisor's assessment short. "The girl, Matilda, found her own champion," the king explained. "Or so half these letters of complaint tell me. She took up with an outlaw, some forest wolfshead called Robin in the Hood, leader of the masterless men of Sherwood Forest."

"Can masterless men have a leader?"

"They do now," the king exclaimed. "England's buzzing with news of them. They beat John's forces when he tried to take them by force. They made his new Sheriff look like an idiot."

"Your brother does have a knack for turning triumph into disaster," Coutances admitted.

"Oh, it gets better. Turns out this Robin Hood is a bastard of the Earl of Huntingdon, and Huntingdon's acknowledged him."

"Isn't Huntingdon sailing out to join us on crusade?"

"Yes. And he's evidently well pleased with his new son. More, Longchamp, my own Lord Chancellor, justiciar set to govern England in my absence, has given Hood a pardon. And my half-brother Geoffrey, supposed Archbishop of York, has given the Sherwood king a blessing."

Coutances frowned. "It's strange, I'll grant. I don't see what I..."

"Oh, that's just the start of it," Richard warned. "I left two justiciars to reign in England in my stead, to keep an eye on my brother and half-brother. De Puiset and Longchamp were meant to work together for my interests. Instead they've gone to war with each other! Then de Puiset versus Geoffrey. Then Longchamp versus John. Then John and the barons. Then the barons and Longchamp. And so on." The king rubbed his forehead. His crown was heavy sometimes. "Mother is furious. The Pope's been dragged into it. And somewhere in the middle of all, in a way I can't quite fathom, this Robin Hood and the Fitzwarren girl keep popping up, interfering."

Walter de Coutances could see where this was going. "You want me to sail to England."

"You'll take my warrant. Find out what's going on. Dismiss or exile any-one who won't listen to you. Work out how Huntingdon's bastard fits into this. *Sort it out.*"

"I'll sail at once," agreed Coutances.

"And send me Sir Mark Fitzwalter," the Lionheart commanded. "I want to ask him about his sister."

Malkyn and Cedony were dragged out of their father's hovel and tied with tether-ropes to the back of the affeeror's[3] cart. Their father knew bet-ter than to protest any more, or he'd get worse than a crop across his face. He had four other children to worry about. His pretty elder daughters were lost to him.

"I'll let you know the price they fetch and remit it from your debt," Cor-vin of Blodworth assured the villein labourer. He gestured for his carter to start the wagon moving.

"Where are you taking us?" Malkyn demand as the cart clattered away from Woodbarrow. She tried to struggle but the ox set a steady, implacable pace, dragging the captives behind the wagon.

"Nottingham," Corvin told her. "You're slaves now, taken in compensa-tion for your family's debt. There's a tavern-keeper on Pilchergate pays fair coin for pretty girls. We've done business before."

Cedony blanched. "You mean a bawdy house? No! We'll not…!"

"You will," the affeeror promised. "There's ways of training new whores, and a month from now there'll be nowhere else fit for you anyhow. A week."

The girls' protests were interrupted as a pair of anxious young men broke from cover and scrambled down a bramble bank to catch the wagon. "Hold! Stop!" one called. "Please, sir! Halt!"

Corvin didn't travel alone. Three archers turned on the newcomers. An-other four burly guards held staves or blades. All of them prepared to deal with the rash interlopers.

"Please, don't take t' lasses!" the other lad cried in a thick Yorkshire accent. "We'll pay thee! We have coin. See?" He held open a pouch and showed gold within.

The affeeror gestured for a guard to bring him the money. The five coins were ancient, so old that the wreathed head of the emperor they depicted

---

3   An affeeror was a medieval manorial official responsible for setting and collecting fines and penalties – for a late tax payment, for example.

could hardly be discerned. But they were gold; Roman gold! "Where did you get these?" Corvin demanded of the youths.

"From the old well," the first lad replied, as if that explained it all. He seemed sharper than the other, but that wasn't saying much. "Is it enough to buy back Malkyn and Cedony? Please?"

The coins were more than enough to settle all Woodborough's debts, but the affeeror wasn't going to tell that to two country bumpkins. "Hardly a quarter of what's due," he snorted. "You'll need a better price than this to save these two little doves from the sweaty stews."

The dumber of the two looked as if he'd object. The guards tensed to hack him down if he attacked. The other lad held him back.

"A hard life for your sweethearts," Corvin predicted. "Shackled to a grubby pallet with twenty men a day climbing on 'em. Raddled and knocked up, used to crones in a couple of years at most, if they live that long. Better to buy 'em free from that life if you can. Better to pay their debts now, before we camp for the night and give 'em a taste of the fate that awaits them."

"We can get more gold," the youth promised. "From t' well."

"What well?"

"Hidden in't wood," the other lad explained. "There's this right old shaft, all covered wi' brambles and such, but if you squirm down it and reach into t' water there's…"

"Hush," the other chid him. "We can get you your gold, master. How much must we bring?"

"Ah, no," Corvin grinned. "That's not the way it works, boys. Y'see, there's eight of us, armed and with authority, and you two yokels all by yourselves. Take us to this well and we won't break your knees. If there's gold enough you can have the wenches and be off with you. Try and run, cross me in any way and there's naught but sorrow for all four of ye."

The lads argued some more, but Corbin could tell from the slant of their shoulders that he'd already won. He left a guard on the cart and took the rest into the thick forest with the boys. His men dragged Malkyn and Cedony along too, to ensure their swains' behaviour.

"Mal," whispered Cedony to her sister as they were bundled down a narrow woodland path. "Those lads are…"

"I know who they are," Malkyn hissed back. "Now shush!"

Much the Miller's Son and David, champion boxer of Doncaster, led the soldiers to the old Roman well. Corvin hadn't expected an old man to be there.

"What's this?" the affeeror demanded. "Who are you?"

"Why, aren't I keeper of the well?" the ragged-robed stranger replied. "If you want to dip into it then you'll need to pay me first."

"And why would I do that? Step aside, dotard, or be beaten."

"If you don't pay then the curse of the well falls on you. Devils rise from the forest and punish the wicked. Judgement comes on those who transgress the ancient laws."

Corvin strode forward to buffet the old man out of the way. The guardian of the well dodged his punch and returned a thunderous fist to rattle the affeeror's head.

Devils appeared from the forest; devils in Lincoln green, with longbows and quarterstaves and bright well-kept swords.

Robin cast back his hood and glared at the affeeror. The guardian of the well hadn't lied. "Take all they have," he told his merry men. "Strip 'em to the skin. John, dump Corvin of Blodworth down this well he was so interested in. Head first. Chances are he'll be able to wriggle out in a few days."

"No!" gasped the affeeror. "Wait! You mustn't…!"

Marion blazed him to silence. "You were ready to sell these girls to destruction! If ever you serve evil men again I swear you'll reap worse than ever you gave!"

There was a scream and a splash, and a round of outlaw laughter.

David and Much cut Malkyn and Cedony loose. The girls hugged the boys. They'd once shared a memorable night in a Woodbarrow barn.[4] "You rescued us!" Cedony gasped, hardly able to believe their turn of fortune. "Like in the stories."

"That's what we do," David assured her.

"We're with Robin Hood," Much explained earnestly.

"With Robin Hood you are," laughed the King of Sherwood. "And now, lasses, you must decide what you're to do. Return to your home, if you will. We'll pay your debts from what this affeeror carried on his person and cart but beware another coming to take you as Corvin was sent. Two fair serf lasses are tempting targets. Or we'll see you safe to kin elsewhere, and a new start. Or there's work at Marion's manors, at Leaford or Verysdale. Or…"

"There's room in Sherwood," David noted. It wasn't often that the city boy blushed.

"A number of girls take refuge with us at the Major Oak for a time," Marion explained. "Safely."

"Safe as they want to be," Gilbert Whitehand chuckled coarsely.

The sisters consulted with each other and made their decision. "Please,

"Step aside, dotard, or be beaten."

Robin Hood and Lady Marion," Malkyn answered, still entwined with David of Doncaster, "May we go into the forest and be free?"

The Chancellor of England, Bishop of Ely, papal legate, keeper of the Tower of London, lawmaker, put down his quill and rubbed his eyes. It was very late. Even his servants and scribes dozed in their cubicles. William de Longchamp worked long hours that few other men could endure.

He was not surprised, though, when his youngest sister Melisend ventured round the door, bearing a fresh candle and a hot posset.

"Gramercy," Longchamp told her. The Chancellor relied upon his family. Each was carefully placed, as abbot, chief clerk, castellan, or other office holder. His sisters were wed in alliance to powerful knights and barons, save for Melisend who awaited such a betrothal. With her angel's looks and delicate grace she was an asset to be spent carefully. The Longchamps were not many generations from obscurity, but by William's efforts they had risen to be the richest family in England, Richard the Lionheart's closest supporters.

"Adam has returned," Melisend told her brother. "Adam Fitzwarren, that is."

Longchamp pursed his lips. He liked the young courier who had been a year in his service. The novice knight had none of the swagger yet all of the courage of the Chancellor's best men. But he was a youngest son, of a crusader great in reputation but not in fortune, and there could be no attachment between him and Melisend.

"Has he word of his outlaw kin?" Longchamp asked wryly.

Melisend defended the young knight. "His sister's wife to Robin Fitz-Huntingdon, a recognised bastard of Earl David, of the Scottish royal line. Didn't you write Robin Hood a pardon and seal it with your own hands?"

"A year since, yes, to prevent civil war in the north and York burning. Prince John overplayed his hand. If I hadn't intervened there'd have been chaos."

"So Adam's brother-in-law brings him no shame. In fact Robin Hood has the goodwill of every peasant in England, whether they're compassed by Sherwood or not."

"And the ill-will of every lord's taxman he halts on the road to steal from, and every rich traveller he dines then tithes," Longchamp objected. "Most men receive a pardon then *stop* breaking the law."

"There's no proof it's him. Anyone can call himself Robin i' th' Hood."

"And anyone can go about with a giant of a shepherd called Little John, and a fat recusant friar named Tuck, and a mad soldier dubbed Scarlet and who knows how many other forest outlaws, drawing squeals of complaint from Sheriffs and Bishops and half the nobility of the land?"

Melisend knelt at her brother's knee, looking up into his tired face. "Those forest men are worth as much to you as an army. In fact they are an army. Robin's people go anywhere and everywhere. The common folk talk to them as they'd never talk to your agents. Through the outlaws of Sherwood you have eyes and ears in every manor, in every castle, in every town and village across England. Through Matilda Fitzwarren—Maid Marion—and her father Sir Richard at the Lee, you have a call on the allegiances of Huntingdon, the Fitzwalters, the Bigods, de Percy, de Manderville, Greystoke, a whole network of interconnected and influential families with strong ties to this country, nor split between here and Normandy. And Hood himself has proved most effective at curbing the ambitions of the Sheriff of Nottingham and many other unscrupulous politicians."

Longchamp snorted. That last part was especially true. It was a measure of the audacious outlaw lord's success that William de Vendenal, High Sheriff of Nottingham, had once placed enough bounty on Robin Hood's head to purchase a small castle.

"Robin Hood is not on my side," the Chancellor recognised. "We simply have mutual enemies."

"All life is a tangle of duties and loyalties," Melisend argued. "You taught me that. But really William, you shouldn't underestimate the power of those tavern songs and village stories. Robin Hood has fired the imagination of the common people and there's a lot more of them then there are of John's army, or De Puiset's, or yours! Do you want to be in the songs along with the Sheriff of Nottingham, butt of every joke? Or do you want a brave, clever, moral ally who'll hold with you as long as you hold with the people?"

"Adam and his family have a passionate advocate, I see," Longchamp observed.

Melisend tried not to blush. "There are many in your service for venal, selfish reasons. Sir Adam at the Lee is not one of them. I just wanted to remind you of that."

"You know, however, that there are limits to how I can favour him," the Chancellor warned. He looked sharply at his sister. "Don't you, Melisend?"

"Of course I do. I'm not naive. I know that... well, I know." The lady looked down, her beautiful face pale in the candlelight.

"Those Sherwood rebels have a habit of stealing away noble women," Longchamp warned. "Lady Matilda was destined for a high alliance. She caught the eye of Prince John himself, before she spoiled the romance by crowning him with a chamberpot. She ran away with a peasant outlaw. The daughter of the knight of Loughborough was supposed to wed the Sheriff of Nottingham. She eloped with Hood's minstrel Alan a Dale."[5]

"That's… I'm not Marion or Elaine," Melisend replied. "Much as I might sometimes wish to be. I know how hard you've had to fight to get here, William. I know how you struggle to stay at the top."

That much was true. Longchamp's enemies were gathering. Last winter he'd clashed with Lackland, sieging and taking John's castles of Tickhill and Northampton. This spring he'd enforced Richard's decree of exile on the Archbishop of York, the king's bastard half-brother, though it had made him few friends. And with Pope Clement's death, the chancellor's legatine commission had expired, leaving his clerical authority diminished.

"It's not that I don't like Fitzwarren," Longchamp made sure his sister understood. "Or his outlaw kin, for that matter. I like a story of derring-do as much as the next man. I even admire them a little for their ethics and audacity. But the next man doesn't have to try and run England while Prince John, the barons, the prelates, his rivals, the French, the Scots, the Welsh, and everyone else tries to tear him down. I can't afford weaknesses, Melisend. I can't afford mistakes."

"I understand, William. Really I do." Melisend was loyal. She abandoned silly affection for a handsome young courier and put him out of her mind. Times were getting darker. There was no room in the world any more for outlaw dreams and heroes. Civil war was coming to destroy all hopes.

For Lord Longchamp and his sister there could be only duty.

"Well, Sheriff, this *is* interesting," Robin Hood told the Sheriff of Nottingham. "What shall we talk about?"

They met together at table, in the Bishop's palace at Leicester, where a perverse seating plan had positioned them next to each other

William de Vendenal eyed the pardoned outlaw who was beyond his reach; for now. "You might tell me which kind of rope you think I should

---

5   Recounted in *Robin Hood: Arrow of Justice*, by I.A. Watson.

reserve for you. Hemp is common for forest wolfsheads, but as an earl's bastard you might qualify for flax."

"Either's fine," Robin assured him, "so long as I can use it to tie you in knots."

De Vendenal sipped his wine. He seemed to find it sour. "There's only one way this can end, Loxley," he warned. "Every Sherwood robbery piles more evidence that you have broken your parole. Every escapade is closer to disaster than the last. Sooner or later, it will end badly for you."

Robin tasted his drink. It seemed fine. "You're overlooking how I get more brilliant all the time, Sheriff."

De Vendenal sneered. "Do you really believe what you promise your peasant worshippers, Hood? Freedom? Freedom from their masters is freedom to starve, freedom to prey on each other, freedom to be conquered by other nations. Justice? Overthrow every tyrant and watch a new generation of dictators rise from those who have taken power from the old. A proper share for one requires less for another because there isn't enough to go around. Shifting wealth about isn't the same as solving the underlying problems. The rights of man? We live short, brutal lives. The strongest of us prosper for a time. Only the weak bleat of rights they do not earn or hold by force; the weak and those who seek to manipulate them."

"How do you live in that head of yours?" Robin snorted. "If we can't offer freedom or justice to all it doesn't mean we can't offer freedom and justice to some. Or just one person. It might not change the wide world, but it changes *their* world."

The Sheriff gestured round the hall. The guests were mostly settled at table now, awaiting the benediction grace before they could break meat and bread. "Your ideals won't change the world, outlaw, but the world *is* changing. King Richard is gone. Even if he returns he has no interest in our foggy little island except as a bankroll for his wars. The noble Norman houses have been established for a century and a quarter now, enough generations for a feudal system to be enshrined in this society. Men have servitude bred into their bones. The lords control men's lives. The bishops command men's souls. Prince John's star rises and those who follow him rise with it." De Vendenal turned his pointed finger to Robin. "You are the last sputtering spark of something that has died in England. Some days I'm pleased to have you out there opposing me. Otherwise my work would be just too easy!"

"Ideals change the world more than anything!" the rebel of Sherwood replied. "Nothing is forgotten. And that spark, that glimmer of freedom and justice for all, that you think is dying, the more you try and tread it out the more it spreads. Hang me if you can. Fifty men will take up my cause. Hang them and watch five thousand take their place." He grinned. "Of course, hanging me's turning out to be pretty much a lifetime job for you, isn't it?"

Lady Matilda of Leaford, new-made Lady of Loxley, glided over to join her husband at board. "I see you've found someone to annoy then, Robin," she observed. "Lord William. Not a pleasure."

"Maid Marion," acknowledged Nottingham. "I was just discussing your hero's forthcoming execution."

The queen of Sherwood wrinkled her nose. "Again? Oh, you might be interested to know, Lord William, that your eloped bride was delivered of a fine daughter some weeks ago. The child's doting father has named the girl Calliope."

"Loughborough's ruined daughter is of no interest to me," the Sheriff replied curtly.

"For her part, she'd like to see you dead in a ditch for murdering her family," Marion replied; and suddenly she wasn't bantering.

"There is another way this can end, you see," Robin warned the Sheriff. "If not freedom and justice for all, judgement and justice for some that deserve it most."

"Kill me and there are orders in place to slaughter every villager I ever suspected had dealings with you," De Vendenal threatened. "Kill me and Prince John will burn down Sherwood to find you. That's your weakness, Hood, and it's why you'll die. You care about those fools you try to save. I am of stronger mettle."

Marion wrapped a hand round Robin's arm. "Well, won't it be *interesting*, finding out?"

De Vendenal drained the dregs of his goblet and tossed it at one of the palace dogs. "You know, while you are here playing knight and lady, you're not with your forest scum," he pointed out. "So if they were discovered, say hiding out in a cave on the border to Derbyshire near Creswell and Whitwell,[6] why there'd be no clever bandit king to sneak them away before

6   Cresswell Crags is a limestone gorge on the Derbyshire/Nottinghamshire border that has been intermittently occupied since Palaeolithic times, with archaeological evidence of Neolithic, Bronze Age, Roman, and even post-medieval activity in its many multi-chambered caves. Along with such colourful names as Mother Grundy's Parlour, Church Hole, and Pin Hole is one of several places across England named Robin Hood's Cave or Robin Hood's Hall. Largest of the Cresswell caves, it has four chambers linked by narrow passages. It has yielded a wealth of ice age artefacts.

Another good Robin Hood's Cave is found at Stanage Edge in the Peak District where Derbyshire and Yorkshire meet, and is also of much archaeological and geological interest, as well as being in a stunning site of natural beauty,

soldiers came on them in force and slaughtered the lot of them." He gave his enemies a think bleak smile.

Robin's eyes widened. "Soldiers at Cresswell, you say?" He paused for a moment before dropping his counterfeited shock. "So not at Lichfield, then?"

The Sheriff's smile froze. "Lichfield?"

"Cathedral city in Staffordshire," Marion prompted him. "Very pretty place. King Richard authorised a royal mint there, I believe."[7]

De Vendenal's eyes narrowed.

Robin returned the Sheriff's ruined smile with a cheeky grin of his own. "Didn't you just send a large consignment of confiscated silver plate there secretly, to be made coin? It's a good thing your soldiers have my outlaws cornered at Cresswell, otherwise who knows what might have become of that shipment as it travelled through the Derbyshire hills?"

"I flayed a beggar to death to learn where your bandits are hiding."

"He wasn't a beggar until you took all he had," Marion accused. "Do you think there are not men who will die for a cause they believe in? Who will strike back at tyrants with their dying breath? You have men who will kill for gold. We have heroes who will die for freedom!"

"And we have another substantial donation to our campaign coffers, Sheriff." Robin added. "You know, while you're here playing villain, you're not with your treasury, guarding it from outlaws."

De Vendenal's face was a mottled mixture of white and red. He rose abruptly as the Bishop was about to pronounce grace. He stalked from the hall, calling for his horse and men.

Marion and Robin touched cups. "To Michael the Porter," the king of Sherwood said softly. "May he be with his family again in heaven."

Marion nodded her throat tight. She glanced after the departed Sheriff of Nottingham. "It will come to an end, Rob. It has to. At the last it'll be you or him."

Robin caught her hand and kissed it "Then you'd better inspire me, Maid Marion."

"And you'd best be as clever as you think yourself, Robin in the Hood."

---

7   Lichfield produced coins under royal charter from A.D. 1189-99. Nottingham's own mint, first opened in the year of William I's conquest, 1066, had cut its last legal coin in 1145.

❧Dramatis Personae:

The Merry Men of Sherwood Forest:

Robin in the Hood, outrageous outlaw rogue, leader of the bandits of Sherwood, the people's hero

Lady Matilda Fitzwarren of Leaford, *Maid Marion,* beloved by the common folk and by Robin Hood.

John Little of Hathersage, Robin right hand man, known for his giant stature as *Little John*

Brother Thomas, a fat monk nicknamed *Friar Tuck*; Robin's boyhood tutor

Will Scathlock, a professional soldier; his violent tendencies earned him the nom-de-guerre *Scarlet*

Alan a Dale, a minstrel who understands the power of legends

Much, the Miller's Son, a handsome lad of limited intellect

David of Doncaster, a fiery young wrestler

Arthur a Bland, a cunning poacher with woodcraft and tracking skills

Gilbert with the White Hand, the band's cook

Riccon Hazel of Flintshire, a handy lad in a fight

Ros of Waltham, a camp follower, mother of the infant Tad

Elaine of Loughborough, a noble damsel who eloped with Alan a Dale, and by him mother of infant **Calliope**

Prince John's Faction:

Prince John, Count of Mortain, Lord of Ireland, younger brother of King Richard I

Benet Rothmere, the Prince's lackey

Sir Marcel of Flanders, Prince John's finest archer

Lord William de Vendenal, Lord High Sheriff of Nottingham

Sir Nikolas Church, newly-appointed Constable of the Tower of London

Madam Clemence de Royce, Prince John mistress, by him mother of infant **Joan**; also mother of malevolent 10-year old **Roger**

Nunchmaun, Clemence's cruel fool

Captain Nacien Vexstaff, thief-taker, leader of a Free Company of opportunist mercenaries

Dan Bellows, his second-in-command

Smeat, Jessop, Nipper, and **the Canker,** Free Company bravos

William de Longchamp's Faction:

Lord William Longchamp, formerly Lord Chancellor, formerly Bishop of Ely, formerly master of the Tower of London, formerly Grand Justiciar in the South; now fallen from grace

Lady Melisend de Longchamp, William's unmarried beautiful younger sister

Sir Adam Fitzwarren, knight courier to Longchamp, brother to Maid Marion; Lady Melisand's most loyal admirer

Sir Richard Fitzwarren, Sir Richard at the Lee, knight of Leaford and Verysdale; Adam and Matilda's father

Other Notables:

Lord Walter of Coutances, Bishop of Rouen, King Richard's emissary sent from the Crusades

Lord Hugh de Puiset, Earl of Northumbria, Bishop of Durham, Grand Justiciar in the North; Longchamp's enemy

Geoffrey Plantagenet, the Archbishop of York, Henry II's bastard, half-brother to Richard the Lionheart and Prince John

Londoners:

Henry Fitz-Ailwin de London-stone, first Mayor of London

Mab Make-Do, hostess of the Turk's Head Tavern in Billingsgate

Longshanks Edwin, a significant thief and whoremaster

Gibbet Drake, master of the Thieves Court of Scabber's Hole

Brother Florian, attending altar-monk at All Hallows Church

Agnes and Clara, young doxies of the Thieves' Court

And a full cast of revellers, rioters, river-men, lavender-girls, dells, mollies, dips, queer-coves, idlers, oglers, Flemings, Aldermen, clerics, warders, and imaginary Switzers.

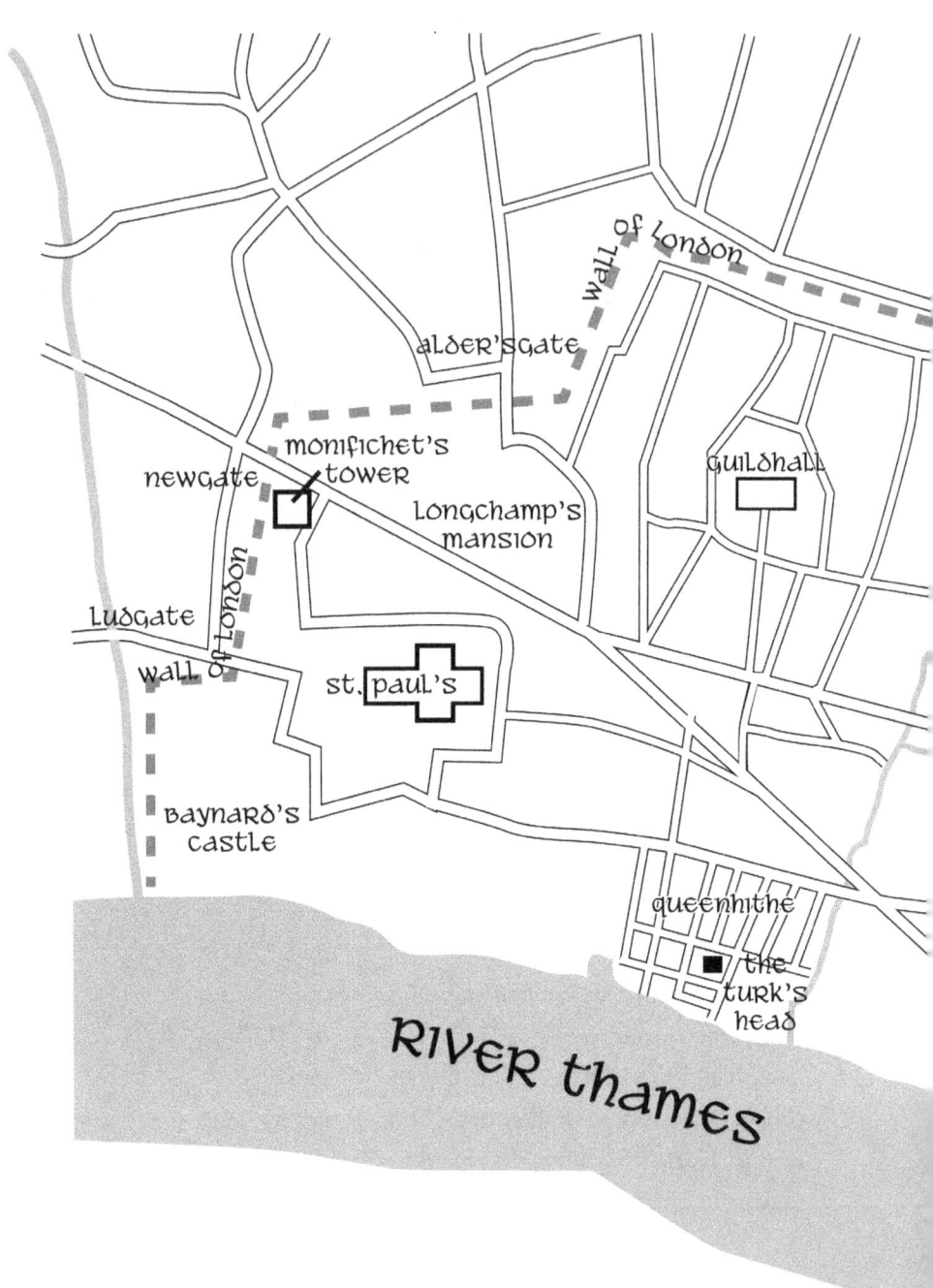

Robin Hood's London

ppLegate

wall of London

moorgate

bishopsgate

aldgate

bigod's estate

scabber's hole

hound's ditch

wall of London

bridge

tower of London

Robin Hood
and the
Maiden in the Tower

I

Soldiers swarmed through the streets. Where the shops were closed up they broke off the shutters to take what they wanted. Shouts and screams came from the invaded houses.

The red-haired young man in the dark blue coat shouldered his way through the people at Hound's Ditch, pushing against the tide of citizens fleeing the Prince's men. The city had fallen. The gates had been flung open to the mercenary army that had returned with John Lackland from Europe. King Richard's brother was reputedly already at the Palace of Westminster.

Rumour ran faster than the burghers of London who sought to escape across the river before the soldiers closed the bridge. For three days, the King's Justiciar, his de facto regent while Richard crusaded in the Holy Land, had been besieged in the Tower of London. Now word came that the Tower was surrendered, Lord William Longchamp himself fled.

That only made the young man's mission more urgent. Sir Adam Fitz-warren pressed free of the retreating citizenry and broke into a sprint towards Moorgate.

A troop of Prince's men marched up Bishopsgate. Adam pressed himself into the nearest alley and watched them pass. It was unlikely that Lackland's soldiery would recognise so minor a courier of England's displaced Justiciar but they might detain a man of noble birth carrying a sword anyway.

He ducked round the back of the houses, scrambling over fences and walls, and rejoined the thoroughfare when he thought it was safe. Safe was a relative term; the Prince's men swarmed everywhere, mostly uncontrolled, taking their vengeance for the capital's support of William Longchamp.

Adam made another long detour around Cheapside and Candlewick, where a house had caught fire. Some of the less drunken of John's troops had formed a chain from the well to quench the blaze. An unchecked fire in crowded London could spread across the whole city. Yet even then Adam could see the red ember glow of other conflagrations over the roofscape.

He was seen once, by a vigilant sergeant who called challenge. "Who goes there? Stand and speak, in the Prince's name!"

Adam simply ran, counting on his speed and superior knowledge of the rats' maze of London alleys to lose any pursuit.

It took too long, though, and Adam Fitzwarren had no time to spare. When he passed St Martin's and found the house in Aldergate Street it was too late.

Lord Justiciar William Longchamp was the richest man in the country. England's Chancellor, Bishop of Ely, until late a Papal legate, master of the Tower of London and its mint; his holdings were lavish and many. The house on Aldergate Street was not the greatest of the dozens of estates he owned; nor was it the least.

That house burned. The roof thatch was well ablaze and the interior was filled with flame-lit smoke. The timbers of the upper floor smouldered. The horn in the windows had either been smashed from without or shattered by the heat.

The front door was broken down, hanging from one bent hinge. Its heavy metal-studded timbers were splintered apart by battering ram.

Adam rushed into the burning building. The heat was intense but the fumes were worse. He used the last of his breath to call out a name: "Melisend! Melisend!"

There was no reply. The young knight pressed his cloak over his nose and mouth and pushed further into the smouldering manor. The upper floor had collapsed over the kitchen block, making that way impassable. The main staircase was already burning. Adam raced into the other wing, hoping for a servant's stair, preferably a stone spiral that would not be devoured by the hungry flames.

"Melisend!"

There was no reply. Even as he shouted, Adam knew that it was futile. If Melisend de Longchamp had been at home when the soldiers came she was taken or dead. If she'd hidden out in some secret chamber on the upper floor she'd have burned.

"Melisend!"

The flames pushed Adam back. There was no way further in to the blazing house. The hem of the knight's cloak began to smoulder.

The great chimney-stack suddenly collapsed, spilling its stonework into the drawing room where Adam called. The young man was forced to retreat, hastily exiting the manor before the rest of the roof came down.

He staggered out into the fresher air of the courtyard, surprised how chilly the October night was on his scorched skin. The whole frontage of the house was ablaze now, but no-one moved to quench this conflagration. The manor stood apart from other buildings so would not easily spread its flames; and this was the property of yesterday's man. William Longchamp's star had fallen.

Adam couldn't help but think of the implications. Since King Richard's coronation and almost-immediate departure to the Third Crusade, England had been torn between the competing authorities of the two Justiciars set to rule as regents and the king's brother John. Longchamp has seemed to be in the ascendant; he had defeated then exiled his rival Justiciar de Puiset. His papal recognition gave him both spiritual and temporal power over England.

But Prince John was cunning. Where Longchamp curtailed the Barons, John whispered of nepotism and corruption. When Longchamp toured the provinces with a train of a thousand courtiers, bankrupting cities and lords to host his progression, John spoke of overweening pride and unbridled ambition. Gradually the masses' mood soured and public opinion turned from the elitist French Norman.

Longchamp had finally overreached himself when he'd imprisoned the Archbishop of York, Richard's half-brother. Although Archbishop Geoffrey had been in defiance of the Lionheart's order of exile, the cleric's over-violent arrest that summer at the very altar of St Martin's, Dover, had stirred bitter memory of Thomas á Becket's murder twenty years earlier.[8] Rich-

---

8   On 29th December 1170, four knights entered Canterbury cathedral and cut down Archbishop Thomas á Becket in the sanctuary as he conducted vespers. They believed they were carrying out the wishes of King Henry II, Richard the Lionheart's father; he is commonly quoted as saying of the clergyman who had excommunicated him and thwarted him at various turns, "Who will rid me of this turbulent priest?" The murder shocked England. Henry denied authorising the deed but did not punish the perpetrators. The outrage almost ended his reign. Within two years Becket was canonised and added to the Calendar of Saints.

Like Henry II, Longchamp denied that the violent capture of his clerical prisoner from the very sanctuary of a church had been his intention. It didn't matter. Prince John had his excuse. Longchamp fled from Windsor as Lackland's armies approached and took refuge

ard's appointed arbiter, Walter of Coutances, Archbishop of Rouen, had returned from the Crusades to demand order and restitution. No other could have clipped the Lord Chancellor's authority and fractured Longchamp's grip on power.

And then the Prince had acted, with a mercenary army paid for by the King of France's gold. His expert generals had won almost every confrontation with Longchamp's forces. Now the Lord Chancellor was forced to take boat and flee, and England was John's.[9]

Longchamp's boat was set to leave tonight, anchored outside the city at Greenwich to sail down the Thames with the receding tide. The fleeing Justiciar waited only to gather up what he could to take into exile with him, his treasuries, his papers, a few favoured allies, and his youngest sister Melisend.

Adam looked despairingly at the blazing frame that had been an elegant townhouse. He wondered what to do next. If Melisend de Longchamp had somehow avoided capture and escaped arrest or murder then where would she go? The whole city was swarming with drunken soldiers and Prince John's elite agents. A helpless girl of quality would have no haven.

The young knight's orders were clear. He was to check Longchamp's Aldgate Street mansion and return with Melisend if he could. He must otherwise report to the Chancellor's galleon an hour before matins and sail with him for Normandy.

Except... Melisend de Longchamp had eyes of purple-blue that shone when she laughed, and a curve to her lips that softened the intelligent quirk of her brows into good-humoured understanding. She listened well, spoke quietly and thoughtfully. She'd spared time to talk with Adam Fitzwarren though he was a youngest son of a poor crusader, and she had aided him at need. And now Melisend de Longchamp was lost and alone and she needed someone to help her.

Adam's father and mother were on that boat, along with Adam's second

in the Tower of London. Even this fastness did not protect him for long.

9   This truncated summary of the complex politics and shifting alliances of 1191 is perforce incomplete. For example it omits the role of Richard and John's mother, Eleanor of Aquitaine, the most powerful woman in Europe, dowager queen by different husbands of both England and France (this is corrected by the essay "Eleanor of Aquitaine: Much More Than a Footnote" elsewhere in this volume). It makes but slight reference to Longchamp's brothers being surrendered as hostage for his quiet retreat. Events have been omitted from reference here for the sake of telling a story. Fortunately for interpreting this complicated period of history, for every expert there is an equal and opposite expert. The author has felt at liberty to select the interpretations that best serve his narrative purpose.

brother and his family and other of Longchamp's allies. They all awaited his return; but Melisend, if she somehow lived, awaited rescue.

A shout from one of Prince John's elite emissaries decided the young man. As the agent rode over to see who was so interested in the Longchamp house, Sir Adam at the Lee hoisted him from his horse and pummelled him to the ground. The young courier leaped into the saddle, spurred the bay to a gallop, and raced off down the street; away from the rendezvous at Greenwich.

Adam Fitzwarren hunted Melisend de Longchamp!

The Tower of London was the greatest of royal fortresses, palace, garrison, administrative base, and status symbol, all in one sprawling stone engine of war. The Lord Chancellor had also been the Tower's keeper. During his time in office he'd strengthened the ancient citadel, extending the curtain wall and adding an outer ward. The last of the wooden structure was now replaced by massive white Caen stonework befitting the treasure house of England and its greatest prison.[10]

It was a shame that he'd spent all that time and effort on a stronghold that was now held by his enemy Prince John[11] and was a prison for his sister.

Melisend de Longchamp tried not to tremble as Clemence de Royce entered her tower chamber again. She had grown to fear and hate Prince John's cold-eyed mistress and her unusual retinue.

Madam Clemence swept into the dark tower cell with her son, ten-year-

---

10   Work on the White Tower, the central part of the Tower of London, is generally thought to have begun around 1078 on the orders of William I, England's new conqueror. Some literary traditions prefer to trace a possible history for the site predating the Norman construction on Roman remains. Geoffrey of Monmouth (c1100-1155), whose hugely popular *Historia Regum Britanniae* was considered the standard history text at the time of our present story, mentions it in his tales of King Arthur in the 6th century. Some mythographers suggest it was the same sacred fortified White Hill where the head of Celtic mythological figure Bran the Blessed was buried in pre-Roman times.

11   The Pipe Rolls, a collection of financial accounts maintained by the English Exchequer, form the oldest continuous series of records kept by the English government, covering A.D. 1130-1933. They record that between 3 December 1189 and 11 November 1190, £2,881 1s 10d (equivalent of approximately £14 million/$20m today) was spent on improving the Tower of London, from a national castle-building budget of around £7,000.

old Roger, and her leering hunchback clown. Nunchmaun licked his lips as he stared at the captive. Roger smirked, anticipating Melisend's tears. He liked it when she cried.

"Good morning Melisend," Clemence bade the captive. "Have you considered your position now?"

The Chancellor's sister shook her head.

"How unfortunate. Unbind your bandage."

Melisend's left palm was swathed in silk. The lady unwrapped the cloth, wincing where it revealed the burned flesh beneath.

"Hold out your hand," Clemence demanded. "We need light to talk by in this gloomy place, do we not?"

Melisend stretched out her arm. Nunchmaun limped forward and laid a thick stubby candle on the prisoner's blistered palm. He winked at the maiden as he touched a taper to the wick. As the wax melted it would dribble down to burn the damsel's flesh.

"When you decide to obey me we can summon proper light, and food, and warmth," Clemence promised.

"I do not obey Prince John's whore." Melisend hadn't meant to speak. She bit back her retort too late.

"Whore?" Clemence de Royce repeated. It was true that she shared Prince John's bed, sometimes alone, sometimes with others. He had acknowledged her younger child, little Joan who was just now learning to walk.[12] But Clemence liked to believe that she was dearer to John than the mothers of his many other recognised bastards.[13] "I could give you to my

---

12   In 1205, John secured peace and alliance with Wales by wedding this fifteen-year-old bastard daughter Joan (1191-1237) to Llywelyn ap Iowerth the Great, Prince of Wales and Gwynedd. Five years later John turned on Llywelyn and backed the Earl of Chester's campaign to "tame" the Welsh. Joan pleaded with her father for her husband's life and received it but on humiliating terms. Joan's obituary in the *Tewsbury Annals* is the only evidence of her mother's name, referring to "Regina Clementina," Queen Clemence. There is no evidence of Joan actually coming from royal blood on her maternal side.

13   John also recognised his paternity of Richard Fitz Roy by his cousin Adela, Oliver FitzRoy by a mistress called Hawise, Geoffrey FitzRoy who died on an expedition to Poitou in 1205, John FitzRoy, a clerk, Henry FitzRoy of whom little is known, Osbert Gifford who was given lands in Oxfordshire, Norfolk, Suffolk, and Sussex, Eudes FitzRoy who crusaded with John's half-brother Richard and died in the Holy Land in 1241, Bartholomew FitzRoy, a member of the order of Friars Preachers, Maud FitzRoy, eventually Abbess of Barking, Isabel FitzRoy, later wife of Richard Fitz Ives, and Philip FitzRoy. Not bad for a ruler nicknamed "Soft-Sword" for his lack of prowess in war and the bedroom.

Fitz is a precognomen meaning "son of" or more often "bastard of".

dwarf's lusts here and now. What would that make you then, Melisend de Longchamp?" She turned to the hunchback. "What say you, Nunchmaun? Do you desire the fair flesh of this wretched forsaken virgin?"

The dwarf made an obscene reply expressing his agreement. Little Roger snickered.

The first trickles of today's wax dribbled down onto the peeled skin from yesterday's candle. Melisend blinked back tears. "If you debase me then I lose my value as Lackland's hostage," she argued. She cursed herself for letting her voice tremble.

"There's plenty of ways Nunchmaun can debase you and still send you to the altar with your maiden seal intact," promised Clemence. "Continue to defy me and I'll take pleasure in watching him show you."

Melisend closed her eyes. "I will not yield to you," she said, although it took every last shred of her courage. "I will not tell you of my brother's plans. I will not name his allies. I will not swear false testimony against him. I will not. I will not. I will not!"

"Then we shall wait here by candlelight while you ponder your choices," Clemence replied.

"Shall you cane her again, mother?" Roger asked eagerly. "Make her blub some more!"

"Let me lick her maiden's tears from her cheeks, mistress," begged Nunchmaun, waggling his tongue.

Melisend sat unmoving as the candle burned down.

"William has fled," Clemence told the prisoner. "It seems that he failed to reach his ship, though. It sailed without him."

The captive showed no reaction. If her brother had missed his planned escape on the night London had fallen then he could be in serious trouble. Or the Prince's mistress could be lying.

"He was traced as he fled in disguise to Dover. It's a shame his lack of English marked him as a foreigner. We have reports of him dressed as a monk and as a woman. There's an amusing tale of a fisherman who thought him a doxy and tried to take him by force. Such an undignified position for a former bishop to be in."

"I bet that brought some colour to his cheeks," snickered Nunchmaun.

Clemence smirked at Melisend. "Did I mention that the Archbishop of York whom your brother previously arrested, the Bishop of Coventry, and other holy men convened a clerical court and excommunicated dear William?"

The prisoner had heard that part before. The trial had been held at

Lodden Bridge, not far from London's walls. Longchamp had not stirred from his Tower stronghold to attend. It had probably been a tactical error. Once the Chancellor began to be stripped of his powers his London supporters had become much less certain that they backed the right side. Within days the most powerful man in England had become a fugitive.

"Did… did they catch him?" Melisend hadn't intended to blurt out her question and betray her worry.

Clemence could have lied, but she thought the truth more hurtful. "It's reported that he finally slunk aboard a ship to the Continent yesterday. He's run away to Flanders or Harfleur or who knows where and left you to your fate. Your other brothers are Coutance's hostages for William's acquiescence. The only messenger William sent to find you miscarried and never returned. Your brother has abandoned you. You owe him nothing."

Prince John's mistress noted a flicker in the prisoner's pained face that was nothing to do with the heat on her palm. "You *expected* a messenger?" she discerned. "A friend? A suitor, perhaps? Well he has failed you too. I've set Nacien Vexstaff to seek him, the best thief-taker in England. If your hero's still alive he'll be hauled here for me to dismantle in front of you."

Clemence had misplayed her hand. Melisend didn't despair at the news; she took strength from it. "You know who it was that William sent for me?"

"Of course. Prince John has spies everywhere, even close to the former Lord Chancellor. We knew of Adam Fitzwarren's dispatch moments after he'd left."

"Adam." Melisend's heart seemed to jump. He was only a young knight, new-made, unlanded, little heeded at court; so why was his clean determined face so bright in Melisend's mind? For a moment the grim cell, John's mistress, crude dwarf, cruel child, all seemed far away.

Clemence recognised her mistake. "He'll be caught and broken," she promised Longchamp's sister. "I'll let you watch."

The candle was a mere stub now. Melisend couldn't ignore it. It seared her flesh. She bit her lip to stop herself screaming out. Clemence was waiting for her to beg.

"Have Nunchmaun stick her with pins, mother!" Roger urged. "She's not crying enough!"

The hunchback offered a variety of crude and explicit suggestions.

"In good time, my pet," Clemence agreed. "We have many days to work on sweet Melisend's resistance. So many ways to break her spirit that we have barely begun to explore. Before we're done she'll crawl to obey and beg to render what she knows about her brother's treacheries."

The last of the candle burned away and extinguished itself in Melisend's hand in a puddle of molten wax.

"Until tomorrow then," Clemence de Royce said to her special project.

Melisend waited until her tormentors were gone before curling up to weep on her thin hard cot.

When she finally found sleep she dreamed of Adam.

The unfortunate tailor was tossed on his knees amidst the half-drunken soldiers. Someone kicked him to keep him down. Others laughed.

He lay on the mouldy straw of the stables that the Free Company of Nacien Vexstaff had claimed as their headquarters for their stay in London. That same company of mercenary opportunists ranged around him now.

"What's this then?" Vexstaff himself asked, ranging forward to look down at the trembling merchant. The thief-taker was gaunt as a pole, his grizzled face angular and merciless.

"A shop-keeper," Dan Bellows answered contemptuously. "A hat maker."

Vexstaff glared down at the trembling prisoner. "Do I need a hat?" he asked Dan.

"He sold one yesterday," Bellows replied. "To a well-spoken Norman lad but for his Saxon hair."

"I didn't do aught!" the tailor promised. "He bought a cloak and cap and some hose from me, that's all. He had a fair price of me!" That last part at least was a lie. The merchant had sensed the young man's urgency and had inflated his costs accordingly.

Vexstaff reached down and grabbed the tailor by his beard. He dragged him to his knees again by it. "What did the boy say to you? Where was he staying?"

"He took the items then and there. He said little, only that he wanted some finery better than the riding clothes he had on." The tailor allowed his professional observations get the better of him. "His attire was mud-spotted and soiled, and though of good quality it was provincial in cut, lacking in proper style. I sold him a fine capuchin in the Frankish fashion and…"

Vexstaff spat in the merchant's face. "I need to find this fashionable youth. You'd best think fast where I can look, tailor. You'll be less adept at your trade if I prick out your eyes."

"But I don't know! I told your men everything when they burst into my shop!"

Vexstaff reached for his poignard.

"Wait! He, um, he asked about tides. About which way the river swelled and when."

"The Thames?"

"Yes. And methought he had a stale fishy smell on his garb. The fish market, perhaps?"

"Billingsgate," Bellows suggested. "Maybe he's seeking passage over the river on one of those leaky fishing barges?"

Vexstaff cursed. If Adam had already crossed into the Liberty of South-wark[14] then he was beyond the guarded containing walls of the city and could have taken a horse to anywhere. "Go down to the market. Break some heads till we know if he was there and if he's around now. I'll take a few lads over to Southwark and tickle a few throats to see if we can't pick up the trail. There's a fine reward for this lad from Milady Clemence Hot-Lap. Let's see it comes our way, eh?"

Vexstaff's company cheered. They were living high, in the Prince's favour and free to plunder and bully in England's greatest city.

The thief-taker looked down at the cringing tailor. "Confiscate his rings and chain in the Prince's name. Beat him as a lesson then throw him out."

Nacien Vexstaff didn't care about the blubbering merchant any more. There was a young knight out there that he intended to coin into gold, alive or dead.

---

14   Across the river Thames from the medieval city of London proper, Southwark was not under London's jurisdiction. The city's various laws against gaming, prostitution, and theatres did not apply there. Despite most of the land ultimately belonging to church or monarch, the Liberty of Southwark therefore became a notorious thieves' den of brothels and entertainment halls servicing the capital. This legal liberty is the reason playhouses were built on the south bank, including Shakespeare's Globe Theatre.

II

"**M**arry," said Robin Hood to the guard on the Cripplegate. "We're a travelling troupe here to help good Prince John celebrate his triumphs. Why we've musicians and acrobats and knife-throwers and wrestlers. Even a giant." He pointed to Little John. "The world's biggest bearded lady!"

"That's a man!" objected the gate guard.

"Sssh. She gets angry when you hurt her feelings," Robin whispered confidentially. "Tore a bear apart last time. Still trying to replace it. Baiting a fat drunken friar's not such a crowd-pleaser."

John Little of Hathersage flexed hands large enough to encompass Robin's entire head and crush it. "I think they'd like the amazing headless jester," the big man speculated.

"Being a drunken friar suggests I should have a drink," objected Brother Thomas, better known to his comrades by his nickname Friar Tuck. "Since the ale ran out at Oxford we'd better get inside the city and find a tavern as soon as possible."

"We have letters of authority from the Lord High Sheriff of Nottingham to Sir Benet Rothmere, the Prince's steward," Alan a Dale said smoothly. He opened a seal-stamped scroll in front of the guard, knowing it was unlikely that the soldier could read what was actually a proclamation taxing farmers on the birth of lambs. "We don't want to keep the Prince waiting, do we?"

"God look down on the noble Sheriff of Nottingham," prayed Tuck, "and give him all he deserves!"

"And may we be the ones to bring it to him," added Little John.

Will Scathlock didn't join in the banter. He just eyed the guards and got into a position where he could slaughter them easily if required. There was a reason he was called Scarlet.

"Can we really get a bear?" Much the Miller's son asked hopefully.

The guard gave up. "Fine. Go in. You'll find all the other troubadours and acrobats and wastrels and whores gathering round Billingsgate. Watch your step."

"We'll be absolute models of good behaviour," Robin Hood promised as he led his merry men into London. "You won't even know where we've been."

36

"The world's biggest bearded lady!"

It wasn't all of Robin's band that followed him through the old Roman wall into the first city of England. Even that dull guard might have objected to two hundred bow-armed men and women arriving at the gate seeking free entry. But Robin had brought enough of his best to answer the summons that had come to Sherwood, and they were his closest allies.

The closest of all took his arm as they emerged from the gateway and looked upon the grubby streets of the city beyond. "Welcome to London," said Maid Marion. "Smelly, isn't it?"

Robin chuckled. "You said the streets were paved with something other than gold. A mere breath tells me this is the capital of tannery, smelting, glue-making, butchery, fullering, dying, and every odorous activity in England. And then they throw their refuse in the gutters!"

Ros of Wickham was quick to defend the most wonderful place she'd ever seen. "But look at the rest, our Rob!" the girl who'd grown up in a tiny rural hamlet argued. "They've put great stone slabs to pave the sides of the main streets where you can walk out of the debris! And see those lavender girls selling pomanders so you can breathe sweet scents? And the buildings! Three stories tall, some of them, big as York! Bigger! And so many churches it makes me dizzy to think about all the bells!"

"It is a place both wonderful and awful," Elaine Lambert agreed. The absconded lady-turned-outlaw had never been allowed to visit the capital by her strict father but she knew about it. "There are places here unlike any other. The great Temple of the Poor Knights who crusade in the East! You can deposit a sum with their bankers here then redeem it from their Temple in Venice or Rome or Cyprus or Antioch! The Guildhall where merchants meet who are richer than princes, the men who own those tall ships down on the river, that travel to Europe and the Middle Sea and even to Afric! The great church of St Paul, largest and most beautiful cathedral in England, bigger even than York's Minster or St Augustine's great church at Canterbury!" The young woman cradled the eight-month infant in her arms to show her the sights. "Look, Calliope! See all the wonderful houses!"

Alan grinned at his wife's enthusiasm and gathered her to him. "They do say there's much to see and do here. For those of low tastes," here he looked deliberately at Little John, "there's cock-fighting and bear-baiting at the Circus. There's theatre-pits where you can hear passion plays and mummer's tales. Maybe even some stories of Robin Hood and Maid Marion. For the well-bred there are courts and stately gardens, shops that sell anything you might wish from anywhere in the world, and enough palaces to fill the whole space of a lesser town."

"My low taste's to kick mouthy minstrels," Little John growled. "Is there a special place for that or will the street do like anywhere else?"

David of Doncaster prided himself on being a town lad, more sophisticated than the serfs who'd grown up in some Nottinghamshire sheep-pen or Lincolnshire turnip field, but even he felt out of his depth in the big city. "We'll need to be careful. There'll be thief-bands and spies, a city watch as well as all Lackland's soldiers, eyes everywhere. We cannot turn our backs for a minute in case... agh!"

Much, who'd just dropped something from the street down David's collar, guffawed. "You need to stay alert," the miller's son agreed.

While David chased his friend to introduce him to the city's midden piles, Robin turned to Gilbert of the White Hand. "We're all enjoying the big city holiday, but we're here for serious purpose. Where do we start looking, Gilbert, to find Marion's lost brother?"

Maid Marion, queen of Sherwood, Robin's true love, was also Lady Matilda Fitzwarren of Leaford and Verysdale, daughter of Sir Richard at the Lee who had sailed a week since with William Longchamp. That made her sister to Sir Adam Fitzwarren who had failed to catch the boat. A final messenger from Sir Richard had delivered a message to a certain Nottingham tailor to seek the aid of his younger daughter's unconventional lover.

Gilbert was a thickset man of middle years, older than Scarlet and Little John but not of the same grey hairs as the poacher Arthur a Bland who'd remained in Sherwood to command the rest of Robin's band. Gilbert had been an Earl's steward in his younger days before some trivial offence had sent him fleeing from a flogging to turn outlaw in the woods. It was Whitehand who had come to London over a year ago as attendant to Sir Adam at the Lee, and the outlaws' cook remembered the vanished young noble affectionately.

Gilbert pushed forward and stared down Cripplegate. The streets seemed crowded to the newcomers to London, but in Gilbert's view they were remarkably quiet, subdued by the soldiers' presence on each corner and by the recent violence and looting. "There's an inn I took Adam to when we first came here, before he received the hospitality of His Grace Lord William. It's a dingy old place down in Queenhithe by the river. I, um, know the landlady."

Friar Tuck chuckled. "Is there any town in England you don't know a landlady, seamstress, sailor's widow, or hostess, Gilbert?"

The cook shrugged. "I get on with people," he excused himself. "Must come of not stealing wine nor swallowing down all food within fifty yards of me without leave nor pause for breath."

"So, this inn," Marion prompted. "Which way?"

"Downhill," Gilbert directed. "You can't get much more downhill than the Turk's Head without falling in Thames."

Robin set the pace, although even he kept stopping to comment on some aspect of the big city. The fashions, the houses, the furnishings, even the manners of the southern city-folk were fascinating and alien.

They detoured round to avoid a herd of cattle being driven to Smithfield market, instead passing down an entire street dedicated to goldsmiths. Most big settlements were lucky to have one good jeweller; here the silversmiths occupied a different yard.

Marion's attention was still on her brother, though. "I hope he's hiding out at this Turk's Head, the idiot. Maybe he's grown the sense to keep his head down when he's caught in a city where every enemy of Prince John is being hunted down for slaughter." She didn't sound hopeful.

Elaine winced. "Aren't *we* enemies of… you know?"

"We are," Robin boasted. "In fact my reward's so high now I'm tempted to turn myself in. But London's as hard to find a man in as Sherwood. We're safe as long as we keep quiet."

Marion looked at the outlaw lord. "So we're in great danger, then?"

They passed under the high spire of Paul's church and carried on through Ludgate. Sometimes the wooden buildings were so close-packed that it was hard to press down the crowded alleys that divided them. Upper stories encroached even more, closing the streets under a virtual tunnel. In other places green estates blossomed behind high stone walls of monasteries or mansions.

The mercenaries questioned them twice but lost interest when Robin showed them the yellow ribbons the outlaws wore and explained them as a minstrel troupe. Entertainers never had any money.

"It was certainly worth robbing that rich haberdasher at Waltham," Little John admitted. He'd quietened the exuberant David and Much by grabbing each by an ear and dragging them with him.

Towards the river the houses got cruder and more temporary. The docks were lined with wharves and warehouses, carefully controlled by the Chancellor's taxmen; presumably Prince John's taxmen now, although the same customs men took the same tolls. Behind the waterfront lay ramshackle rows of fishermen's huts, wharfmen's cots, drinking houses and whorepits.

The Sign of the Turk's Head lurked amongst them; a two-storied wooden tavern that looked like it had been constructed from marine salvage, complete with a figurehead of a naked-breasted siren protruding over the lintel.

"I'm surprised they didn't call this place the Mermaid," Marion admitted, until Will Scarlet tapped her shoulder and pointed upwards. A rotting tarred head was stuck on a pike. "Oh," the maid responded.

"Brought back from the Second Crusade, they say," Gilbert commentated. "Although I hear it's been stolen and chuckled in the river a couple of times. They always seem to get it back or find another head that serves as well!"

The cook pushed his way through a low door to the inn's dingy interior. A long common room was mostly empty at this time of day, its trestles set out for the evening trade. A little ingle-nook at one end was curtained off in case any of the quality came slumming. Beside the wooden stairs that led to the balcony and guest rooms a plump slattern in a low-cut gown guarded the beer-kegs while she wiped out her wooden cups.

"Mab Make-Do!" Gilbert called out to her. "Swear ye've been faithful to me and I'll promise as much to you!"

The hostess looked up and squeaked in surprise. "Gilbert of the White Hand! Have they not hanged you yet? There's no justice in the world!" But she put down her cloth and hurried over to give the bandit-cook a bosomy hug and a smacking kiss.

"Nin o' Barnsley says it's not that he can make friends easily," Much reported to the others. "She says it's 'cause he's got an enormous..."

"Introduce us to your ladyfriend, Gil," Robin cut in quickly.

Gilbert detached himself from the landlady's embrace, although he kept one hand clasped on an ample buttock. "This is Mab o' Queenhithe, mistress of the Turk's Head. Mab, here's some sworn comrades of mine, and good men all. Robin, Marion, David, Much, the big fellow's John, the fat friar's Tuck, Alan a Dale and his Elaine, Ros, and the sour silent streak's called Will Scarlet. We've come for lodging and to meet a friend of ours."

"Lodging you can pay for?" Mab checked. Old friends were one thing but business was business.

"We're good for it," promised Little John. "We don't let Tuck look after the money."

"Even though I can count past ten," the friar replied.

"I can count," the giant growled. "Want to see me give a hundred drubs to a fat drunken monk?"

"He can get to twenty-two if he takes his boots off to help him keep score," Tuck told the landlady with a mocking wink.

Mab Make-Do laughed. "You'll be good company all right. You're all welcome at the Turk's Head." She glanced at Ros, Marion, and Elaine. "Although if you plan to ply a trade while you're here I expect a fifth part of what you earn," she warned them.

"What trade?" Elaine puzzled. "I can sew a little and know some midwifery of Constanza, but…"

"She means whoring," Ros explained. To Mab she said, "There'll be none o' that. My days are past and these two are of a different quality. And married as well."

"Like that ever made a difference," snorted Mab. But she measured the women up and took Ros' word.

"I'll be plying my trade, with your permission, mistress," Alan said, holding up his lute, "and I'll gladly share a tithe of my fees with you."

"Well then," agreed Mab, satisfied, "what brings Gilbert of the White Hand and a likely gang of trouble to the wicked city?" She poured cups of dark stout ale for her guests.

"I'm looking for my brother," Marion explained. "He stayed here once. Adam Fitzwarren."

"The handsome well-spoken lad with Saxon hair like yours?" the landlady remembered. "Yes, I can see the likeness. He was here till three nights ago, but then he vanished. I've kept 'is gear safe in store, but if he's not back to pay his rent I'm selling it at Bread Street market."

"We'll redeem Adam's debts," Robin promised. "But we're concerned for his safety. What was he doing here, with London teeming with soldiers?"

"And him Lord Longchamp's man?" Mab had to be sharp to survive in her profession. "Yes, I know what he was. A knight, they claimed, when some long sour piece called Nacien Vexstaff and his men came to hunt for him. I told 'em nothing. He wasn't here anyway, by then. They searched."

"Somebody came looking for Adam?" Little John worried. "By name?"

"By name and with an official warrant, from what this Vexstaff said. A thief-taker, I thought him, though he led some Prince's men as well as bravos of his own. I'll have naught to do with that type! But the lad's hunted. Maybe he caught wind of it and decided to vanish?"

"That doesn't explain why Adam was still in London at the first," Marion said. "He was due to take the Lord Chancellor's ship, the night the Tower fell, but he never made the galleon. Nor, by your account, did he flee with Longchamp when the Chancellor missed his boat. All the gossip has Longchamp travelling south in disguise alone. Adam remained in the city, alone. *Why?*"

Mab shook her head knowingly. "What reason did young swain ever have for doing dangerous things?" she asked with a sly smirk.

"A girl," guessed Robin, from personal experience. "They can make you do all kinds of ridiculous, dangerous stuff. Fight tyranny, champion the helpless, brave certain death to finally get a kiss."

Marion elbowed him in the ribs. "Alan did speak of someone. A lady beyond his reach."

"Melisend de Longchamp," Alan a Dale supplied. "I wrote him some verses for her. She's the Lord Chancellor's sister."

"And destined for a greater marriage than to a landless younger son," Elaine guessed.

Alan took his wife's hand. "Sometimes love overcomes shackles of birth and breeding and two hearts find each other through every adversity."

"They're doing it again," David cringed to Much.

The miller's son was handsome but not quick. "No. We can tell when they're doing it again because the noise…"

"They're being poetic and lovey again," the Doncaster boxer clarified.

"That is because we are in love," said Elaine, blushing. Little Calliope cooed.

Marion brought matters back to the point. "Father wrote that Adam was sent to fetch Longchamp's sister to escape with them. She was lodged at the Lord Chancellor's house on Aldgate Street. Adam rode to find her and he never returned."

"Is it too much to hope they just eloped together?" Little John wondered.

Marion gestured to Robin. "Hasn't the House of Fitzwarren seen enough trouble from unfortunate romantic entanglements?" she asked, hugging the young outlaw even as she accused him. "Lady Melisend is sister of the richest man in England, and until late the most powerful man too. She's a massive asset to him. Remember that for all his pre-eminence William Longchamp's of humble origins. He wants to carve a noble dynasty through service and alliances. When Melisend's given in marriage it will be to a high lord, probably an earl or prince. Not my idiot little brother."

"If she was in that house and Prince John's soldiers came she might have already been given in Danish marriage[15] to the whole lot of 'em," Ros pointed out.

"Not while Adam lived," said Alan grimly.

---

15   The Norman custom of "Danish marriages" referred to the traditional Viking dating techniques that avoided ceremonies, oaths, and priests and concentrated more on a short-term sexual encounter, consensual or not. Some Danish marriages were more than mere rapes though, where the woman became a long-term concubine. William the Conqueror was conceived in just such a Danish marriage, explaining his early soubriquet of William the Bastard.

The outlaws became graver as they considered the implications of the new-made knight's disappearance.

Robin snapped them out of it. "This Lady Melisend, then, Adam's amour. We need to know what became of her. We need to find out about this thief-taker that's hunting Adam by name. We want to know where Adam went when he quit the Turk's Head. And some general gossip about the way things are in the capital now Lackland's strutting tall wouldn't be amiss." He clapped his hands together. "So go find out! Shoo!"

The merry men dispersed, planning visits to taverns and guilds. Marion stayed with Robin. "We'd best go to Longchamp's manor," she suggested. "Better to know the worst."

Robin nodded and held out his arm for her to take.

"Hold a moment!" Mab Make-do called after him, suddenly piecing things together. "Robin… and Marion. And a giant called John and a fat friar…"

"Is there a problem?" Robin asked the hostess.

She shook her head and grinned. "Only a discount in my boarding rates." She looked outside her door to where brutal soldiers occupied the street corner. "You are most welcome in London, Robin in the Hood!" she told the outlaw and his lady.

III

The Tower of London's officers had changed but the warders remained. These were the experienced career watchmen who understood the guard rotas, who knew the routines of the castle in peace and war, and who served whichever lord officially held the Tower. Since Prince John convened parliament in Westminster and the Justiciar had fled charges of treason and peculation, the warders obeyed Lackland now.

When the Prince's courier arrived they followed procedure and called for a superior. That didn't sit well with the weary traveller at the drawbridge.

"Dullards? Do you not know 'oo I am? I am Sir Marcel de Flanders, envoy of Prince John 'imself! You will admit me immediately and bring me to your commander!"

The Tower warders[16] had seen princes and prelates come and go, some of them after a long stay in the dungeons of their fortress;[17] but they had just survived a three-day siege that had earned them the Prince's ire. They hastened to fetch their new Constable.

Sir Nikolas Church was a greying man with a limp he'd won after the Cutting of the Oak.[18] He'd served with Lackland in Ireland and had been amongst the last to flee when the country rose against the prince they

16   The Tower of London's famous order of Yeoman Warders, often nicknamed Beefeaters, date from 1485 and remain custodians of the fortress and its treasures today. The use of the term warder to describe much earlier Tower guards in our present story is for euphonic convenience only.

17   The first recorded prisoner in the Tower was Ranulf Flambard (c1060-1128), Bishop of Durham and at one time of sixteen other bishoprics and abbeys, probable composer of *The Domesday Book*, keeper of the king's seal. After service to William the Conqueror and Rufus I he was imprisoned by Henry I in the Tower that he had helped to build. on charges of embezzlement and financial extortion. Flambard also became the first person to escape from the Tower (AD 1101), climbing from a window with a rope that had been smuggled to him.

18   For centuries an old oak tree at Gisors near Paris was the traditional neutral meeting ground between the warring kings of England and France. In 1188, Philippe II of France had the tree destroyed to indicate that he would have no more talk with England nor allow them any quarter. A lengthy and bloody altercation followed "the Cutting of the Oak".

called "Soft-Sword".[19] He came to the gate to meet the knight who was disturbing the watch.

"What do you want?" Sir Nikolas asked bluntly. He didn't approve of the mincing fops that Prince John surrounded himself with and sent out to interfere.

"I am sent to see the Lady Melisend, sister of Longchamp. The Prince 'as questions he wishes put to her."

"I thought the Lady Clemence was her interrogator."

"The Prince is unhappy with 'er progress. I am sent from him direct."

"Have you brought papers?"

"I do not need papers. I am Marcel of Flanders. I ride for Prince John."

Sir Nikolas had heard of the knight. It was said that Marcel was the best bow-shot in Normandy and had only once been bettered at the lists. It was also said that Marcel was charming when happy but could be vindictive and spiteful in adversity. The Constable of the Tower mused on the idea of sending the preening peacock back to his Prince for written orders in the proper form. He decided it would probably be a mistake.[20]

"I was told to keep the lady held close. She's in the Lanthorn Tower,[21]

---

19   John was appointed Lord of Ireland when he was ten years old but did not visit until 1185. His inexperience and lack of tact quickly alienated the nobles there, culminating in his ignominious retreat. In 1210, then-King John returned with a massive army to crush the rebellious Anglo-Norman Lords and force English law and customs on the nation.

20   Up to the time of our narrative, October 1191, the Constable of the Tower was the most powerful man in London, commanding the city almost like a military governor. Previous Constables had held and sometimes exploited significant political power, in particular Geoffrey de Mandeville during the civil war of King Stephen and Empress Maude where he sold and resold his loyalty. After displacing Lord Longchamp, John stripped the post of Constable of many of its powers, investing them instead in the newly created post of Mayor of London.

The official list of Constables (cited, for example, by W.L. Rutton in *Notes and Queries 10 S. IX*, 1908) does not include Sir Nikolas' brief tenure. Our present narrative may reveal why. By the end of 1191, Walter of Coutances (see footnote 45) was Constable of the Tower.

21   The Tower of London has undergone many alterations and expansions over its long history, which makes it difficult to offer complete accuracy when depicting the site in a fictional historical narrative. In particular, the names of some of the early parts of the complex which were later replaced by other structures have not survived.

The Lanthorn Tower proper was erected by Henry III between 1238 and 1272 and took its name from the beacon placed atop it to guide ships along the Thames by night. It was the second largest tower within the multi-building military complex that made up the Tower of London. Originally built as personal chambers for Queen Eleanor, this tall structure was later used to imprison prisoners of quality. That version of the Lanthorn Tower, the last part

watched day and night."

"You will take me to 'er."

Sir Nikolas nodded to the warders to let the Frenchman in. The Norman noble spurred his horse to the inner bailey and waited for grooms to help him dismount.

The interior of the castle looked like a construction site. Lord Longchamp's expansions had not been finished when Prince John's return had interrupted the works. The outer wall was not yet topped off, and a moat intended to bring the Thames around the fortress remained dry. Inside the curtain defence, huge piles of stone and timber were stacked ready to add to the halls and houses lining the interior.

Sir Nikolas caught the royal envoy's wandering stare. "Work will begin again when everything's back to normal. We're hard-pressed right now to keep the peace. For an unpopular man, His Grace the Lord Chancellor left plenty of supporters to make trouble for us. A few more guards and a bigger budget wouldn't harm."

The herald didn't reply to the obvious hint. Sir Nikolas took him past the timbered palace that nestled in the shadow of the central White Tower, to a new-built turret topping the old Roman stonework of the riverside wall. A smoky brazier belched from the top of the Lanthorn Tower, for at night its high point served as a guide for river shipping.

The Warder led the visitor up a flight of outer steps into the first floor of Lanthorn Tower, then up two tiers of spiral staircase to the garret where the prisoner was confined.

"I will speak wiz 'er alone," the envoy declared.

Sir Nikolas almost protested but there was something in the visitor's stare that warned him that he was in danger. There was an intent focus in the envoy's movements and speech, which betrayed either a suppressed rage or a deadly contempt. "I'll place a guard within call, Sir Marcel," he said. "She's not to be severely harmed, not without a warrant from his highness. Is that understood?"

"I 'ear you. Open the door."

---

of the medieval palace that still remained, burned down in the 18th century.

It is assumed for this story that the predecessor of the Lanthorn Tower shared its name and purpose. An earlier tower of some kind did formerly stand on the same spot, part of the expansion and improvement of the old Roman wall that formed two sides of the original curtain around the fortress. It was probably erected at the same time as the distinctive octagonal south-western Bell Tower, as one of three such defences along the river-side of the castle. These early constructions were replaced in the early 13th century with the named Lanthorn Tower, Wakefield Tower, and Bloody Tower around the time when a river gate was created.

The Constable turned the lock and allowed entry to the circular room. Lady Melisend stood slowly, eyeing her visitors cautiously.

"I'll have to lock you in, Sir Marcel," Sir Nikolas warned.

"As you will. Now go."

The knight stood motionless until the Constable had secured the door and retreated down the spiral stair. Only then did he speak to the captive in the Tower. "Melisend!"

The maiden flung herself across the room and into his arms. "Adam!"

Clemence de Royce fed her son sweetmeats while she listened to Nacien Vexstaff.

"We traced the boy to Billingsgate," the thief-taker announced. "He was sleeping rough over a cobbler's hovel since he quit the Turk's Head. When we questioned the cobbler he was quick to betray the lordling's hiding place."

"You have him then?" the Prince's mistress said.

"He wasn't there. His possessions were. I've left good men to watch for him when he returns."

Young Roger shifted discontentedly on his mother's lap. "You should order that cobbler to be punished," he insisted. "Tell them to punish him! Make them nail him to something!"

"The cobbler won't hide fugitives again," Vexstaff promised. Behind him the hunchback Nunchmaun mimed a man having his fingernails, ears, tongue, and genitals removed.

"It's important that you find this young man," insisted Clemence. "The Prince has old scores to settle with his family. John would like him dead. Even more than that, John would like to supervise his death."

"He can't hide forever," Vexstaff answered. "Now we know he's not skipped London it's only a matter of time. The ways out are closed and the places he can hide are fewer and fewer."

"'Tis a poor fool who must caper for a living, but a poorer one who dances as he dies," jested Nunchmaun.

"Why are you here? How are you here? This is folly, madness!" Melisend de Longchamp clung to her unexpected ally as if she'd never let him go. Adam didn't mind at all.

"I'm in disguise, of course," the young knight told her. "I got the idea from my sister's husband. He impersonated Sir Marcel of Flanders before. Twice." Adam thought carefully. "In fact I don't think I've ever actually met the real Marcel of Flanders. But he is a Prince's envoy, so while the guards here are still working out their new protocols his name was enough to get me to see you."

"But what if it had not? What if you had failed and been caught? There's a headsman's block down there in the yard. I've seen it used nine times in the few days since I was caught. I could have been you! It still could be."

Adam stroked Melisend's ebony hair. "I had to try it. I can't plan an escape for you unless I know where and how you're held."

Melisend tried to pull away. "There is no escape for me, Adam. This is the Tower of London, the most secure gaol in England. I am watched every moment, locked in a tower with a window too small to pass through, behind a guarded door atop a guarded stair, inside walls and gates greater than any in our country! No force of arms, no bribe, no trick can set me free."

Adam held her closer still. "Shhh. There's a way. There has to be. I just don't know it yet. You are not forgotten or abandoned, Melisend de Longchamp."

"Then William sent you?"

"Yes."

Some hesitation in Adam's voice betrayed him. Melisend looked more closely at her Perseus. "William sent you to bring me from the Aldgate Street house to flee with him, but you were to return to him with me or no," she guessed.

"I used my judgement," the young knight said. "When I was dubbed knight, at that desperate time of which I have told you, my father bade me comfort all women in distress and protect all ladies. Surely you are in distress, sweet Lady Melisend, and surely I must needs stand for you?"

Melisend snorted, something between a laugh and a sob. "Distressed I am, but I won't ask you to go to your death for me, Adam at the Lee."

Adam caught her hands, then noticed the bandage covering her burns. "What's this?"

The maiden shivered. "I am questioned. They want to know my brother's secrets."

"They're torturing you?"

"Not yet. Not compared to what she will have them do to me."

"She? Who?"

Melisend was reluctant to speak the name. "Clemence le Royce, mother of one of Lackland's bastards, and of another little monster who laughs to see pain. It is she who is set as my interrogator, she and a vile hunchbacked thing who leers and paws and ever threatens to steal my maidenhead."

Adam looked round as if he could find an exit to lead Melisend to then and there.

"There's naught you can do, my sweet fool," the lady told him. "I'm confined here, hostage for my brother's compliance until they learn that William will not bend to save me, or any but his King Richard."

"And then?" Adam worried.

Melisend shuddered. "Then William will be stripped of his lands and titles and all his goods and wealth. If John Lackland does not feel secure enough to steal them outright then he'll let them revert to me and to my husband."

"Your husband?"

"Whichever of his toadies John decides to grant me to. De Lacy perhaps, or de Vendenal, any of that set. He can make me a very rich prize and ensure my brother's wealth and power come to his control with the flick of a quill."

"You do not have to give your consent to marriage."

Melisend snorted. "Ladies have been raped into wedlock before, Adam. It's an old custom." She blinked away tears. "The prince's mistress says she will break me to obedience. She is very good at it. I… my courage is growing very thin, Adam. I fear I might yield."

Adam shook his head. "That won't happen. Take courage from me. Hold to yourself, your wonderful self. I'll see you out of here, Melisend, and safe to Normandy and your brother's side."

"You keep saying that, but it's impossible."

"I was in the oubliette beneath Nottingham," the young knight reminded her. "I was freed and escaped from a place as strong as this; near as strong. If I can, you can."

Now Melisend did pull away. "If only it were so. I wish it were. But cannot be."

"I'll find a way. I swear it!"

"Or die trying," Melisend feared.

Adam thought fast. "Could I take you with me now?" he speculated.

Surely his bluff could not stretch so far? And yet he considered it.

There was movement below, a clatter of guards returning and the flickering of a torch.

"They're coming!" Melisend de Longchamp gasped. She stared straight at the mad knight who'd braved the Tower to see her and she kissed him.

They broke apart as the door opened, too soon.

Sir Nikolas Church re-entered with Lady Clemence de Royce and her retinue.

"Sir Marcel de Flanders," the prince's mistress said to Adam at the Lee, "How you have changed since I last saw you at court!"

The first the guards knew about trouble was when the new Constable of the Tower spilled down the spiral staircase. He was followed by a fleeing dwarf screaming for help, and then a young sword-wielding maniac.

The two warders raised their polearms but Adam at the Lee was well trained in dealing with infantry. He pressed in close past the iron-tipped guisarmes and pommelled the first man down before bringing his blade back to prick the throat of the second.

"Yield or die," the young knight offered. The warder dropped his weapon.

It took mere moments for Adam to pinion the men, a few seconds more for him to check that Sir Nikolas Church was properly unconscious. Then he headed back to the tower.

Clemence le Royce was livid with anger and anxiety. Lady Melisend held the screaming Roger by the throat as hostage.

"You will be quartered for this, Fitzwarren!" the prince's mistress promised Adam.

Adam ignored her. "We have to go," he told Melisend. "There'll be lots more guards."

"You can't fight all of them," Lady Clemence scorned. "You'll be cut down before you reach the first barred door!"

"We have you and your monstrous son," the Chancellor's sister pointed out.

Clemence sneered. "You think that will mean anything to these men? I don't doubt but John would sacrifice me, the infant Joan he planted in me, and all the courtesans in Lambeth Palace without flickering an eyelid."

Melisend had to confess that sounded truthful. She made a decision.

"Adam, you have to escape. Leave me and get away."

"I'll not abandon you," the knight swore.

"I didn't say abandon me. I said escape. You're no good to me dead, Adam at the Lee. I don't want you dead."

Adam glanced at the stairs, nervous of new pursuit. "I can try to get you out with me," he ventured.

"You can go where I can not, and defending me would hamper you," Melisend owned. "Go now…if you love me."

"I do love you!" The words bubbled unconsidered from the young knight's lips. He should not confess his affection for so high a lady, but the need was overwhelming.

"Then for my sake, at my command, go. Keep all your vows to me, if you can, but go now. Live and love me!"

Adam ignored the brat squirming in Melisend's grasp and kissed her again. "I will not fail to return," he vowed. To Clemence he warned, "Every harm this lady takes I will return on you and yours. If she bleeds you will bleed. If she burns you will burn. If she is shamed then you will die. I swear it by Jesu, Mary, George and Michael! Doubt me at your peril!"

If Lady Clemence had held a dagger she would have stabbed him. "I don't doubt you. But to threaten me you have to live, and I doubt that will be a concern for much longer. Once you are fallen I shall take my revenge upon your fair Melisend."

"She's trying to delay you," the fair Melisend warned. "Go now, Adam. God speed!"

Adam took one last look at the lady. Melisend was pale, dishevelled, wounded, frightened, and yet he had never seen so beautiful nor noble a damsel. Young men die for such a girl; or fight and live!

He cast her a salute and barrelled down the stairs.

Other guards had just discovered the fallen warders. They saw Adam and shouted the alarm. The young knight charged them, barged through, and ran onto the battlements.

The alarum bell sounded. More of the Tower's protectors looked to see the fugitive trying to escape. Some ran along the parapet. Others atop the central White Tower drew back bows.

Adam pelted along the top of the curtain wall. He crashed right into the first guard, knocking the man off his feet, rolling him over the edge to plunge through the roof of a cookhouse below. The second carried a sword and engaged Adam while the archers found his range.

Adam was well-versed in swordplay. He used a trick his father had taught him and disarmed the soldier, then downed him with a left hook. The first arrows rattled off the stones near the knight as he continued his escape.

Warders appeared from everywhere. As the gates were sealed more men appeared with dogs. Efficient sergeants sent soldiers up each of the staircases to the wall-top. Adam was hedged in.

He glanced up at the Lanthorn Tower where Melisend was confined. He looked over the battlements to the brown ribbon of the Thames that flowed far below.[22]

He dropped his sword and dived into the river.

---

22   The Thames came much closer to the Tower before the thirteenth century expansion that created the Water Gate and a proper pier beneath the southern curtain. Before the expansion, high tide brought the waters right to the foot of the old Roman wall.

IV

William Longchamp's house was a scorched wreck of charred timber frames. There weren't even any guards on it; there was nothing left to guard.

"This was always likely," Robin told Marion.

The queen of Sherwood looked at the ruin. "What do we do now?" she worried. "We don't even know if Adam got here. We don't know if he came before or after the mansion burned. We don't know if he found Melisend de Longchamp. Where do we even begin?"

Robin winked at her. "Well, we could start by letting those fellows secretly watching the place creep up on us and ask their questions," he suggested.

Marion discretely followed the outlaw's gaze and saw the two men lurking in the shadow of the burned out stable. "Good idea," she admitted.

Robin moved up to the charred wooden threshold and amplified his Northern accent. He spoke in tones loud enough for the hidden listeners to overhear. "This is no good, milady. We'll need more than a tale of a burned-out manor to bear back to our Lord de Vendenal."

Marion's eyebrow twitched at Robin's casual namedropping of the Lord High Sheriff of Nottingham, and its implication that they might be his agents. She played along anyway. "We'd best find out what happened, at least. William's not one to like incomplete reports. Or indeed, anything at all."

"He's a sour scourge of a man to have to call master, but better we find out what he wants than have the skin taken of our backs."

"Maybe was can discover for him whether any in this place were taken alive?"

Robin and Marion were so enjoying their game that they had difficulty feigning alarm rather than disappointment when the men with the long knives accosted them. "Don't move," warned a rough one-eyed man called Jessop. "Try and flee and I'll cut your throat."

"Well, we wouldn't want that," Robin admitted. "Is this a robbery? Because if so you'd be wiser to choose other prey."

The second watcher, Smeat, grabbed Marion by her hair. "Don't hurt us!" she gasped, acting quickly before Robin filleted the man. "We'll pay you!"

"It's secrets we'll have first, before gold or ought else," Jessop declared.

"Starting with who you are and why you're poking into the former Lord Chancellor's house."

"We are agents of Lord de Vendenal, good Prince John's Sheriff of Nottingham," Robin warned. "Get your hands off us if you don't want to be drawn and quartered."

"And we have the same interest in this place that you evidently do," Marion added. "What happened here? Who do you serve? Why are you set to watch it now?"

Another yank at her red tresses made her grit her teeth. Smeat leered at her. "We ask, you tell. For now we'll see your purse and any token you carry."

Robin shrugged. "Show them the package," he told Marion. "Then we can get on."

Marion reached into her scrip and produced a small silk pouch, tied at the end with a ribbon. "This is what you need to see. Look."

Both men watched closely as she undid the tiny parcel. Smeat was the nearer so she flung the pepper into his eyes.

Robin slapped Jessop's knife away and butted his head into the thug's nose. When the bravo staggered back clutching his face, Robin drummed a rain of blows to his exposed midriff. As the man folded Robin's rising knee caught him in the head.

Marion rammed a pair of fingers into her thug's pepper-stung eyes. He yelled and jerked away. The maid hooked his legs from under him and kicked him as he fell.

In less than half a minute, Robin and Marion each had an enemy pinned down and a blade holding them steady.

"I think you should apologise for pulling my lady's hair first," Robin advised Smeat. "Then tell us everything you know about Melisend de Longchamp."

"It's getting so a girl can't walk the streets," Thin Nellie complained to Ros of Wickham. "It's not that you can't find a soldier. It's finding a soldier as will pay for what he has!"

"It was the same in Nottingham when the Prince's troops visited," the headwoman of the Sherwood refugees said. "O' course, they hadn't strutted in all conquering, like, but still they didn't come with pleases and thank-yous."

The two women were part of a crowd at the cockpit watching the wrestling match in the sunken arena. The assembly was cheering and jeering as local champion Nick Hardstaffe took on the Northern contender who'd come with Ros.

David of Doncaster was getting the worst of it or seemed to be. He had to keep taking blows and appearing to lose or Much couldn't get the best odds betting on his friend's eventual victory.

"Speaking of women on the street," Ros went on, guiding the conversation in the direction she needed it to go, "my cousin vanished that night the soldiers took the Tower. She went off with her mistress, their house burned, and she's not been seen since."

"Dead, most like," Nellie admitted sympathetically. "Lots of dark deeds done that night, and more'n one body floating in the Hound's Ditch next morning."

"Her lady would have had jewellery," Ros suggested. "If she'd been robbed where would her necklaces end up?"

Nellie leaned in confidentially. "See the lanky fellow in the corner with the bravos round him? Longshanks Edwin sees a piece of every dip and grab in Broad Street and Langbourne. He's close to the bullies and beggars in Scabber's Hole and every throat-cutter in town. If your cousin's lady miscarried here, her gemstones will have passed his hands sooner or later, or somebody's fingers will be feeding the pigs."

"He's the big man round here, then?"

Thin Nellie nodded. "But don't go talking to him. Not unless you want to be back in harness as one o' his trivets and thirty men a day on top of you. Without a strong protector he'd have you away to the stews before you told him good morning."

"I have a protector," Ros said. She turned round to the table nearby. "John of Hathersage!" she called, then pointed at Longshanks. "It's that one."

Alan a Dale finished his song then finished his story. "So the Sheriff had the three poachers brought out to be hanged by his clever new executioner. But the executioner was cleverer than even the Sheriff expected. It was Robin Hood himself! And he sliced the three brothers' ropes and set them off running into the forest. With a cheery wave and a doff of his feathered cap, Robin leaped after them laughing. Then they and their old widowed mother vanished into Sherwood to join Hood's merry company, and the three squires live there still!"[23]

The crowd breathed again, then laughed, then clapped.

And a pretty crowd it was. Alan sat at Billingsgate market at sunset, just as the flower-sellers and lavender girls were finishing their long day's labours and returned to render their earnings to their masters. His clever songs and sunny countenance easily charmed a crowd of the little creatures, as well as a few sad night-moths desperate enough to take to the streets so early.

They clustered round the minstrel and clapped and giggled at his story; but they also cooed at the infant the minstrel's wife carried, sleeping Calliope who charmed by doing nothing more than breathing peacefully at her mother's breast.

"Speaking of Robin Hood," Alan went on now he'd gathered the street-girls with his siren songs, "did you know that Robin's own Maid Marion has a handsome young brother, and a knight no less? And that the lad's running for his life from wicked thief-takers right here in this very city while he strives to find his lost love?"

"It's true," Elaine agreed as the flower maids gasped and pouted. "This Sir Adam Fitzwarren was at the Sign of the Turk's Head until the guards came for him, but he escaped."

"What's he like?" asked one pert little miss, dimpling her cheeks. London maids liked a handsome lad.

"Saxon haired, Saxon-tempered, bold, noble, foolhardy," Alan described his friend. The minstrel and the young knight had first met in the deepest dungeon of Nottingham castle at a time when the future looked bleak for them both. Alan loved Adam almost as much as Marion did and shared her worry for his fate.

"The men who've taken the city are hunting for Adam," Elaine added. "If they should find him first..."

"They mustn't," one of the flower-maids insisted. "They shan't. Why, we and our sisters go everywhere in London town, see everything. And if we should miss anything, why we know the wharf-lads and the street peddlers, the clerks' boys and the runner pages. If this handsome young knight is to be found then *we* shall find word of him for you."

---

23   This summarises the climax of one of the oldest tales in the canon, *Robin Hood and the Widow's Three Sons*, Child ballad 140. When Pyle retells the story in *The Merry Adventures of Robin Hood* he makes Little John the hero instead of Robin.

The minstrel reached for his lute again and smiled at them. "Then you shall have another song," promised Alan a Dale.

Brother Florian looked down his nose at the itinerant hedge-friar who had shambled into All Hallows,[24] The oldest and richest church in London did not have much welcome for dirty mendicant beggar-monks who were little better than vagabonds. He moved down the aisle to send the fellow on his way.

"You are not…" he began before Friar Tuck caught him by the throat and kicked his knees out from under him.

"Forgive me. I'm about to sin," the wandering friar smiled nastily.

"What are you doing? This is a house of God!" protested Florian.

"I was about to ask you the same question," said Tuck. He hoisted the brother up, locked Florian's head under his armpit, and dragged him to the rear of the church where a vestry and undercroft allowed more privacy.

"I'll have you defrocked for this! Excommunicated!" Brother Florian warned.

"Too late, I think," Brother Thomas told him. He'd walked many a mile since Fountains Abbey. "Now be still or I'll box your ears. I have questions."

Florian hadn't got much choice. The friar's fat arms were stronger than they looked, with muscle under the flab.

"A seven-night since, when John Lackland's soldiers took the Tower, some flower-girls saw a cloaked lady slip into this church by the side-door. Who was she?"

"I don't know what you're talking about. I have… ouch!"

"Lying is a sin and it is a monk's duty to reprove sinners. I'll ask again, who was she?"

24　　　　All Hallows by the Tower is well worth a visit. Founded in A.D. 685, with Roman pavement beneath, the nearest major church to the Tower of London received the beheaded bodies of many of the executed, including Thomas More, Bishop John Fisher and Archbishop Laud. William Penn, founder of Pennsylvania, was baptised in the church and educated in the schoolroom. All Hallows survived the 1666 Great Fire of London which started only a short distance away, through the efforts of William's father, Admiral Penn. Samuel Pepys watched the city burn from the church tower. John Quincy Adams, sixth president of the Unites States of America, was married in All Hallows in 1797. Although partially destroyed by blitz bombing, the restored church continues as a working Christian community and a fascinating historical landmark. The undercroft is now a small museum and the Roman paving can be seen in situ.

"A lady. She sought confession. She… ouch! Brute! She sought sanctuary as well."

Took looked around. "She's here?"

"No. She left."

"Tell me when and how."

"I don't remember… ow! The soldiers took her. To the Tower."

"And how did the soldiers know she was here? By what right did they drag her from God's temple when she'd claimed right of sanctuary?"

Brother Florian trembled and didn't answer.

"You sold her, then," Tuck concluded. "Her name was Melisend de Long-champ and you gave her up to Prince John after she claimed the Church's protection."

"It wasn't just me! There were soldiers everywhere, looting and burning. We had to protect the plate and the sacred relics! We had to *ouch!* Aaagh! Aah!"

"If it wasn't just you then you'll need to pass this lesson on to your brethren," Tuck said wrathfully. "You didn't save the church that night, you betrayed it. Christ will forgive you if you ask it, but I'm not so good as Him. I'll settle for giving you a drubbing!"

Brother Thomas passed on his liturgical lesson to the unfortunate Florian; but it did not bring back Lady Melisend from the White Tower.

V

There were two armed men lurking in Bread Street, watching the ramshackle stairs to the upper floor rooms. They blended well into the shadows where low arches led to tiny planted plots behind the bakers' row. If Adam hadn't been looking for them he'd have walked straight past them and blindly to his destruction.

Instead he jerked aside into one of the narrow alleys that made this part of London so profitable for cutpurses and bandits. He pressed himself against the wall and considered his options.

Melisend's rescue from the Tower had not gone to plan. Any hopes of bluffing the lady out of her cell had been shredded when Clemence le Royce had arrived. His desperate escape had cost him his chance at saving the girl, his sword, and his anonymity. No wonder Mistress Clemence's bravos had been able to find the tiny attic he'd bespoken as a final hiding place.

What I need, he thought, *is a weapon. What's a knight without a sword? And what good am I to Melisend if I can't be her knight?* He considered the maiden, close-bound in that deadly and terrible fortress, tormented and tortured by Clemence and her minions, with only ignominy and indentured marriage in her future. *It shall not be so!*

The two thugs who watched the baker's stairs had weapons. One even had a longsword, dirty and antique but good.

Adam considered what his father would do. Sir Richard at the Lee, that old crusader paladin, would boldly stride before the villains, damn their eyes, and fight them to the death weaponless and defiant.

I'm not my father, Adam reflected. *He took the cross, fought across the Holy Land, earned respect and regard. He stood alone at the Lee and did not allow the Saracens to pass. He saved many lives and a great and sacred treasure.* The young knight could not find any deed of similar merit in his own spotty history.

Adam revered his father but he could see that charging to his death in an uneven brawl wouldn't aid Lady Melisend.

What would Robin Hood do? The question slithered into the young man's mind and would not depart again. It was a speculation that appeared more and more often. When Adam had bluffed his way into the White Tower it had been the King of Sherwood in his head.

Adam heaved up a rotting grain barrel that had been discarded in the alley. It stank of mould and fish bones and squirmed with maggots. He hefted it to his chest regardless, holding it high so it concealed his head, and waddled towards the thugs as brazenly as he could manage.

Nipper and the Canker were expecting a furtive fugitive, not a laden night-porter. Adam was alongside them before they thought again. He smashed the barrel round into the Canker's face. The old wood splintered and shattered. The pock-skinned man toppled backwards, stunned, covered in rubbish and maggots.

The bravo with the sword reached for it. Adam had been counting on it. Those fateful seconds of drawing were enough for him to hammer home a perfect right hook on his adversary's nose. He felt the cartilage splinter under his knuckles as Nipper went down.

Adam didn't rely on that, though. The Canker was already stirring. The young knight set on the swordsman with swift brutal blows, allowing him no time to recover. As that bravo went limp, Adam pulled the sword he carried and turned to meet Nipper.

The second man had risen. He wielded a knife and bill-hook and knew how to use them, but he was up against an adversary who had been trained in using a sword three hours a day since he was five years old. Adam could afford no mercy.

When the combat was over, the young man caught his breath and came to terms with the idea that he'd just killed a man. It wasn't the first time, but he was not so seasoned that taking a life was easy for him.

The Canker was merely unconscious. Adam refused to murder him in his sleep, so he trussed him with his own belt, hogtieing wrists and ankles together, then gagged him with his hose. He dragged him to the midden-pit in the baker's yard and dropped him in. The dead man went down the hole after him. Someone would discover them soon enough.

Adam sheathed his new sword, concealed it under his new cloak, and hurried away from his latest discovered refuge, worrying what to do now.

The little girl selling lucky heather on the street corner watched him go with wide, fascinated eyes.

Clemence de Royce sat opposite Lady Melisend with her too-old son on her lap, her lust-slavering hunchback crouched at her feet. "Tell me about Adam Fitzwarren," she commanded her captive.

"He is a man of his word," William Longchamp's sister answered. "If you

The bravo with the sword reached for it.

harm me more, you will suffer for it."

Prince John's mistress snorted her contempt for Adam's threat; yet she did not produce the waxed candle to scorch Melisend's hand. "I already know all about the boy. Your brother's courier, they say, though not so close or trusted as some. Too young and untested to be certain of, I'm told."

"Told by whom?"

Madame Clemence smirked. "Do you think all the former Lord Chancellor's aides and allies crowded aboard his ship for the Continent? Some were never even summoned. Others were as late for their departure as your brother. More considered the way the tide was turning and judged John a better patron than a fallen bishop. Many voices are now eager to tell what they know, in hope of favour or to avoid an inquisitor's steel."

Melisend pursed her lips. "I am not amongst them."

"They say young Fitzwarren came to your brother's attention through you. It was you who secured him an interview with the Lord Chancellor, to plead some trivial suit."

"His case was not trivial. He deserved to be heard."

"It is also reported that this Fitzwarren is of the same kin as Sir Richard at the Lee, Henry II's bold crusader. And that his sister is that Maid Marion of whom the tavern-bards sing."

"You would know better than I what tavern-bards sing," replied Melisend.

Roger de Royce glared malevolently at the captive. "Whip her," he urged his mother. "Whip her bare arse!"

Nunchmaun sniggered.

"So your bold Sir Adam is kin to forest outlaws, Melisend" Clemence went on. "Hardly a proper match for so high a lady as you think yourself."

The maiden looked away from her captor's stare for the first time. "No," she confessed.

"So this lovelorn swain eschewed escape with his patron and remained behind in a hopeless quest for one he could never fairly win," Clemence purred. "I wonder whether he hoped to seduce you after he rescued you and so claim you as wife, with all your dowry? Or even take you by force and claim a marriage by the old customs?"

Melisend locked stares with her tormentor again. "You might wonder such, for your mind ever goes in crooked dishonest spirals. He does not think so. He sought to save me because I was in need and he is good."

"Or would it be you who disgraced yourself, casting away your virtue and your good name to rut with your gallant? How could even your paragon resist the charms of your spread virgin thighs?"

"You speak poison. You fear to touch me while Adam lives and might make good his threats so you try to hurt me with your spiteful tongue. I do not fear your words."

Madame Clemence stroked her son's cheek and smiled cruelly. "Fear these words at least," she advised Melisend. "I've spoken with Prince John. Your fate is decided. Your husband is appointed and sent for."

"What?" Melisend wanted to ask: *who?*

Nunchmaun made a crude remark about Melisend's bridal night.

Clemence de Royce supplied the vital information. "Mere days from hence you will be the wedded wife of William de Vendenal… Prince John's Lord High Sheriff of Nottingham."

The shabby man with the red caul-mark across half his face slunk into the Free Company's stables just after dark. He favoured one leg and held a shoulder high, as one ill-born. When the rough soldiers bade him be off or take a beating he pleaded in a thin whining voice to speak with Master Vexstaff.

"Please, good masters! It's said there's a reward for word of a noble lad hiding in the stews of Queenhithe. I have a sister who sells trinkets on the street, who saw such a one but two hours ago!"

That was enough to have the kern hauled before the captain of the Free Company. Nacien Vexstaff looked up from a scrawled plan of the captured city and sized up his visitor. "What?"

"Good sir, they say there's a fee for information about…"

One of the informant's flanking guard struck him in the belly. He folded over and whimpered on the floor.

"There's maiming and death for those who don't talk," Vexstaff promised. "What have you to tell me? Make it good."

The caul-marked man didn't scramble to his feet, but he managed a kind of half-grovel on his knees, the best a twisted leg could manage. "Please, master, I'm but a poor man doing his duty."

"Break his finger."

"No! No, sirs, I'll tell all! It was on Bread Street, good master, Bread Street where my sister saw the youth. He fought two who lay for him at a house there, killed one and bound the other in a cess-hole."

Vexstaff glanced over at Dan Bellows.

"Nipper and the Canker," Vexstaff's second supplied. "They were watching that attic we had word on. They've not come back."

The captain of the Free Company scowled. "So he was there. Why did we send but two men?"

"Who knew he'd be so handy?" Bellows objected. "Besides, it's only one of a dozen places we've set watch. But two hours? He cannot have gone far."

"No, my masters," the grovelling informant promised. "He has not."

Vexstaff glanced down at the ragged heap that cowered before him. "You know more?"

"My sister, she followed him," the beggar blubbered. "She knew there'd be a reward, see? Thought there'd be…"

"Where did he go?" There was promise of pain not gold in Vexstaff's tones.

The informant's voice fell to a mere whisper. He closed his eyes as he confessed. "Scabber's Hole."

Vexstaff looked to his deputy for clarification.

"A robber's den, set up in the old workings under the city. A rookery of dispossessed scum, thieves, tramps, whores and cripples. Gallows-fodder, the lot of them. Nobody goes there by choice, and few that go come back to daylight."

"Why haven't we searched there before?"

"Who knew he'd be so desperate? Besides, to search that maze would take our whole company. Any less would be lost or gutted."

"Whose writ runs down there? Is there a master-rogue to treat with?"

Bellows shrugged. "Whichever knife-man's ascendant this week, I'd say. Best we seal up the entrances and set fires in all the tunnels. Smoke the lot of 'em to death, like weasels in their dens."

Vexstaff shook his head. "Milady Prince-Warmer wants the boy alive, so she can peel him before her hostage maiden. There'll be a far fatter purse if we can drag him to her in chains than as a suffocated corpse. No, we'll have to take this Scabber's Hole with men and dogs. We might even pick up extra reward for ridding Prince John's city of its surplus scum."

"Tonight?"

"When else? If we leave it long those mendicants might do anything with the lad; kill him, sell him on, probably eat him in a stew if they're hungry. No, we go in with every man, we go in hard, and we go in now." He glanced down at the quivering informant. "You know the way?"

The cringing beggar thought quickly and carefully, assessing his chances before venturing a hesitant nod.

"Bring him. Call up everyone."

The guards flanking Robin Hood seized him up and dragged him with them to invade Scabber's Hole.

VI

Ragged gutterscum guarded the rat-holes into the ancient tunnels that laced England's capital. The shabby beggar guards were taken down swiftly and silently, before they could give any warning.

There were traps and deadfalls set within to cripple and kill the unwary. They were found and deactivated with precision skill.

Inner watchmen were taken by surprise by intruders they did not expect, in numbers they could not withstand.

Within a third of an hourglass, the underground hive of Scabber's Hole was infiltrated, ready for the taking.

Gibbet Drake, master-thief, sat in the high seat beneath the streets. He'd reigned since he'd sliced Chapelyard Tobin's throat three months before. The company were mostly gathered with him tonight; the streets weren't safe for honest thievery when Lackland's soldiers prowled for what they could take. The hall was crowded when the intruders marched in.

Little John was at their head. He strode through the smelly assembly and planted his quarterstaff firmly down in challenge to every man present.

Gibbet Drake looked up from his doxy and glared with mad piggy eyes. "What's this? What is this?"

The giant stared back. "John Little of Hathersage am I. Some call me Little John. I'm here to take command of your thieves and cut-throats."

"Little John, is it? And I'm King Arthur!"

John shook his head. "Arthur would surely know how to bathe. Step aside, laddie, and you'll walk off without a broken head."

Drake pushed his whore away and scrambled to his feet. "You think you can just walk in here all alone and…"

"Not alone," Gilbert of the White Hand noted. He stood in another of the doorways with his English longbow nocked and ready.

"Not alone at all," agreed David of Doncaster, similarly prepared at another of the entrances.

Much the Millar's Son wasn't as good at timing his dialogue, but he had his bow drawn to full stretch with the others. "So there," he added, lamely and late.

The denizens of Scabber's Hole rose in alarm as they realised they were surrounded by archers. The remainder of the Merry Men swarmed into the underground chamber.

Longshanks Edwin recognised some of the intruders. "That's the boxer who set Hardstaffe on his back!" he blurted, pointing at David. "And the big one, he asked me about some lady's rings that a hunchback sold me!"

Gibbet Drake turned red, then furious white. "You'd challenge me? *Me?*"

"It's the old code," Little John replied. "But I don't cut throats of sleeping men. Face me here or step aside."

"John of Hathersage," considered Longshanks Edwin. "Not the real…"

He was interrupted by Drake's cry. The master-thief leaped from his crude dais and sprang full at John, knives in each hand. The giant caught him in the belly with the end of his stave, driving the wind from Drake, sprawling the cut-throat back to the rotten straw flooring.

"Stay down," the big man advised.

Drake came back again, more furious than before.

Longshanks Edward reached through the seam of his cotte for his concealed throwing dagger. Little John's back offered a broad target.

A sharp point pricked the fence in the side of his neck. "Don't," advised Friar Tuck. "There's no time to shrive you."

Drake came against John more cautiously now, circling and choosing his moment. When he closed it was quick and skilful, accepting a numbing crack on his upper arm to get inside the quarterstaff's reach, to close range where blades could tell.

John was forced to discard his polearm. Instead he caught the master-thief's head in a massive fist and squeezed.

Everyone present in the room heard the skull crack.

John dropped Gibbet Drake's body to the ground and looked around. "Anyone else? No?"

Nobody felt the need to avenge their fallen leader. He hadn't been well liked.

"Then I'm in charge," Little John insisted. "And we don't have much time. Listen well, because there's more visitors on the way, and they're not as well-mannered as me."

Construction had begun again on the Tower of London. Wagons of material were drawn up outside the fortress gates for the time when the drawbridge would lower at dawn and the new timbers and stone could be taken inside. A night-watch of soldiers kept an eye on the laden carts to prevent them vanishing into the tangle of ramshackle slums that pressed to the perimeter of the outer moat.

The guards were alert, and at need they could call upon help from archers on the battlements of the Tower gatehouse itself. They were quick to spot the arrival of a small mounted party that rode along the West Causeway towards the gate.[25]

"Stand!" warned the watch. "Identify yourselves."

There were a pair of men on horseback, flanking a cloaked and hooded third. One of them slipped from his saddle, kept his hands where the covering archers could see them, and approached the soldiers' brazier. "Easy lads, I'm from the Sheriff of Nottingham. Here's his writ on the scroll in my belt."

He allowed the guards to take the case from him and examine it. The heavy vellum manuscript was weighted with a lead and wax seal showing a cross, crescent, and six-pointed star.[26] A sergeant was summoned to inspect the document.

---

25   The Tower of London was a long work-in-progress. At the time of our present narrative much of the outer workings and many of the inner towers of the complex were not yet present. The west, "land" entrance described here was significantly remodelled and improved by Edward I almost a century after our story. In his time the impressive Lion Tower Gate and drawbridge, Middle Tower, Byward Tower and Postern replaced the simpler previous arrangement, and made the West Causeway a spectacular and even more formidable approach to London's greatest royal fortress.

26   John Speed's Map of the Countie of Nottingham, dated 1610, has the earliest surviving depiction of the heraldry of Nottingham. Guillim's *Display of Heraldry* (1679), describes it thus: "…argent, two ragged staves in cross vert, between three coronets, two in chief and one in base or, the ragged staff in pale, passing through the coronet in base."

The current Nottingham coat-of-arms was recognised by the College of Heralds in 1614, and then depicted (in non-heraldic language) a rough cross of green wood and three crowns on a red shield. Later a crest of a walled, three-towered castle with a crescent and a six-pointed star topping the spires was added. At the time Nottingham received its modern city charter in 1898, supporters on each side of the shield were allowed; these figures were originally foresters but have since been replaced by stags. The motto was "Vivit post funera virtus" – virtue outlives death.

However, heraldry was a long time developing, so it can be properly supposed that Nottingham's arms and seal, and that of its Sheriff, was assembled piecemeal over centuries before it was formalised. The crescent moon and star are contentious (as are all heraldic matters; long and passionate correspondence passed over the version of the arms finally awarded by the Victorian College of Heralds). They may represent day and night or may refer to Islam and Judaism, harking back to Nottingham's crusader links.

The coat of arms of Nottinghamshire was granted in 1937 and is not of ancient origin. In older times the heraldry of Nottingham also covered the county as a whole.

For the purposes of our present tale it is assumed that the cross, crescent, and star are ancient symbols associated with the city, and that it is therefore not unreasonable that they might form the images on the Sheriff's seal.

"What do you want?" the veteran asked the night riders suspiciously. He looked carefully at Will Scathlock and found a soldier who would pass muster.

"We're hunting a man," Scarlet answered. "The Sheriff sent us to search these wagons."

The sergeant eyed the dozen laden carts under canvas outside the Tower gate. "It'd be a fool who sheltered under this cloth for the night. If he overslept he'd find himself in the prison ward by morning."

"And that's his plan," the supposed Sheriff's man declared. "You've already had one visit from Sir Adam at the Lee, from what I hear. Wasn't that intrusion embarrassing enough for you?" He indicated the paper he held, which was the same tax charter Robin had used to gain entrance to the city. The seal was genuine, just like the tax gatherer they'd taken it from.

The sergeant looked at the carts stacked high with timber, slate, pitch, rope, and stone. A man might possibly conceal himself beneath the canvas, amongst the tar barrels or between the chests of tools. "We'll check them," he conceded. "If your lad's there be sure we'll give him the beating of a lifetime and have him in the torture cellar before he can even scream for his mother."

"My warrant's to take him straight to the Palace of Westminster, to my lord Sheriff and to King John himself." An old campaigner like Scathlock knew exactly how to appeal to meaningless authority. "But let's find him first, eh?"

The sergeant gestured his men forward, and signalled the archers atop the gate to stand ready. Scarlet waved Alan a Dale to join him. The minstrel wasn't as convincing a soldier, but he could assume a clerk's air very well.

"How do you know there's a man hidden under these sheets?" the sergeant enquired as the guards began their search.

"From a little flower-girl who followed him earlier," Alan answered honestly. "He slipped into the builders' yard and hid himself 'neath the wagon covers before they were hauled here. We think he planned to use tools and rope from the carts to release the Longchamp girl and lower her over the wall. Say what you want about Adam Fitzwarren, he's ingenious."

"Bloody suicidal's how I'd call it," rumbled the sergeant. "He'd be taken ere he ever got to Lanthorn Tower."

There was an alarum at the furthest of the carts. The fugitive had been found. A young man scrambled from shelter under timber chords and tried to break.

Scarlet was amongst the men at the spot. Before any other could act he'd laid his sword at Adam's throat. "Hold it right there," he warned the young knight. "You're coming with me."

Adam's face passed through a series of expressions that included fear, defiance, recognition, shock, surprise, puzzlement, then a fixed attempt at deceit. He struggled to find words but contented himself with a silent nod.

Alan a Dale hurried over to his old companion. "You're coming with us, Sir Adam," he told the fugitive as he bound Adam's hands. "Our commander is very eager to meet you."

Alan's eyebrows rose. "He's here?"

"Oh yes. Did you think you wouldn't be sought?"

"Not by him."

Scarlet clapped a hand on Adam's collar and hauled him from the nest he'd made under the timbers. "Well he is, and you're wanted. This way, my lad." He dragged the prisoner away to tether him behind a horse before the sergeant could think again about matters of jurisdiction.

The hooded figure who'd remained on horseback leaned down to address the captive. "What in holy Mary's name did you think you were doing, *idiot*?" Marion hissed to her brother.

Nacien Vexstaff's Free Company were led into the tunnels under London by the man they didn't know was Robin Hood. The passageways were as various as their origins. Some were old sluices. Others were forgotten cellars, long abandoned and now linked by secret tunnelling. Some were siege trenches from forgotten defences. A few were even lined with cut Roman stonework. In 1191 London was already a thousand years old, and its history contained many phases and more secrets.

"Where are the guards?" Dan Bellows muttered. So far they had passed unchallenged.

"It's not so organised as that down here," Robin told them in the mumbled whine he'd affected. "If there's a good haul of food, a feast, then everyone will crowd in to get some while they can. Happen they've sold that fellow you're looking for and are celebrating their fortune?"

Vexstaff didn't like that idea. He cuffed the guide for it. "Keep your opinions to yourself. Just take us to the thieves' rookery."

Robin cowered and tugged his forelock in assent. He kept forward, picking up on the forest marks his comrades had helpfully scratched on walls to indicate the way he should take.

The ramshackle burrowings opened into the dressed stone of some ancient and forgotten abbey foundation. Vexstaff observed the lit torches ahead and heard the distant sounds of voices and concluded that he had reached his target. "Quietly now, boys," he told his bravos. "Spread out. Mark as many exits as you may. When I go in charging you all advance with me. Cut down any you can. I want fear and chaos in there. I want everyone running blindly, not standing to fight. We'll still collect a purse for each mill-ken's[27] carcass."

The Free Company crept forward. The sounds of a crude peasant song echoed down the low passages:

"Here safe in our skipper let's cly off our peck,
And bowse in defiance o' the Harman-beck.
Here's pannam and lap, and good poplars of yarrum,
To fill up the crib, and to comfort the quarron.
Now bowse a round health to the go-well and come-well,
Of Cisley Bumtrincket that lies in the strummel."[28]

Vexstaff crept forward, blade in one hand, Robin in the other. Even the very archways into the subterranean hall, former ecclesiastical cellars of a lost priory, were carelessly unguarded. The Free Company were fifty strong and well armed.

"Here's ruffpeck and casson, and all of the best,
And scrape of the dainties of gentry cofe's feast,
Here's grunter and bleater, with tib of the butt'ry,
And Margery Prater, all dress'd without slutt'ry.
For all this ben cribbing and peck let us then,
Bowse a health to the gentry cofe of the ken.
Now bowse a round health to the go-well and come-well

---

27   Thief

28   Actually, this song is out of period, coming as it does from *A Jovial Crew* by Richard Brome, 1641, as reported in *Musa Pedestris, Three Centuries of Canting Songs and Slang Rhymes [1536-1896]*, collected and annotated by John S. Farmer, but it is included here as an example of the kind of cant-rich drinking chorus that might have been current even at this earlier time. The words actually mean:

"Safe in our barn let's eat,
And drink without fear of the constable!
Here's bread, drink, and milk-porridge,
To fill the belly, and comfort the body
Drink a good health
To Cisley Bumtrincket lying in the straw."

Of Cisley Bumtrincket that lies in the strummel."[29]

As Vexstaff drew breath to call the attack, Robin kicked him in the back of the knees to drop him to the ground. "*Now!*" the outlaw shouted, and the lights within the chamber were suddenly covered.

Darkness confounded the Free Company. They had left their own torches some way back so that their light would not betray their stealth. Now they found themselves in sudden blackness, unsure who was friend or foe. They milled around, some striking blindly, others shouting for order.

Then the lanterns were uncovered again. The Merry Men had been ready for the sudden darkness. Now they stood lined in a row, with bows at stretch, nocked arrows ready. Gilbert Whitehand and Riccon Hazel came up from behind to roll in the stragglers.

"Fight them, damn your eyes!" snarled Vexstaff, lunging at Robin.

The grinning guide was no longer halt and lame. He held out his palm and Much tossed a sword to him. Robin met the thief-taker's attack on steel of his own.

Vexstaff's eyes narrowed as he realised he faced a canny trained fighter. "Who are you?" he demanded.

"The last man you'd want to meet," the king of Sherwood promised him. "The last man you will meet if you can't use a blade better than that."

Some of Vexstaff's men followed him into the fight. Dan Bellows surged forward to aid his commander and slammed into the immovable wall of Little John. The giant hammered a piston fist into the bravo's ear and went at him with his stave. The Canker made straight for Tuck, confident he could overwhelm a fat friar. The monk cudgelled the bravo's legs from under him and planted the full weight of an ample hedge-preacher on the villain. Smeat lunged for Much and went down with an arrow through his thigh. Jessop, a step behind his comrade, thought better of his escape and yielded.

The regular denizens of Scabber's Hole cowered at the far end of the hall, absurdly protected by a young mother nursing a babe at her breast and a bold-eyed country woman. Elaine hummed to little Calliope to soothe her as the fighting went on at the other end of the chamber, but also to calm the

---

29   "Here's bacon and cheese
And scraps from the gentleman's table
Here's pork, mutton, goose,
And chicken, all well-cooked.
For this good food and meat let us
Drink the gentleman's health and
Then drink a bumper
To Cisley Bumtrincket that lies in the straw."

ragged denizens who'd had a traumatic night of surprises in their buried rookery. Ros of Waltham kept a careful eye on the rogues who might turn on them if things went bad.

When it was clear that the thief-takers were taking the brunt of the beatings, a few of the locals decided they'd join in as well. Nobody liked a bounty-hunter.

Vexstaff came at Robin with mounting fury as he understood that his ambush had been turned into a trap. "I'll see you dance at Tyburn[30] for this!"

"I bet I'd get a really good crowd," admitted Robin in the Hood. He capered back a step, doing a jig with his feet as he deflected the thief-taker's assault, then pressed in again to slam Vexstaff to the wall. "I think I owe you for a cuff earlier."

Between the archers of Sherwood and some close-quarters brawling from John, Much, and David, the fight went out of the Free Company. Half their number were dead or wounded. The rest were surrounded. Bellows lay sprawled on the stinking matted straw with a broken head. Friar Tuck moved forward to take charge of the prisoners.

Robin saw that the rest of the fight was done. He pressed Vexstaff into the middle of the room then neatly disarmed him, flicking the thief-taker's blade out of Vexstaff's hand and over into Little John's. The mercenary captain stood surrounded by grinning outlaws.

"Prince John will hang you all for this," Vexstaff warned.

"This and plenty more," Tuck admitted. "What's the bounty on you now, Robin?"

"Who keeps count?" the young rebel shrugged.

"I do," said Little John. "Someday I might need a nice sum to retire on."

"Robin?" Nacien Vexstaff heard. "*Robin in the Hood?*"

The laughing outlaw took a bow.

---

30   "Doing the Tyburn jig" is old slang for being hanged. Tyburn, named for the boundary stream ("teo bourne") that once ran there into the Thames, was for many centuries a traditional place of public execution. The first recorded execution there was in 1196, when William Fitz Obsern, leader of a populist uprising in London, was corned in the church of St Mary le Bow, dragged naked behind a horse to Tyburn, and hanged. The infamous Tyburn tree was a wooden gallows for mass execution erected in 1571. Highwayman John Austin was the last man to die there in 1763; thereafter death sentences were conducted privately in prison grounds. Tyburn itself was extensively remodelled in the Victorian era and is now the location of Marble Arch, where Park Lane, Oxford Street, and Edgeware Road meet.

VII

"**I** am not an idiot!" Adam Fitzwarren told his sister. "What are you even doing in London?"

"My idiot brother went missing," Marion answered fiercely. "When he didn't turn up to sail for safety, father sent word to Sherwood so that someone could go seek him before he got himself killed."

"Did he also mention *why* I couldn't run away and leave an innocent girl in danger?"

"Nobody knew anything. You could have been dead in Hound's Ditch or clapped in the Tower yourself. So we came to look for you; idiot."

Marion's brother wasn't going to accept sibling criticism that easily. "So when you ran off to chase Robin Hood through the forest it was all right, but when I had to risk my life to save someone who's been abandoned to torment and shame I'm stupid? Matilda, there are no cool heads in our family!"

Marion had to concede that Adam had something of a point. "I did need to help Robin to become the people's champion," she admitted. "But that's very different from…"

"Didn't Robin creep in to Nottingham Castle and snatch you away from the Sheriff himself, despite all the guards and every precaution? I know he did, sister, because I was there and he saved me too! And you admired him for it so much that you wedded him. So how can you find the gall to criticise me for trying to save Melisend de Longchamp likewise?"

Alan a Dale intervened before the sibling bickering fetched the watch down on them. "It's exactly what a young knight is supposed to do when a damsel's in distress, Lady Marion, but we so rarely see the deed match the ideal."

"That's because anyone who tries it ends up hanging from a battlement or pincushioned with arrows in a cess moat," Scarlet noted gruffly. More practically he loosed the tether that dragged Adam behind Marion's horse. "You've balls the size of catapult stones, lad, but you'd scant chance of getting to the lady you seek by sneaking in on those wagons. You'd have been caught before you'd got anywhere near the inner ward."

"Scant chance is better than none," Adam insisted. "She needs me, Scarlet. She needs me and I promised."

"Love," grinned Alan a Dale, punching his friend on the arm. "With it all things are possible."

74

"Better to have five hundred men and siege equipment as well," grumbled Will.

Marion hadn't finished paying her brother back for the scare he'd given her. "You are *not* Robin Hood!" she insisted to him. "Robin has some kind of… devil inside him that lets him get away with stuff that no sane man would even consider. You, from what I hear tell, had to dive in Thames from the Roman wall of the Tower."[31]

"I nearly had her free," Adam protested. "If Clemence de Royce hadn't turned up with her imp-brat and homunculus at the wrong moment I could have bluffed Melisend away. Instead I fear I've made it worse. I *have* to get back to her."

Marion opened her lips to protest, then closed them again. There was something in Adam Fitzwarren that she had not seen before. An echo of their father, perhaps? Or an even more familiar bravado?

She nodded slowly. "Best come and see Robin, then," she advised. "Maybe he'll lend you his devil?"

"I'm not saying it's impossible," Tuck told Robin Hood. "Just that Weaselly John has five thousand men in the city, sentries at all the gates, galleys on the Thames, watchmen in the streets. He's arrested every Longchamp sympathiser he can find, and a few other men he simply doesn't like. He's got control of the White Tower, the Mint, Baynard's Castle,[32] Montfichet's

31   The original Roman city wall was used for two sides of the first construction of William the Conqueror's Tower of London; the other two sides were wooden palisades. The wood was quickly replaced by Caen stone, but the Roman materials were retained until the Tower was expanded in the 13th century. A section of the Eastern city wall built by the Romans is still above ground east of the exit from Tower Hill underground station.

32   The second great castle of London once stood on the River Fleet at the city's western boundary. Extant long before the Norman invasion – King Canute is said to have had an enemy executed there at Christmas 1017 – it was rebuilt by Ralph Baynard, Sheriff of Essex, after William I's conquest. By the time of our story the castle was property of Robert Fitzwalter, who became King John's adversary (some near-contemporary sources cite John's lust for Fitzwalter's daughter). John had the castle destroyed in 1213, but Fitzwarren led "the Barons Revolt" of 1215 that curbed John's power through the Magna Carta.

Fitzwalter is sometimes identified in Elizabethan Robin Hood material as Maid Marion's father. For the purposes of this story and other of I.A. Watson's tales it is assumed that the Fitzwalters are kin to the Fitzwarrens but that Marion is the daughter of Sir Richard Fitzwarren, the crusading Sir Richard at the Lee who appears in the title role of the oldest recorded Robin Hood story, *Robin Hood and the Knight*.

Tower,[33] London Bridge, every strong point and guard-place. Every third man is Lackland's spy. It seems like the Prince might have us at a bit of a disadvantage."

Robin embraced Marion and for a few moments neither had any interest in addressing the fat friar's concerns. At last the outlaw rebel reluctantly put aside his lady-love and returned to the point. "Weaselly John has the soldiers and the strongpoints. We have the flower-girls and the cutpurses, the dock porters, the night-soil collectors,[34] the linkboys[35] and the street performers. We have the taverns and the bawdy-houses, the secret tunnels and the forgotten cellars. We have eyes and ears everywhere and ways of travelling unseen and unsuspected."

"And we have a name," Little John admitted. "Even here in London, folks have heard of us."

"After last night they'll talk about us being here whether we want it or not," Alan a Dale warned. "News about the capture of Vexstaff and his thief-takers will spread like wild-fire. What did you do with them, by the way?"

Ros answered. "The big man's still our guest in Scabber's Hole," she grinned. "The rest we disarmed, stripped to the skin, then turned loose down by the Fleet; them that could walk after the drubbing they took. Last we saw of 'em they were fleeing in all directions from angry Londoners who'd taken a misliking to 'em for past sins."

Some of the Merry Men still held that rank underground warren. Gilbert Whitehand was enjoying himself, Ros said far too much, playing underworld king-pin. David and Much guarded the prisoner.

"I'm grateful that you all came," Adam Fitzwarren admitted, "Even Matilda. But I'm not leaving London without Melisend. I swore to get her free or die trying, and I shall."

Robin nodded. "Wouldn't have it any other way, old lad! Even if this Lady Melisend of yours hadn't helped us at a time we desperately needed

---

33   The third of London's castles stood on Ludgate Hill (St Paul's). Little is now known of Montfitchet's Tower, except that it too was demolished by King John in 1213. The land on which it stood was eventually sold by the Fitzwarren family for the foundation of a Dominican abbey that gave the area its modern name of Blackfriars. A series of recently rediscovered underground tunnels that may date back to the time of the castle remain closed to the public and even to archaeologists because they are in private ownership.

34   Men who carted faeces from the city by night for use as fertiliser in the countryside.

35   Children who carried torches for rich men as they travelled after dark.

it,[36] she's in the clutches of Lackland's cronies. That makes her our business anyhow."

Marion sighed. "How much tougher than Nottingham Castle can the White Tower be?" she asked.

Scarlet scowled. "Quite a bit tougher, actually. This place is the King's greatest fortress. Garrison, prison, headquarters, and palace all rolled in one. John's mercenaries might have caught it unprepared and ill-provisioned once, but be sure they've learned from their adversaries' mistakes. And after Sir Adam's intrusion by disguise they'll be more than ready for tricks too."

Adam winced. "We'll still go for her, though?" he checked.

Marion rolled her eyes. "Of course we will. We're with Robin Hood. If it's stupid and dangerous he *can't* turn away." She squeezed Robin's arm and shot him a secret smile.

Robin had Adam describe all he'd seen and done inside the great fortress. Little John laughed at the part where the youngster had leaped from the wall. He clapped Adam on the back so hard as to almost topple him. "God's wounds, lad, if the girl doesn't want you after that there's no hope for any of us!"

"There's no hope for some anyway," sniped Ros sharply.

Elaine picked up on another facet of Adam's account. "This Clemence de Royce. I think I've heard of her. She was mentioned at table in Nottingham when I was... visiting the Sheriff.[37] She's one of Lackland's mistresses, part of his entourage. I believe she bore him a daughter."

"It's the son who's a malevolent spawn of the devil," Adam judged. "Anyway, John's set this Madam Clemence to cow Melisend to compliance. If Longchamp's estate is distrained then it might be simpler for John to let it pass to a sister rather than just confiscate it. That makes the lady a very attractive gift to pass on to one of the Prince's followers."

Robin thought for a moment, staring into the open space of the Turk's Head tavern beyond the nook where the outlaws made conference. Then he hailed over Mab Make-Do to check on things.

"Hostess Mab, how happy would you say people in the city are with Prince John and his soldiers right now?"

The blowsy landlady blew through her lips. "May they all rot on spikes in hell for eternity," she suggested. Longchamp had been surprisingly pop-

---

36   Another reference to events in *Robin Hood: Freedom's Outlaw*.

37   Elaine of Loughborough is speaking of her broken former betrothal to the Sheriff of Nottingham.

ular in some quarters of London despite the tight grip he'd kept on the nation for his absent King Richard. Prince John's looting thugs had done little to endear Lackland to the metropolis.

"I know the commonality aren't pleased at the invasion. But what about the quality? Are the merchant guilds and holy houses backing John? Or the local lords?"

Mab shrugged. The real quality weren't likely to venture into a wharfside tavern like hers unless they wanted their purse-strings cut. "Nobody's speaking a word against the Prince now. There's still plenty of rope in London."

Robin drummed his fingers on the table and thought some more. A slow smile spread over his face.

"This is going to hurt," predicted Little John; but he didn't seem too put out that his chief might have derived another mad plan.

"What this time?" asked Friar Tuck, braced for the worst.

"Scarlet's right," Robin conceded. "We can't siege the Tower, nor even sneak in there. We're not really an army to break down a fortress or invade it by stealth. What we are is bandit rogues. Thieves. We rob from the rich…"

"And give to the poor," Marion completed the mantra. "Yes, so what?"

"So we do what we're good at. We steal things and we give them to the deserving and needy. Now we have to snaffle the biggest thing we've ever stolen."

"The Crown Jewels?" Meg suggested.

"The Royal Mint?" speculated Little John.

Robin spread his arms out wide to encompass the whole metropolis. "We are going to steal the city of London from Weaselly John Lackland," he promised. "White Tower, Melisend de Longchamp, and all!"

"There'll be a rich reward for men who return me to the Prince," Nacien Vexstaff encouraged Much the Miller's Son and David of Doncaster. The thief-taker struggled with the ropes with which they'd bound him. "Men like that wouldn't just avoid hanging and quartering. They'd be made for life."

"You won't go anywhere," Much told him fiercely. He didn't like bullies. "Robin says we're to hold you here, so here you'll stay."

"And us watching you to see you don't do anything," David replied, though in truth he was somewhat distracted by a couple of giggling minxes from amongst the desperate hangers-on at the beggar's court. The women here had mostly long since graduated from flower selling to selling themselves, but Agnes and Clara were still in bloom and seemed interested in the bold lads from Sherwood.

Vexstaff argued on. "Hood made a mistake when he released my company. You think they won't return, with others, with dogs, with the Prince's soldiers, in enough numbers to swarm this place and slaughter everyone here?"

"Not before the Lord Chancellor's army gets here," Much answered defiantly.

David nudged him in the ribs. "Shut your mouth, dummy."

Much frowned. "But Rob and White-Hand were talking about it. Twelve thousand men in arms, they said, and not just villeins and peasants. Three thousand Swiss and Florentines with coat-mail. And some of the Northern Lords who used to follow that Hugh de Pussy."

"Hugh de Puiset. He was Justiciar up north like de Longchamp was here, 'till Weaselly John and Longchamp got rid of him."[38]

"It don't matter who he was. It's his men that count, and Rob said they were a-coming to take back London, coming sneaky like."

David sighed. "And that's why we're not supposed to talk about it in front of a prisoner who's working for Weaselly John's mistress, isn't it?"

Much's face paled and his mouth formed a dismayed O.

Vexstaff took the news with concern. "Another army?" He calculated whether the Prince's stretched force would hold both Westminster and London's damaged walls against a well-armed and ordered force. "So Longchamp didn't flee for the Continent!" If the rumours of the justiciar's desperate flight were false, deliberate lies, then Longchamp's absence from his escape ship made sense. The fallen Chancellor had been, might still be, the richest man in England. If anyone could afford Switzers or mercenaries it was him.

"Much good may the knowledge do you, trussed there like a Christmas

---

38   Hugh de Puiset, (1125-1195) Bishop of Durham, Earl of Northumbria, did not get on with his fellow Justiciar William Longchamp. In 1190, Longchamp, Bishop of Ely, arrested de Puiset and confiscated his "castle, earldom, and hostages".

After Longchamp's defeat and flight from Prince John it was de Puiset's turn to take the field against Richard I's usurper brother. In 1194 he laid siege to Prince John's much-captured Tickhill castle, for example, in a joint operation with Richard and John's bastard half-brother the Archbishop of York. More about that in "Robin Hood and the Black Monk" later in this volume.

goose," David told the thief-taker.

"Anyway, there'll be boats sailing up the river to attack before that, most like," blurted Much triumphantly.

David whacked him on the side of the head. "Why not give the Prince's man the names of all the captains while you're at it! Just close your bone-box. Don't talk to the prisoner. He's hung hundreds of fellows like us. We're just to guard him till he swings the same way. And don't repeat what you hear Robin say in secret. There's other ears than his present, you know."

Much rubbed his sore ear. "I'm getting ale," he told the Doncaster boxer, and stomped off.

David growled and went back to his vigil alone until the London minxes came to talk to him.

Vexstaff watched them carefully as Agnes and Clara whispered in the lad's ear. David must have liked what he heard. The youngster cast a sideways glance at his bound captive, then a longer one at the nubile chests pressed up against him.

David reached a decision. "Don't go anywhere," he told Vexstaff with a smirk, then folded his arms around the ingénues waists and hurried them away to a distant dark corner. Giggling echoed back from the darkness.

The thief-taker's moment had come. He worked the hidden razor from his sleeve-hem and sawed quickly on the hemp that restrained him. He sliced through the fibres quickly; the moon-calf boy might return with his flagon at any moment.

The ropes gave. The thief-taker was free. He slipped away for the exit he knew, the one by which he'd arrived in Scabber's Hole. He avoided the armed guards who'd been badly posted and who watched with little discipline, and he slid out to daylight without a single confrontation.

Then he set off at full pelt for the Tower of London to give warning to Sir Nikolas Church that another siege was on the way.

Gilbert Whitehand watched him go. "Well done, lads," he told David and Much. "And you lasses an' all. He'll bear that tale to Lackland himself!"

The girls with David tittered again. "Our pleasure," Agnes simpered, then squeaked as David pinched her behind.

Much was more bothered. "But he got away! Robin'll be that mad! And I told him all about that army!"

David patted his friend's shoulder and handed Clara over. "God love you, Much, but it's as well you have brawn and good looks for you'll never be a scholar."

Gilbert chuckled. "You've done naught that Robin didn't want, laddie.

In fact you've given him an army and a navy that he didn't have before, for all its no more than rumour and conjecture. Now let Captain Vexstaff do his part."

"I still don't understand," complained Much, until the girls of Queenhithe comforted him.

VIII

Nobody really knew the origin of the London-stone. Some said the great block was the last dolmen from a pagan ring that had once topped Ludgate Hill before St Paul's cathedral had been raised. Some claimed the Romans had set it to mark the highest point at which the Thames could be forded, and from there the distance to Rome was measured. Others believed it the stone from which King Arthur had drawn the sword that proclaimed him rightwise born ruler of all England. Romancers claimed Brutus the Trojan had set it when he had settled Britain and given the land his name, at the founding of New Troy, Trinovantium, the city of London.[39]

Whatever its origins it was the heart of the metropolis, planted outside Guildhall, which stood where King Lud's royal palace had once been and was the centre of the economic and political life of England's capital.[40] And

39   This almost-forgotten but most ancient landmark of London still exists, albeit moved slightly from its original location. It, or a portion of it, can be found today part-hidden behind glass and an iron grille in a wall niche at 111 Cannon Street, beside what was formerly the offices of the Overseas-China Banking Corporation and is now a branch of W.H. Smiths newsagents. The stone's glass case is obscured inside the shop by a magazine rack and is not usually accessible. Two buildings down is the London Stone pub, where a slight dip in the road denotes the covered course of old Walbrook River, one of the city's 'lost' waterways. The stone may move again soon; planning permission was sought in 2011 to relocate the London-stone to the retail frontage of a proposed new building on the same site.

London-stone was formerly of great significance. Mayors of London struck the stone to claim office. It was a site to pass laws, make oaths, pay debts, and make proclamations. Striking papers to the stone made them "official." Jack Cade's rebellion against Henry VI travelled England to the London-stone, which Cade struck with his sword before passing on to Guildhall and the Tower of London to present his demands. The event is commemorated in *Henry VI part 2*, act IV, scene VI. Queen Elizabeth I's mystic Dr John Dee wrote of the stone's occult properties. When the Worshipful Company of Spectacle Makers inspected their members' shops under their royal charter, lenses of an unsatisfactory quality were taken and shattered on the London-Stone.

40   The first written reference to a Guildhall is dated 1128, confirming the traditional use of the site long before the 13th century rebuild that vestigially endures as the current west crypt, or the 1411 rebuild that survived the 1666 Great Fire of London and still stands today behind an additional 1788 grand entrance in "Hindoostani Gothic". The building's name may come from *gild*, the Saxon word for payment, indicating the hall's function as a tax office.

At the time of Robin's visit the vast old Roman amphitheatre behind the Guildhall was

a pair of Flemish mercenaries leaned on the London-stone and spat wads of bitter chewing weed as they guarded the building behind.

It wasn't difficult for Robin and his group to get past the sentries. Many of the freemen of London had clustered at the Aldermen's meeting house to loudly discuss what was happening in the city. They protested their dismay at soldiers' looting, at battle damage, at lost business or personal outrages. Inside Guildhall the lesser guests were shepherded into the great moothall and left to complain to each other, while the Aldermen of the city met behind closed doors to decide how best to reconcile themselves with the conquering Prince who waited in triumph at Westminster.

Robin Hood arrived with Maid Marion, Alan a Dale, and Friar Tuck as the Aldermen reconvened after a brief and troubled luncheon. William de Vendenal's much-abused seal got the outlaws past the ignorant gate-guards. Alan's fluid tongue convinced the ushers of the hall to admit Robin to the presence of the Mayor of London.

A harried liveried retainer shepherded the visitors through to an inner court, under a balcony arch that held two crude carvings of London's mythical protectors Corineus and Gogmagog.[41] Marion was amused that the images resembled a forest hunter and a shaggy giant.

Beyond the crowded halls the Mayor awaited them in a private chamber. "Greetings!" Robin bade Henry Fitz-Ailwin de London-stone.[42]

London's first mayor looked at the grinning rogue in the hunting clothes

---

probably still visible and may even have formed part of the site. The positioning and unusual pre-Great Fire layout of adjacent 12th century church St Lawrence Jewry may well have conformed to the amphitheatre's curves. A portion of what was probably the largest amphitheatre in Britain is still preserved in the basement of the Guildhall Art Gallery.

41   Effigies of the Guildhall giants have processed through London in the annual Lord Mayor's Parade since at least the reign of Henry V to contemporary times, and may well have very ancient provenance. They are variously named Corineus and Gogmagog after the legendary founder of Cornwall and the last giant of Albion whom he tossed into the sea (c.f. Geoffrey of Monmouth, *Historia Regum Britanniae* and John Milton, *History of Britain*), or Gog and Magog after the Biblical giants. The earliest descriptions of these sentinels suggest images of a Saxon and a Briton (Celt), the one armed and bearing a halberd, the other shaggy and wielding a spiked ball, both garlanded with spring flowers. Various conflicting legends exist to associate them with Guildhall, where images of them reside to this day. They are often viewed as guardian patron spirits of the city.

There is no evidence to support the giants' statues being present as early as 1191. Conversely there is no evidence to refute it.

42   London's very first Mayor lived, as his suffix suggests, right at the London-stone on Ludgate Hill. He took office in 1189 and served through to his death in 1212. He is credited with setting up ordinances to deal with boundary disputes and for encouraging fire-prone London to be built up in stone. His abilities as a politician may be inferred from his survival and prospering in troubled times.

and hood and at the party with him with mild annoyance. "What's this information you have that's so important that I have to leave my Aldermen at council to hear it?" His tones suggested that what he was really asking was *What's gone wrong now?*

The forester leaned over Fitz-Ailwin's desk and said, "Have you heard rumour of a fleet gathering in the Estuary to sail up and retake the city for the Lord Chancellor?"

Speculations abounded, but there was no firm evidence anywhere. "Sage men doubt that Longchamp would break truce with his brothers hostage, but Prince John has ordained that the great chain be drawn across the Thames to prevent any warship from passing," the Mayor replied.

"And the stories of a column of knights and commoners descending from Lincoln under the banners of the Northern barons?"

The Aldermen had also debated that. "It's unlikely that Archbishop Geoffrey would lift a finger to aid Longchamp," Fitz-Ailwin scorned. "It's only last summer that the Lord Chancellor arrested and imprisoned Geoffrey for trying to re-enter England after King Richard's ban. Earlier this month the Archbishop was part of the court who had Longchamp excommunicated. I deem Longchamp has few friends left."

"But there's plenty of men still don't want Prince John in charge of London and Westminster," Marion interjected. She was well versed in politics of state. "You and your Aldermen made a deal with Prince John for London to recognise him as Richard's heir, but others in London and beyond may not agree."

"What other deal was there for us to make with John's forces at our gates? Within our gates?" the Mayor demanded.

"Besides, John is only Richard's heir-presumptive," Alan-a-Dale clarified. "He'll only inherit if Lionheart has no legitimate issue." And the King had recently wed in Palestine.[43]

"All is rumour and conjecture," Fitz-Ailwin complained. "If you have certain news, not mere gossip, then deliver it. Otherwise stop wasting my time."

---

43   In the winter of 1190, Richard the Lionheart set aside his long-standing betrothal with Alys, the French king's sister, possibly because she had been the lover of Richard's father Henry II and borne him a child. The following Easter, Richard's mother Eleanor of Aquitaine arranged his marriage with Princess Berengaria, eldest daughter of King Sancho VI of Navarre. En route to the East, Berengaria and Richard's sister Joan were shipwrecked in Cyprus and menaced in proper villainous style. by its ruler, Isaac Komnenus. The Lionheart attacked and captured the kingdom and overthrew its ruler to rescue them. Berengaria wedded Richard and was crowned queen of Cyprus and England. She followed her husband on crusade, but is famous as the only English queen never to visit England during her reign (she did get to England as a widow and dowager queen) After Richard's death she ended her days as the abbess of L'Épau in Le Mans.

"Firm news, then," the king of Sherwood agreed. "Have you heard that Robin Hood's in London?"

The Mayor frowned. "The outlaw? The forest bandit?"

"Aye, a right rogue," confirmed Friar Tuck.

"The same," agreed Robin. "I can confirm that he's in London and he's got a plan."

"Robin i' th' Hood. In London?" Fitz-Ailwin swallowed.

"Robin Hood and his Merry Men. Here to confound Prince John."

The Mayor swallowed. "And what does he want?"

The outlaw smiled. "You could start by offering us a drink!"

Melisend de Longchamp knew things were serious when Clemence de Royce did not return with her retinue alone, but with the Constable of the Tower and with Prince John's closest steward, Benet Rothmere.

"Speak quickly and truthfully," Madam Clemence demanded. "What do you know of a French fleet in the Thames, ready to assault this city?"

Melisend's eyebrows rose.

"Or of a column of men from the North marching for the capital?" interrogated Sir Nikolas Church.

Melisend shook her head. "I know nothing," she told them. "If I did, I would not speak of it."

"The rack!" shouted young Roger de Royce. "Put her to the rack!"

Melisend stood at bay, surrounded by her questioners.

Benet Rothmere stepped between the lady and the others. "Excuse me," the prince's man told them, "but I see no value in all of us shouting at Lady Melisend. It's not only bad manners but it is counter-productive. Let us have some order and decorum and then we may get some sense."

"This is the Tower," Clemence responded. "Order and decorum are not the rule here. This is a place of pain and penury, of shame and destruction. This is where wilful silly maids are broken to the wheel and the lash to learn hereafter that their value is not so high as they once thought."

"This place is only stones," Melisend answered. "It is those who come here that bring evil or pain with them."

"Well said," assured Rothmere. "Madam Clemence, perhaps you might allow me to speak with Lady Melisend?" Without interruption, his tone implied.

The Prince's mistress shook her head. "John gave me watch over this partridge. I'll not surrender her. I'm tasked with questioning her, disciplin-

"You could start by offering us a drink!"

ing her, and then delivering her to her husband chastened and obedient. And I shall."

"What would you know of chastity or obedience, Prince's whore?" Melisend snapped. "I am captive here but I am not abandoned. I have kin and friends who love me."

"Adam at the Lee?" Clemence sneered. "He's dead."

Melisend shook her head fervently. "If it were so you'd have shown me his head to make me weep. No, he's still free and you can't find him. His threats restrain your malice. His liberty haunts your nightmares."

"My lady has better things to do in bed than fret over a pale landless boy," Nunchmaun snickered, and was cuffed for it.

Melisend had watched her Justiciar brother for years. She knew that she must command the conversation so that others could not. "If, Master Rothmere, what you say is true and there are ships or men coming to London, then the Lord Chancellor's power holds. That makes me too valuable a hostage to surrender to a royal bedmate's spite."

Rothmere nodded at the sense of it. "You must admit though, milady, that also makes it imperative that we learn what you know of your brother's intentions."

"Am I a man to be in the Lord Chancellor's council? Do you believe my brother so ill-supplied of counsellors that he would discuss his plans with me?"

"A woman has ways of listening and learning in any household," Clemence insisted. "And of cozening truths from eager men close to a leader."

"A woman of character might hesitate to use them though," Melisend scorned. "Master Rothmere, I will take oath upon a bible that I do not know naught of fleet or army closing on London. Master Rothmere, I will take oath upon a bible that I know naught of fleet or army closing on London."

"Frightened women will promise anything," Sir Nikolas sneered. Nunchmaun passed another off-colour remark.

Rothmere looked closely at Melisend. "I do not believe that this lady would speak false before God. If she will make a vow, of my wording, then I am content. Send for a priest and a gospel."

Clemence's glare at the captive promised new and terrible torments when the steward's hand was no longer protecting her. Melisend stared back.

The priest of St Peter-ad-Vincula was hurried into the Tower.[44] He heaved a heavy tome into Melisend's cell and took her oath as Rothmere dictated.

"I vow before God and on peril of my immortal soul that I know nothing of an army from the north nor a fleet in the river, nor of any plan my brother William de Longchamp might have laid to retake London or resist his exile," the damsel repeated.

Rothmere was satisfied, but Melisend kept her hand on the book and went on: "I also attest that I am unlawfully held captive in durance vile by Prince John of England and his creatures. I call upon our Saviour to place His blessing upon His true knight, Sir Adam Fitzwarren of Aniston, who stands as my champion against those who do me injustice. May God protect his steps and guide his hand as he comes to save me from those who wrong me. Amen!"

"Prince John forced your agreement," Robin Hood told the Mayor of London. "Everyone knows it. You opened your gates because it was better than having them battered down. You let his soldiers plunder so they wouldn't burn. But if you really believe that Lackland will take seriously any promise he might have given you while he needed to chase Longchamp out of the capital…"

"Of course we don't," snapped Henry Fitz-Ailwin. "But we walk a very thin rope here between defiance and destruction. John's not known for his forbearance and he's in the ascendant. He has garrisons in the castles of London. Longchamp's fled, as ordained at the Council of Lodden Bridge,[45]

---

44   St Peter-ad-Vincula is an ancient church of 9th Century Saxon origin. It stood close by the perimeter of the original Tower of London, but within thirty years after our present story's date the Tower was expanded and the walls encompassed both church and graveyard. Rebuilt in 1286-7 it became a royal chapel and the parish church for the community living inside the Tower. The current version of St Peter-ad-Vincula was constructed circa 1520 after a fire destroyed the older church.

45   This was the fateful meeting called by Walter of Coutances, Bishop of Rouen, on 5th October 1191 where Longchamp's fortuned irrevocably shifted. At that meeting, Longchamp defied Coutances, unaware that the King's representative had documents authorising him to depose and exile the Lord Chancellor if Longchamp did not accede to Coutances' council. In modern terms, Longchamp was sacked and tossed out of England.

and he'll help us no more. By all rights I should have you outlaws arrested and turned over to the Prince to win his favour."

"That wouldn't be as easy as it seems," Alan a Dale warned. "We've men all through the city, and the commonality love us. If Robin doesn't return to them safe there'll be rioting to make the soldiers' sport seem mild."

"And it would be bad policy, too, to surrender any advantage you might have to just appease Lackland," advised Friar Tuck.

The Mayor's eyes flicked up. "Advantage?"

"Think about it, Fitz-Ailwin," Maid Marion urged. "What other force can you call upon that would be sympathetic to you and oppose Weaselly John? Who else has defied him again and again, to the nation's joy and Lackland's fury? Who else can act against him without seeming to be set on by you and your Aldermen absolutely deniably? Why, Robin can cause more trouble than you could believe and you'd have your hands clean to sympathise with Prince John afterwards and help him dab his bloody nose."

Fitz-Ailwin was no fool. His shrewd eyes narrowed as he considered the possibilities. "Why should I trust a robber outlaw?" he wondered.

"Because I'm brilliant," Robin explained to him. "And because I've never stolen a whole city before. I'm really looking forward to taking it from Prince John."

And giving it to the poor, he didn't mention to the Mayor.

Robin Hood strode out of the Guildhall across Candlewick Street[46] towards the church of St. Swithin. There in its forecourt stood the London-stone, that tall ancient monument of Kentish oolitic limestone. The young outlaw elbowed the Flemish guards out of the way, clambered up onto the plinth that ringed the dolmen, and winded his horn. Traffic stopped.

The guards outside Guildhall came to wary attention. A crowd began to gather. Little John passed Robin his bow.

Marion and Tuck watched from amongst the casual passers-by. "He does love an audience," the Saxon-haired woman sighed.

"And you love him loving it," the fat friar chuckled.

"Good people of London!" Robin called to the crowd. "They tell me that

---

46   This road is now called Cannon Street.

since time immemorial[47] men with grievances have brought them here to Brutus' stone. Protesters have struck the rock and told all who would hear it what injustice was done. I'm here today to expose such an injustice and to set it right!"

That grabbed attention. The Flemish mercenaries began to move in to break up the crowd before things got out of hand. Little John and Will Scarlet got in their way.

Robin smacked his bowstave onto the London-stone. "Prince John Lackland has bullied his way into this city, coercing by force what Londoners would not offer him freely!"

There were murmurs of agreement from the throng. More were gathering.

Robin hit the dolmen again. "Prince John's foreign troops have arrested many good men of the town. Amongst them he's imprisoned the fair Lady Melisend de Longchamp, the Lord Chancellor's sister. She is held close for torture and forced marriage in the Tower and her future is bitter."

This was news to most of those gathered. Few had known or cared that the fled Bishop of Ely had a sister. But suddenly Robin had put a face to the injustice that the Londoners suffered, a name to go with the cause. A damsel unfairly held in a Tower went straight past logic and rhetoric to some deeper, older part of the listeners' imaginations.

"Out of the way," Lackland's guard warned Will Scathlock.

"Why not make me?" growled Scarlet, his voice betraying anticipation.

"Best not make a fuss, lads," Little John advised the mercenaries. The big man leaned on his seven-foot quarterstaff and looked down at the Flemings. "You're not getting paid enough for broken heads."

Robin struck the London-stone a third time. "Prince John means to usurp the Lionheart's throne while the king fights for God in the East. He takes by force what he does not possess by right. London isn't his, any more than England is his. What he does to Melisend de Longchamp he will do to this city and to the whole of the realm. Except that I shall not allow it. Not today. Not when I stand here, at this oldest of rallying points, and I call for justice!"

---

47   This phrase may be an anachronism. The first *Statute of Westminster*, AD 1275, described time immemorial as "a time before legal history and beyond legal memory", then practically defined such a period as before the accession of King Richard the Lionheart on 6th July 1189, a mere two years back from our present narrative. From the 14th century onward the Court of Chivalry defined time immemorial as before the accession of William the Conqueror in 1066. The rarity of an English phrase where the adjective is a postmodifier marks the phrase as Norman, so it may well have been in customary use long before it acquired a written legal definition that has survived down the years to us.

"You're not from London," a voice called from the crowd. "Who are you to speak for us?"

"I'm a free-born Englishman who bows to no tyrant and will never turn my back on a lady in peril!" Robin called back.

"I know him!" Alan a Dale called from amongst the assembly. "That man is Robin Hood! Robin Hood of Sherwood!"

A sensation rippled through the crowd. The mercenaries, seeing more of their number finally arriving, decided that their moment had come.

Scarlet didn't wait. He moved. Something red and gory happened to the man opposing him. Little John followed in and felled his own opponent with a single blow.

Robin pulled back the bow he'd used to smack the London-stone, and suddenly an arrow was in flight. Before it had even passed over the crowd to bring down the first Flemish horseman another shaft was loosed and a third being drawn back. Three incoming soldiers toppled from their mounts, injured but not dead.

"Yes, I'm Robin Hood," the archer admitted. "And I'm here to see London free from John Lackland, to fetch Lady Melisend free from the White Tower, and to deliver England free from the nobles' death-grip that taxes us to oblivion. Who's with me?"

A slender red-haired beauty climbed the plinth. "Maid Marion's what they call me. I'm with you!" She threw her arms around the outlaw's neck and kissed him. "For better or worse," she whispered in his ear, then squeaked as he goosed her.

Adam Fitzwarren pressed forward. He climbed the London-stone, cast back his hood and cloak, and called at the crowd. "I'm Adam at the Lee, Knight of Aniston. I was Lord Longchamp's courier. Now I'm Melisend de Longchamp's man. They're hunting me high and low. Well here I am! Let him take me who durst try. *I stand with Robin Hood!*"

Perhaps it was the staged theatre. Perhaps it was Robin's rebellious words, or Marion's fervent endorsement, or Sir Adam's earnest determination. Perhaps there really was some ancient magic in that old stone that defined the heart of London. Something shifted the crowd. A mood washed over them like the first gusts heralding a storm. They changed from passive spectators to active participants. London awoke.

London roared.

By the time more soldiers arrived to quell the disorder, the riot had already begun.

The same cross, crescent, and six-pointed star that had appeared at the bottom of the outlaws' stolen identification was moulded in sterling silver on the chain of office around the newcomers' neck. In dark travelling robes that were costly but sober, mounted on a quality stallion, flanked by a travelling guard of fifty soldiers, unsmiling and ever-scheming, the Lord High Sheriff of Nottingham had come to the city.

It would have been an unwise guard who did not throw open the doors of Bishopsgate and allow him access.

Lord William de Vendenal led his retinue under the city wall archway, towards the Tower of London.

IX

London was complicated. Its twisted cluttered streets followed paths defined in Saxon times by cattle straying to the rivers, by long-forgotten field boundaries and ancient rights of way. Its ramshackle wooden houses leaned against each other and interjoined, allowing secret passage from one to the next under the thoroughfare, or across gaps between facing upper floor windows. The very geography of the city made policing it hard, rendered military tactics useless. Horses could not charge down crooked streets with overhanging eaves. Soldiers could not kettle insurgents who could melt away through front doors and appear again streets away to begin their protest anew.

London's people were a strange mongrel mix of classes and trades, of freemen, serfs, runaway slaves and new-money merchants; yet somehow when they moved together they became an unstoppable fellowship, united by some collective identity that made them a force to give even a monarch pause.

Rebellion blossomed as the resentments of the past few days welled up. Soldiers who had been confident of their mastery of the city found themselves retreating to Baynard's Castle, Montfichet's Tower, and the Tower of London. City officials who had previously facilitated Prince John's new regime grew sullen or went absent. The Mayor, summoned peremptorily to Westminster to explain London's sudden intransigence, was unable to leave the city to attend upon the king's brother.

That didn't stop Henry Fitz-Ailwin from fretting though. "I didn't expect this amount of uproar," the Mayor worried as he paced the gallery at Guildhall. "The Prince will be furious. If he gives his troops licence to sack…"

"Then he'll lose the advantage that Longchamp's intractability gave him," Marion insisted. "John's in the ascendant right now, but Walter de Coutances holds Richard's letters of authority. Walter could make things very unpleasant for Lackland. No, if John wants to hold the capital he's going to have to deal."

"And that's where you need to be ready," Alan a Dale encouraged. Elaine passed him a scroll-case with some suggested provisions for a new agreement about London's future. "Take a look at these terms for a charter that will assure the city's rights and privileges. If Prince John wants order again then he needs to make good on those vague promises he made you when you surrendered your gates to him."

Fitz-Ailwin scanned the document. "Right to elect a mayor, right to appoint our own sheriff and beadles, right to raise taxes…? Prince John would never agree to this, and King Richard will surely not ratify it."

"The Lionheart is well away and his attention is far from the city of London," Elaine suggested. "I'd think a sufficiently large donation sent to his war-chest might win his support."

"And John hasn't seen how bad things can get," added Marion. "If he loses London now he'll be a laughing stock yet again. They'll never stop calling him Soft-Sword."

"How bad can things get?" the Mayor worried.

"Robin's involved," Marion warned him. "They can get pretty bad."

A snotty-nosed wretch half-ran, half-slithered into the crowded common room of the Turk's Head. Mab Much-Do caught hold and steadied him. "Slower, Gad. What news?"

"Soldiers!" the boy blurted between his gasping breaths. "Lots of 'em, coming down Bishopsgate. With archers."

Mab looked over to the ingle-nook where Will Scarlet and Riccon Hazel had chalked a crude street map on the trestle-top and were studying it.

"Ros!" Scarlet called. The outlaw wench turned from bandaging those who'd been wounded in the intermittent brawling and hurried over. "We need a barricade here, between Cornhill and Leadenhall Street," the soldier told her. "And another cutting off Walbrook. Get those drays turned over in the road then stack furniture behind them. Riccon, take some lads and sneak round behind the Flemings. Keep 'em jumpy, stop 'em organising. Gilbert…"

Whitehand had just returned, leading some of the thieves of Scabber's Hole who'd carried out the burglaries Robin had authorised on those rich men who'd been most happy to receive Prince John's invaders. "I'll take some of our own lads up there on the roofs," the outlaws' cook agreed. "If its bowmen they want its bowmen they'll get."

"Disperse them," Scarlet ordered. "Not too many dead, or they'll send reinforcements. Scattered and scared is how we want 'em."

"We'll have them timid as foresters near the Major Oak,"[48] Gilbert promised. He bussed Mab and hurried out again, drawing his Lincoln green cloak about him. Riccon drained his flagon and called half a dozen likely locals to follow after.

"See this booty's divided good and proper," Ros instructed Mab. "Our Rob wants this to feed the needy, not lining bandits' pockets. Can I leave you to see to it? I've barriers to erect across half the city."

"It'll be done," promised the landlady, flushed with the excitement of the night, "And done aright, or someone'll feel the back of my hand!"

A flower girl rushed in. "There's some bad men on a boat putting in at Tower Wharf," she reported.

"That's no threat to us yet, unless they venture the garrison out of the castle," Mab judged. "Go back to watch, Dot, and tell us if any come near to our streets."

As the child departed the tavern doors clattered again. Three men bore in a fourth, bleeding from a blow to the head. "The Flemings are getting nasty," one called.

Scarlet nodded and reached for his sword. "Best we go and have a word with them about that then," he said with a terrible anticipation.

Retreating soldiers escaped from the conflict on Cheapside by withdrawing past the corrals where cattle were kept on quiet semi-rural Milk Street. Concealed behind the row of shops and byres were larger and richer estates, including the confiscated townhouse of Roger Bigod, 2ⁿᵈ Earl of Norfolk.[49] When a half-dozen of the mercenaries approached that estate they were challenged by liveried men in the Prince's colours.

"We're from Nacien Vexstaff," the bravo's commander responded. "We're sent from the White Tower to see if Lady Clemence needs escort to safety there."

---

48   Tradition has long held that the giant Major Oak in Sherwood Forest was the centre of the outlaws' kingdom. Tourists today will be shown a vast ancient tree that is claimed as the site.

49   Roger Bigod (c1144-1221) was one of Richard's staunchest supporters during the Lionheart's life, transferring his allegiance to King John only after Richard's death. He married Ida de Tosny, Henry II's ward and former mistress, who brought with her impeccable royal connections that ensured Roger's sons were major figures in English politics at the turn of the 13ᵗʰ century. His son Hugh Bigod, 3ʳᵈ Earl of Norfolk, was one of the signatories of the *Magna Carta*.

The sounds of conflict were close now, as rioters looted rich houses nearby. The guard sergeant hurried inside to consult with his mistress. Shortly she emerged from Bigod's mansion clutching her jewel case and her son, trailing her hunchback on her tails. "To the Tower then, and quickly," she commanded.

The combined force of mercenaries and Prince's men was sufficient to keep looters and small roving bands of rioters at bay. The Free Company commander skirted the Hound's Ditch and Aldergate to avoid conflict further west where a platoon of Lackland's levies was being repulsed along Bishopsgate.

They were a bowshot away from the walls of the sealed Tower when they were challenged by a warning shot. "Who goes there?"

"Lady Clemence de Royce," roared back the commander. "Open a postern before we're taken by these scum!"

There was still a pause as someone went to consult with the Constable. Clemence's guard stood uneasily as the street-fighting moved nearer. Some gutter-urchins began to pelt them with stones.

Sir Nikolas must have been able to identify the Prince's mistress because at last a small door was opened in the huge timber gate. The visitors hurried over the stone bridge across the unfinished moat and so through to the outer bailey. Even then the lady was scarcely able to rush inside before the mob caught up.

"Rebellious scum," Clemence spat as she stormed into the wide turfed space before the White Tower. "John should hang every third man in London for this!"

Her guards were relieved to be behind the safety of stone walls. Clemence hadn't minded risking their lives so she could collect her jewellery. Inside the thick Caen stone of the Tower there was little that the rebel mob could do to harm them.

Others had taken refuge in the fortress too. The outer bailey was full of dignitaries, churchmen, and rich hated merchants who had decided that flight from home was their best option. A collection of handcarts in one corner was ringed around London's Jewish settlers; it wasn't the first time they'd had to hide out in the great bastion.

Clemence ignored them all and spurred her horse on for a situation report from the Constable. Her retinue had to jog hard to keep up with her. They halted in the inner ward beside the same loaded wagons of building supplies where a desperate young knight had recently tried to conceal himself. The Prince's mistress vanished into the White Tower itself to find Sir Nikolas Church.

The mercenary commander who'd escorted her turned to the young man next to him. "And that," Robin Hood told Adam Fitzwarren, "is how you break into the Tower of London."

Sir Nikolas Church wasn't able to immediately attend to Madame Clemence. He ignored her demands for an audience and continued to look to the defence of his charge.

From the heights of the Tower the extent of the riots was clear. Ugly black smoke rose from dozens of plots across the city. There was open fighting in Bishopsgate and along the Billingsgate waterfront. If the defenders of Baynard's Castle or Montfichet's Tower had ventured far from their fortresses there was little sign of it.

He returned from the crenulations of the White Tower to find another distinguished visitor had unmounted and was waiting in the great hall with an impatient arrogance. "You chose a bad time to visit London," Sir Nikolas noted dryly.

"I was eager to meet my bride, of course," replied William de Vendenal, Lord High Sheriff of Nottingham. His smile never reached his eyes. "What's the commotion?"

"Unrest in the city," the Constable answered. "Lots of wild rumours about an army of Northerners in Longchamp's pay descending upon us, or else a French fleet. There's even some claim your Robin Hood's in London, looking for his lost brother-in-law."

The Sheriff's expression changed. Any sardonic amusement at a chaos he was not responsible for controlling vanished. "Hood? Here? Explain."

Sir Nikolas updated de Vendenal on the doings of Sir Adam at the Lee. "He's still fugitive," the Constable concluded, "But the lady's close-held here and the Tower's secure and well provisioned this time."

The Sheriff's lips curled back into a snarl. "Fool. This whole riot *stinks* of Robin Hood!" He turned to look around him, as if expecting the laughing outlaw to be hiding in the courtyard. "Send for a priest now. I intend to be married within the hour."

"Your grace…?"

"You heard me. I'll wed and bed the Longchamp girl now, before witnesses, before sunset. Before aught can go amiss. Keep a watch on her till then." De Vendenal's dark eyes thinned. "Who was that rode in through the gate a few minutes since?"

"That was Clemence de Royce, one of Prince John's playthings. She's set to question your bride and beat some obedience into her."

"And with her?"

"Her guard, and some Free Company men who escorted her hither."

The Sheriff almost struck the Constable. "Dolt! Call your troops! Gather up every man who came with that courtesan and keep them close! Do it now!"

Sir Nikolas gestured for a sergeant to obey. "I don't understand," he confessed.

"Robin Hood or Adam Fitzwarren or both are probably within your walls right now!" de Vendenal fumed. "See to it that they do not leave alive!"

Nacien Vexstaff had not had a happy time since he had escaped from Scabber's Hole. Paraded before Prince John's commanders at Whitehall then hastened back to the Tower, he'd had to endure a series of humiliating interrogations about his failure and disgrace. His professional pride was wounded and his reputation damaged.

He was in a foul mood when he was summoned by a mere sergeant of the Tower to vouch for some men of his company. Vexstaff made ready to pass on his distemper to his troops in a blistering outburst about their uselessness.

Except that the soldiers weren't in the inner bailey where they'd been left.

Melisend rose as her door clacked open. The old woman set to make sure she didn't harm herself remained knitting in the corner.

"Good news, my dear," Clemence de Royce announced to the captive maiden. "Your husband has arrived. Your happy day will come sooner than we expected."

Longchamp's sister paled. Nunchmaun snickered.

"The bad news," Clemence went on maliciously, "is that time has run out for my soft approach to training you. We'll have to break you the hard way."

Melisend flinched at the expression on her captor's face. That same cruel anticipation was reflected in the face of her dwarf as he licked his lips in anticipation of what was about to happen, and on the hate-twisted countenance of young Simon.

"Why do you despise me so?" Longchamp's sister asked the Prince's mistress. "What has been done to you that you must envy and destroy me?"

Clemence's cruel grin twitched a little. "Perhaps I'll show you. Nunchmaun, strap her down. The next hour or so is going to be *very* unpleasant."

The lustful clown snickered and stepped towards the maiden of the Tower, but one of Clemence's flanking mercenaries grabbed him by the collar and slammed him off a wall.

"It is going to be very unpleasant," agreed Sir Adam. "I promised you that, Madam de Royce." He and Robin turned together and dropped the pair of royal guards flanking Lackland's mistress. Young Roger squealed as the soldiers tumbled to the floor.

Clemence took a step back as she recognised the knight. Whatever words she'd intended to speak to him failed her. Fear closed up her throat.

Melisend stared at her rescuer as if he'd dropped from heaven. "Adam?" she breathed, unable to comprehend by what miracle the man she most wanted and needed stood by her now in her darkest hour.

Clemence backed away. She finally found voice to summon the remainder of her guards into the cell.

No guards came, save the supposed Free Company mercenaries she'd travelled with to the Tower. Little John and Friar Tuck peered in and waved. Much the Miller's Lad and David of Doncaster kept watch on the stairs.

"The *really* bad news," Adam's companion grinned, "is that I'm Robin Hood." He winked at Melisend and made a short bow. "Well met, my lady."

"I came back," Sir Adam told her simply. "I brought friends."

Melisend flung herself at her knight. "Adam!" She half-sobbed, half-laughed as they embraced.

Something snapped in the dwarf Nunchmaun. Seeing the damsel cling to her rescuer, being robbed of the debaucheries he had so keenly anticipated, the lust-crazed clown hurled himself at the couple. A dagger from his sleeve came to his sweaty grip and aimed at Melisend's back.

Robin was faster. His sword-tip caught the fool mid-leap. The blade punctured the fool's stomach. Nunchmaun made a rough gurgling noise as he slid down to the hilt. Before Tuck could hurry in to offer the rites the dwarf was dead.

Young Roger watched in fascinated delight.

Adam had whirled Melisend behind him and pulled his own sword into his hand. As the evil clown perished he turned to Clemence. "I warned you," he spat at woman, livid and frightened by Melisend's near-murder. "I gave you a chance."

The Prince's mistress backed away more, looking round wildly for any escape. There was none. She cowered into the corner with the old woman and clutched Roger to her. "Mercy," she begged. "Have pity on me! For the boy's sake." She dropped to her knees.

Adam stood over her, blade ready to strike. Then his better angels mastered him. He turned to his lady for guidance. "Melisend?"

The maiden came to his shoulder. She looked down on the pale trembling creature who had tortured and humiliated her and who had planned much worse. Clemence gazed back with teary eyes, waiting to hear her fate from one who represented everything she had learned to despise.

A range of conflicting expressions played over Melisend's face. In the end a cold Norman nobility won out. "Spare her," she commanded Adam, rubbing the silk cloth that bound her palm. "She is nothing. I would not have you blacken your blade on her."

Clemence collapsed on the ground, hugging Roger. The alarmed, confused knitting woman gave her a useless pat on the shoulder.

Adam and Melisend turned away.

Robin nodded. "Probably best we were off, then. We've soldier's clothes for you, Lady Melisend, and then we'll head out with you through the main gate, sent on a mission by our good Mistress Clemence here. Easy!"

Little John snorted.

A clattering on the stone stairs below shattered the outlaws' good humour. Much and David drew back their bows.

The first men to round the spiral of the staircase died. Other soldiers behind them fell back. There was much shouting. "He's here! In the Lanthorn Tower! He's cornered."

Tuck looked uneasily back at Robin. "I don't remember this being part of the plan, lad."

Little John shifted his quarterstaff. "When is it ever easy for us, Tuck? What's happened now?"

Much hastened up the curve of the spiral stair to blurt a report. "They're on the stairs below and at the doors onto the battlements! They've got us, Rob!"

And then a cold calm voice called up from below: "Robin in the Hood.

I'm delighted to have the chance to speak with you again. Especially since this time you have no way of escaping my revenge."

"The Sheriff of Nottingham!" Alan Fitzwarren recognised. "What's he doing here?" He clutched Melisend to him.

"My betrothed!" the lady shuddered. Her life swayed crazily from nightmare to dream and now back to nightmare.

Clement de Royce looked up from her corner triumphantly. "Your deaths," she hissed.

Tuck peered through an arrow-slit. "Soldiers everywhere," he warned. "Nottingham's too bad for hanging but he knows his business. They've got us surrounded all right."

The outlaws peered at one another in the gloom of the besieged turret.

Little John looked across at the king of Sherwood. "Rob… what on Earth can we do now?"

Towards sunset a lone rider made his way unmolested up Ludgate Hill to parley with the rebels. If he was surprised to see a woman waiting to treat with him he did not show it.

He doffed his cap gallantly. "Benet Rothmere."

"Marion of Sherwood."

The Prince's steward breathed a sigh of understanding. "Ah, of course. Marcel of Flanders speaks well of you."

"Please apologise to him for us taking his name in vain for our ruses."

Rothmere gestured around. "This is your riot then?"

"I'm looking after it for Robin in the Hood."

The steward nodded appreciatively. "You probably expected him back from the Tower by now, with your brother and Lady Melisend de Longchamp?" he suggested.

Marion failed to keep her face blank. "I did," she confessed.

"They will not come. There was an unforeseen complication."

Marion kept her voice even. "What complication?"

"The Sheriff of Nottingham. He arrived earlier than any expected. He discerned what was happening."

"De Vendenal!" The lady of Sherwood nearly spat the name.

"The same. He has cornered your Hood and his men in Melisend's turret. There is no escape."

"You do not know Robin," Marion replied.

"I know that his life is forfeit," answered Rothmere, not without sympathy. The lady was very fair. "Your revolution is over. It cannot survive the night. At dawn my master's troops will march in force from Westminster and from the fortresses of London. If there is still resistance then, we *will* fire the city. Do you think the citizens will burn and die for a bandit trapped in a high cell in the Tower?"

"I doubt it," Marion responded. "But it is not for Robin that they fight, so it is not about that which we should negotiate."

The steward's brows furrowed a little. He had expected news of the outlaws' downfall to break any resistance.

"The citizens of London have a number of legitimate concerns and grievances," Marion explained. "Some hot-headed few have taken to the streets with their complaints. The sober majority wait to see if Prince John will keep his word to them before they decide which way to turn."

"Prince John has given assurances."

"Then let him now make them good. Here is a charter to guarantee the rights of the city that were previously discussed. Churchmen are here who will witness the Prince setting his seal to a legal document securing those articles. If John puts his name to this paper then he can have London back tomorrow, whole and unspoiled."

"And if he will not?"

"Then he will turn all the cities and towns of England against him, for each will think they may be next. John will hand to William Longchamp the very tool that's needed to win back all the support the Lord Chancellor has lost. John will alienate the opinion of King Richard's man, Walter of Coutances. John will not be recognised at Lionheart's heir." Marion smiled thinly. "Better he set his seal to what is asked."

Rothmere received the scroll from the maid. "This will not save Robin Hood," he warned.

"I do not ask that," the forest queen declared. "Nor would I trust John's word if he gave it. This is a bargain between the Prince and the city, and a fair one at that. Will you tell him so?"

"I shall," promised the steward. "But as for your Robin Hood…"

"He must find his own way home," admitted Maid Marion.

X

"**h**ello, de Vendenal, you grasping, mean-spirited, penny-pinching, whey-faced scheming bastard!" Robin called down the stairs at his old enemy. "How like you to turn up where you're not wanted, just when it's most inconvenient."

"I imagine it must be sobering for you to discover that you are not so clever as you like to think," the Sheriff called back from the landing below.

"Certain I'm not so clever as you at licking my way back into a Prince's graces," the outlaw admitted. "It must have cost you a lot of other people's gold to get out of Weaselly John's black books after the last time you crossed me."

"I imagine handing him your head for a spike on London Bridge will adequately compensate me," de Vendenal surmised. "How helpful of you to imprison yourself in the Tower of London and save me so much trouble."

"I don't see myself as a prisoner so much as a guest, Sheriff. In fact I've just liberated your only captive, Melisend de Longchamp, another poor girl you intended to inflict marriage upon."

"My betrothed is going no further than you are, Hood; that is to say, nowhere. Your departure is blocked. You've run out of places to flee from me."

"Actually, Melisend's here with another suitor who'd be more than happy to be joined in holy matrimony with her. I've even brought a friar that can perform the ceremony."

"Perform it then," snorted the Sheriff. "Apart from the mild amusement of breaking in a virgin, she'll be just the same a widow as a maid for my purposes."

"But you only gain her lands if she's alive to wed. Try to charge this tower and take her then she's got a good sharp dagger to rob you of her dower."

The Sheriff sneered. "So you'll threaten a woman to try and barter an escape, will you? Isn't that's at odds with the legend of Robin Hood?"

"Oh, there'll be no deal between you and me, de Vendenal. I wouldn't trust you if you swore an oath to Blessed Mary, in person, to her face. But try and charge the Tower and first you'll have a lot of dead guards and last you'll have a lady who prefers death to dishonour. So what we have is a stand-off."

"Until you run out of food and drink, of course. Or until the Prince's men hunt down the rest of your gang in the streets of London. Doubtless some of your cut-throat followers are still out there causing trouble. And dear Marion must be near, of course. I imagine you'll surrender handily enough when we start slicing bits off your lady-love."

"You're welcome to imagine whatever you like. If you actually try it then you'll find out what I'd really do."

Sheriff and outlaw were so caught in their private dialogue that de Vendenal was irritated when Sir Nikolas Church intervened. "Nottingham, he's got Prince John's fancy-woman up there too. Ask him to let her go."

"Stay out of this," de Vendenal snapped. "Do you think Lackland values his doxy over Robin Hood's pelt? He'd throw a dozen like her to the wolves to have this outlaw's head. Just see this Tower secure, with no admission save that I authorise, and we'll finish Hood for good. It ends here."

"Says you, Sheriff," called Robin Hood.

"I think you'll have your charter by morning," Alan a Dale told the Mayor of London.

Fitz-Ailwin had listened to Marion's parley with Rothmere from the doorway of the Guildhall. "I think I will. The Prince's man was convinced and he'll convince his master." The Mayor stared out into the torchlit city where alarums sounded and armed men raced about. "I didn't expect rioting this severe though. Reports are coming of many rich men's houses looted, of money-lender's shops broken into, of noble mansions plundered…"

"You got your charter. Think of the rest as a collector's fee," Alan told the Mayor.

"And charity to the poor of London," added Elaine. "This way everybody benefits from their efforts."

Fitz-Ailwin's gaze turned towards the ever-present silhouette of the White Tower. "Everybody except your Robin Hood," he reminded the outlaws.

Sir Adam's heart pounded in his chest. Was it the danger of being closed up and surrounded in England's greatest fortress, or the welter of emotions that coursed through him as he held Lady Melisend near?

Melisend hadn't let go of Adam since he'd first appeared. She hugged him tight now. "Have I just got you killed?" she whispered.

"No. You bring me to life," her knight promised. "Better an hour with you than a bitter lifetime without."

Clemence de Royce watched the couple maliciously. "How quaint. Happy ever after. As if there was ever any future for William de Longchamp's sister with a nobody youngest son."

Adam fumbled for a reply, but he had never been taught to be rude to women. It was Melisend who turned on the courtesan. "This is the noblest knight on life, and the best man I know! Of good parents, of full honour, a bold heart and a kind one too."

Adam soared. For all the chance he would not see out the night he could imagine no better place to be and no other he might want in his arms.

Melisend wasn't finished. "If I had my will I would be his wedded wife, and let the world tumble as it may!"

"Milady!" the young knight gulped. His grip on the maiden slipped but she caught his hands and firmly replaced them around her waist.

"Well now!" chuckled Friar Tuck. "There's a thing. And at the moment this young lady's the sister of a disgraced man, former Justiciar, an excommunicated bishop, without lands or wealth at all. I'd say she was a fair match for a youngest son, and he for her."

"She's a bitch, and he's a stupid..." Roger de Royce began, before Little John caught him a clip on the ear. "Owwww! Mother!"

"Keep your rat in order," Little John warned Clemence.

Melisend clung to Adam as if he were her last chance in the world. Perhaps he was.

Little John went back over to his leader. "Do you have a plan then, Rob?" he asked in subdued tones.

"No," the outlaw champion confessed. "Not as of this moment. I expect I'll get one soon, and it'll be amazing. But right now... no."

"He'll think of one, though," Much assured David of Doncaster. "He always thinks of one, our Robin."

"'Course he does," David comforted his friend. "Famous for it." He bit his lip.

Robin Hood called the room to order. "Right, we need to think. First thing, John, let that old lass with the knitting go down. We don't need her and she's taking up space. Call to let the Sheriff know she's coming or she'll get an arrow in the chest when she descends."

"Let me go too," pleaded Clemence de Royce.

"No-oo," considered the outlaw. "You, your horrible son, and your jewel case can stay with us for the moment."

Little John returned from delivering Melisend's watcher. "You know that old biddy heard you admit you didn't have a plan?" he warned the outlaw.

"She did, didn't she?" Robin replied.

The answer seemed to have a sly twinkle to it. "So you *do* have a plan?" Adam wondered. Melisend clung to Adam. Adam clung to a desperate faith in Robin Hood.

The Sheriff of Nottingham laid his own plans quickly and well. He summarised the tactical situation for the slower-thinking Sir Nikolas. "Hood's hemmed up in the Lanthorn Tower. We hold the only ground exit but he commands the two upper floors. His only ways out are through the sally-ports onto the curtain wall battlements east and west."

"The Fitzwarren boy escaped along the ribbon wall before," the Constable admitted. "He raced across to the unfinished part where the old Roman stonework is lowest then hurled himself into the river."

"That won't happen again," de Vendenal replied. "I've set men on the shore and archers in a skiff on the Thames. If Hood ventures onto the tower-top there's a good line of sight down from the White Tower. So we need to come at him along the walls. He may be a lethal bowman but he's only got so many arrows. Have your men carry wooden trestles before them and keep them going in until the outlaws' quivers are empty. If any of the wolfsheads poke their heads out, have 'em off."

"That will be costly in men," Sir Nikolas worried.

"There always more lackeys," the Sheriff replied. "The Prince will expect every effort made to bring Hood down. I want the wolfshead out of that turret before darkness falls."

"And his hostages?"

"Longchamp's sister, Lackland's hussy and her brat? I doubt he'd harm a woman or a child. He might allow the girl to take her own life if things go ill, I suppose." The Sheriff considered the problem. "I don't suppose you can get me some orphans?"

Sir Nikolas blinked in surprise. "Orphans?"

"Yes. Villein waifs, urchin beggars, ragged snotty-nosed gutter children. If we had a dozen of them here and slit a throat every five minutes until

Hood yielded up my bride she'd be with us soon enough."

The Constable wasn't sure if the Sheriff of Nottingham was joking with him. "There's a major riot outside our gates," he reminded de Vendenal. "I doubt we could find any… subjects for you just now."

"I suppose not," frowned the Sheriff. "Just a thought. We'll have to rely on brute force then. Send your men in along the walls."

Melisend was well trained for her station. She knew the duties of a chatelaine under siege. Yet here there were no supplies to husband, no wounded to treat, no records to maintain. If Robin Hood's outlaws had their fears and doubts in their inescapable trap they kept them silent; their trust in their leader seemed implicit.

The maiden could offer little but support for her knight and the friends who had placed their necks in nooses beside him. She found the role of passive rescued victim sat uncomfortably on her.

A brief calm had come upon the Lanthorn Tower. The first forays along the ribbon wall and up the spiral stair from below had been repulsed. Little John had deterred the most enthusiastic invaders by dropping furniture from the windows above. One ambitious guard sergeant had got his ram right up to the eastern wall-door before a well-aimed and full brass commode had ruined his day.

Melisend held her breath until Alan and Robin returned from the flat turret roof. They had ventured to test how good a range the White Tower archers had to shoot at men atop the Lanthorn Tower. Now they knew: the lines were too good. William de Longchamp had designed his ring-defences well, so that if an outer tower was taken it could still be covered from the high battlements of the central White Tower. There was no escape from the turret's top.

For the moment there was only waiting.

Adam made for Melisend. Her fears melted. The maiden slipped into the young knight's arms as naturally as if she'd been made for it by God. Her lips brushed his cheeks then found his lips. In this strange crisis it seemed the only thing to do.

"Everything has changed," she whispered in Adam's ear.

"Things are moving fast," he agreed.

"Not just that," Melisend confessed. Here, at the end, confession to the knight seemed as important as owning her sins to God. "Adam, I liked you before; I mean before William fell and had to flee, back when you rode courier for him on all those dangerous adventures. Right back to when I first saw you, desperate for your kin and determined to save them at any cost. I liked you... but that was all."

"You were...are...too high above me," the young knight recognised. "You could not give, nor could I ask, affection. But I could give devotion, and that I offer still."

Melisend pressed to him. "You love me. I know it. And I have changed." A breath for courage. A prayer for honesty. A surrender to destiny. "I love you too."

She felt Adam shudder in her arms. He sought her purple-blue eyes with his own honest sea-grey gaze. "You... mustn't say that, Lady Melisend, though it's my heart's wish to hear it. You have been imprisoned and misused, terrified near to death. You do not know your own mind."

"Adam..."

"My lady, if you were safe away from here, in your brother's care, surrounded by your friends and servants in your proper estate, you would bethink that you spoke this only from the strange relief that comes with respite from harm."

It was a strange kind of intimacy, there in that crowded tower, in each others arms yet separated by fortune and family and history and custom. Melisend knew she had to somehow bridge the void.

"Do you think me so fickle, then, Adam at the Lee? Look here..." She unwrapped the silk bandage from her scorched palm and showed the red scar. "That harlot tried to make me tell what I knew. It hurt so much, and she threatened me with much worse. It was everything you say, terrifying. I had not suffered torture before, nor been at the mercy of such people."

"You did not speak. I know it."

"I was more frightened than I can tell. Each day eroded me more. After a while I... I so wanted to do what she demanded, to yield and confess, to obey rather than face Clemence's ordeals." The maiden shivered. "I did not give in. Do you know why?"

"Because you are the noblest and bravest girl in Christendom."

Melisend shook her head. Her loose tresses spilled across Adam's chest. "At first it was pride that kept me from surrendering. A Norman lady does not bend to threat or pain. Then my love for William and King Richard sustained me, for I would not harm them for all the world. But then Clemence's candle burned through even that defence, and I was almost lost. There was only one thing held me firm." The maiden touched her fingers to Adam's cheek. "She told me of you."

"Of *me?*"

"Yes. That you were looking for me, though all alone and hunted. Of all men in this world, *you* were the one who sought me."

"How could I not?" It was a natural response. It was Adam's nature.

Melisend smiled. "Then I remembered you, saw you in my mind's eye. How could I not have seen you before as I saw you then? Always so kind, so honest, so fair to others. You never abuse a servant or speak crude jokes or leer and paw. You never push yourself forward for preferment or riches. But always you do your duty and hold to your fealty and love your kin."

Adam blushed. "Lady, I think you hold me in too much esteem."

"Will you contradict a lady then? I say you are a good man."

She saw him struggle to choose his words. *He is as new to this as me,* Melisend realised. *He has dared the Tower of London to reach me. What else will he dare to bring me safe to him?*

His grip on her tightened. "If I have tried to be such a man it is my father's example and lately your inspiration, Lady Melisend! Ever since I begged the fetching of you from your brother on his ship I have burned for you brighter than the flames of your mansion."

"Adam, why I didn't let Clemence break me… I did not want to let you down. I did not know, until that time, how much your opinion of me meant. When I realised that I was being strong so you would not be ashamed of me…" She pressed her lips to his throat. "That is not a foolish girl's reaction to danger and fear. It is a naked soul's discovery of what is most precious in all the world."

Adam stroked her hair as she trembled. He took her burned hand and laid the gentlest of kisses on the scabbed palm. "It is likely that we will not live out the night," he warned. "Melisend de Longchamp, will you go to your grave my wife?"

Marion, Alan, and Elaine arrived back at the Turk's Head as the sun set over the south bank. The fighting was beyond direction now, a hundred private brawls that filled the streets and kept Londoners and invaders alike from planning anything.

Ros was bandaging Whitehand's bloody head. Gilbert brushed her aside and hurried over to the lady of Sherwood. "Have you heard about Robin?" he asked urgently.

"Melisend de Longchamp, will you go to your grave my wife?"

"We have," Alan replied. "Who knew de Vendenal would turn up now? Damn the man!"

"He has the devil's gift of turning up when it can do the most harm," Elaine agreed. "Aye, and Lucifer's cunning to twist the knife and make whatever happens that much worse."

Scarlet came over. "We've done what we can with this chaos," he reported to Marion. "It'll run the night but if Lackland's men march come morning there'll be a massacre in the streets."

"There's an agreement sealed between the Aldermen and the Prince," Elaine revealed. "Marion won it. Order will be restored tomorrow, under terms as close to just as any could hope for."

"So this fighting and chasing in the streets wasn't for nothing," Ros concluded. She washed her bloody hands in a bowl and moved on to the next wounded rioter, relieved.

"We won a concession," Alan judged. "For a little while the poor of London will eat and Prince John will walk quietly."

"And we'd best be gone," Gilbert warned. "Don't imagine that our part in this will be forgot. We need to be on a barge downriver tonight and vanished into Essex marshes before they come looking."

"Not without Robin, Adam and the rest," objected Alan.

Gilbert shook his head sadly. "I'm not one to desert my fellows, but there's no help for Rob and John now. And they'd not want us all to hang with them. Rob would expect us to get Marion away and safe. No, it's a boat we need. If we stay here we're done for. We'll just get Mab and all that helped us in a noose as well."

"Ye've been welcome guests," confirmed Mab Make-Do, "but I've a misliking for dangling on a rope."

"There's nothing else to win here," Whitehand sighed. "Only more to lose."

Scarlet saw the sense of the argument but he didn't like to run from a fight. "Lady Marion?" he asked.

The lady of Sherwood hadn't spoken since she'd entered the Turk's Head. She'd allowed the conversation to wash around her while her thoughts were in the Tower with her life's love. Now she thought for a long moment then made her choice. "Get a boat," she ordered. "Get everyone together to leave. I want to be on the Thames in an hour."

Ros bit her bottom lip. "We're leaving them, then?" she asked, blinking back tears.

Marion frowned. "Leaving them? Not yet, we're not. We're just gambling everything that Robin really is as clever as he thinks."

XI

Robin ducked his head back from the clatter of arrows shot from the White Tower.

"Seen what you wanted to see?" Little John asked him.

"I have. Now I know how impossible escape is."

Tuck noted the little smirk on the bandit leader's face. "So you've got an idea?"

"Possibly. It's risky."

"Is it as risky as getting starved out by the Sheriff then hung, drawn and quartered while molten led in poured into our innards?" checked Little John.

"I'd have to say no," Robin adjudged.

"Then I'm for it."

Tuck clapped the big man and the laughing outlaw on the shoulders. "So, is this plan able to wait for a few moments before we all die horribly?" he checked.

"We'll need to hold out for full darkness," Robin admitted. "The Sheriff will try and take us before then, of course, get us to exhaust our ammunition so he can brute-force his way in. We'll have to be careful to keep the warders at bay without using up our arrows. I'll need some for the escape."

"How many?" asked John.

Robin chuckled. "Say three? And one of them's a spare."

"Then if we've some time to fill before our grand last charge, there's a ceremony needs performing," Tuck reported. "Robin, come and witness the wedding of your brother-in-law."

"But if we then escape won't there be trouble because Melisend wed Adam?" asked Little John.

"Yes," agreed Tuck. "They both expect to die here. That's why they're willing to make their vows." He glanced at Robin. "Try not to mention that you've a possible way out until the service is done."

"You can't marry them!" insisted Clemence de Royce. "The girl's brother isn't here to give consent."

"Isn't William de Longchamp disgraced and excommunicated?" Tuck pointed out. "That strips him of all rights in the matter. I promise you, this marriage will be more real and consecrated than anything you might have forced the lady to with William de Vendenal. And what God has joined together let no man set asunder."

"What shall we do while Tuck's misusing the authority of the church, Rob?" Little John wondered.

Robin set his men to work. "Bring up the bedding from the guards' chamber and tear it to make a rope that'll bear our weight. Find me a good-sized bolster and some straw. Make sure we've got at least one good torch we can carry with us. Find a bar we can seal the spiral staircase door with when its time. Oh, and Madam Clemence, I'm sure you must hear this a lot, but we need you to strip off your gown."

"This is not acceptable," hissed the Sheriff. "Send more men."

"They won't go," replied Sir Nikolas Church, "and small wonder given what became of their fellows before. Those archers must be inspired by the devil. And that strong fellow can heave things with appalling accuracy."

"It's getting dark. Hood will seek his escape then."

"Let him try, Nottingham. Guards at the foot of the outer wall, bowmen on the river, our best shots atop the White Tower, pikemen to block the stairs down to the inner bailey. There's no way out."

"You don't know Hood. He's plotting something." De Vendenal looked around the inner bailey, trying to work out what. "Have men move that builder's scaffold. I can't see how he'd use it but I want it removed. And set more torches so we'll see if they try to creep out through the shadows."

The Constable of the Tower looked askance at the Sheriff's taut thin face. Nottingham seemed to believe Robin Hood some kind of magician that he could escape so tight a noose.

De Vendenal jabbed a finger up to the wall-walk that connected the Lanthorn Tower with the fortress' southeast corner-turret, the Salt Tower. "There!" he cried.

A dark bulky figure had darted through the sally port, running full-pelt away from the besieged defence.

Robin Hood's harsh voice echoed down to the watchers in the court-yard. "Adam, stop! It won't work! We need her here!"

The fugitive raced past the torches tossed to light the gantry. It was Adam Fitzwarren. Slung over his shoulder in a fireman's lift, shielding him from the Tower's archers, was the limp shape of Melisend de Longchamp.

"Hold your fire!" roared de Vendenal. "That's my wife!"

"Adam, halt!" thundered Robin Hood. "Last warning!"

The young knight struggled on, making for the same spot where he'd dived to safety before.

An arrow slammed into him. It wasn't the archers atop the White Tower, nor those who manned the slits of the other wall turrets. The shot came from Robin Hood himself. It avoided the form draped over the young knight's shoulder and smacked home at his left shoulder blade. It dropped Adam in his tracks, sending him tumbling to the ground.

Adam's limp burden slipped from his shoulders as he fell. Melisend's shrill scream filled the courtyard. The trussed body rolled, then toppled over the lip of the parapet. She fell the forty feet into the inner bailey and crashed atop the wagons of building materials lined up by the wall. The scream ended abruptly.

"No!" shouted de Vendenal. He and Sir Nikolas raced together towards the fallen lady, though there was scant chance of her surviving so deadly a drop.

The Sheriff stopped short. Going to Melisend would bring him in range of Robin's bow, and already the outlaw archer had another arrow nocked.

And then the Sheriff realised what Robin Hood's target would be. The fallen woman, if indeed Melisend's gown contained more than bolsters and stuffing, had brought soldiers running in all directions to gather in one place. "Church! Get back! Get away! He's…"

Robin's hundred-and-twenty pound pull launched the burning shaft downward with a force that could punch through plate armour. His target was not Sir Nikolas Church, nor any of the other soldiers who raced towards the fallen bundle beneath the outer wall. The arrow went straight at the builder's cart that carried barrels of pitch for waterproofing the Tower's new construction. It sliced through the planks of the container with ease and seared into the thick flammable resin within.

The barrel exploded. Burning tar sprayed in every direction, showering the nearest guards with black, boiling pitch. The fireball consumed the other barrels. Each detonated in turn, adding its own load to the conflagration.

The inner bailey turned into a blazing inferno. Wooden sheds lining the walls caught and burned. Choking black smoke welled up to engulf the sentinels on the White Tower.

The Sheriff picked himself up from the cobbles where the blast had hurled him. Sir Nikolas was down, stunned by the explosion. His soldiers were milling around, panicked by the flames, undirected.

Robin Hood was making his escape.

"Time," called Robin. Much dropped the linen rope over the side of the parapet and secured it.

"Me first," called Little John. If the rope held his weight it would take the rest. More importantly, guards waited at the base of the wall. John of Hathersage intended to discourage them.

The big man rappelled down to meet the soldiers with the Thames lapping at their heels. David of Doncaster hurried after him.

A vigilant sentry pointed at the descending giant. "A man there!" he shouted. Little John hammered him down but that alarm was given. There were plenty of other guards on the mud strand.

John and David were forced back towards the wall even by the sheer numbers of attackers. "How many men did the Sheriff send round here?" David wondered as more and more guards loomed from the darkness.

"Quite enough of them!" came the crowed reply. Nacien Vexstaff emerged from the gloom. His twisted smile was not pleasant. "I do hope you won't try and surrender. I'm spoiling to pay you scum back for shaming me before."

The thief-taker gestured and his men went in.

"They're escaping over the wall!" the Sheriff of Nottingham called. "Send more men round the riverbank. Signal to the archers on the Thames. Now!"

Hasty signal lantern warnings from the Salt Tower warned the Sheriff's boat that escapees were down on the shore, fighting in the darkness.

"Get lights over there!" de Vendenal called. The great courtyard blaze was destroying any chance of night-vision for the remaining bowmen on the walls. "Get reinforcements! Move!"

Adam scrambled to his knees. He pulled the arrow from the plank he'd concealed under his cotte. Robin had used expert judgement to place that shaft so accurately yet to prevent it splitting the board and the man behind it; even so the young knight felt as if he'd been kicked by a horse.

He tucked the shaft into his belt and ventured a peek down into the roiling black smoke that filled the courtyard. The heavy bundle of rags dressed in Melisend's clothes burned merrily along with the carts of building timber, the half-demolished scaffolding, and the more unfortunate of the soldiers.

An arrow clattered off the battlement beside Adam. He was halfway between the Lanthorn and Salt Towers, in range of the archers in the southeast turret. He hurried to his feet and closed the distance back to the spot where the outlaws were climbing down to the Thames shore.

Only Robin and Melisend remained when Adam rejoined them. Robin hauled up the makeshift cable and looped it for Melisend's heel so she could be lowered from the castle.

Melisend kissed Adam hastily, reassuring herself that her paladin was somehow, miraculously in one piece. "They're trying to force the door from the stair below," the lady warned. The sound of axes on reinforced wood echoed from the Lanthorn Tower.

"We need to get down quickly," Robin warned. "It sounds like there's quite a fight going on and the lads might need help. Melisend, set your foot in this. Adam, help me pay out the line to set her down gently."

Another explosion bloomed in the inner bailey as the fire caught the last of the tar barrels. For a moment the wall was choked with smoke and bright straw sparks.

Clemence de Royce made her move. In the confusion she'd slipped her bonds and seized up Nunchmaun's unregarded dagger. Now she darted from the sally port and brought the blade to Melisend's throat.

"Hold, all!" the Prince's mistress called. Her voice was thick with hate and triumph. "None will leave if they wish this bitch's neck unslitted!"

Robin froze. Adam slid to a halt, too many paces distant to prevent his new-made wife from being the cruel courtesan's hostage.

Clemence pressed the knife tight enough to draw blood. It trickled down Melisend's neck to stain the hem of the gown that the outlaws had confiscated from the woman who now held her. "Cast away your weapons and yield," Prince John's mistress demanded of the outlaw and the knight. "Do it now."

Adam didn't stop to see what Robin would do. He dropped his sword and dagger onto the battlement walkway.

"Over the edge," Clemence insisted.

Adam nudged his weapons down to the fume-choked courtyard. Robin tossed his bow and sword down to the Thames shore.

"Roger, come out!" the Prince's mistress called. Her pale vicious son slunk from the shadows. "Unbar the door, my darling, and let the soldiers in," the Prince's mistress commanded. "Quickly!"

Adam instinctively braced himself to grab the child and prevent him granting access to the warders. Clemence twisted the knife at Melisend's neck. "Hold fast, bold hero. It would be no hardship to me to slice this spoiled princess' face."

Melisend saw that they would comply. Adam, Robin, all of them would be lost because of her. She saw the fear and despair in her true love's face.

"Robin?" asked Adam, desperate and bleak.

"As she says," the outlaw advised. "We can always escape later."

"There will be no more escapes," vowed Clemence de Royce.

The Canker roared as he charged Little John. The wild mercenary had a shortsword in each hand and he came in low, aiming at the giant's legs. Behind him, sneaky Jessop manoeuvred for a stab at the big man's back.

Little John ignored the assassin. David intervened as he knew the lad would, slamming Jessop into the shallows and grinding the mercenary's head beneath his boot while fending off the bravos who followed after. John concentrated on the blood-crazed Canker. He fended with his stave while the pock-riddled killer exhausted his first fury, then caught the thug a gut-smack before breaking his back.

Friar Tuck dropped to the muddy shore beside John and David. "Oh, this doesn't look good," he admitted, crossing himself.

Much climbed down behind him, wide-eyed at the number of fallen attackers lying round Little John in the shallows.

But there were more soldiers still. Vexstaff ranged them to surround the outlaws. "Take your time, boys. They're not going anywhere."

Little John flexed his staff. "Come on, then, thief-taker! I'll split you like I did your second!"

The Free Company captain shook his head. "I don't play fighting games, you stupid oaf. I take wolfsheads down, hard, fast, and any way I can. You're a big man with a quarterstaff, Little John. How do you cope with a score of arrows?"

Now the archers with Vexstaff loomed into view, each man with a nocked shortbow, every one ready to take the escapees down.

"Cripple them, but don't kill," Vexstaff ordered. "I want them alive for torture."

The whirr of arrows filled the night.

XII

No more escapes. Clemence de Royce had said it and Melisend had heard the death-intent in the woman's voice. She also heard the bar being drawn back from the stairway door and the clamour as Sir Nikolas Church and his men entered the Lanthorn Tower. Clemence had made Melisend her victim again, and this time the courtesan would make sure there were no happy endings.

Fury welled inside the hostage. The anxiety, the pain, the shame, the fear all surged up, but above them were passion and duty and a shimmering desire to be *worthy* of Adam's love. With no conscious thought she jerked her hand over her shoulder and jabbed her fingers into Clemence's eyes. The courtesan screeched and shied back naturally. Melisend bit the hand that threatened her. For a moment the blade was clear of the maiden's throat.

"Kill her!" screamed Melisend de Longchamp.

Robin seized the forgotten arrow that Adam had slipped into his belt. He leaped to the entangled women and jabbed the shaft into Clemence's neck.

John's mistress flinched backwards. Blood welled from her wound. She tottered. Then Melisend slammed into Clemence, toppling the dying courtesan over the battlements. Adam caught the maiden before she fell with her tormentor. Clemence's shift-clad body splashed lifeless into the shallows after the escaping men of Sherwood Forest.

"*Mother!*" screamed Roger de Royce. He rolled hate-filled eyes at Robin Hood. "I'll kill you for this!" he promised. "I'll *kill you!*"

Sir Nikolas Church elbowed the boy aside and came at the unarmed bandit.

Adam shouldered into the Constable of the Tower, knocking him back into the sally port so no other men could achieve the wall-top. The young knight seized up the same dagger that had been at Melisend's neck and went in close to engage his fully-armoured adversary.

"Hood... get her out!" demanded Sir Adam.

Adam Fitzwarren's father had been a great crusader. In his youth, at a forest clearing outside Damascus, the elder Fitzwarren had held the breach alone for five hours against the cream of Nur ad-Din's warriors, and had won renown and the name Sir Richard at the Lee.[50] His son was sometimes accorded that same title, but he had never stood against impossible odds where any sane man would flee, stemming uncountable enemies for an unbreakable passion. Until now.

Robin Hood was often inspired to daring folly and foolhardy heroics. He did not grudge Adam at the Lee his moment now. "Come on," he told Melisend de Longchamp, new-made Lady of Aniston. "He knows what he's doing!"

Sir Nikolas hammered Adam back, trying to force his way onto the wall-top so that others could follow after. Adam held in close, knowing that his only hope with a dagger was to keep inside his opponent's swing.

"He'll die!" gasped Melisend as Robin helped her over the crenulations.

"Give him something to live for," the outlaw told her. "Hold tight."

The lady had a rapid descent.

At the foot of the outer wall the outlaws stood at bay, surrounded by Vexstaff's bowmen.

The whirr of arrows filled the night. The thief-taker's archers screamed as they fell.

Vexstaff whirled round as his men were shot down. "What?" He waved his arms at the incoming boat. "You fools! We're the Prince's men. It's the outlaws you want!"

"Right you are," Maid Marion's voice came back from across the water. "That's why we borrowed the Sheriff's skiff to come and collect them."

"She knew Rob'd try something," Tuck surmised. "So she waited for us."

"And he knew she'd be waiting," Little John replied. "That's Robin and Marion for you."

Vexstaff stared in horror as his remaining troops broke and fled. Armed men before them with more descending the wall, archers behind them in the darkness; they ran for their lives.

Little John waded into the water for Vexstaff. "I hope you won't try and surrender," the big man echoed the thief-taker's earlier words.

---

50   The culmination of the Second Crusade was the 1148 Siege of Damascus, wherein Christian crusaders attempted to take the Moslem city. A counterattack from Nur ad-Din, ruler of Aleppo, caught the besiegers unprepared and led to many individual battles in the orchards west of Damascus. *Lee* is a Saxon word for a wooded area.

Melisend de Longchamp descended on her makeshift tether to alight close by Clemence de Royce's shattered bloody corpse. Tuck hurried over to guide her away. "Where's Rob?" the fat monk checked.

Robin Hood swung down from the battlements. "Right here," he called to his men. "I see you've been keeping busy. Marion?"

"On the water," came back the lady of Sherwood's reply. "And hauling you from trouble as usual. Where's my brother?"

Robin glanced worriedly at the battlements. "It was his turn to be hero," he admitted. "I hope he survives it."

Sir Nikolas Church was perhaps past his fighting prime, and had suffered somewhat in the courtyard explosion, but he was a canny and experienced warrior. He quickly brought his skills to bear, knocking aside his young opponent's short blade and slamming Adam back with a straight shield-push.

Adam's dagger skated uselessly over the wood-and-metal surface of the Constable's shield. Without intending it, the youngster had to give back a pace. Sir Nikolas pressed his attack.

"Yield, Fitzwarren," the Constable demanded. "Maybe you can save your life."

"I am saving my life," Sir Adam at the Lee replied with a sudden surge of joy. "I'm fighting for her!"

Adam dropped Nunchmaun's weapon and instead locked his hand round the Constable's sword-wrist. They closed to wrestle. That brought Adam near enough to twist the Constable's blast-scorched helmet and obscure Sir Nikolas' vision. Adam hooked a leg to the blinded fighter's ankles and tipped him to the ground.

The next man behind the Constable surged in. Adam planted a foot on the fallen knight's chest to keep him down and seized up Sir Nikolas' discarded sword.

The nature of the battle had changed, though. Adam's new opponent had a heavy mace that could shatter any bone it connected with. The Tower guards mostly carried halberds. The men behind could stab forward with their polearms, past their fellow. Any one of them could pierce the young warrior or knock him from the ledge. Thick black fumes from the courtyard conflagration masked Fitzwarren from White Tower archers but also concealed guards creeping at him along the wall-top.

Sir Adam was forced back another step. The front soldier stepped aside to allow a second to join him through the sally port. Adam made a desperate calculation, ducked under a mace-swing that could have splintered his skull, and crashed low into the first guard. That warder was knocked off-balance and barrelled into his fellow. Adam heaved and both men toppled from the parapet. Their cries ended suddenly as they dropped through the burning straw roof of the wooden building below.

Sir Nikolas grabbed Adam's leg and tried to skewer it with a stiletto. The young knight kicked out and caught the Constable in the front of his helm, displacing it again.

More soldiers thronged through the undefended doorway. Behind them the hysterical Roger de Royce was screaming for them to slaughter Sir Adam. More alarming were the cold sober commands of the Sheriff of Nottingham, co-ordinating men to fold in on the fugitive from both sides, sending others to the roof of the Lanthorn Tower to take him down with bows.

Robin Hood's horn sounded from the river below. Adam took it as a sign that the need for obstruction was now over.

Even as he looked to the ragged sheet-rope, Sir Nikolas anticipated his escape route and sawed through it, sending it falling after Clemence de Royce and the escaped outlaws.

Adam hammered a last boot into a knight he was heartily coming to dislike and set off at a run along the parapet. The first arrows from the Lanthorn Tower splintered on the flagstones beside him. The soldiers through the sally port were two paces from his back.

"Stop him!" he heard de Vendenal call. "Bring him down *now!*"

In the darkness and the shroud of fumes, with the blazing glare of the courtyard inferno to his left, Adam could not judge whether he'd reached the spot where he'd previously jumped for his life. He only knew that he was out of time.

He leaped up through a gap where the old Roman wall was crumbled and launched himself into the night.

For a moment that stretched far too long he was in free fall. *Melisend*, he thought. Then the Thames hit him with a breath-stealing force.

He floundered, struggling for consciousness. The cold November water sucked him under.

"Archers!" shouted William de Vendenal. "Pepper the water. Keep firing 'till you *kill someone!*"

Robin steadied himself on the swaying deck of the Sheriff's skiff. He hefted his retrieved bow. "Arrow," he prompted, holding out his hand. Scarlet passed him a shaft.

Robin fired at extreme range, upwards onto the Tower wall where his old enemy stood silhouetted by the blaze inside. The shot passed between the crenulations and sliced through de Vendenal's neat small beard. The Sheriff yelped and hastily dived behind a buttress.

"That'll discourage him from standing around giving orders," the outlaw laughed.

Melisend didn't care about her supposed-husband's discomfit. She wanted her actual one. "Where's Adam?" she demanded urgently.

Slender hands hauled Adam to the surface. He breathed, choked up water, and breathed again. A hand across his chest hauled him over the river.

"Not bad for my idiot brother," Marion told him as she swum him back to the barge.

By the time the Sheriff reached the shore the outlaws had taken the archers' launch and rowed away. Vexstaff's body floated face down and unmourned in the shallows beside the corpse of Clemence de Royce.

"Launch the Prince's galleys," de Vendenal commanded. "They're in a small vessel. We can catch them."

"There's a chain drawn across Thames," someone reminded him. "They'll pass it but big ships won't. They're gone."

The Sheriff of Nottingham kicked Vexstaff's corpse for ten minutes. It didn't make him feel any happier.

Dull grey morning found Robin and his band in cover at Swanscombe, far enough downriver that pursuit was impossible. Adam and Melisend appeared from the shepherd's hut they'd shared for the night, holding hands and blushing. The Merry Man gave them a hearty cheer.

Marion hugged her new sister for support and slipped her a wink. "How's marriage?" she whispered.

Melisend flushed more. "Marriage is good," she whispered back. "Marriage is… very good!"

Adam and Melisend's hands remained locked together. Somehow in the nightmare chaos of the Lord Chancellor's fall and Prince John's ascendance these two had come together and salvaged something invaluable from the wreckage. And if they had found hope for a future then was there not a chance for others too?

Sir Adam dragged himself from his blissful haze to consider the reality of the situation. "We must return Lady Melisend to her brother," he decided. "And we must explain to Lord William what has… occurred."

"My brother always intended me to secure him a valuable ally, some resource to strengthen him and prosper our dynasty," Melisend declared. "That I have done. Sir Adam many not be rich nor hold grand estates, but he is great in valour and unmatched in honour. If William cannot see how that is of greater value still then he is a fool; and my brother's no fool."

"Mine is," Marion told her, "but I've learned there's sometimes a special blessing in loving the right kind of fool."

"Whatever William may think, I am Adam's lady now," Melisend insisted. "I have vowed it and God has witnessed it. All else may fall where it will."

"I warrant Lord Longchamp will be glad to have his sister back and out of Prince John's hands whatsoever her condition," Alan a Dale promised his friend. "He might even be glad to have one heroic deed to add lustre to his hasty retreat."

Friar Tuck passed round a wineskin he'd somehow acquired. "I expect Lord William desperately needs kin he can rely upon right now. A bold young fellow like Sir Adam at the Lee might have a good future in his service."

Robin tossed a pouch of coins over to the newlyweds, along with a few choice pieces from Clemence's jewel case. "We'll see you to Dover. After that you'll have to adventure on your own, for we're Sherwood-bound."

"Or come with us," Melisend offered. "My brother will grant you refuge and pardon."

"We need no man's pardon," insisted Scarlet.

"And Sherwood's our refuge," added Gilbert. "The Sheriff can seek us there if he durst."

"Prince John has all the power now," Adam warned the outlaws. "Everything has changed. The alliances and politics that have held him back before have all gone away."

"Then we're needed more than ever," replied Robin in the Hood.

"Because we haven't annoyed the Sheriff enough yet?" checked Little John.

"Because this wasn't a close enough scrape?" suggested Friar Tuck.

Robin looked across the winter land, looking further than even an archer's keen vision could see. Across the whole country men and women laboured and suffered without freedom or choice. Barons, bishops, and princes revelled and plotted without regard for those they ruled. Men toiled and died without voice, without hope, without champions.

"We're needed…" Robin breathed, "because people still hunger, and labour without rights, and suffer without justice. Because the rich grow richer and the poor grow poorer. Because someone has to stand against the law when the law does wrong. Because…"

"Because you enjoy it," teased Marion, nudging him.

"Well, yes," conceded the outlaw. "Obviously."

Melisend looked at the Merry Men, wild and unafraid despite the forces arraying against them. "So this is freedom," she said to Adam. "Terrifying and exhilarating."

"Like true love," the young knight answered her.

"We're needed. We are the free men of Sherwood," concluded Robin Hood. "It's what we do."

THE END

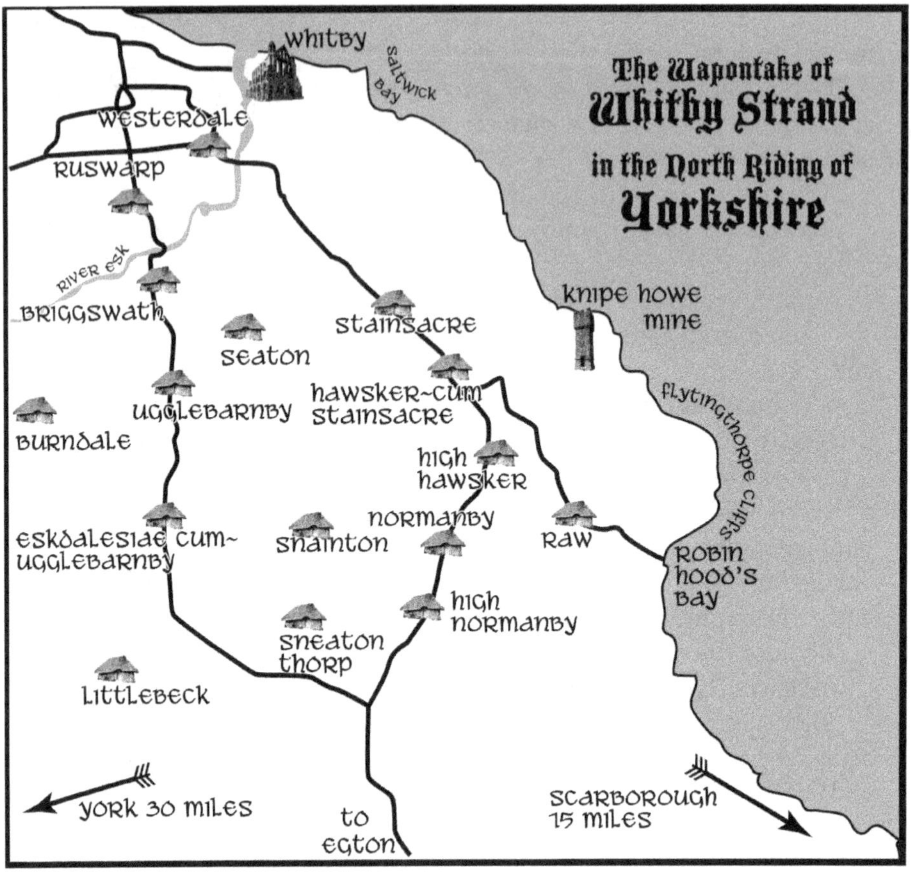

The Wapentake of
Whitby Strand
in the North Riding of
Yorkshire

Whitby

Saltwick Bay

Westerdale

Ruswarp

River Esk

Briggswath

Seaton

Staimsacre

Knipe Howe Mine

Flytingthorpe Cliffs

Ugglebarnby

Hawsker~cum Staimsacre

Burndale

High Hawsker

Normanby

Raw

Robin Hood's Bay

Eskdalesiae Cum~Ugglebarnby

Snainton

High Normanby

Sneaton Thorp

Littlebeck

← York 30 Miles

to Egton

Scarborough 15 Miles →

Robin Hood and the Slavers of Whitby

I

The Bishop of Hereford danced. It was an absurd jig, capering around the immense tree that would henceforth be called the Bishop's Oak.[51] Whenever he slowed down, Robin Hood hastened him with another smack on the backside with the flat of a sword.

The Bishop's attendants and guards watched helpless to intervene. They'd been brave enough when they'd spotted the half dozen ragged peasants gutting a deer at the side of the road, ruthless in pursuing them into the bushes. They'd lost their taste for the hunt when the disguised outlaws had led them to the spot where two score of well-armed bandits waited with nocked arrows.[52]

The portly divine ran around the wide tree trunk until he was red in the face and gasping. Only when he was about to drop did Robin relent enough to let him stop.

"Now you'll have less energy to flog serving boys for spilling your cider," the young outlaw told the Bishop. "But we'll take your treasury off for you to save you the strain of carrying it."

The raid was done. Much the Miller's Son and George a'Green fastened the servants' arms behind their backs. Will Scathlock, who'd earned the

---

51   The remnant of this famous oak, called the Bishop's Tree Root, is found in Skelbrook Park near Wentbridge.

52   This opening summarises the ancient tale *Robin Hood and the Bishop of Hertford*, ballad number 144 in the 19th century collection *English and Scottish Popular Ballads* by Francis James Child. Version A of that popular ley concludes, "Robin Hood took the Bishop by the hand/And he caused the music to play/And he made the Bishop to dance in his boots/And glad he could so get away."

name Scarlet the bloody way, divested the clergyman of his rings and chains.

"The poor thank you for your donations," Maid Marion assured the Bishop. "Next time don't wait for an outlaw to force your Christian duty on you."

The Bishop looked like he wanted to make a rude and noisy answer, but he glanced at Robin Hood and held his peace. He didn't want to dance again.

"Ware!" called David of Doncaster, on lookout. The bandits of Sherwood were careful to set a watch. They were about to made a hasty departure into the greensward when David called all clear. "It's Little John."

Robin patted the Bishop of Hertford on his cheek, thanked him again for his contribution, and set off down the road to meet the returning lieutenant.

Marion fell into step beside her forest lord. "John went north to see how things lie now Baron de Puiset's been deposed," she remembered. "Is the Sheriff's writ unchallenged now?"

Up to last summer three powerful men had contested the control of England. Richard Lionheart had appointed two Justiciars to rule during his absence on crusade. Hugh de Puiset, both Bishop of Durham and Earl of Northumberland, had been displaced and demoted by his fellow Justiciar, Lord Chancellor William Longchamp, who had in turn been dispossessed by the scheming Prince John. The Sheriff of Nottingham, sour William de Vendenal, now had authority over the vast tracts of Yorkshire and Derbyshire as well as his own county.

"The Sheriff won't be unchallenged," Robin promised his lady. "I'm easily bored."

The unmistakable figure of Little John came over the crest of the road. He was huge and sheepskin-clad, his seven-foot quarterstaff barely topping his shaggy head. Riccon Hazel and Gilbert Whitehand trailed behind him; and one other.

Old Arthur a Bland recognised the lithe young woman with the streaming black hair. "Uh oh," the wiry poacher breathed

Marion glanced at Robin, then back to the maiden approaching with John of Hathersage. The stranger was clad in green velvet decorated with yellow ribbons. She walked confidently, assured and collected, and she carried a crook.

"Clorinda, Queen of the Shepherdesses, I presume," Marion said to Robin.

"I think that's her name, yes," the young outlaw answered in casual tones. "I, er, met her once."

"I heard the ballad, Robin. 'Met' is a pretty tame word if everything Alan sings is true." Clorinda of the high peaks and hidden valleys, the outlaws had called her.[53]

"Alan a Dale should shut up," said Robin with feeling.

Little John approached with the lovely shepherdess. He looked sheepish. "Look who I found," he ventured, trying to sound casual.

"Hello, Clorinda," Robin bade the maiden.

"Hello, Loxley. Or do I call you the king of Sherwood now?"

"Rob's fine," Marion answered for the young outlaw. "Or Mud. Either name's right."

The queen of the shepherdesses regarded the outlaw lady. "You must be Matilda."

"I must. My friends call me Marion." The Queen of May didn't extend that invitation to Clorinda.

"Well, isn't this nice?" Little John said nervously. "A nice meeting of old friends and new. Nice."

Scarlet intervened. "As great as it is to watch Rob squirm, could we do it back at camp? Those Bishop's men will get loose from their ropes sometime and summon help. These awkward pauses will be a lot less funny when we're dangling from gibbets."

"An excellent point," Robin Hood agreed. "Clorinda, good to see you. Meet my heart's love, Marion. Marion, this is the shepherdess queen who made a man of me. Let's all get some supper."

---

53   Child ballad 149, *The Birth, Breeding, Valour, and Marriage of Robin Hood*, is one of the earliest ballads, from before Marion enters the Robin Hood canon. In it our hero meets with the huntress Clorinda, Queen of the Shepherdesses, whom he weds. The old song describes her thus:

"As that word was spoke, Clorinda came by;
The queen of the shepherds was she;
And her gown was of velvet as green as the grass,
And her buskin did reach to her knee.
Her gait it was graceful, her body was straight,
And her countenance free from pride;
A bow in her hand, and quiver and arrows
Hung dangling by her sweet side.
Her eye-brows were black, ay, and so was her hair,
And her skin was as smooth as glass;
Her visage spoke wisdom, and modesty too;
Sets with Robin Hood such a lass!"

The remorseless tide pulled back from the crumbling cliffs at last. When it was safe enough, Captain Aelstan of Osmondthorpe climbed the rope ladder down to the cove to see the damage.

"It's brought t'whole entrance down," said Mickle the foreman, gloomily. "No way to open that 'un up again. We'll need to tunnel in a bit along, happen up by t' Gnipe Howe."

The Sheriff of Nottingham's guard captain inspected the tumbled rockfall that had closed the tunnel into the sea-cliffs. Massive blocks of friable stone had completely blocked three months' diligent digging. He spat and swore.

"We'll need new scaffolding and that," Mickle went on. "T' flood's washed all away. And t'miners are refusing t'dig owt now after them lads and lasses were lost."

Captain Aelstan had been a handsome man once. That was before the fury of the York riots and the hot flames of the brazier where the mob had held his head. Now his face was a pink mass of scar tissue and purpled blisters, one burned eye blackened and sightless. He was not an enemy to cross. "They'll work, by Mary, or I'll slit the noses of every child in the camp! Aye, and take their ears if I have to!"

Mickle nodded, satisfied. "That'd do it, most like. I'll need the menfolk down here to get't rig set up. We'll need to drill some holes in't back of yon hollow and drive a shaft that way. We'll catch the jet layer about ten feet in, I reckons."

Aelstan had to be satisfied with that. The Sheriff wouldn't like the delay, but even he must understand that the sea's aggression could not be controlled.

"There'll be jet fragments all along this strand where the tide washed out the cave," Mickle added. "Best have t'lasses walking this shore to collect 'em. They won't want to step where their kinfolk drowned but we've plenty of whips."

The Captain nodded. "See to it. Maybe we can get back on quota before Lord de Vendenal gets here." It would be better for everybody if they did.

Mickle leaned down to the shingle strand and picked up a black pebble. He dropped it into Aelstan's hand. "There y'go. That's Whitby jet[54] for you.

---

54   180 million years ago, fallen Jurassic Monkey-Puzzle trees were compressed and fossilized into layers of the mineraloid that the Greeks called *lithos gagates*, which became the French *gaiet* and the English jet. England's great deposits, generally considered the best quality in the world, are along the sea cliffs of North Yorkshire around Whitby. The decorative black stone was valued in the Neolithic era and appears in many gravebarrow hordes. The value of Britannia's jet deposits was one economic reason for Julius Caesar's invasion. The Romans carved the "black amber" into pins, brooches, and religious talismans. Unsatisfied with beach-combing as a means of gathering jet they began the cliff-

Another half ton and you're back on schedule."

Aelstan looked at the rounded stone in his palm. True jet was rare. It could be carved and shaped. When rubbed on porcelain it left a brown mark. It was sovereign against evil magic, popular for use in clerical jewellery and the mourning garb of princes.

It was certainly worth the lives of a few nameless nobodies.

"Set them to work, Mickle," the Captain commanded. He pocketed the jet-stone. "Work them hard. There's plenty more where they came from!"

All eyes were on Clorinda's bosom. She dipped her fingers down into her cleavage and pulled out a tiny carved cross of Whitby jet. "This is what I've come to show you," she told the outlaws.

"Your boobies?" asked Much hopefully. Arthur a Blank swatted him across the ear.

"This," the shepherdess clarified, passing the little icon to Robin Hood. "It's jet. Lignite. Black amber. It's found in the cliffs of North Yorkshire and along the pebbly beaches. It's valuable."

Tuck knew about the polished black stone. "Pliny the Elder[55] mentions it," he recalled. "He said kindling it drove off snakes and relieved constriction of the uterus. He wrote that it also discovers attempts to simulate virginity."

"How?" Little John asked, curiously.

"We'll deal with the fake virgins later," Robin promised. "Right now I want to know why Clorinda's come all this way to show us some jewellery. Cloe?"

"Up in my part of the world, the high grassy North Riding moors, people have always beach-combed the sea-shore below for jet. If you know the trick of shaping this stuff for setting it in silver there's a good living. That and scrimshaw[56] are the local specialities."

"But?"

"But now the Lord High Sheriff has other ideas. There's demand for jet on

---

mining that continues to the present day.

55   Gaius Plinius Secundus (A.D. 23–79), Roman author, naturalist, and natural philosopher, author of arguably the first encyclopaedia, *Naturalis Historia*.

56   Sculpture or engraving using the teeth or bones of whales.

the continent, you see. There's money to be made. The Sheriff's reopened the old Roman cave-mines down at the cliff bottom. It's difficult, dangerous work, crawling through low tunnels gouged down through what they call the top jet dogger, a limestone layer that's always just above the jet seam. Scarcely a day goes by without an accident, some crushed limb or a sudden death by pitfall or drowning."

"The Sheriff's set men to work in his perilous jet mine?" Marion understood.

Scarlet shrugged. "Labourers face dangerous tasks everywhere. I don't see what this has to do with us."

"The Sheriff doesn't send in men," Clorinda answered. "Not when children can squirm into much smaller spaces. And he doesn't use labourers. He uses slaves."

Robin's head came up. Slavery was still legal in England under old Saxon law, but it rarely happened these days.[57] Serfs were tied to their master's land, unable to leave or wed or own possessions without their lord's permission, but even they had rights. Slaves had none. They were property, no more protected by law than a pig or a handcart. Their owner had the right to trade them, loan them, breed them, and kill them.

"William de Vendenal is enslaving boys and girls to die in his jet mines," Marion summarised. Her face was bleak and dangerous.

Robin mirrored her expression. "We head north."

The great forest of which Sherwood was the heart ran almost the whole length of England. It ended where the Yorkshire moors began, surrendering to league after league of turf-topped highland. Tiny villages sheltered from the winds in steep river valleys. Only hardy Northern sheep ranged across the desolate hills.

Three riders came out of the treeline and looked over the undulating landscape. "That way," Clorinda told Robin and Marion. "The old Roman road takes us down to the White Village. We'll be able to find out there what's happening along the coast at the Sheriff's mine."

"I'm very keen to know," the young outlaw confessed. "Lead on, Cloe."

---

57   The *Domesday Book* census of 1086 recorded more than a tenth of England's population as slaves. As Norman feudal customs were enforced slaves became rarer, replaced by the villeins or serfs that made up eighty percent of the population by the end of the 12th century. Slavery remained legal in England until the 1833 Slavery Abolition Act.

The queen of the shepherdesses turned to Marion. "You didn't have to ride with us, you know. You can trust me with Robin."

"I know that," the lady of Sherwood replied. "But I can't trust Robin to rein in his tendency to hatch very stupid schemes and plans."

"You think you're going to stop him from dangerous adventures?"

"I think I'm going to be with him when he has them."

Clorinda snorted and spurred her horse forward.

Robin reached across and squeezed Marion's hand. "You really don't need to worry about me and the shepherdess," he promised. "It was a long time ago. Those tavern-songs are old. Before you filled my world."

"I'm not worried." The red-haired beauty winked at him. "By now I have lots more verses than she has."

They rode after Clorinda down the steep trail to one of the tiny hamlets between the rolling hills. Then their good mood evaporated.

"What happened here?" Marion asked.

The village was deserted. The thatch was gone from most of the cottages, whipped away by the fierce coastal winds. Already the wattle-and-daub dwellings were crumbling back to mere mud and sticks. The stone-built chapel stood empty and desolate.

"This was Egton," the shepherdess said. "It defaulted on its taxes."

Robin looked at the sad remnants of the weed-choked settlement. "And then?"

"And then Lord de Vendenal bought up the debt. And he invoked the old law."

Marion had been brought up in a noble house. She knew judicial process. "Slavery for debt? Is that still legal?"

"It is with the consent of the manor's lord and of the creditor and with permission from the Lord High Sheriff."

Robin bunched his fists. "This is not just. This is not right."

"I could ride you round half a dozen deserted villages like this, maybe more," Clorinda warned him. "The incomes from marginal estates such as Egton are far less than the profits of exporting jet to France and Holland."

"De Vendenal is nothing if not a shrewd businessman," Marion scowled.

"Let's show him the hidden costs of his enterprise," suggested Robin in the Hood.

"Pirates. They're now't but by-the-Lady pirates," the ruddy fisherman in the seafront tavern complained to Robin, Marion, and Clorinda. He nursed his mug of warmed sour ale and glared out to sea from under his bushy eyebrows. "They calls themselves king's marines, but they comes ashore with swords and bows whenever they please to take whatever they wants. Livestock, beer, sometimes a maid. We can't stop 'em."

"These are the men on the ship that collects the jet?" Marion checked.

"Aye. They say as they're lawful sailors and they gather necessaries in the king's name by right. But I'd heard t' Lionheart was overseas, in the Holy Land by all accounts, a-fighting of the heathen. What's his mariners want to be coming here disturbing our peace for?"

"Richard's not in Palestine any more," Robin reported. "They're saying in London and York that he took ship home when he heard of Prince John's treacheries. But he was shipwrecked, then captured by the Duke of Austria for ransom."

Clorinda wasn't interested in high politics. "No concern of ours what the great and mighty do. Richard's no better than John. The whole lot of 'em can jump off Fylingthorpe cliffs and crash on the rocks below!"

"It does matter," Marion argued. "Richard's ransom is set at sixty thousand pounds, three times the taxes of England for a whole year.[58] His mother Queen Eleanor is chivvying the chancellery for new levies of scutage and carucage[59] and to squeeze the church for a quarter of its wealth to set him free, and Eleanor's a hard woman to ignore. But taxes on the rich mean more taxes on the poor."

"So Sheriff de Vendenal's mining Whitby jet to pay for Richard's return?" the shepherdess asked, failing to hide her contempt and anger at the aristocracy's tax farming.

Robin shook his head. "De Vendenal's pinned his advancement on Weaselly John. Richard's return would wreck him. There's gossip though that Lackland and the King of France have offered a different fee to Lionheart's captives, £40,000 to keep him locked away. I bet that's why the Sheriff's chasing money."

The old fisher drained his mug. "Kings and princes and Sheriffs and all that, they don't mean a thing t'me. But pirates robbing my catch, raiding my boat, carrying off our Dorrie, that's too much. Someone should do something about it, they should!"

---

58   This has been calculated as about $3.5 billion in modern money.

59   A tax in lieu of rendering feudal military service and a tax on farmed land.

Robin looked from Marion to Clorinda and saw the expectant expression on both their faces.

"All right!" he surrendered. "I volunteer!"

Captain Aelstan stood at the water's edge and spoke with Captain Makebliss as the tide turned. They watched the ragged men and women who dug the top jet dogger drag their naked grazed children out of the mine tunnel before the waters washed back in.

"You've started a new hole," the sea-captain noted to de Vendenal's scarred guard officer.

"The waves took the last one," Aelstan replied. "The mine engineer was too greedy and skimped on the support columns. Mickle flogged him."

"Will you meet your targets?"

"We have to. I've got the slaves working night and day now, whenever the water's low enough. Four full teams. It'll kill a few extra but we can always get more."

Makebliss grinned. His teeth were brown and rotten. "Get some more pretty ones. They sell well in Harfleur and Normandy. There's a demand."

The captain fingered a silver chain of jet beads at his neck. The Sheriff didn't need to know about Aelstan's lucrative sidelines. A disfigured guard captain had to plan his own retirement. "We'll get back to that after we've sorted out production problems. Lord de Vendenal's coming to check up on the work. He'll want to get the jet shipment away to London as soon as he's inspected it."

A rough palisade at the top of the cliff enclosed the work-barracks of the captives, with a guarded strong-hut to store the precious black stone itself. When the time came the chests would be lowered by rope to the shore and loaded into Makebliss' two-masted warboat. From there it was an easy sail down the east coast of England to the Thames and London.

The two captains watched as the last of the children was hauled out of the working. A pair of ruthless soldiers checked the slaves for hidden jet and seemed to enjoy doing it.

The final child was a boy no more than six or seven. He bled where he'd grazed all down his left side squeezing into the tight seam cleft. His desperate mother set up a wail before Mickle the Overseer brought his crop down on her back to silence her.

"I'll get my ship ready," Captain Makebliss decided. "It'd be just like de Vendenal to decide to inspect it." That would mean casting the stolen girls overboard, but it was no hardship. All the fishing villages could do if the pirates took more prizes was complain to the Sheriff!

"It's best to keep on the Lord Sheriff's good side," Aelstan agreed. "He can be creative when people fail him."

A shout came from the top of the cliff. Somebody hailed the guard captain, beckoning him up the rope ladder.

"What is it?" Aelstan shouted through cupped hands. When the guardsman above yelled a reply the Captain winced. "Z'ounds![60] Speak of the devil! What the hell's de Vendenal doing here two days early?" He hastened to the cliff ropes so he could be up top to greet his employer. "Be sure you're ready, Makebliss. The Sheriff's come. Something must be wrong!"

Robin joined Marion and Clorinda atop the Fylingthorpe cliffs. He took off the disgusting floppy-brimmed hat he'd disguised himself with and span it over the edge so the wind took it to fly off with the gulls.

"You weren't caught then," Marion noted.

"No," Robin told her with a mock apologetic expression. "Luckily, I'm me. I went into the slave camp, delivered the beer to the soldiers' mess, got a look round, then headed back to the warm embrace of my beloved." He glanced at Clorinda. "Er, Marion, that is," he added apologetically.

The dark-tressed shepherdess snorted. "Still with a high opinion of yourself, Loxley. There's other men."

"But none of them could creep into that compound, spy out the land, work out a plan to save all the slaves and make the Sheriff cry himself to sleep, and still be back in time to enjoy the view of this fabulous sunset with the two fairest maidens in the land!"

"If you feel the need to throw him off the cliff I won't object," Marion told Clorinda.

"No. He's yours now," relied the shepherdess. "You should do it."

Maid Marion looked as if she was considering it. "While you were off playing dress-up I went to the Abbey," she reported. "I spoke to the Abbot, asked him what he was doing about the Sheriff's nasty scheme at Gnipe Howe."

---

60   A contraction of "God's wounds", a blasphemous medieval profanity.

"Doing something would require him to stand up," Clorinda snorted. "He's far too fat for that!"

"The Abbey's lands border on some of the royal estates de Vendenal controls. I got the impression he was afraid of trouble from his neighbour. He wasn't about to upset the Sheriff or the Prince, even with a war-boat full of raiders robbing his settlements in the king's name." Marion grimaced to indicate her opinion of the cleric.

"You should have brought your men with you, Loxley," Clorinda told Robin. "What can three of us do against a pirate ship and Captain Aelstan's thugs?"

"Did I mention I met the Sheriff as well?" Robin added casually.

"What?" Marion cried out. "De Vendenal's here? Since when?"

"Since about an hour ago. With an extra forty guardsmen, because otherwise rescuing sixty-odd exhausted injured prisoners and four chests of jet would be too easy."

"Can you shoot him?" Clorinda wondered. She knew how good a marksman Robin was.

"Not without reprisals that would see half the villages of Nottinghamshire burned. If it was as simple as putting an arrow through de Vendenal's throat he'd have been in his grave years ago."

Marion agreed. "We just have to settle for making the Sheriff wish he were dead."

The sun sank down behind the Yorkshire hills. The sea turned grey. Three quarters of a mile up the coast torches flared where the slaves still laboured to dig the Sheriff's jet.

"So what's the stupid dangerous scheme going to be this time?" Maid Marion asked the outlaw lord.

"Well, from what I've seen and Clorinda's heard, the Sheriff of Nottingham has a hundred or so guards with ugly Aelstan, an impenetrable stockade, one of the king's war galleys with a ruthless cut-throat crew, threescore battered peasants in dire straits, and four boxes of jet to keep the Lionheart locked away for a long time. I've got two lovely wenches and a longbow." Robin Hood grinned. "Isn't it obvious what we should do?"

11

akebliss' first mate was effusive about the wenches. "Two of 'em, Cap'n, and each as lovely as an angel. The one Saxon-haired and dainty, the other black as a raven and ample as you please. They were down at the harbour in the White Village[61] under the abbey, seeking a boat to take them and a small chest along to Scarborough Castle."

The Captain was intrigued. "To Scarborough? Why? Of what quality were these vixens? What men attended them?"

"No companions at all. Alone, they were, with a sealed box the size of a Bible. Like to be a jewel casket, I thought. The red minx, she spoke like a Norman noble. The other was more local, but she bore herself well. A lady and her maid perhaps, separated from their lord and seeking passage to safety."

"Did they appeal to the Abbot?"

"No, Cap'n. They were asking amongst the fishermen, promising silver for their passage."

Makebliss considered his options. De Vendenal's caskets were ready to move once the tide reached its outer range. In the half-hour of calm the warship would beach on the shingle bank, load the chests, and be gone before the waters turned to push it hard onto the shore. But that was four hours off yet; time enough before that to consider another source of profit.

"They might be worth something, the wenches and their box," Captain Makebliss mused. "If naught else they'd brighten the sailing to London. Even if there's no ransom to be had they'll still fetch a price in Harfleur."

"One of the fishers took them out in his single-mast herring boat," the first mate told. "The way those things move we could overhaul it in an hour and be back to catch the tide."

Makebliss looked at the men on his twin-masted warship. Two dozen sea-hardened sailors could defeat any resistance a frightened fisherman could make. They had before.

---

61   This is an Anglicised version of the Old Norse *Hweitebi*, from whence the name Whitby derives. The prominent ruins of the Abbey still stand on the high cliffs above the town and are well worth a visit. The Abbey, its graveyard, and the winding steps up to it are perhaps best known in popular fiction for their appearance in Bram Stoker's *Dracula*.

"Bring her around," the Captain ordered. "Make for the fair wenches, best speed!"

The fisherman laughed at Robin. The people's champion hopped on one leg and tried to untangle his boot from the unexpected knot he'd made of the line he was supposed to be hauling. The boat rocked and the young outlaw sat down heavily, narrowly avoiding being spilled into the sea.

"I thought Robin i' th' Hood was never caught?" Marion giggled as Robin rolled in the belly of the fishing boat and slithered on the detritus of the morning's catch.

A helpful sailor unhooked Robin's leg with an easy twist of the rope. "Tha'll ne'er be a seaman, lad," the fisherman warned. "If I were thee I'd avoid owt much bigger than a puddle."

"I have other talents," the forest lord protested. "I'm a remarkable lover, for example!"

The boat caught some chop again, sliding him back into the slippery fish pile.

"You'd have to be pretty damn brilliant at it to bring your average back up after demonstrating your seamanship," Marion commented.

Robin looked at her challengingly. "And?"

Clorinda interrupted the banter. "Is that a ship over there?"

The fishermen's' attention had been on dragging up their nets and on Robin's rope handling. At the shepherdess' words they all turned to look where she was pointing.

"It's them!" the master-fisher spat. He swore, then apologised for it to the ladies. "Get them nets in fast, boys! Weigh the anchor and let's be gone. We don't want to let them buggers catch us again."

Robin, Marion, and Clorinda said nothing. It was exactly what they were wanting.

The fishermen lugged the half-full hemp nets into the boat. The little skiff rocked alarmingly. Robin didn't try to help them. They thanked him for that.

Marion kept an eye on the approaching vessel. "So that's the war-ship. It's designed to be small and fast; a courier, probably. Ideal to transport small valuable cargo like a few chests of gems."

"Those are the reavers who've been preying on the coast," Clorinda reported. "It's the Sheriff's job to stop men like that, not commission them."

The craft was closing fast. It had more sail and the wind was behind it.

"Lift t'sheet and make for land, lads!" the master-fisher called. He sounded tense but he kept his head. "Break out oars an' all." He looked worriedly at the two women at the stern, imagining their fate at the pirates' hands.

The two ladies seemed unconcerned. Marion reached under the rear bench and brought out two long cloth-swathed bundles. She passed them to Robin and Clorinda, who unwrapped them to reveal English longbows. The chest contained no treasure but broad-headed arrows.

"What's this?" demanded the master-fisher. "Tha can't fight! That's a warship. There'll be a score of men wi' bows on board."

"Perhaps," said Robin Hood, stringing his weapon. "They've got men and bows. We've got an archer."

"Two," Clorinda corrected him, preparing her own yew-bow. "Or have you forgotten those Scots raiders we took down in our reckless youth?"

"Wait," said Marion. "I thought this was his reckless youth?"

The warship hove closer, cutting across the fishing smack's course, stealing its wind. "They're gonna catch us!" the master-fisher warned.

"I hope so," replied Robin Hood. "I really want to talk to them." When the ship was two hundred yards distant he drew his bow and loosed his first red-fletched arrow.

The shot was at long range, in a sea breeze, on a pitching deck. It curved in a high parabola over the North Sea and embedded itself in the arm of the war-boat's pilot.

"Show off," said Clorinda.

"That wasn't showing off," Robin told her. "This is showing off." He loosed a second shaft, putting it through the throat of the lookout who was warning the warship of the attack.

"They'll kill us for this!" the master-fisher fretted.

"Bring us alongside them, captain," Marion told him. "Whitby wanted rid of the pirates? This is the time to do it."

Robin fired again, and again. Each shot took down another sailor. Clorinda joined in as the range closed.

When the men on the war-ship pulled out their own bows Robin targeted them as a priority. A few enemy arrows splashed into the water around the fishing ship. One embedded itself in the port hull. Robin allowed the marauders no time to aim. He kept them scared.

"They'll run soon," Marion judged. "They never expected a fight and they've taken serious losses." She'd counted at least eight men down, probably several more injured. All the sea-marauders were taking shelter behind the ship's wooden walls now. She finished knotting a cord onto an arrow that was longer and thicker than the regular ones Robin was dropping into the warship. Marion had no problem with the knots but didn't distract the young outlaw to point it out just then, and passed the shaft to the archer.

Robin checked the steel-tipped missile. Its broad head was designed to punch through a knight's armour then stick there, its wide triangle shape making it difficult to dislodge without shredding the flesh it had penetrated. It would be equally effective lodged through a war-boat's side.

"They're turning!" the master-fisher saw. The men aboard the skiff had gone from terror to amazement to a wild elation as their persecutors had sailed into a rain of death. "They're heaving off!"

"Not without us, they're not," said Robin determinedly. He aimed the special arrow low above the waterline and released the hundred and eighty pound pressure on his bowstring. The missile sped almost too fast for the eye to follow and slammed through two inches of hardwood like it was nothing.

Marion passed the other end of the line to the fishermen. "Secure this well," she ordered. "We don't want them getting away."

One of the enemy sailors tried to lean over the side of his hull to sever the line. Clorinda got him.

"Prepare for them to try and board us next," Robin warned. "That's what I'd try."

Captain Makebliss had the same idea. The ship veered in, looming close to the fishing vessel.

Robin kept the enemy sailors ducking for cover as the distance closed.

Marion unpacked her flint and tinderbox and a flask of black sticky oil. She struck a spark with special care because shipboard fire was deadly, and ignited a small lamp.

"They're coming!" the master-fisher shouted, alarmed again. He'd seen many of the mariners fall but the warship still steered so there must be more.

Marion passed the lamp and the remainder of the flask to Robin. "Don't even try to be careful," she sighed. "Just be… you."

Robin blew her a kiss. As the warship loomed beside the fishing boat he surprised the pirates by jumping up and boarding it.

Captain Makebliss already had a cudgel ready to invade the skiff. He came at Robin and got a faceful of black oil as Robin shattered the flask on him. The heavy tar spilled down onto deck and formed a pool.

Robin held up the lantern he'd brought. "I'm told fire's very bad on a ship," he advised the surviving raiders. "If anything happens to me I'll be dropping this light right onto that oil. And your captain's soaked in the stuff."

Clorinda and Marion scrambled aboard. The surprised fishermen found the courage to follow them.

The five sailors who'd survived the archer's onslaught well enough to still fight suddenly found they'd been beaten by a lone outlaw and two women.[62]

The master-fisher took control of the warboat. Marion opened the rear cabin and released the three girls who'd been stolen away for Harfleur.

Robin had his back to Makebliss. Seeing an opportunity, the marauder captain leaped at the young outlaw from behind.

That was what Robin had hoped for. He whirled round and brought his horn-tipped longbow up into Makebliss' nose. There was a crack of cartilage and the captain fell down heavily in the gunwale. Makebliss clutched his bloody face, screeching.

The master-fisher kicked the pirate captain in the ribs. "You're no sailor but you're a trueborn archer, lad," the fisherman told Robin. "I've ne'er heard tell of one man catching a pirate warship wi' naught but a quiver of arrows."

Even Clorinda was surprised. "Does he do that often now?" she whispered to Marion.

"Stopping him from doing these things, that's the hard part," the lady of Sherwood replied.

Robin Hood wasn't a bloodthirsty killer. Even men who'd enslaved children and sold captives to lifetimes of bondage overseas got the chance to surrender. The nine wounded men on the captured warship were tended, despite the fishermen's willingness to toss them overboard with the corpses of their fellows.

Marion insisted no harm came to the prisoners. "They're to be tried by your elders in the old fashion," the queen of Sherwood instructed. "Let their accusers come forward and a jury decide their fates."

It was hard for the half-dozen Whitby fisherfolk to pilot the prize Robin had won and their own vessel back to shore. Robin conscripted three of

---

62   These events echo the ancient ballad *The Noble Fisherman, or Robin Hood's Preferment*, collected as Child ballad 148.

the prisoners to help and stood at the prow with his bow ready in case they tried to fight.

Clorinda was surprised when the outlaw ordered the boat be beached in an empty bay a few miles south of the natural harbour at Whitby.

"There's nothing in this cove, and we're near the Sheriff's mine," she objected.

"I wasn't sure what we'd find here," Robin told the shepherdess, "so I arranged for some aid."

The outlaw winded a horn at the shore. An answering blast came from somewhere in the foothills, and within five minutes a dozen outlaws in Lincoln green were assembled at the strand.

"Little John," Clorinda said, recognising the giant by his size alone. She waved at him. The queen of the shepherdesses had always liked the shepherd from Hathersage. "Why didn't you tell me you'd brought your men up here?"

Robin looked sheepish. "Honestly? I wasn't that sure you were telling me the truth about everything until our fight today with the pirates. You didn't mention that Egton was where you come from, for example."

Clorinda was shocked. "How did you know...?"

"There was a time when I wanted to know everything about you. I'm a smart lad. I asked folk. But if the Sheriff has all the people of Egton enslaved then he probably has kin of yours. He might have sent you to lead me into a trap. It's the sort of thing he does. Anyone would try to save their parents, brothers, sisters..."

"Husband," said Clorinda. She managed a faint smile. "Did you think you'd ruined me for other men, Loxley?"

"Does de Vendenal know he's got such good hostages?" Marion wondered.

"De Vendenal's not been here before today," the shepherdess pointed out. "Now he is."

"And he's sharp," Robin admitted with a frown. "We'd better hurry before he's got time to work out I'm here."

Little John splashed out to meet them, with Scarlet, Tuck, Alan a Dale and the others. "You've never stolen a whole war galley before, Rob," the big man noted. "Where are you going to keep it? It won't really fit in the little beck beside the Major Oak."[63]

"I expect I'll give it to the poor," Robin laughed. He embraced the giant.

---

63   Many folk stories and local tradition place the outlaw's hideout at a huge oak tree near Edwinstowe in Nottinghamshire. The nearby stream is narrow enough to jump and shallow enough to paddle.

"Did you think you'd ruined me for other men, Loxley?"

"There's some bad men on board. Do you think you could keep them occupied while we do clever things, then leave them for the elders of Whitby to try and punish afterwards?"

Will Scarlet moved forward, grim as ever. "I'll see to them," he promised.

"Why do you need a ship, exactly?" Alan a Dale ventured. "Not that I mind. There's lots of things will rhyme with ship when I come to make a ballad of this." He thought a moment then looked less certain. "Drip, dip, flip, nip, tip, snip, blip… hmm, perhaps you could stick to horses. They have much less ominous rhymes."

"We need to get this ship back out to sea with the master-fisher's help," Robin proclaimed. "Captain Makebliss tells me its time to load the Sheriff's jet chests aboard and when his nosebleed stops he's volunteered to help us. Well, he's volunteered not to be tossed overboard in a weighted fishing net, which is the next best thing!"

"We can't just sail up to the Sheriff's stockade and pick up the treasure, Robin," Friar Tuck objected. "Captain Aelstan knows us. Even with this pirate pretending he's not got a dagger at his back we couldn't fool Aelstan. And there's word that the Sheriff's there too. Sorry, lad, but he won't fall for it."

"I agree," Robin admitted. "That's why there needs to be a better, bigger plan!"

William de Vendenal had a glare that could freeze water. The Lord High Sheriff was both powerful and competent, a dangerous combination. Fools learned quickly that he was not a man to fail or deceive. Now that gimlet stare was turned on Clorinda of Egton.

"Robin Hood?" de Vendenal repeated her words. "Robin Hood is here?"

"Yes," agreed the queen of the shepherdesses. "Nearby."

"To seek my jet?"

"Of course. You know Robin. Those chests must be worth a thousand pounds or more."

"And you come to betray him to me from a sense of public duty?"

Clorinda shook her head. She tried not to falter. She knew the Sheriff was a frightening man. She'd not anticipated how hard it to keep calm was under his attentive gaze. "I want something. A reward. I can tell you where to find Loxley, but it's for a price."

Captain Aelstan shifted to stand behind the shepherdess. "I can have the truth out of her in two hours, my lord," he promised. "Less, if she's keen to keep her looks."

"And Hood'll be gone in half an hour," Clorinda warned scornfully.

"What reward?" de Vendenal asked her. "It is rare that any of Hood's people try to coin him. He seems to inspire universal folly in his minions."

"I'm not one of his merry men," Clorinda answered. She smoothed her hands down her ample curves. "You can see that plain. What I was to him once… well, he's with the Maid Marion now. And I've a man of my own."

"Your name?"

"Clorinda."

De Vendenal had studied his enemy. He'd heard the tavern song. "You're the so called shepherd queen."

The dark-tressed woman shrugged. "With my dogs and a crook I can make my flock do anything. I can shear a sheep in less than a minute. I can charm the lambs out of ewes. But there's some wolves I can't fight."

De Vendenal was fast. The maid spoke bad Norman French with a local accent. "Not money, the reward you seek," he discerned. "A man of Egton, perhaps? A lover? A husband?"

"Aye. Give me my man, free and safe, and I'll give you Robin of Loxley."

Aelstan was sceptical. "How do you know where the wolfshead is? Why should we trust you?"

"I know his location because I fetched him here. He's planning to take your treasure and free your captives because I asked him to. But his mad plans won't work." The dark-tressed shepherdess shook her head. "I knew all along the only way to free my love would be to trade you Robin Hood. So I brought him for you, far from Sherwood's safety. Let fair Lady Marion save Loxley if she can. I'll see my husband free."

William de Vendenal stroked his pointed beard and considered. "If what you say is true then it's a chance we must not miss. Prince John will be much consoled at the hanging and quartering of that particular rebel and my life will be considerably bettered. If you lie, it's your belly we'll slice open and draw out your innards while you still live."

Clorinda paled.

"Who's your man?" de Vendenal demanded.

"I'll tell you when Hood's caught and the bargain's done," the shepherdess answered. "I'll not let you threaten my love to loosen my tongue."

The Sheriff had thought the gambit worth the attempt, but he was willing to make the deal. "You have a bargain, wench. But you'll remain here until Hood's caught or slain." He turned to the camp overseer. "Lock her with the jet chests, Mickle. There's nowhere more secure. See she's fettered too, and a pair of incorruptible guards on the door." To Clorinda he said, "You'll tell Captain Aelstan where to find the wolfshead. Be precise. Your life depends upon it."

The shepherdess blinked back tears she hadn't expected and confessed. "Five miles south there's a small bay. There's a sea-cave there. That's where Loxley's waiting for me." She hung her head. "God forgive me for selling him to his death."

III

The cave was unoccupied; but not empty.

Captain Aelstan liked to report the obvious. "He's not here. The wench lied!"

The Sheriff of Nottingham was sharper. "He's not here now, but he was. And he wasn't alone. Look at the bedrolls stowed here. There are, what, fifty or sixty of them? The shepherdess lass lied, yes, but her lie was omitting the fact that Hood was here with the greater part of his wolfsheads."

Aelstan looked around to check the forty men they'd brought with them were still there. Robin Hood hadn't spirited them away.

"These fire pits are still warm," de Vendenal added. "Hood and his fanatics can't have been gone long. But why...?" The Sheriff looked up suddenly then whirled to one of his squires. "You! Ride back to camp. Warn Mickle that the girl's information was a ruse to draw our forces away from the stockade. Tell them there are three-score outlaws, expert archers all, loose somewhere in the countryside. He's to seal the gates, turn out every man to watch, and prepare for Hood's deceit or overwhelming force."

The squire raced for his horse and galloped away.

De Vendenal pointed to two more men. "You and you. Go after him. Ride separately. Hope Hood isn't able to kill all of you en route. Aelstan, assemble the column. We'll head back quickly but in good order. Send out screen riders to avoid unfortunate ambushes."

"Yes, my lord! But no amount of outlaws could overcome the stockade without terrible losses."

"Hood's clever. There'll be a trick." The Sheriff thought hard. "What deliveries have you received of late?"

"Captain Makebliss brought us supplies yesterday. And there were some barrels of ale from the brewer of Briggswath."

"The drayman! Was he known to anyone?"

Aelstan shrugged. "I don't know. Mickle sees to the stores. I don't see..."

De Vendenal jabbed a finger at another rider. "Back to Gnipe Howe," he ordered. "Tell them not to drink the beer. Pour it away. Hood has a liking for drugging it with poppy syrup to quieten guards."

Aelstan gasped. "You don't think he intends to attack the camp while our men are disabled.?

"I think Hood's got more wits than everybody at Gnipe Howe put together, and that includes you! We need to get back at once so that..."

De Vendenal's explanation was cut short as an arrow skimmed past his ear and embedded itself on his saddle.

Aelstan looked up at the archer on the cliff above. The outlaw in Lincoln Green waved a feathered cap down at the soldiers. "Robin Hood!" the guard captain recognised. "After him!"

The Sheriff made the order more specific. "Six mounted men up there after him. Six more range out looking for the rest of his wolfshead scum. Return in half an hour to report. Six form on me. Rest of you line up and make for camp. Now!"

Aelstan appointed himself at the head of the squad chasing Hood. The horsemen galloped up the winding channel where a shallow beck trickled out into the sea, tracking back towards the high promontory from where the archer fired. One horseman grunted and fell as the outlaw's arrow took him in the arm.

"Faster!" Aelstan called, bending low over his horse to offer a smaller target. "Spread out!"

Another arrow toppled another rider. But then misfortune struck the young outlaw. His bowstring snapped loose!

Aelstan spurred his horse up the slope. Hood was only two hundred yards off now.

The outlaw chose not to try and restring his bow with five horsemen closing on him. He ran to his own horse, a sleek chestnut borrowed from some unsuspecting manor, and rode away.

Aelstan gave chase. His scarred mouth twisted into a gory grin. Hood might be the better archer; Aelstan of Osmondthorpe was the better rider. The guard captain would wager Hood's life on it.

Two messengers made it to the mining camp. The others fell to outlaw arrows.

Mickle the overseer wasn't happy at the prospect of a bandit siege. With forty men away with the Sheriff he had only sixty guards remaining to protect the jet and keep watch on the slaves who laboured in the cavern below. Even reducing the watch on the miners to a bare minimum left him with less guards than he'd have liked to man the walls.

When news came that the ale might be poisoned it was Mickle himself that took an axe and stove in the barrels. A disheartened groan came from the soldiers. They'd have been even unhappier to know that there was nothing wrong with the beer.

A horn sounded away to the south. Replies echoed from west and north.

Sixty wolfsheads, the Sheriff's squire had said. Sixty of the notorious Sherwood bandits, each a deadly shot, each able to rain down flight after flight of arrows into the rough compound. The crude huts and canvas dwellings would not survive if the arrows were lit ablaze.

There was a garrison at Scarborough, but that was fifteen miles away. Help could not come in time.

But then the tide reached its furthest ebb and the yellow-and-white sails of the royal warship appeared around the headland. Mickle remembered that Captain Makebliss was coming to collect the treasure.

The horns sounded again, nearer. There was no sign of the sheriff's return. The overseer had to make a decision.

"Get the chests out of the strong-hut," he commanded. "They're to be strapped and lowered down to the strand. Tell Makebliss he can load them but he's not to leave with them till lord de Vendenal's inspected them again, unless there's an outlaw attack."

The warship pulled up onto the shingle beach in its customary harbour. Sailors jumped off and beached it. Looking down from the clifftop, Mickle saw Makebliss and a couple of men move over to speak to the sergeant who was guarding the slaves.

Mickle found he was sweating. He watched each of the four treasure boxes be lowered down the cliff and hardly dared breathe until they were safely received at the bottom.

A couple of Makebliss' men climbed the long twisting rope ladder up into the compound to speak with him. "Captain Makebliss' compliments," said one of them, "and he says if you're shifting the goods to his ship for safety you'd best empty the wench from the strong-hut as well."

"He's sent us to fetch her," said the other in blunter terms.

It made sense to Mickle. He was more concerned at the smoke that was now rising not far from the camp. The sailors dragged Clorinda from her prison and lowered the shackled shepherdess down the cliff face after the strongboxes.

"You'd better go too," the politer sailor suggested to the overseer. "You'll want to keep an eye on the Sheriff's treasure."

Mickle decided it might be best to be closer to the ship in case the outlaws came. He handed over defence of the camp to a competent sergeant and accompanied Alan a Dale and Will Scarlet down to the strand.

Robin kicked his heels into his chestnut's sides to keep it moving. The horse was tiring as it tore along the incline. Aelstan and his riders were staying close, less than a hundred yards behind.

The young outlaw followed the natural curve of the land, letting his mount choose its own path, concerned more with speed than direction. His job was to keep Aelstan busy and to convince the Sheriff that outlaws intended to assault his camp.

It was the terrain that betrayed him. The Yorkshire sea cliffs had unexpected gullies and sudden drops. Robin's horse had the sense to shy away from a steep fall it couldn't survive, veering sharply left at ninety degrees to its precious course. That allowed the pursuing Sheriff's men to cut a corner and close the distance.

Robin pushed his horse on, back towards the Fylingthorpe cliffs, knowing his tired steed was nearing its limits. He pulled out his bow and refastened the string he'd deliberately released earlier. Stringing a new cord at the gallop would have been impossible; reattaching the loose end of a good catgut thread was only very difficult.

The nearest rider was close now, less than fifty yards away. Robin twisted in his seat, holding his bow horizontally. He couldn't draw the string fully back, but at that range he didn't need to. The arrow caught his pursuer in the belly.

Four horsemen remained to chase him. One tried to fire back from the saddle. It was a mistake. He lost his balance, dropped his shortbow, then fell from his horse to roll heavily on the turf. Aelstan and the remaining pair continued to close in.

Robin waited until the riders were sure he was making for Fylingthorpe then veered suddenly left towards a narrow track down into a stand of woodland. Once there he could find cover and fend off horsemen as he pleased.

On the bridle-road below, the Sheriff of Nottingham rode out with another six horsemen.

Robin cursed himself. De Vendenal was clever. The Sheriff had anticipated Robin's escape plan, had ignored the ruse that would have sent him scurrying back to the mine, and had closed off the young outlaw's best line of escape. Now fresh riders galloped up from the track he'd hoped would be his getaway.

Robin shot again, taking down another of Aelstan's original horsemen. The last of them pushed forward, no more than a horse's length behind the outlaw as they climbed the hill again towards the sea.

Aelstan looked ahead and saw the cliff edge. In an inspired moment he decided to cut right and block Robin from slipping away along the clifftop path.

The other rider drew out a boot knife and held it by the blade, ready to throw. Robin turned and fired again. The arrow missed the guard but injured his horse. The creature bucked, spilling his master. Robin spurred his own blown ride onward.

He'd lost track of Aelstan. Suddenly the guard captain barrelled his own horse into Robin's mount, side to side. Both horses reeled then fell, tumbling their riders to the turf.

Robin rolled as he landed, but the breath was knocked out of him. His bow skittered away out of reach. By the time he'd scrambled to his feet Captain Aelstan was already running at him, naked sword in hand.

Robin pulled his own blade, a new longsword liberated from a proud knight on the Leicester road. He barely had time to get it up before Aelstan's blade sparked off it.

The Sheriff's squad topped the ridge and saw the outlaw and the guard captain fighting.

"Hold back!" Aelstan shouted to them. His burn-scarred face was livid with rage and hate. "Let me take him! Robin Hood is mine!"

Mickle hadn't expected a woman at the mine; at least not a woman wearing more than rags or doing more than cringing or wailing. He certainly hadn't expected her to turn on him with incandescent fury.

"What have you done to these people? How could you do it? What kind of monster are you to treat them so?"

The overseer took a step back. The guards chuckled nervously. One of them told Captain Makebliss to control his wench.

Makebliss said nothing. His face was drawn and pale save for his swollen scabbed purple nose. Much the Miller's Son stood very close behind him.

"I'm not his prisoner," Maid Marion told Mickle. "He is mine."

And suddenly the shingle shore became a battlefield. While Much held Makebliss the other outlaws stopped pretending to be sailors and turned on the guards they mingled with. David of Doncaster hammered down a whip-wielding sergeant with scientifically-accurate blows. Gilbert Whitehand tripped his target and stamped on him while he was down. Little John picked up two of the Sheriff's men and slammed them together. Scarlet pounced on the nearest foe, broke the man's jaw, then sank his teeth into the guard's ear.

Alan a Dale had climbed back up the rope ladder to the top of the ridge. Now he severed the cords that held it in place, sending it coiling down to splash into the shallows. None of the garrison above could get down to assist the guards who battled below. The minstrel made his own escape down another double-loop of rope that he could pull down after him.

Mickle staggered back, tripped on the pebbles, fell into the washing waves. Marion loomed over him. "You've done terrible deeds, slavemaster. Now Robin Hood has come to bring you to justice."

"W-what justice?" the overseer stammered as the reduced guard force at the cliff bottom were overcome.

"Me," Marion told him.

The prisoners had realised that something remarkable was going on. A few of them even joined in to subdue the guards.

Mickle sprang up and scrambled towards the child slaves. "Watch out! Clorinda shouted, but her fetters prevented her from stopping the overseer grab a young girl and press a knife to her neck.

"All hold!" Mickle screamed, "Or I'll slit t'lass's weasand!"

One of the enslaved Egton men struck him from behind with a heavy lump of shale. The overseer crumpled. Marion dragged the child away from him. The prisoners raged forward and fell on Mickle, grabbing up stones to strike him with vengeful fury, over and over again, until he was a gory red pulp.

The savage execution took whatever fight remained out of the other guards on the shore. They dropped their weapons and begged quarter from the outlaws; they begged protection from the slaves.

"On your knees, then!" Will Scarlet growled at the surrendering soldiers. He hammered one in the belly and crumpled him into the surf to demonstrate. The other men knelt down quickly.

The man who'd downed Mickle broke out of the huddle of captives and raced over to where Clorinda sat in chains. "Cloe!"

"Brom!" the queen of the shepherdesses cried out, struggling to her feet. "You live!"

Little John snapped the shackles that restrained her. "Nicely played," he congratulated the black-haired beauty. "You fooled the Sheriff. That's not easily done." Clorinda fell into her husband's embrace.

The confused prisoners huddled together, unsure what was happening. Some of them still held the bloody stones that had transformed the overseer into a grisly feast for the wheeling seagulls. Some looked nervously at the supposed pirates, confused that Whitby fishermen freely aided them, uncertain why the dread Captain Makebliss was trembling and silent.

"You're being rescued," Friar Tuck announced to the slaves. "Get the other children out of the caves. Everybody needs to board the ship before the tide turns."

"Rescued?" a harried, pinch-faced women asked. "How? We're enslaved now, by law. There's no escape nor rescue for us."

"I think we've got a way," Marion promised. "The bad news is it's a Robin Hood plan."

An arrow clattered down on the shingle beside her. The soldiers in the camp had worked out what was happening on the shore.

"Time to go," Little John announced. He beckoned for Much to drag Captain Makebliss aboard. "Anybody who wants to leave get on the ship now."

Another pair of arrows thrummed down from above.

"It'll take time to get all the children out, John," Tuck warned. "Some of these people are very ill." He stepped over Mickle's pulped corpse and went to help the weakest captives limp onto the ship.

"Then break out the longbows, lads," John of Hathersage decided. "If those Sheriff's guards want to match shots with the merry men of Sherwood then let's have at it!"

Aelstan had earned his position as captain of the Sheriff's guard the hard way, by fighting for it. The dispossessed Saxon had clawed his way up by being tougher and fiercer than the men around him. He knew how to kill.

He closed on Robin Hood, knowing his Sheriff was watching him. De Vendenal and his escort drew close to watch the show.

Robin gave ground at first. The captain was stronger and he wore chain-mail beneath his uniform tabard. Aelstan came in fast, pressing the outlaw towards the crumbling cliff's edge.

The young outlaw dodged his first three strokes then caught the fourth, shivering his own steel into the captain's blade. "How many died in your mines?" Hood demanded. "How many children have you murdered? How much gold did their blood buy?"

"Always so righteous!" spat Aelstan. He pressed harder, flicking his blade at the bandit's exposed face and arms. "Life's not a ballad, wolfshead. You'll learn that today. It's bloody and it's brutal, and for you it's short."

"You make it like that, captain. I prefer my ballads." Robin managed to cut through Aelstan's guard for a moment and jabbed at the captain's head. Aelstan shied away from losing his good eye.

The Sheriff's man renewed his attack with fresh venom, angry at having his secret fear exposed. He pulled a hunting dagger from his belt so that Hood must watch for danger from two ways. And always the steep precipice above the sea-dashed rocks loomed closer.

"When you're dead your spell will be broken, Hood. They'll all see you were nothing, nobody. All those stupid worthless people in their stinking hovels, they'll know how much you misled them. How you fooled them into thinking they were anything other than cattle."

"When I'm dead they'll remember," Robin Hood promised. "And where one rebel falls five more will rise, then fifty more, then a thousand! This land was meant to be free. Until there's fairness and justice, men like you and your rat-bearded Sheriff can never sleep safe. England won't bow forever. Tyrants are not for us."

Aelstan got in close where his strength could win him advantage. "Sheep bleat but it won't make them free. The strong will always rule. The weak will always be slaves." The captain's blistered face screwed into a red snarl. "I wish I could take all their children and crush them just to hear the noise their stupid parents make! Then they'd know what this world is."

Robin punished him with a left jab to the nose, sending the soldier backward, bloody. "That York mob didn't disfigure you," the outlaw realised. "They revealed your true face!"

William de Vendenal sighed. "Get on with it, Aelstan. There's no time for ethical debate. I want Hood finished quickly so I can catch his insipid friends as well. Hamstring him helpless and drag him back to camp."

Aelstan renewed his attack. Heedless of the minor cuts it would cost him he hurled himself at Robin Hood, clutching him round the waist, lifting him from the ground then tossing him down.

Robin landed hard but rolled aside from the sword-cut that followed. He almost tumbled over the cliff's edge. Stones and turf broke loose and dropped into the troubled sea that dashed on the killer rocks. Hood's sword slipped over the precipice and vanished in the spume.

Aelstan leaned down for a final stroke. Hood reached up and caught the necklace of jet dangling round Aelstan's throat. He twisted it round, choking the captain.

Aelstan wrenched backwards by instinct. The silver chain snapped, scattering his retirement across the grass and over the edge of Fylingthorpe cliff.

"No!" he shouted, losing all sanity. His dead eye was blood red now. Flecks of spittle dripped from his blistered lips. "Die, Robin Hood! Die!"

Hood was on the ground beneath him. The outlaw reached up and stabbed two fingers into Aelstan's good eye. As the captain screamed, Robin used his hook-hold to throw his enemy off him.

Aelstan rolled sideways, misjudging or forgetting the line where the turf dropped away. Too late he scrambled for purchase. His fingers caught a tuft of grass. It came loose in his fist.

The guard captain fell, his body clawing at air as the rocks came towards him. He crashed onto the jagged stones, bounced once, then lay sprawled in a broken bloody pile.

Robin rolled from the edge. His fingers closed around one of the discarded jet beads from Aelstan's chain. He dragged himself to his feet.

The Sheriff of Nottingham was there, with six men. Four of them had arrows nocked at the outlaw.

"You've nowhere to run, Robin i' th' Hood," de Vendenal pointed out.

"You've nowhere to hide, Sheriff. I'll always find you and stop you. One day I'll stop you for good."

William de Vendenal swept his arms along the bleak cliff-top, indicating how the outlaw had exhausted his options for escape. No welcoming forest waited to shelter him. No clever tunnel would allow his exit. There was only the Sheriff's guard ready to take an unarmed man, or the remorseless rocks by the churning sea. "This story has a different ending, wolfshead. This story's called 'The Death of Robin Hood'.

The young outlaw stood at bay. The sea wind whipped his blonde locks towards the azure horizon. He grinned. "Are you sure, Sheriff? I mean, that's quite catchy, but is it accurate? Why not call it 'Robin Hood steals the Sheriff's jet'? Or 'Robin Hood frees the Sheriff's slaves'?" He pointed over the waters where the royal warship was bobbing over the waves. "That'll be my men taking your treasure chests and prisoners away from you."

De Vendenal stared out to sea. The war-boat had pulled down the Prince's colours. Now it sailed a white stag on Lincoln green.

The Sheriff frowned then sneered. "I would sacrifice a thousand pounds to have you in my grasp, Robin Hood," he declared. "There is more black amber. There are always more infants to enslave. But when you have died a death that makes men shudder in the night there will be no more resistance."

"You'd be surprised, de Vendenal. There are things you don't understand about the heart of England. I tried telling Aelstan but he was blind even before I put his eye out."

The Sheriff wasn't about to let Robin plot a clever escape later. "Seize him. Break his fingers and kneecaps now. Bring what's left of him to the camp." He considered further. "Take his sight, too. Let's see how good a shot he is after that."

Robin hurled the jet bead with an archer's accuracy. It shot like a bullet into De Vendenal's eye. The Sheriff cried out, fell back, clutching his bloody face.

While the guards reacted to their master's sudden injury Robin turned to the sea. "I know what this story's called now," he told the Sheriff. "This is 'Robin Hood's Leap.'"

And he jumped.[64]

Aboard the warship the outlaws had seen the tiny figures fighting above the bay. Sharp-eyed Much was the first to identify the combatants as Robin and Aelstan.

"We have to get to him," Little John insisted. He turned to the borrowed fisherman of Whitby who sailed the boat for the outlaws. "Set in. Rob needs help!"

"It's too late," Scarlet said with a soldier's pragmatism. "By the time we got there we'd be too late for Robin, just in time to be cut down by the Sheriff's guard ourselves."

Clorinda shielded her eyes from the sun's glare and tried to follow the action. It was clear Hood was surrounded. "I wanted you to meet Robin of Loxley," she told her husband Brom. "Now you never will."

Marion said nothing, merely clutched the sail-ropes and watched as her forest king duelled the Sheriff's captain.

A cheer rose up from the outlaws of Sherwood when Aelstan toppled from the cliff.

"But what's he doing now?" Much demanded as Robin's unmistakable figure backed towards the edge where the captain had fallen.

"He's at bay," guessed Friar Tuck. "They've got him surrounded. There's no way out."

---

64   Many places claim to be the location of "Robin Hood's Leap", including some that are actually named that. In selecting this location for story purposes the author was mindful that the coastal cove where Robin meets his men described in this narrative, with the steep jagged cliffs above it, is nowadays the picturesque fishing village called Robin Hood's Bay. Robin Hood tourists are recommended to visit this tiny unspoiled location themselves and make their own judgement on the matter.

"But one," said Maid Marion. "Watch."

Robin Hood turned and leaped from the cliff. As he fell he twisted, turning his drop into a dive.

"There's dozens of rocks down there," Clorinda objected. "The water's full of them."

"Watch," insisted Marion.

Robin vanished between the jagged boulders at the waterline.

"He'd dead," whispered David in a small shocked voice. "What do we do now? Robin's dead!"

"Watch," Marion repeated. Her voice was less calm than she'd hoped.

"It's a million to one shot," Little John owned. "That's our Rob's speciality, for sure."

"Come on, Robin!" Marion hissed. "Make it work!"

A wet blonde head broke out of the water fifty yards beyond the rocky shore. Robin Hood waved to the distant boat.

"Come about," Tuck told the sailors. "Prepare to take aboard the madman."

"See him safe," Marion agreed. "Then I'll kill him."

Clorinda nodded. She grasped Maid Marion's hand briefly. An understanding passed between them.

The boat of stolen jet and rescued slaves hove in to pick up the prince of thieves.

The boat didn't put in at Whitby, where the abbey's writ ran, nor at Scarborough where a royal castle and garrison commanded the promontory. Robin had the fishermen take the vessel down the coast to the Humber estuary then up the river until the broad Trent branched off to the north.

"This is our stop, for most of us bandits," the young outlaw told Clorinda, Brom, the refugees of Egton and the fishermen of Whitby strand. "Alan and Tuck will be sailing with you all the way up river to York."

"York?" puzzled Brom. "Why…"

"The law is clear about slaves and runaway serfs," Marion supplied. "If you can live free inside the boundaries of a charter city for a year and a day you are freemen forever. Be sure to get some helpful clergyman to notarise it for you."

"And you'll make your way in York with this," Alan added, patting one of the heavy strongboxes of Whitby jet. "You mined it so you should spend it. There's enough here to set up every family with a home and trade inside the city walls, where the Sheriff can never find you."

Little John tapped his seven-foot quarterstaff on another of the chests. "This one's for the smallfolk of Whitby, to compensate them for their pirate woes. You'll be taking Makebliss back with you to face local justice with that captured crew and neither Abbot nor Sheriff need know how that trial goes."

"Make if fair, though," insisted Marion. "We have to be better than De Vendenal."

"And don't forget that you can claim salvage fees if you return a royal boat you happen to find abandoned and drifting," Will Scarlet pointed out to the fishermen. "A quarter of the vessel's price. That'll be a nice little windfall."

Alan a Dale laid claim to the third chest. "This for His Grace Geoffrey Plantagenet, Archbishop of York, to help remind him that slavery's wrong. A prohibition from him in the Church's name will end this particular scheme of the Sheriff's. If de Vendenal wants jet hereafter he'll have to pay a wage to miners full grown."

"Archbishop Geoffrey's very moral," Tuck told the peasants, "where large chests of treasure are involved."

Robin perched up on the final trunk. "And this for the poor of Sherwood. We're behind on deliveries. It's been a nice holiday but we need to get back to work."

"Holiday?" Will Scarlet almost yelped.

Marion had heard Robin's account of the clifftop confrontations by now. She laid her head on the outlaw's shoulder, her red locks twining with his blonde hair. "They were wrong you know. You will be remembered. This rebellion of yours, showing that tyrants can be fought, that wealth can be used for good, that everybody has worth; that rebellion will never end. Nor should it."

"So we can work out a couple more verses to those songs about you and me, then?" Robin asked her speculatively.

She squeaked as his hand closed on her. She glanced over at the beautiful Clorinda, queen of the shepherdesses. "I want four more verses at least, Robin Hood," Maid Marion insisted to the lord of Sherwood. "And they'd better be good long ones. See to it!"

THE END

Robin Hood and the Lionheart's Gold

2

3

5

Eleanor of Aquitaine: Much More Than a Footnote

Comic books don't really lend themselves to lengthy footnotes. My use of Eleanor of Aquitaine in the graphic story in this volume left me with an irresistible itch to tell her backstory. So here goes! Eleanor of Aquitaine was the most powerful woman in the twelfth century, and a direct cause of Robin Hood! Here's why.

At 17, Eleanor was the most eligible heiress in Europe. Her father had just died, leaving her Countess of Anjou and Aquitaine, roughly 1/5 of modern day France, then separate kingdoms. Not only was she rich she was also said to be the most beautiful woman in Europe. Within three months of coming into her titles she was invited to visit the son of the King of France. Two weeks later she was his wife. Two years later he was King and she was Queen of France.

But Elaine wasn't content to stay home. When the French King went on the Second Crusade, Eleanor went with him! In fact she organised what today we'd call the logistics, leaving her husband free to hit people in tin cans with heavy objects.

But things didn't work out well between Eleanor and the king. She bore him a daughter but found him an indifferent and unskilled lover - historians now suspect he may have been homosexual - and a bit of a loser generally. She asked the Pope for a divorce on the grounds that she and the king were third cousins, and after the birth of a second daughter the marriage was annulled.

Three months later she married Henry, Duke of Normandy (whose father she may have bedded first). Two years after that Henry II was King of England! Eleanor went from being Queen of France to Queen of England; the French weren't too happy.

Eleanor fought with her new husband like cat and dog but they made an effective partnership stabilising England after decades of civil war between the contending would-be rulers King Stephen (Henry's cousin) and Empress Maud (Henry's mother). Eleanor bore Henry eight children. The three girls all went on to become queens. The four boys who lived to adulthood all went on to attack their father, with their mother encouraging them.

What caused a final rift between Henry and Eleanor was the Fair Rosamund, twenty-five years Eleanor's junior, the new most beautiful woman in Europe, and somebody who hadn't got any interest in scheming or power-struggles and seemed to genuinely care for Henry. Eleanor put up with Henry's other mistresses, who were venal and corruptible and easily disposed of. Rosamund was something out of a fairy tale and became the nation's darling. In fact the greatest love ballads of the age were all about Henry and Rosamund.

So Eleanor decided Henry must go. She encouraged her sons to make it happen. The eldest, also Henry, known as "the Young King" because he was crowned co-ruler even though he never actually got to England's throne, was set on to his father. Henry senior had provoked the murder of Bishop Thomas a Becket, who'd raised Young Henry since infancy. Henry Jr. might have won too, had he not died of dysentery. The third son Geoffrey also fought his father but died in a tourney.

That left two potential heirs: Richard, called by some Lionheart for his bravery in war, and John, called Lackland for his poverty (youngest son inherits least) and Soft-Sword for his war skills and possibly bedroom deficiencies. Richard went to war with Henry II. John came in on Henry side, then defected when he thought he might lose. Henry was broken-hearted, lost the will to fight, and died shortly thereafter.

When Richard became king he also went on crusade. During his ten year rulership of England he spent less than seven months in the country. Eleanor was left to keep an eye on things, including the two Justiciars Richard left to run the administration - and to keep John out. When John did take over it was Eleanor who sent for her favourite son to come home. When Richard was captured and ransomed on his way back, it was Eleanor who terrified the barons and the church into finding three times the annual tax income of England to pay for his release. In fact Eleanor was formidable enough to *force* the church to part with a quarter of its wealth! John's attempts to pay for Richard to stay locked up were stomped flat by his mother.

The French had captured Normandy while Richard was imprisoned and John was being John. Richard set off to reclaim the territory. Eleanor went with him. Richard and his mum scared the hell out of the French - she knew exactly where their weak spots were. Richard spent the last seven years of his life campaigning in Europe. He died of an infected crossbow wound, in his mother's arms.

And even then Eleanor wasn't done. She returned to England and "advised" John for the rest of her life. It was only after she was dead that the Barons rose against John and imposed the *Magna Carta* on him. I'm not sure any of them would have dared try it while Eleanor was around to glare at them.

Arguably Eleanor put Henry II on the throne. She certainly put Richard I on the throne. She was responsible for at least a portion of the crippling taxes that are the backstory of many a Robin Hood tale. She was behind the Lionheart's return, which is the culmination of many a Robin Hood movie. There's even old ballad stories of a queen summoning Robin Hood to seek his aid - Eleanor would be as good a candidate as any; she certainly had the charisma and intelligence to consider it (had Robin been real).

In an age where noble women were often traded as commodities, Eleanor turned the system to her advantage and played major league politics with the top rank of European rulers - the Pope, the Holy Roman Emperor, the Kings of France and England... and Eleanor of Aquitaine.

Meanwhile, back with the Forbidden Legend...

By 1194, King Richard the Lionheart had been gone from England for four years, first to fight the crusades, then latterly held ransom by the Duke of Austria and the Holy Roman Emperor. In his absence his surviving brother, Prince John 'Lackland', had outmanoeuvred and replaced the two Justiciars set to rule England and had taken command himself. While his mother sought ways of freeing the Lionheart, he plotted to pay Richard's captors to keep the monarch locked away. Seizing on England's weakness, King Philip of France avenged Richard's jilting of his sister by snatching away the Lionheart's Normandy territories.

While kings, queens, and princes plotted and postured, John's officers undertook a systematic looting of the lands under their control; except in Nottinghamshire, Derbyshire, and Yorkshire, where Lord William de Vendenal's ambition was curbed and thwarted by forest outlaws under the command of the people's troublesome champion, Robin in the Hood. Hood and his merry men of Sherwood stood against the nobles' tyranny, robbing the rich and giving to the poor.

But nothing can last forever, and change was coming to England…

❧ Dramatis Personae:

The Merry Men of Sherwood Forest:

Robin in the Hood, outrageous outlaw rogue, leader of the bandits of Sherwood, the people's hero

Lady Matilda Fitzwarren of Leaford, *Maid Marion*, beloved by the common folk and by Robin Hood.

John Little of Hathersage, Robin right hand man, known for his giant stature as *Little John*

Brother Thomas, a fat monk nicknamed *Friar Tuck*; Robin's boyhood tutor

Will Scathlock, a professional soldier; his violent tendencies earned him the nom-de-guerre *Scarlet*

Ros of Waltham, camp headwoman, mother of the infant Tad

Alan a Dale, a minstrel who understands the power of legends

Elaine of Loughborough, Alan's wife, mother of his children Calliope, Adam, and Eurydice

Much, the Miller's Son, a handsome lad of limited intellect

David of Doncaster, a fiery young wrestler

Arthur a Bland, a cunning poacher with woodcraft and tracking skills

Gilbert with the White Hand, the band's cook and quartermaster

Riccon Hazel of Flintshire, former beggar, handy lad in a fight

George a' Green, the jolly pinder of Wakefield

Betris of Bradford, George a'Green's wife

Wat o' the Crabstaff, tinker

Malkyn of Woodbarrow, a pretty runaway who's fond of David

The Sheriff and his Staff:

Lord William de Vendenal, Lord High Sheriff of Nottingham

Ralph Murdac, Castellan of Nottingham Castle

Matthew Shankshard, Chief Constable of Nottinghamshire

Gill o' th' Red Cap, the finest archer in the Sheriff's service

Lewis of Newark, herald and messenger

The Sheriff's Guests:

Roger de Montbegum, Philip and Ralph de Worcester, Eustace de Mortain, John Crocan, Walter Avenel, Ralph de Wellbuef, William de Kellham, Richard de Camera and many others, two score of villains in all.

The King and his Retainers:

Richard I, King of England, Duke of Aquitaine, Normandy and Gascony, Lord of Cyprus, Count of Anjou, Maine, and Nentes, Overlord of Brittany; called *the Lionheart*

Queen Eleanor of Aquitaine, the Queen Mother, the most powerful woman in Europe

David of Scotland, Earl of Huntingdon, Robin's probable father

Ranulf, Earl of Chester, Huntingdon's brother-in-law

William, Earl of Ferrers, Richard's ally and friend

Lord Hubert Walter, the new Archbishop of Canterbury, Justiciar, and Lord Chancellor of England

Hugh De Puiset, Earl of Northumberland, Bishop of Durham, former Justiciar

Sir Mark Fitzwarren, crusader, Marion's eldest brother

Edgar, Lord Greystoke, Marion's brother in law, wed to her sister Anne, newly father of infant Aline

Master Elias of Oxford – a renowned siege engineer

Also:

Master Peata Whatton, Alderman of Nottingham, father of Tercie

A Large Bull of indeterminate ownership and temperament

An Angry Badger of low character and bad temperament

With a full cast of townsmen, retainers, mercenaries, lackeys, leeches, recusants, office-seekers, chroniclers, churchmen, gibbet-bait, and onlookers, blended to taste.

Nottingham Castle A.D. 1194

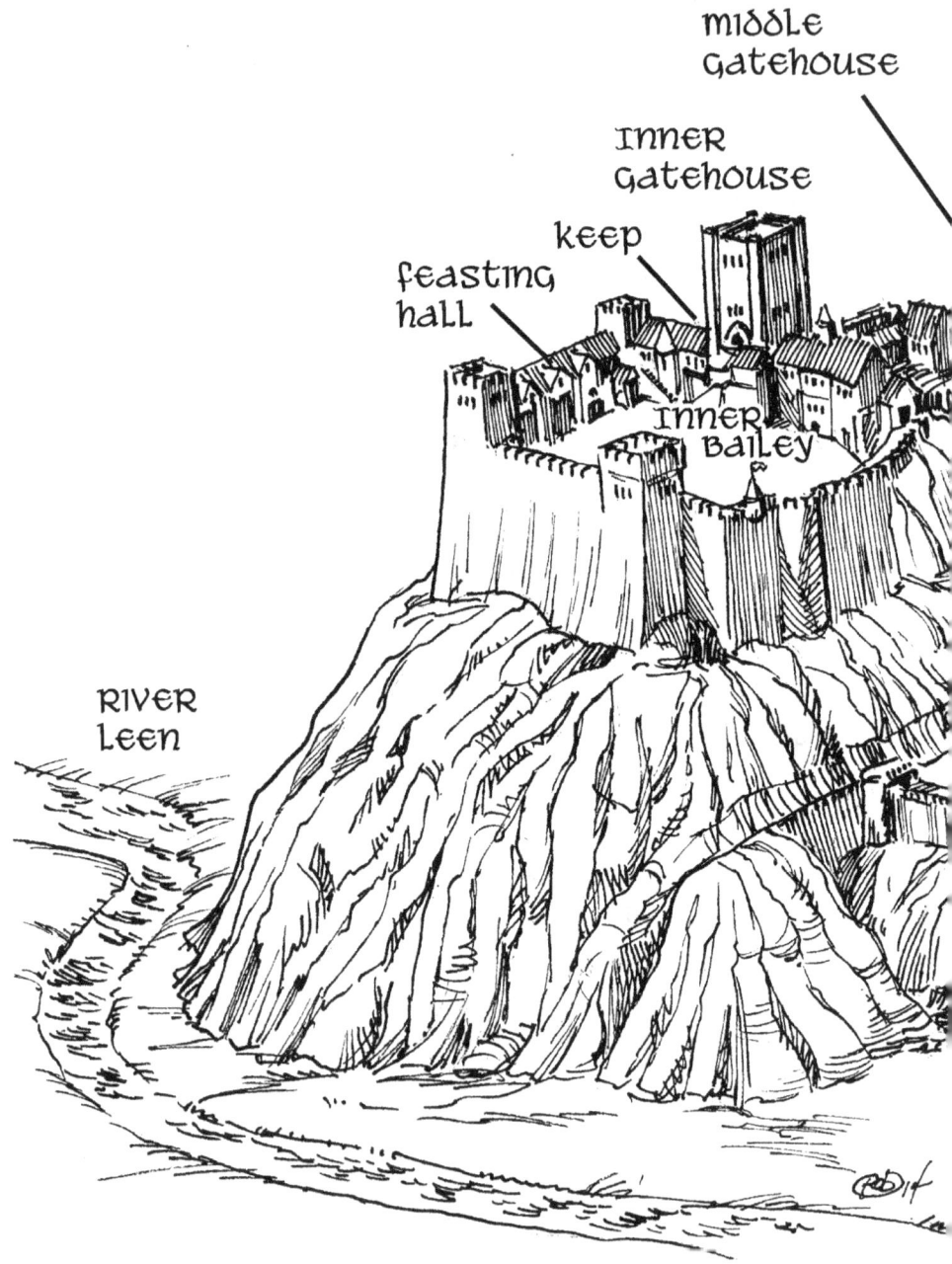

middle gatehouse

inner gatehouse

keep

feasting hall

inner bailey

RIVER LEEN

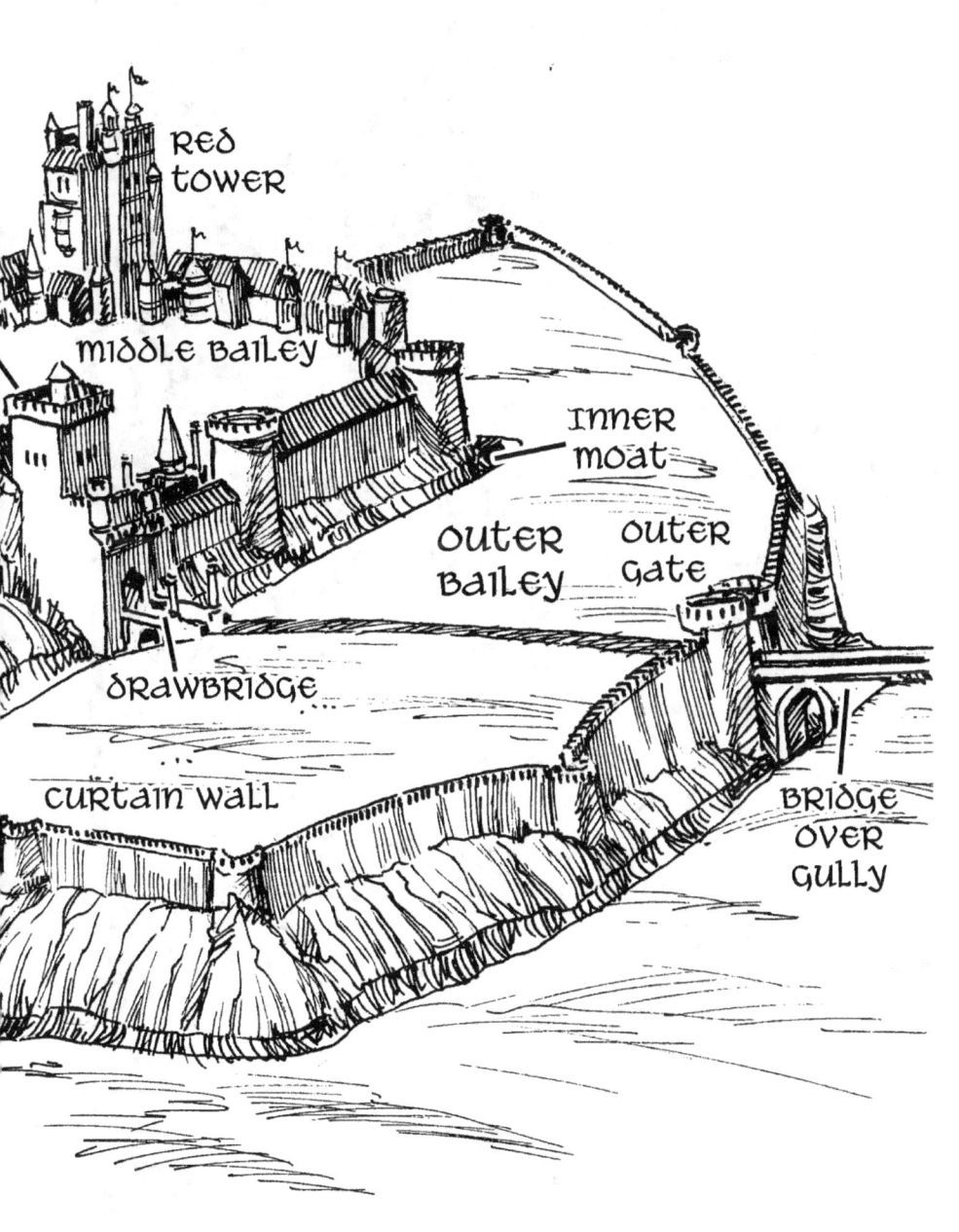

RED TOWER

MIDDLE BAILEY

INNER MOAT

OUTER BAILEY

OUTER GATE

DRAWBRIDGE

CURTAIN WALL

BRIDGE OVER GULLY

Robin Hood and the Black Monk

I

There were still bandits in Sherwood Forest. The best efforts of the Sheriff of Nottingham and all his men had failed to catch them.

They cheated, those so-called merry men who served the forest lord, the bandit-king who called himself Robin Hood. They struck from the unmapped depths of the greenwood, alerted to rich travellers by their network of peasant sympathisers. Their skilled archers were sufficient to overcome all but the strongest of guard troops; an arrow from an English longbow could punch through plate-mail. Before armed response could be sent from any of the garrisons, the thieves had melted away again, taking whatever loot they found and hostages for ransom.

But that wasn't the end of their perfidy. Not content with disrupting the safe passage of merchants, nobles, and priests, and the Sheriff's own tax gatherers, these scofflaws distributed the wealth they'd taken amongst the poor of the towns and villages of Nottinghamshire and Yorkshire. Serfs worked near to death and taxed almost to oblivion naturally welcomed food and coin that would see them alive through the next winter. Men without hope would place their faith in even forest rebels when they could hold to nothing else.

It was the spring of 1194 and everything was wrong. The commonality of England hated their overlords and loved Robin in the Hood.

Brother Leroy reflected on that as he stared into his campfire, feeding the occasional branch into the hypnotic flames. It was a cold March after a bitter winter and the nights were still chill. He took another sup of the flask beside him and looked over his shoulder.

"Friend or foe?" he asked in good Norman French.

The outlaws ghosted from the shadows. "That depends on you," one of them replied.

Brother Leroy still sat on his pack before his fire. He had a heavy broadsword across his knees, an old sturdy blade that had seen some action, but he didn't go for it. "And that depends on who you are and what you want," the monk replied.

The dark figures moved closer and became distinguishable. Their leader was a blonde-haired young man with a neat pointed beard. He wore hunting leathers dyed Lincoln green, perfect camouflage for Sherwood's depths. A quiver of red-fletched goosefeather arrows and a long bow were slung across his back. A pair of likely lads flanked him, each armed with quarterstaffs, ready for trouble. The monk guessed that beyond the circle of firelight other men held taught-drawn bows aimed at his heart.

"We want a talk to start," the lead outlaw said. "They call me Robin Hood. These are my woods."

"I thought this was the king's royal forest?"

"He's busy right now. We're looking after it for him."

Brother Leroy snorted. "And if I asked you to produce a charter granting you authority in these lands?" he challenged.

"I'd get it from the same place King Richard got permission to invade Normandy and Flanders."

"King Richard holds those lands by ancient right. He merely asserted his authority to restore them to lawful rule."

Robin Hood gestured to the dark tracts of Sherwood. "I hold this forest by ancient right too, by customs and privileges older than the Normans, older than the Romans. I'm only asserting my authority to bring true justice where the law has failed."

The black monk took another pull at his flask and held it out to the bandit. "So you're the king of Sherwood, then?"

Robin accepted the drink. He hunkered down on the other side of the fire, took a long swig, and returned the flask. "Some call me that. I prefer to be the people's champion. A ruler should protect and care for his subjects. The aristocrats and prelates that tear England between them have forgotten that."

"So you take on the burden?"

"I do."

"Why?"

Robin chuckled. "Because of a woman. She has this way of forcing you to be more than you are."

Brother Leroy nodded. "This would be the Maid Marion they sing about."

"It would. But let's not repeat all the verses in front of her, shall we?"

"You don't want her to hear the more graphic ones?"

"I don't want to give her ideas." Robin shifted and pointed to the monk. "You're not a humble hedge-friar moving from village to village. You're dressed plainly but you're armed and you're well-spoken. Are you ready to tell me who you are and why you're in Sherwood?"

"I'm passing through on my way to Nottingham," Brother Leroy replied. "I'd like to get there with my purse intact."

"We can all dream. Pass your coin-pouch over. If you're a needy mendicant preacher we'll fill it for you. If not, then you can make a donation to the poor."

The black monk was surrounded. He unlaced his leather scrip and tossed it to Robin Hood.

Robin passed it to one of the lads behind him. "David?"

The burly youngster with the quarterstaff opened the moneybag and counted it out. "Eighty marks!" he cried, happily. That was a useful haul. A single mark bought eight months' work from a basic labourer.

Robin looked at the black monk discerningly. "Take half," he decided. "Give him the rest back."

Brother Leroy raised an eyebrow.

"We don't rob more than men can afford," the outlaw lord told him. "Think of this as a tithe, a forest tax, to pass safely to Nottingham."

The monk received his lightened purse back with mixed feelings. "I thought the merry men of Sherwood were against taxes?"

"We're against taxes that break men or are used to keep them slaves. But your silver, that'll buy corn and bread, nails and hides, that'll keep somebody going until his luck changes. Some of it will even go to the king after all."

"Really?" Brother Leroy was sceptical.

"Really. It's our own personal Richard tax. Haven't you heard that the Lionheart was shipwrecked on his way back to England? He had to travel right across Europe by land, and he was taken captive by Duke Leopold of Austria and sold on to the Holy Roman Emperor. There's a ransom demanded of £65,000."

"That much? That's thrice England's royal income each year!"

"Which is why King Richard's mother has the Lord Chancellor screwing every penny out of the barons and the church. A quarter of all clerical wealth and yet more scutage and carucage[65] from the Barons. But that gets passed down to the peasants and the serfs and they suffer worst of all."

Brother Leroy had heard that the Sherwood outlaws had stolen some of that financial muster. "If you oppose the collection then why claim my money for Richard's release?"

"We don't approve of squeezing the smallfolk," Robin explained, "but we still need Richard home to check his brother and restore order. John

---

65   The previously footnoted tax in lieu of rendering feudal military service and a tax on farmed land.

Lackland's running the country into the ground. He can't control the great lords and they do as they please with no check on their greed and lusts. He can't defend our borders or protect us from crime; I don't mean our Sherwood kind of crimes but murder and rapine and brutal robberies, extortion, piracy, slavery. So we're collecting for the Lionheart too, in our own way. Thank you for your donation."

The black monk had to smile at Robin's audacity. "Richard's the lesser of two evils?"

The king of Sherwood thought for a moment. "Richard's still unknown to us in England. Since he took the crown he's been in this country for less than six months. Maybe he's as bad as his little brother. Maybe he's the best king ever. We've never had a chance to know." He shrugged. "Besides, Weaselly John and the King of France have offered the Holy Roman Emperor £40,000 to keep Lionheart imprisoned, so we've got one reason at least to see him free."

Brother Leroy nodded. "Well, enough of high politics. It's not a conversation I expected when I camped in Sherwood. What are your intentions for me now you've thinned my purse?"

Robin smiled at him across the campfire. "Why don't you join us for dinner?"

The outlaw camp wasn't what the black monk had expected. The squalor and chaos he thought to see amongst landless rogues in the wild forest was notably absent. The merry men had laid out their temporary settlement in good order. Wattle-and-daub shelters and good canvas tents were arranged away from dug latrines. A picket line of well-curried horses stood beside a makeshift smithy. Lanterns were strung from the trees to illuminate the clearing where the feast was prepared.

"How can you get away with this?" Brother Leroy wondered. "Surely the High Sheriff's men can find you here?"

A huge man shifted out of the shadows where he'd been standing unseen. The black monk was tall and broad but the hairy giant loomed over him. "Finding us is one thing," said John Little of Hathersage, "getting away to tell's another. And at need we can be gone into the forest without trace in an hour."

"You'd be Little John, then," the monk surmised.

"Someone has to be," mocked a rough-looking fighter in studded leather.

"Bad luck on the fellow who got the short straw!"

"Better Little John than Will Scarlet!" the big fellow jibed back. "At least I'm tall enough to see over my own sour moods."

"Big enough to plant your feet where they're not welcome," chided a fat friar trying to pass the giant with a heavy platter for the feasting trestle. He'd already helped himself to a hefty handful of minced mutton. "One side!"

"I *can* see my feet though, Tuck," Little John shot back. "My belly doesn't block my view."

"Why would the Sheriff want to find us here," Robin asked Brother Leroy, "when he'd have to put up with these rascals?" He led the black monk through the camp towards the banquet.

The monk looked around the busy clearing. "You have women here," he noted. "And children."

"We offer refuge to any who come to us honestly," Robin told him. "Some come fleeing a cruel landlord or a noble's malice or an overlord's lust. Others join us for the free life we live, with few rules save of fellowship. Some come for a season, while the hue for them dies down or to recover their strength or wits. Others stay and swell our outlaw ranks."

The black monk tried to count the host. He couldn't. "There are hundreds here."

"And more ranging far beyond. Sherwood runs as far as the sea in Yorkshire's North Riding and to the fens down south, and we've bands roaming the greensward keeping an eye on things. Where a cruel lord unjustly flogs his servant, where a starving widow struggles to survive, where a savage knight abuses some poor village maid, we try and set things right."

"A secret army," Brother Leroy understood. "No wonder the Sheriff of Nottingham fears you. Mobile, organised, supported; for all the Sheriff's troops you have him surrounded."

A red-haired beauty looked up from the table she was dressing. "That's exactly the idea," said Maid Marion of the Greenwood.

Brother Leroy had heard that the Queen of May was lovely. Nobody had told him that she radiated sovereignty. He bowed low and kissed her hand. "Lady Matilda at the Lee," he greeted her, calling her by her old name from her life before she'd become Robin's forest love. "I am most pleased to meet you. Even if it means the loss of half my purse."

"Robin's doing his job then," the lady of Sherwood approved. "Welcome to our revels, sir monk."

"Our guest seems surprised that we're not hiding in caves cutting each other's throats," Robin explained. "I can only assume that he's been out of

England for a time, not to know that Sherwood has become the last bastion of free civilised men."

Marion looked at the black monk. He'd travelled, for sure. He had an old tan that was faded away now, and the pallor of a man who'd been confined for a while. He was of middle years but hale and hearty, handsome in a bullish kind of way. At six foot five he was near as tall as Little John. He wore his friar's robe and hood like an ermine gown.

The forest queen shot a glance over at Robin. He grinned back and winked.

Much the Miller's Son came over with a message. "Ros says can we get sat down, please. Gilbert's ready to serve the venison up." The lad's honest face folded into a grin. "I like venison!"

"The king's deer," Brother Leroy pointed out. It was forbidden to hunt in the parts of England set aside as royal parks. The price in law was a hand or an eye.

"We always set aside a portion for the king if he chooses to collect it," Robin promised.

Dinner was a surprise as well. The feast would not have shamed an Earl's table. Rather than the simple stews and peasant fare the monk had expected, Gilbert of the White Hand and his cooks served up a five-course banquet for the two hundred residents of the outlaw camp.

Marion caught the monk's thoughts. "We don't always eat like this. But tonight is a special occasion."

"What occasion?" Brother Leroy felt compelled to ask.

"A donation from a rich greedy merchant who met me disguised as a potter and followed me into the wood to buy more of my ridiculously cheap wares," Robin grinned. "He won't abuse his apprentices again, nor have his debtors' widows cast from their homes. It turns out the pottery wasn't so cheap after all."[66]

Marion explained. "Every so often Robin feels the need to do something ridiculous and dangerous. Then we have to have a party to celebrate our surprise that he's still alive."

"You're the one who commanded me to look after the oppressed," the outlaw objected.

"I never said champion the oppressed by playing dress-up and dodging the Sheriff's men as they chased you back through Sherwood!"

Robin Hood took his scolding in good part and grasped his lady's hand.

---

66   This exploit may be a variant of one of the earliest Robin Hood ballads, *Robin Hood and the Potter*. It is collected as Child Ballad 121. An almost identical ploy is told in *Robin Hood and the Butcher*.

"It's coming on to four years since I stole Marion away," he told the black monk. "How was I to know that no-one would take her back?"

"Nigh four years since I had to make do with a lunatic wolfshead for a true-love," Marion parried. "Too late now to find a better champion for the people."

The minstrel Alan a Dale sat close by with his wife and children. "No better champion could be found in all of Christendom!" he proclaimed, "nor a fairer lady at that champion's side."

"Don't get him started," Little John cautioned the monk. "He'll sing for hours about sylvan ideals and forest romance. We'll be knee deep in pastourelle. And then Tuck'll start in on the theology of banditry."

"Whereas the best we can hope for with John is that he'll keep drinking and pass out early," Friar Tuck responded. "If he ever had a thought in his head, the fleas in his sheepskin ate it."

Ros of Waltham, the camp's headwoman, smacked the friar on his pudgy arm. "You mind your tongue on Little John, my lad," she warned. "He might be dull as a millstone and ugly as a stump but he's got his uses."

John roared in protest at this outrageous insult. Ros suffered herself to be hauled across his lap and thoroughly kissed. The yet-small curve of her belly betrayed one of the giant's uses.

Brother Leroy watched the good fellowship and sipped his wine. "This cannot last," he said. "You have rebelled and survived for four years, but the Prince's forces muster against you."

Marion turned serious. "Lackland must be curbed. My father and others wrote to King Richard to warn of John's ambition. The Earl of Huntingdon must have reported all when he joined Richard on crusade. The nation crumbles. Already France has taken Normandy. And here at home our every escape comes that little bit harder."

"That's what makes it interesting, of course," Robin added.

"It's said that the Sheriff of Nottingham hates you," reported Brother Leroy.

"If William de Vendenal didn't hate me then I'd be doing something wrong," the young outlaw replied. "That Sheriff is everything that's amiss with the kingdom. He uses his power to control not protect. He's greedy, cruel, bitter, vicious and those are his good points!"

"I'm to Nottingham to see him," Brother Leroy confessed.

"Then maybe I should have had more of your purse," replied Robin Hood.

"You want to see how we survive?" Maid Marion asked Brother Leroy. "Then watch this."

Dinner was over. It was time for games. The outlaw company gathered by torchlight to enjoy the show.

First came the wrestling. David of Doncaster put down Riccon Hazel easily enough but struggled against the huge mass of Little John. The three-times champion boxer finally managed to throw the giant, but once John sat on him it was all over.

The crowd laughed. A pretty runaway called Malkyn helped David back to his seat and comforted him.

"Anyone else?" John challenged. He spat on his huge hands. "I'm just getting started."

"I'll see you get your come-uppance another night," Friar Tuck promised him. "For now I'll take on my fellow monastic if he's got the belly for it. He's near as tall as our Hathersage sheep-chaser."

Brother Leroy rose. "I couldn't match that belly," he quipped to the portly friar, "but I'll take three tosses with you and may the best man win."

"We should really hope it's Tuck instead," called Scarlet.

Tuck kilted his robe. Leroy doffed his sword and scabbard. They closed together in a tight clinch.

And then it was over. Friar Tuck was in the dust gasping for breath. The black monk held out a hand and hauled him up.

Two more falls happened in quick succession.

"This is turning into a right good night," chuckled Arthur a Bland. The old poacher softened his words by tossing Tuck a wineskin.

Brother Leroy still held the ring. "I'm ready for the big man now," he said, gesturing to John of Hathersage.

"Don't break him," Marion told Little John. "He's our guest."

"I'll be gentle," the giant lied, flexing his arms and joining the black monk in the circle.

This was a much closer match. John won the first fall, finally scooping Leroy up and hammering him to the turf. But the monk learned from his mistake and hooked a leg under the giant while Little John was off balance. The big outlaw crashed to the ground for one fall all.

"There's not many can do that," Robin admitted. "Must be the power of prayer."

The third meeting was the longest, each man cautious now, each straining to get the advantage that would mean victory. John was the stronger, but the monk was cunning and well-versed in wrestler's tricks. At the last he managed to take John by the waist and hurl him down.

A mighty cheer went up from the crowd. None could remember Little John ever taking a second fall.

"How did he do that?" Much wondered. Five-year-old Tad sitting on his lap didn't know. The boy clapped his hands anyway.

Then came the archery. A willow stick four fingers wide was set up at fifty paces, lit by a lantern. Marion announced the game. "One shot each and a forfeit for who misses!"

"A smack from me," Scarlet clarified. The former soldier was the camp's trainer. Likely lads quickly learned to respect and obey the hard ex-mercenary's discipline.

All the men in the company and some of the boys and women took a shot. Most hit the target, despite the distance and the darkness. The boys who failed got a slap on the rear. The women who missed suffered a kiss from Friar Tuck. The men that were delinquent in their archery took a hard punch from their displeased taskmaster.

Brother Leroy declined a chance to shoot. "The bow's not my weapon," he confessed. "But I would like to see the famous Robin Hood flight a shaft."

"Robin!" called Alan a Dale, and soon all the outlaws were shouting for their leader to show his skill.

Robin fetched his bow and nodded to the crowd. "On one leg or not?" he asked.

"Try one-armed!" Little John called out, laughing.

But Robin nodded. "One armed it is, then," he agreed. He nocked the arrow and drew it back then took the string in his teeth so he only needed a single hand.

"Show-off," said Marion. As Robin released the shaft her fingers twitched Robin in a sensitive area. The outlaw yelped and his shot went wide.

"That's not fair!" Robin objected. "I demand a recount!"

"It does you good to remember you're not unstoppable, Robin i' th' Hood," his lady chided him. "Take your blow from Scarlet like a man."

Robin's eyes shifted from the soldier to the black monk. "No. I'll take a punch from Brother Leroy," he announced. "Moreover, if he can knock me down with a single fist I'll return all we took from his purse and set him on his way."

"That's a fair wager, and a brave one," the monk agreed.

"Let's to it then," Robin said. Aside to Little John he muttered, "John, check the perimeter. Now." The giant nodded and ghosted into the shadows.

Brother Leroy made a show of rolling up his sleeve and flexing his fingers. Robin smoothed down his hair and preened his beard. He took a good defensive stance with his left leg behind his right for support.

Brother Leroy hammered a fist into his chin. The blow lifted the young outlaw right off his feet and toppled him on the turf on his back.

Robin rubbed his face and sat up.

"Stay down," said the black monk. "I command it."

Little John burst back into the clearing. "Soldiers, Rob! A lot of them! Not the Sheriff's louts. These are orderly and quiet and hard by!"

"Who commands it?" Maid Marion demanded of Brother Leroy.

"To arms!" cried Scarlet. "Every lad grab a bow. Ros, break camp and make for the Skellow Well."[67]

"Wait!" Marion countermanded. She stared at the black monk. "Well?"

Brother Leroy pulled back his hood. His red-brown hair was ringed by a crown. "We are Richard," he said, "by God's grace King of England, Duke of Normandy, Aquitaine, and Gascony, Lord of Cyprus, Count of Anjou, Maine, and Nantes, Overlord of Brittany."

Scarlet lowered his sword, stricken. Little John stood open-mouthed. Tuck crossed himself.

Marion made a perfect curtsey and knelt at the king's feet. One by one the outlaws followed her example until all knelt around Richard the Lion-heart.

Robin still sat where he'd been dropped. England's King looked at him. "And you?" he asked the King of Sherwood.

"You said you were going to see the Sheriff of Nottingham," Robin Hood replied. "Why?"

"To strip him of office for supporting John's rebellion against us. To call him to account for his misadministration of our lands. To take our castle of Nottingham which our brother denies us."

"And then?"

"And then to show England what manner of king I am. A good one, I hope."

---

67   Six miles north-west of Doncaster on the Great North Road (A1) near the villages of Skellow and Skelbrooke, the tiny river Skell bubbled up and filled a pool called Robin Hood's Well, with an iron ladle chained to it and a stone seat. The later rustic dome covering the site was designed by 18th century architect Sir John Vambrugh, but the whole edifice has since been shifted to accommodate the modern highway and no longer covers an actual water-source. In 1634 one traveller wrote, "We tasted a cup at Robin Hood's Well; and then were in his rocky chair of ceremony dignified with order of knighthood and sworn to observe his laws." Little John's Cave is only a short distance away between Wrangbrook and Skelbrooke, although the carving identifying it as such has eroded away.

Robin climbed to his feet then knelt before Richard.

The first soldiers arrived, pushing past the camp's bewildered watchmen, surrounding the outlaws.

"Your majesty," prompted Marion, challenging the king with her stare.

"Hold off!" the Lionheart called to his officers. "These are no bandits but our loyal subjects. They have kept our realm better in their forest fastness than any baron or bishop in castle or palace. These are the heroes of Sherwood, bold men of bold Robin Hood!"

Robin knelt beside Marion and kept his head down.

"When did you know?" the damsel whispered to him.

"Oh come on. Leroy? Le roi? French accent, six-foot-five, warrior priest? What about you?"

"When he ate with us I knew of sure. Such royal manners, throwing his bones to the dogs like that. I saw him when I was a girl. He was a young prince when father took us to old Henry's court at Windsor."

"Show off. Now ssshhhh!"

Their hands tangled together before the king.

"Rise, Robin," King Richard bade. "Rise, all you great hearts of the greenwood! Your outlawry is at an end, pardoned and forgotten. Although you've cost me a hundred gold ducats in lost wager."

"How so, your majesty?" Marion asked.

"My comrade the Earl of Huntingdon warranted that I'd not need relieving from the Sherwood rebels. He said his natural son would prove true and fair, and he has!"

Robin shrugged. "I'm me." Marion elbowed him.

"You're free of the Emperor, I see," the lady addressed the king. "Does Prince John know you're back in England?"

"Oh, he's discovered it by now," Lionheart promised. "He and all his toadies and lickspittles. And they'll learn of my ire. Starting with Lord William de Vendenal, I hope. But I've few men yet to retake my country, save these loyal companions from the Holy Land. My forces are spread thin and far. I need allies. I need an army." He looked at Robin. "And you have one, Sir Robin FitzHuntingdon of Loxley."

Robin looked at his merry men. "I suppose we could steal a kingdom for you, majesty," he offered. "For a price: liberty and fairness hereafter."

Richard clasped Robin Hood's hand. "A bargain," he agreed. "Now let me invite *you* to a banquet, with the Sheriff of Nottingham in Nottingham Castle!"

11

arion took charge. She ordered the appearance of a king and his attending retinue at the Major Oak as she might have had she been chatelaine of an earl's palace. She directed royal stewards and surprised outlaws alike to see to the necessary business of expanding the camp for a hundred extra visitors. Nobody else in Sherwood, and few amongst the Lionheart's retinue, could have managed the problems so well.

She was directing the squires where to raise King Richard's pavilion when a tall thin knight in weathered armour approached her. "Tildy?"

She turned round. Her eyes widened. "Mark?" She rushed over and embraced her crusader brother. Her eldest sibling had followed his monarch to the Levant. Now he had returned with him.

"Tildy... this isn't where I expected to find you when I got home. What in heaven have you been up to?"

Marion snorted. "Oh, you know. Running off with a bandit-lord to be his wife, starting a rebellion, robbing the rich to give to the poor. You?"

Sir Mark Fitzwarren shook his head. "I heard the stories before I ever reached England. They're talking about Robin Hood and Maid Marion across the continent!"

"Good. I hope it gives them some ideas about truth and justice."

Marion's eldest sibling looked incredulously at her, then laughed. "I thought father was considering wedding you off to Sir John Stokely or Roger de Montbegum. Only Stokely's dead now, and Montbegum's with the gang of villains who've fled to Nottingham Castle to plot and scheme. Instead..."

"Instead I'm wedded and bedded to Sir Robin FitzHuntingdon," the Queen of May declared defiantly. "You heard his majesty. Prince David, Earl of Huntingdon has acknowledged Robin as his bastard. King Richard has proclaimed him knight. You can call me my lady."

Sir Mark snorted. His expression became more serious. "I rode through Leaford."

Marion sobered too. "The Sheriff confiscated all of our estates when father and mother got out of England with Lord Longchamp. Adam went after, with Longchamp's rescued sister Melisend... as his wife."

"So we heard. Longchamp helped raise the ransom that bought Richard free. Father sent word to Lucas that an army was mustering to harry King Philip of France in Normandy. You know that the French king invaded and took Normandy while the Lionheart was in an Austrian dungeon?"

"I know it's rumoured that Prince John didn't oppose him, or couldn't, because Lackland was more intent on making sure his brother didn't ever return from his imprisonment. Eleanor the Queen Mother called on Robin to help sort out some ransom issues."[68]

"Eleanor of Aquitaine called on your outlaw?"

"He's not just my outlaw, Mark. He's the people's outlaw." She beckoned across the camp, gesturing for Robin to leave directing the tethering of war horses and join her. "Rob, this is my biggest brother. Now you're in trouble."

The king of Sherwood grinned and held out his hand in greeting. "I was in trouble from the moment I met you, Matilda of Leaford, and you'll have me in trouble to the day we die. Well met, Sir Mark. I'm the poor fool who tries to tame your sister."

Mark gave in and shook the bandit's hand. "Pity you," he admitted, returning the outlaw's smile.

"How come you to be with the King again?" Marion asked her brother.

"Word came to us from Walter de Coutances that Richard was found, by an adventuring troubadour called Blondel, if you can believe it[69] and a ransom was ready to be paid. I was part of the force that guarded it and retrieved the king. We sailed for Sandwich and the Lionheart headed for Canterbury to the seat of St. Thomas Beckett. By the time we got to London it had already risen against Weaselly John. The Great Council had declared all his lands forfeit and the bishops had excommunicated him."

"Good for them," Robin responded. "So did Lackland just sit down and cry? Even if he did, I bet some of his followers had more steel."

"John was warned of Richard's coming," Mark admitted. "Philip of France sent him word: *Beware, the devil is loose!* Nobody's sure where John is now. He may have fled to Normandy."

---

68   As recounted in *Lionheart's Gold* in our present volume.

69   According to the A.D. 1260 *Récits d'un Ménestrel de Reims*, Blondel de Nesle was a heroic troubadour who combed Europe searching for his master Richard the Lionheart's place of imprisonment. He verified the King's identity by singing the first part of a love-ballad the two had composed together; Richard responded with the remainder. Blondel then assisted in securing Richard's release. Although the historicity of this is doubtful, there was a real French trouvère Blondel de Nesle (c1155-1202) who is presumed the author of a couple of dozen courtly songs, a few of which have even been recorded in the modern age. Blondel's modest medieval legend grew with the 1874 opera *Richard Coeur-de-lion* by André Ernest Modeste. Romantic English poet Eleanor Anne Porden (1795-1825) contributed *Coer de Leon*, an epic poem in which faithful Blondel is revealed to have actually been Richard's young wife, Berengaria of Navarre, in disguise. In recent years the tale has been popularised by Stephen Oliver and Tim Rice's rock musical *Blondel*, recently reworked and retitled *Lute!*

"It doesn't really matter where he is if he's not captive," Marion judged. She frowned as she worked through the situation. "Lionheart has the popular support, the initiative, and a small loyal army. Lackland's chief thugs have most of the castles, all the money, and a lot of standing troops at their disposal. Most of the barons and a lot of the churchmen will be waiting to see how well Richard fares. If he has a string of victories then they'll all flock to him loyally, with gifts to buy his forgiveness. If things go ill, or just too slowly..."

Mark had forgotten how sharp his youngest sister was. "There's more men mustering for us. And though Richard's forces are less in number, they are great in experience. Men who have fought the Turk these four years, men well used to war. Engineers who can reduce Saracen castles in days."

"And now archers of Sherwood who can cut down any number of mounted opposition," Robin added. "I can see why Richard sought us out. He really needs us, and he really needs to take Nottingham Castle. Fast."

For all the night's revels, King Richard was up at dawn, striding naked down to the stream that watered the outlaw camp to splash himself clean, then calling for his gown and breakfast.

"He really is the king, then?" Much the Miller's Son checked with Robin as he watched the large man striding back to the magnificent silk tent that dominated the eastern side of the clearing. "He looks like a king."

"He's the king," the outlaw lord assured his anxious comrade. "Elder surviving legal get of old King Henry, and King of England because his mother said so and because he had armies and Lackland had none. And maybe for more than that. We'll see."

"I've been talking to his soldiers," Will Scarlet reported. "Old campaigners, nearly all of 'em. Fought with him from Messina and Cyprus[70] all the

---

70   Richard's travels to the crusades were adventures in their own rights. The slighting of the king's sister Joan led to his conquest of Sicily, as referenced in our prologue. Later, a storm separated part of Richard's fleet and Isaac Komnenos, despot of Cyprus, captured Joan and Richard's then-fiancée Berengaria of Navarre. The Lionheart conquered Cyprus and had Komnenos paraded in silver chains – Richard had promised not to put him in irons.

"If things go ill, or just too slowly…"

way through Acre, Arsuf and Jaffa.[71] We might actually stand a chance in a battle, Rob."

"This isn't the Holy Land," Friar Tuck warned. "Poor Nottingham's been sacked and burned, what, three times in the last fifty years? Four? We don't want a massacre there."

"And we won't have one," Robin assured him, frowning. "Look, this is the endgame. Depending on how the next few days go we'll either win the freedoms we were fighting for or go back to a war of attrition until we're eventually caught and hung. And it's not as simple as taking Nottingham Castle…"

"Taking Nottingham Castle won't exactly be easy," objected Alan a Dale. The minstrel had been confined in a donjon there. "In fact it's never been captured in battle."

"But that's not the win," Robin insisted. "We, the free men of Sherwood, we set out to preserve and establish the rights of every Englishman; to law, to a livelihood, to freedoms and protections. It's not enough to get rid of John. It's not enough to get Richard his throne back. What happens then?"

"The Lionheart taxes England pale again and heads off back to his Crusade," predicted Gilbert Whitehand. "Or else he goes to Normandy to win it back off the Froggies."

"We have to get a new idea into King Richard's head. We have to show him something he needs to see." Robin turned to Little John. "How are the lads coping with the idea of being pardoned king's foresters?"

"Bit of a surprise to some of 'em," the big shepherd admitted. "Me amongst 'em. Odd to think that if I wanted to I could head back to Hathersage and buy some land with my loot and settle down with a herd and a home."

"It's not the first time the archers of Sherwood have been called on," the old poacher Arthur a Bland recounted. "Right back in the War of Stephen and Maude, the Archbishop of York called for the yeomen of Sherwood to bring their bows to chase off the Scots – and they did, at Northallerton, harrying 'em all the way back to the Wall."[72]

71　　　　Richard suffered from scurvy during the siege of Acre. He killed men on the walls by firing his crossbow from a bed carried by servants. The Battle of Arsuf was a definitive clash against the harrying forces of Moorish leader Saladin, in which Richard's tough and skilled leadership won him a way forward towards Jerusalem and allowed the reconquest of Jaffa as a Christian port.

72　　　　In 1138, the Scots took advantage of the disorder during the civil war between rival English monarchs King Stephen and Empress Maud to invade and ravage northern England. Thurstan, Archbishop of York, sent an appeal to the "men of Sherwood" to bring their bows and stop the marauders. The forces clashed at the Battle of the Standard two

"A few of the men are a bit nervous," Little John admitted. "Some of our folks are more used to running from soldiers than sitting down and sharing a bowl of venison stew with 'em."

"There was a little trouble with king's men chasing the women last night," Ros admitted. "Scarlet discouraged them that needed discouraging."

"So we're going to Nottingham?" David of Doncaster checked. "We're matching right up to the Sheriff and demanding his surrender?"

"He won't surrender," predicted Elaine of Loughborough, Alan's wife, who had once been betrothed to Lord High Sheriff William de Vendenal. "He'll have some twisty devious cruel scheme up his sleeve. He always does."

"And Robin will stop him," predicted Maid Merion, joining the group that watched the swollen camp. "His majesty requires your presence, Sir Robin. There's to be a council of war."

"Then his majesty can have my presence," the outlaw agreed. "John, Scarlet, come with me."

"And what about me?" demanded the Lady of Sherwood indignantly.

"I didn't expect I needed to ask," chuckled Robin in the Hood.

"Nottingham Castle," sighed Will Scarlet. He leaned over the trestle table and etched lines on a calfskin page. "This is Nottingham, right? River Leen to the south, defensible, with three guarded gated bridges. Walls or cliffs defending the other three sides, with five other gates on the main roads. English Town on the high ground inside to the east around St Mary's, mostly Saxon. French Town to the west near the castle, mostly Norman. The castle itself on a natural promontory here in the south east corner."

"That accords with our other charts and maps," agreed William de Ferrers, Earl of Derby, who was senior officer of the men Lionheart had brought on his forest hunting trip. "What of the fortress itself. You've been in there?"

"Oh aye. And John's even been in the guard up there, in disguise." Scarlet sketched in more detail about the castle. "The river's been diverted to act like a moat to the south. It comes pretty much up to the foot of Castle Rock. South and west are 130 foot cliffs, pretty sheer. The other sides are steep and defended with high walls."

"How high?" demanded King Richard.

---

miles north of Northallerton, with the Scots at a significant numerical advantage. However, the English archers devastated King David's Galwegian infantry and did sufficient damage to the Scots to force their hasty return home.

"Well first you'll come to the outer curtain. Forty feet high, fifteen feet thick, with battlements on top. Six bastions to defend it. That's a hundred yards either side of the only gate."

"What about the gate?" asked Sir Mark Fitzwarren.

Little John picked up the description. "There's a stone bridge across the ravine, leading to the outer gate. There's a wooden drawbridge that'll be up. Twin towers flanking it, with good lines for defending archers."

"It'll be a right bastard to take," added Scarlet.

"What then?" the Lionheart asked.

More drawing on the calfskin. "You're past the outer curtain. There's a steep hill, mostly grassed, where they graze their livestock. Another curtain wall, defended by another moat and drawbridge."

"That's the moat that doubles as a midden," Robin Hood contributed. "You don't want to fall in there."

"Ideal place to drop William de Vendenal though," suggested Marian.

Sir Mark looked uncomfortable at having his sister present in a council of war. "That's a significant fortress," he admitted, trying to keep to business.

"We're not done yet," Scarlet cautioned him. "Break the second gate and there's another wall to the Inner Bailey. There are several towers there that can all be individually held, each with a line-of-fire at invaders in the courtyard below. Every one of them will have to be taken before anyone could get across to the keep proper. The keep has fifteen foot thick walls, naught but loop-holes for windows, four stories high with towers on each corner above that."

"The final approach?" Richard enquired. The formidable fortress didn't deter him. The Saracens made fortifications at least as terrible.

Marion had most experience of the castle's keep. She took the lead stick from Scarlet and added annotations to the drawing in brief accurate strokes. "A straight staircase here, outside and exposed, then a sharp right turn to three successive gates. Arrow loops above the first door, slits over the second, a last flight of steps to take you to the first floor portcullis with holes above for pouring lead."

The king was amused that a woman could supply such details, and said so.

"When I was at Nottingham Castle I devoted a good deal of time planning ways to kill the Sheriff," the lady of Sherwood replied.

"Time well spent," Robin approved. "There's the usual internal keep defences as well, narrow staircases and choke points, all of that kind of thing. In summary, the castle was built as a fortress of war and it was built well. De Vendenal knows how to use it."

"And we need it taken before our credit runs out with the barons and prelates who are watching us," the Earl of Ferrers confessed.

Lionheart nodded gruffly. "I've sent to London for Master Elias of Oxford and his stone-throwing engines. And I've summoned the Archbishop of Canterbury to excommunicate all the castle's defenders."

"We may not have time to reduce the walls," Ferrers warned.

"I hope we can intimidate the defenders to surrender," the king confessed. "I've sent Huntingdon on ahead to start up the scare."

Robin noted his father's role in the siege. "William de Vendenal doesn't scare easily," he cautioned. "He'll know that his best chance lies with a prolonged defence. He'll have laid his plans."

"And you'll have to wreck them, Robin," Marion told the outlaw, hugging his arm. "What else are you for?"

Robin considered the question. "Well, I'm a fantastic lover," he suggested to the Queen of May. "And an inspiration to all who know me. But yes, I don't mind wrecking the Sheriff's plots once and for all."

"It's a major fortress," objected Sir Mark. "We need archers for siege cover and to maintain a full perimeter but..."

Robin turned to King Richard. "Your majesty, Scarlet here's more of a soldier than I'll ever be. He and Gilbert Whitehand will bring our merry men to you at Nottingham. I'll go on ahead with Marion and Little John."

"Good plan," agreed Marion. "We need to do a bit of scouting and a bit of spying. Maybe we can find a way to bypass those walls and gates after all."

"There's a passage up from the brewery and alehouse in the cave under Castle Rock," John remembered. "But that'll be known and guarded.[73] And Alan a Dale once found a way out through a cess-hole in the dungeons. De Vendenal knows about that one too."

King Richard looked from the cunning outlaw to his radiant lady and the towering giant that guarded them. "He's your enemy," he told Robin Hood. "If you can stop him, then do it. Your king commands it."

Robin bowed. "Majesty, it will be my pleasure."

73   This passage ascends from *The Old Trip To Jerusalem* tavern that occupies a natural cavern beneath the castle. The tunnel exists today and leads up into the Renaissance palace that replaced Nottingham Castle and is described as the Castle today. The current Castle is open to the public and for an additional fee there are guided tours of some of the tunnels below.

This "secret" entrance changed English history in 1330, when Queen Isabella and her lover Roger Mortimer had effectively usurped the country from her 15-year old son King Edward III. The lovers met and plotted at Nottingham Castle. William de Eland, who had grown up in the castle, led his friend King Edward and twenty-four comrades in a swashbuckling night raid from the tavern tunnel into the secured fortress. Edward fenced with Roger Mortimer in his mother's bower and the usurper was captured and subsequently executed at the Tower of London.

III

William de Vendenal, technically the former Sheriff of Notting-ham, strode through his hall to meet the clamour of men call-ing for instruction or making complaint. He half-turned to the tall cruel-looking man that flanked him. "Murdac, the next person who paws at me or shouts unbidden, execute him."

The chamber fell silent. The Sheriff looked contemptuously at the crowd of nobles, soldiers and clerks that stood suddenly bashful in his baleful presence.

"Shankshard, Montbegum, the two Worcesters, Lewis of Newark with me. You too, Murdac. I may still want somebody beheaded before the day's done. The rest of you, go do the things you are supposed to do in a sieged castle. If you don't know what they are then report to Murdac later for hanging. That will be all. You are dismissed."

The Sheriff led off towards his private solar, where he could confer with his counsellors and guests in privacy. The officials and attendants of the castle hastily scattered, trying to look too busy to be hanged.

Ralph Murdac, the new Castellan, glared at them as they disbursed; Murdac's first job had been to execute his predecessor Mereward and he had clearly enjoyed it. Nobody in the castle, no matter how high their de-gree, crossed Murdac.

De Vendenal waited until his chosen guests were seated in his inner of-fice. He paced the Frisian carpet before the long fireplace. He turned at last.

"I will hear your objections now, but in an orderly manner. You first, Montbegum."

The Marcher lord was a thickset warrior in his late forties. He insisted on wearing his plate-mail even in the fortified keep of the sealed castle. Perhaps he liked it. He gestured in a wide circle to indicate he was talking about the world beyond the sturdy walls. "Chester and Huntingdon are outside our gates. Richard has returned. His mother has whipped up the barons for him. The church has endorsed him. He will be here soon in per-son to demand our capitulation."

The Sheriff shrugged. "Someone *claiming* to be Richard has returned. All men of quality know that the true Lionheart died in Leopold of Aus-tria's prison. This pretender is some lookalike groomed by the Holy Roman Emperor to seize control of our nation. He has fooled a bereaved and doting mother and has been raised up by factions who think they have reason to rebel against the rule of King John the First. It is the duty of all right-thinking men of quality to resist the usurper and defy his aggressions."

The men in de Vendenal's solar were stunned to silence for a moment at their host's audacious claim. Philip de Worcester[74] responded at last. "Impostor or… not, he has some powerful friends backing him. A lot of them are mustering outside this castle. And where's 'King John', eh? Where's any relief that will stop Richard Lionheart or whoever he may be from starving us out?"

"That's another problem," Ralph de Worcester chimed in across his older brother. "Why is the outer bailey filled with peasants and womenfolk? If there's to be a siege then we need all the provisions we can get. Unless we're to eat haunch of serf I don't see the point in keeping all those useless mouths inside the castle. Military doctrine…"

De Vendenal held up a finger to silence him. "I said one at a time. Philip, our beloved John Soft-sword has fled to Normandy, to the court of the monarch of France. He's accepted an offer of refuge and relief from your namesake King Philip."

"He's run away?" de Worcester was infuriated. "Damn him. I should have known. He's thrown us to the lions; to the Lionheart."

"He's done exactly as I advised him," the Sheriff reported. "An 'alliance' with the man who claimed Normandy off Richard is precisely what we need. Two weeks from now the French fleet will sail for Dover. Philip is pleased with a pretext to bring his armies to English soil. He'll 'reclaim' John's crown for him and destroy his old enemy Richard once and for all, while Richard hasn't yet reconquered his realm or gathered a strong enough military force to repel the French. Of course, I imagine King Philip will claim quite a reward off John thereafter." *And I will receive a tithe of everything Philip gets*, de Vendenal did not add.

"The French will invade?" Montbegum asked nervously.

"In two weeks. Then Richard, whom we will have kept busy here gnawing at our gates, will have to take his rag-bag army of malcontents and fortune-seekers across the length of England to the south coast to face Philip's fresh forces. I think we've seen before how that works out."

Constable Shankshard was a student of history. "Saxon King Harold fought the Danes at the Humber then had to fast-march his reduced armies more than two hundred miles to face a Norman invasion at Hastings. Duke William defeated the exhausted, diminished royal forces, killed Harold, and was crowned King William the Conqueror."

---

74   Worcester is pronounced "Wuss-turr" to rhyme with buster.

The Sheriff nodded. "So the monk chroniclers remind us, Constable. Who are we to deny history?" He pointed to the thick studded doors that led back to the hall. "Out there are two score of the most powerful knights in England, each with their retinues and personal guard. Not just powerful, though. Those are the men who have most to lose if Richard displaces John. All of them have committed crimes in John's name, for his pleasure or their own profit. All of them would be ruined by the Lionheart's victory. And all of them have their principal lands and interests in this country, with few Continental estates that divert their attention or whose confiscation could be used as a lever by Philip to command their obedience. Who have we got, Lewis?"

De Vendenal's herald jumped up to speak. "Sire, mustered here are many great and renowned knights: Eustace de Mortain, John Crocan, Walter Avenel, Ralph de Wellbuef, William de Kellham, Richard de Camera…"

The Sheriff cut off the list. "Brigands and opportunists all," he told his immediate guests. "Just like you. Not as powerful as the great barons like Chester who yaps at our walls; not yet. These are the men who will rebuild England after Richard's fall. *We* are the men who will replace those broken barons that war will destroy."

Montbegum shook his head. "You speak as though Richard's return and Philip's coming are good things, de Vendenal. You act as if they were opportunities that you always expected."

"I did!" snapped the Sheriff. "Use your head, man, for more than propping your helm straight! Once Richard took up the Pope's call to go bother the Turk, it was an easy calculation. If Richard died on crusade then John was king; a weak, pliable king who could be manipulated and directed, a king worth me cultivating. If Richard returned, there would inevitably be conflict between the brothers, one who had overreached, the other who had neglected his soverign realms to go play at soldiers. Add in the ambition and loathing of Philip of France, who despised Richard even before the Lionheart jilted his sister and shamed him before all Christendom, and the rest was obvious."

De Vendenal gestured to the plotters in his solar. "It is in times of crisis and change that men of vision have opportunities to seize what they desire. Arranging those crises in such a way as to maximise our opportunities is the logical course. For a few bribes, a few letters to John and Philip, a little study of the politics of nations, I have arranged matters very handily."

Ralph de Worcester was unconvinced. "And yet we're still all penned up here in Nottingham waiting for Richard to arrive with siege engines. And if he's the real Richard, that's a man who tore down Saracen fortresses stronger than this castle as he rampaged across the Levant."

"But not in two weeks, before King Philip pays a visit."

Shankshard had survived all of de Vendenal's reign as Sheriff of Nottingham, the only senior offical to do so. He did not lack wits. "King John has two fortresses in the north-east that are loyal to him," he reasoned. "Nottingham is one, of course. The other is Tickhill. When rumours of Richard's return reached us you dispatched many summonses in John's name. Some of those brought knights here. Others were directed to Tickhill Castle."

Lewis of Newark was the other man present in the room who directly served the Sheriff, and he too had a sharp mind. "Those who will be most useful to exploit a wounded kingdom under a John subject to Philip are here with us," he realised. "Those who might make trouble or who are less likely to follow Lord William's advice are at Tickhill."

"And Hugh de Puiset, Earl of Northumbria, Bishop of Durham, Richard's former Justiciar, has brought his army and laid siege to Tickhill," Shankshard remembered. "Tickhill will fall."

"Tickhill will fall, along with those who might be inconvenient in a new order," de Vendenal confirmed. "I have hopes that hot-tempered de Puiset might yet hang the lot of them. He will if my defiant threats to him have the proper effect."

"You sent word, threatening the Earl with terrible venegance if he killed any knight in Tickhill Castle," Lewis of Newark realised. He whistled admiringly.

"I believe that I did," admitted the Sheriff smugly. "Now de Puiset will have to decide whether to swallow my insult or to show his disregard for me by making an example of the defenders of Tickhill."

"Many of Prince John's closest advisors have fled for sanctuary there," Montbegum noted. "I almost took refuge there myself."

"Then it is fortunate that you decided it was better to heed my summons," de Vendenal observed.

"I see the point of holding the Lionheart here while the French cross the Channel," Ralph de Worcester admitted. "But if we are to survive even a short siege I see no point in indulging those commoners in the Outer Bailey."

"Still gnawing on that one?" the Sheriff scorned. "Who's guest in our outer bailey, Shankshard?"

The Constable replied. "At least one son or daughter from every significant household in Nottingham, French or English. All of them close-confined in the prison pits we have dug. Any of them at hand to hang from our battlements at a moment's notice."

"Hostages?" Philip de Worcester scorned. "Richard will care nothing for…"

"Richard is not the anxious father, mother, or husband of the hundred or more captives in my further ward," de Vendenal pointed out. "But those kin are out there in the city beyond our gates. What welcome do you think the king will find from the people of Nottingham whilst their sons and daughters are mine to hold or destroy? Nottingham will hold no parades for the returning Lionheart, even if they believe it to be truly him. Nottingham will yield no help to the besiegers that is not wrung from them at sword-point. And at the last, if Richard has no ear to the pleas of desperate burgers for the lives of their children, perhaps one of his lieutenants might. Chester and Huntingdon can be sentimental on occasion. Or Canterbury, if he is not a typical prelate."

"You really have thought this through," admired Roger de Montbegum.

"He always does," contributed Ralph Murdac. They were the only words the dour enforcer spoke during the meeting.

"I have done everything for a reason," the Sheriff assured his chosen confidantes. "Other plans have yet to begin, but are no less laid ready for when the time is right. All proceeds as I desire it."

"You gathered together so great an assembly of John's hangers-on here as bait for Lionheart," Shankshard recognised. "He could not allow Nottingham to go unattended."

"And later you have resource to break whatever diminished siege force Richard leaves behind when he flies to face King Philip Then the knights here to take control of the north while France and England clash in the south," Lewis recognised.

"As you say," acknowledged the Sheriff.

"You seem to have considered everything," Ralph de Worcester admitted. "What about Robin Hood?"

The Sheriff's smile froze in place. "Perhaps when this is over I'll comb the forest once and for all and see him drawn and quartered for my pleasure," he answered curtly. "The forest bandit has no part in this."

The meeting was over.

"It's a bull," Robin Hood explained to the guard at Nottingham's Goose Gate.

"I can see it's a bull," the exasperated guard captain answered the limping yokel who held the huge creature on an inadequate piece of string. "I can't let you in with it."

Marion had perfected her dim wide-eyed peasant lass impression. "But he's got to go to cow!" she objected. "He gets cross if he can't go to cow."

The bull snorted and tossed his massive head. Little John stood behind the animal, where no watchman could see him squeezing the beast's testicles.

The guards exchanged nervous looks. "Whose bull did you say it was?"

"'Tis master's bull," Robin offered helpfully.

"And master's cows," added Marion with equal earnestness.

"And who's your master?" the guard demanded with fraying patience. The bull sidestepped skittishly and began to sniff him.

"Oh, that's Master Peata Whatton," Little John added helpfully. "Him as is Chief Alderman of English Town."

The guards conferred hastily. "The Earl's order were nobody in but has a pass."

"The Earl's orders didn't say stop a randy bloody bull."

The guards glanced at the peasants and their animal. Marion gave them a little wave.

"The Earl did say as we were to not upset the locals. We need the city on our side during the siege."

"That'll do for me. Let 'em through, before that brute decides he's coming through anyway to get his heifers."

"Thank'ee kindly, masters," Robin acknowdged as the watchmen stood aside. Marion have them a dainty pert curtsey. The travellers passed the Goose Gate into the city.

"What was the point of all that?" Little John grumbled. "We could have just got a letter of passage from Richard Lionheart. Do you just enjoy tweaking guards' noses? Or have you always harboured a secret desire to steal a bull?"

"I'd prefer if word of us arriving didn't get out just yet," Robin admitted. "And yes to the questions about guards and bulls."

"And what do we do with our rustled livestock now we're through the main gate? We can't just let it loose in Nottingham."

"We take it to Peata Whatton of course. Give the poor thing some cows. The bull, that is. I don't know the alderman's preferences at all."

"We need to know what's happening in the city and in the castle," Marion explained to Little John. "Who better to tell us than the civic leader himself?"

Guided by Arthur a Bland, the best woodsman in Sherwood, King Richard's retinue threaded south through Arnold and Thorney Woods, past the wondering villagers of Hisperley, and so on into the Leen Valley where Nottingham lay. It was an unusual journey for the outlaws of the forest, marching in ranks behind the mounted knights and disciplined footsoldiers of the royal retinue. Some were nervous until Alan a Dale struck up a rude walking song, but eventually even Richard's men joined in with the chorus as the ditty's abbot searched for his missing duck in more and more unusual and anatomically unlikely places.

"Don't mind us," David of Doncaster boasted to the householders who came cautiously to watch the banners march by. "We're just off to Nottingham with the king to sort out the Sheriff. Robin knows all about it."

"That's the king up front," Much added helpfully. "Him with the crown on his helmet."

"And that fellow with his nose in the air is the king's alms-bearer," Friar Tuck tipped off the beggars they passed. "He'll be needing prayers for the success of his venture and will want a good word in the county. Go try your luck, boys!"

As the procession passed through thinner woodland down to the fertile farmed river plain, Richard's curiousity got the better of him. He left Ferrers and Fitzwarren in the vanguard and trailed his horse back so he could ride beside the free men of Sherwood.

"You, fellow," he called to one at random. "What's your name?"

"George a'Green," replied the sturdy fellow with an outlawish grin. "Pinder[75] of Wakefield."

"How comes a pinder to be marching for Robin Hood?"

The man beside George blinked in disbelief. "Bless you, King Lionheart, but don't you know George a'Green's story?"

"I've been abroad chasing the heathen," the monarch excused himself. "Who are you?"

---

75   A pinder is a pound-keeper, that is a civic collector of stray animals, the medieval equivalent of a dog-warden. He received a fee from a town council for each unpenned animal he recaptured. The owners of the straying sheep, cattle, poultry, horses, or untethered dogs were fined for their return.

"Please, King Lionheart, I'm Riccon Hazel of Flintshire, from Holywell by River Dee. I were a beggar till Robin changed clothes with me for a plot of his, and after we fought, but then he brought me to Sherwood to be his man and here I stand."[76]

"Well, Riccon Hazel, it seems I've missed some important events. What should I know about George a'Green here?"

The pinder of Wakefield shrugged depreciatingly, but his fellows encouraged Riccon on. "Well, King Lionheart, it all began when the Earl of Kendall sent his troops to Bradford demanding food for his rebels so he could aid the Scots. And George a'Green tore up Kendall's charter and made him eat it. Then mean old Grime tried to marry his daughter Betris to one of the rebels, that Bonfild, only she'd love none but our George of course! So then George, he goes and…"[77]

King Richard listened intently as the saga of love, treachery, courage, and sacrifice poured out. He was unsurprised when Robin, Marion, Scarlet and Much turned up in the narrative to confuse matters further. It became clear that the wicked Kendall and the lustful Bonfild were not going to end happily.

"And so George won his Betris, and don't they live happily with us at the

---

76   *The English and Scottish Popular Ballad,* Francis James Child's Victorian collection of 17th century ballads includes two entitled *Robin Hood and the Beggar.* (Child ballads 133 and 134). In both of them Robin encounters and is bested by a beggar. These versions follow a popular tradition of later Robin Hood comedy stories in which the outlaw encounters and is initially thwarted by some tradesman. In many of these tales Robin and his adversary are eventually reconciled and his opponent joins Robin's band.

Howard Pyle develops this tradition in *The Merry Adventures of Robin Hood,* chapter VXII, "Robin Hood Turns Beggar". As far as the present author can tell, it is Pyle who first names the beggar as Riccon Hazel and gives him a recurring presence amongst the merry men. Out of respect for Pyle and his massive contribution of Robin Hood legendeering, the beggar's name is retained in our present account, the latest "modern" accretion that I.A. Watson feels comfortable in including in his source materials.

77   The story begun by Riccon Hazel in our present narrative, along with many other events, forms the substance of the 1599 stage play *George a Green, the Pinner of Wakefield.* George's story was elaborated and expanded upon in *The History of George a'Green, Pinder of the Town of Wakefield, His Birth, Calling, Valour and Reputation in the Country,* by "N.W", printed in 1706. The whole story cannot be reconciled into the version of things presented in I.A. Watson's accounts however, being set in an earlier period than that of Richard and depending upon a disguised King Edward appearing to resolve all disputes at the end of the adventure. The Pinder also appears in Child's Ballad 124, entitled "The Pinder of Wakefield," wherein a jolly pinder boasts that no-one trespasses upon his watch, Robin tests that, and the pinder joins the merry men.

Major Oak to this very day?" concluded Riccon triumphantly.

"We do," confirmed the pinder of Wakefield. "Except on days when she's cranky."

"I can see that Robin Hood has gathered together many fellows of character and courage," Richard observed. "Here's a half-crown[78] for your story, Riccon Hazel, and another for George and his Betris, and may they long be blessed, e'en on her cranky days."

"Thank'ee, King Lionheart. And may our Robin help you to stamp down that wicked Nottingham, as well as he did with all the evil men who vexed the rest of us."

Richard returned to the vanguard amused and enlightened.

"Who are you?" demanded Alderman Peata Whatton, "and why is there a bull at my forecourt?"

"Come now," Robin scolded the civic leader. "Haven't you been reading your wanted posters? A likely forest archer fellow with blond hair and good looks. A Saxon-haired beauty with noble manners and a sharp temper. A big ugly brute that could carry that bull over his head and eat it in one sitting? Think again. You know who we are."

"And one of us won't be so handsome if he keeps on about another of us being an ugly brute," growled Little John.

The alderman went pale. "Robin i' th' Hood!" he gasped.

"While he lives, yes," agreed Marion, unreining that sharp temper for a moment on her grinning lover.

Master Whatton looked around him as if deciding whether to call for help to save his strongbox.

"We're not here for a donation today," Robin comforted him. "We've come to ask what's happening in your town, that's all. We thought there were things you might like to draw to our attention."

"I've already been summoned before the Earl of Huntingdon and his officers," the alderman replied. "I've given full and fair accounting of the numbers and assets of English Town, down to the last soul and the last horse-shoe."

---

78   That is, a coin valued at two shillings and sixpence, an eighth of a pound sterling. In Richard's time it would most likely have been rendered as a silver crown coin (five shillings) clipped in half. In an age where a basic labourer might be paid a penny a day, a gift of thirty pennies was a substantial tip.

"That's very... civic of you, Peata," Maid Marion assured him. "We're more interested in other things. How are the king's soldiers behaving?"

"Not so bad as they might do," Master Whatton confessed. "Huntingdon and Chester hold them in check, so there's no worse pillaging and molesting than you might expect when two hundred men compass a castle."

"Two hundred?" Little John checked. "That's all they have?" It wasn't much to box in a major fortress like Nottingham. It became clear why King Richard needed the archers of Sherwood.

"There's more expected, they say."

"They?" prompted Robin.

"Soldiers talk in taverns. Tavern-wenches talk to their innkeepers. The innkeepers talk to me. It's rumoured that Richard Lionheart himself will attend the siege. But others say that Richard's dead. Yet others believe that a pretender now wears his crown and robes in hopes of seizing the country for the Holy Roman Emperor."[79]

"Richard Coeur de Leon is alive," Marion assured the alderman. "I've seen him before, several times since childhood, and I saw him yesterday throwing Little John around. Expect hearing about him very soon."

Master Whatton winced. His day was getting worse and worse.

"Don't tell me you're sorry to see the Sheriff go," Little John scorned.

The alderman was pale and frightened. "Not de Vendenal, no, and none of those rogues holed up with him, nor his thugs who've terrorised this town these four years past. Question is what harm will he do before he falls?"

"What harm could he do?" asked Robin, serious now.

Whatton chewed his bottom lip while he decided whether to confide in the outlaw. "You faced down the Sheriff once," he remembered. "At the archery match, when you won this lady."[80]

"I've faced him down a few times," the outlaw answered, "though never for such a pleasant prize."

"Master Whatton, if you need aid against the Lord William de Vendenal

---

79   This was Henry VI (1165-1197), at first King of Germany then also Holy Roman Emperor and King of Sicily. Henry was a talented opportunist. He convinced Leopold, Duke of Austria, to surrender up the captive Richard the Lionheart to him. Despite being excommunicated for holding a crusader captive, Henry imprisoned Richard at Triefels Castle in Southwest Germany until he received a ransom of 150,000 silver marks. Henry used this money to secure his power base in Italy and to gain control over the valuable incomes of Sicily by having its eight-year-old king blinded and castrated.

80   As described in *Robin Hood: Arrow of Justice*.

then Robin Hood's your man," Marion advised. "All the world knows it and you saw it for yourself."

The alderman decided. "Well then, you know that the Sheriff's gathered together the worst rogues in the five shires to him, to hide from the king's justice? There's the Worcester brothers, who plundered the coffers of the Irish churches. There's Eustace de Mortain, the count's natural son, who they say murdered that woman in Normandy before he fled to John's court. Ralph de Wellbuef who burned a whole village for failing to bow to him fast enough. Roger de Montbegum, whom John Lackland sent to strip out the estates of those that displeased him. Plenty of unpleasant fellows, a double score of them."

"Bottle 'em all up and send in the terriers to tear them to bits," Little John advised. "Works with weasels, works with bastards."

"But… that's not all who're in there. Before he sealed up the gates, de Vendenal gathered up sons and daughters from every major household in Nottingham and the main estates beyond, a hundred or more hostages, some as young as eight or nine. They're close held, confined to prison pits in the outer bailey where arrow-storms will kill them first. If any citizen of Nottingham aids Lionheart too conspicuously then his child will hang from the battlements."

Marion gasped. Little John gripped his quarterstaff hard enough to turn his knuckles white.

"Does Huntingdon know this?" Robin asked.

"I don't know. I and my counterpart from French Town told as little as possible at our interview. Who knows what spies the sheriff has in the king's camp?" Master Whatton pressed his head into his hands. "He's got my Tercie, Robin Hood. She's but thirteen years old, a clean innocent virgin, and she's locked there in chains, frightened and friendless, amidst desperate soldiers, confined where the siege missiles will fall." The alderman looked up, crying. "Kings and lords don't care. It's told that Lionheart executed thirty thousand hostages in Acre because it was inconvenient to keep them. His men slaughtered whole cities in the name of God. Will he then hold back his attack for a townsman's child?"

"I doubt it," Marion admitted. Her eyes turned to Robin.

"Yes," he promised her. "I don't know how yet, but we have to save them."

IV

King Richard progressed into Nottingham. Heralds blazed trumpets and sounded alarums. The king's knights wore their formal finery, bright crusader surcoats over shining armour. The royal troops marched in unison, their steps echoing across the Leen valley to the defenders in besieged Nottingham Castle. It was an approach intended to intimidate, and perhaps it did.

The crowd was subdued. Most there knew of the Sheriff's hostages. Perhaps they also believed the rumours that the Lionheart was not really himself.

The king reinforced the guard set at the city's gates, to prevent those citizens who had been the most eager to carry out de Vendenal's commands from leaving without facing justice. He prudently set a guard on the water, too. The Leen was not so broad that natives born on the riverfront could not swim it despite checkpoints on the bridges.

Richard's precautions fanned the outlaws' suspicions of his intention to fine and tax the town as part of a major fundraising initiative to finance his next foreign wars.

The king billeted his soldiers in tents where Long Row and Angel Row forked, in the marketplace, but he pitched his own pavilion castleward of the tents of Chester and Huntingdon, provokingly close to the range of the fortress' archers. "I want them to see I'm here," he announced as his banner was flown. "I want them to smell it!"

David, Earl of Huntingdon and his father-in-law Ranulf, Earl of Chester, greeted the king with proper ceremony. Huntingdon's keen eye spotted Tuck and Alan a Dale amongst the royal party. "I see you found my son, then," he noted wryly.

"You'll get your wager," Richard conceded with good humour. "We think the lost crowns to you will be well worth it to add Robin Hood and his woodsmen to our number."

"Your grace," Friar Tuck acknowledged Huntingdon; they had old acquaintance.

"Where is he, then? Off on some madcap plan to blow the walls of Nottingham Castle down?"

"It's possible," the fat friar conceded.

Alan checked around the gawping crowd. "Robin should already be here," he puzzled. "He should…"

Someone behind the minstrel held out an arm and handed him back his purse. "Did somebody mention me?" Robin Hood asked.

The citizens of Nottingham recognised Robin Hood and Maid Marion. "Robin!" "Robin i' th' Hood!" "Robin and Marion!" "'Tis Robin Hood, come to kill the Sheriff at last!"

"At least they have a welcome for you," Richard observed.

"There's a reason their hospitality is restrained, your majesty," Marion warned him. "We might want to discuss this with less ears listening."

Richard nodded. He gestured for his principal retainers to follow him inside his pavilion, ignoring the arrow flights that fell exhausted of force mere yards from his tent-flap. Only when trusted guards had cordoned off the canvas and made sure none could overhear what was said did the king lay aside his helm, settle in a wooden throne, and say, "Well?"

Robin, Marion, and John summarised what they had learned about the Sheriff's hostages. Richard was more excited about the list of villains assembled behind the castle's walls. "We can take the lot of them!" he marvelled. "I can weed out the worst half of my brother's nastiest cronies at one action!"

"We'll need to be careful where we plant our shots, Scarlet," Robin told his companion. "Make sure the lads know to be sure of a target before loosing their shaft. No firing blind. No arrow-storms. This'll require skill and cunning, not brute force."

"I'll see that they know it," the soldier agreed.

"The Sheriff's bravos will think themselves safe behind those loop-hole slits, able to fire on us without fear of a return shot," Little John judged. "We'll show 'em different."

"We cannot allow the lives of a few prisoners to deter us from making war," King Richard insisted.

"That's not Robin's intent, majesty," Marion assured him. "It just means we have to make a different kind of war."

"Hear me out," Robin pleaded. "You won't be surprised to know that I've given breaking into Nottingham Castle a good deal of thought over the years we've feuded with de Vendenal. Marion was prisoner there for a time, and I went over all kind of mad plans to rescue her."

The lady of Sherwood smiled at him. "Fortunately the one you actually used was so sane."

Huntingdon considered the possibilities. "They say there are tunnels under the castle, secret ways in and out. There's a shaft from the alehouse..."

"All of Nottingham's built on chalk and riddled with tunnels," Little John admitted. "It's easy to dig. The citizens link up their houses cellar to cellar. But count on the Sheriff to know what's there and to have it properly guarded."

"All the same, those tunnels will be important," Robin considered. "Meanwhile, I want to work on a way to get just one man inside the walls; me."

"Why?" demanded Scarlet. "I mean, what will one man accomplish? De Vendenal's too well defended for an assassin to get through."

"Oh, there's plenty of mischief a lone intruder could get up to," the outlaw lord promised. "The winding mechanism for the outer drawbridge, for example. If someone were to sabotage that, send the bridge crashing down into place, that would open up certain possibilities, wouldn't it?"

King Richard sat forward, interested. "I have men experienced in taking down portcullises in minutes," he admitted. "With archer cover to prevent my experts being cut down as they go in, and a bridge already in place to give them access to the stonework...yes, we could reduce that gatehouse and gain the Outer Bailey, a week or more before the war engines even arrive!"

"I'll do that then," Robin agreed.

"By committing suicide?" Marion chided him. She gave him a suspicious glance. *What are you really planning?*

"I'll need a day's preparation, to get some special equipment," the young rebel warned.

"It'll take that long to deploy our combined forces to best effect," Ferrers admitted. "I'll see to it now."

"Then go we all our ways and make our preparations," Richard commanded. "Huntingdon, look you to call a parley with those who defend the castle in despite of our royal will. Offer no terms to them save abject surrender, but say I shall temper my wrath with justice if they accede now. Set up gallows by the gate for those who do not heed my command. Scarlet, see that the forest archers keep good discipline and are properly placed. Fitzwarren, see them supplied with extra shafts and a ration of ale. Ferrers, get me word of de Puiset and his siege of Tickhill." He clapped his huge hands together. "Tonight we shall feast, friends, in sight of the castle walls. Let de Vendenal tremble and know his doom is come!"

Robin and his men retreated from the royal presence to where Tuck and Gilbert had mustered the rest of the Sherwood faction. "What's the real plan, our Rob?" Little John demanded when they were sequestered.

"What I said," the outlaw leader declared. "With just a few additions. I'll be going into the castle. John and Scarlet will be leading our lads through the gate."

"And?" demanded Marion.

"And you and Tuck will be taking some folks to grab the prisoners from the pits and see them safe."

"*And?*" demanded Marion again.

"And I'll be going into the keep for a word with the Sheriff of Nottingham."

"Because somehow sneaking into a fortress on war-watch and making a one-man assault on a guarded gate-tower wasn't dangerous enough?" Scarlet snorted.

"I'll need some things. David, you're heading for Rughford Abbey. I need poppy juice, as much as the monks can give you. Alan, I need *aqua fortis*, the etching fluid that smiths use to engrave steel; that burns through near aught metal but gold. Pay what you have to. Arthur a Bland, I need a badger, alive, as big as you can find and as furious as you please."

Tuck crossed himself. "Oh Lord, it's one of *those* plans!"

Late afternoon brought word that Tickhill had fallen. Roger de la Mere's defending force had entered parlay with the Earl of Northumbria's besieging army. Assured upon de Puiset's honour that King Richard had truly returned, they offered to return the castle to him. The attacker insisted on unconditional surrender. Faced with the prospect of a lengthy siege with no hope of relief, Prince John's supporters threw themselves on Lionheart's mercy.

Roger de Puiset wasted no time in retaking Tickhill. He bundled his captives off to the king, so that Richard could parade them before the gates of Nottingham Castle the following morning. The Earl left a garrison force at the recaptured stronghold and brought his men south to add to Lionheart's strength.

The news came to William de Vendenal before it reached King Richard. The stone mantle of the Sheriff's solar fireplace swivelled aside to allow de Vendenal access back to his deserted office. The passage closed again seamlessly, concealing the escape tunnel that none save the Sheriff now knew of; those who had helped in its construction now lined the walls with their bones. The Sheriff had received word of de Puiset's triumph from a messenger he had met in an anonymous townhouse near the Chapel Bar, not two hundred yards from the tents of Richard's soldiers.

"Shame Richard didn't execute the Tickhill knights," he mused. "It would have been better if they'd defied him longer, provoked him more." He made a note to have Murdac and Montbegum be ruder at future parleys, in hope that the Lionheart might hang a few prisoners to show his displeasure.

The other news de Vendenal had picked up was that King Philip was mustering his ships and assembling his soldiers. The next fair crossing to England would bring a French fleet with it.

"Keep looking this way, Lionheart," the Sheriff mocked as he looked down on the gaudy royal pavilion beyond his gates. "Just a little longer, and you will see how a lion is hunted."

As the sun dipped low and the March weather brought a spring squall, another retinue of soldiers reinforced King Richard's siege. This time the banners were of *gules, a lion passant guardant or, armed and langued Azure,* a yellow lion walking on a red background, and *gules, with three lions passant guardant in pale or armed and langued azure,* three lions like the other, in column; the arms of Aquitaine and of England itself. Only one personage could legitmately weild such flags. The most powerful woman in Europe had arrived; Eleanor of Aquitaine had come to join her son, the King of England. In her train she brought another two hundred men and the new Archbishop of Canterbury.

She met privately with Richard. What passed between them was unrecorded. Afterwards she returned to her lodgings, having conmandeered the finest house in Nottingham, and she summoned Lady Matilda at the Lee.

Maid Marion attended the Queen Mother and made a full courtly greeting.

"So you still keep company with that outlaw," Queen Eleanor observed, regarding the Queen of May's forest garb and plaited tresses. The two had

met before, when she had summoned Robin Hood to liberate ransom boxes intended to bribe Richard's captors to keep him imprisoned.

"And it please your majesty, he is my husband," Marion replied. "And I
love him."

"Love," winced Eleanor. "What a devil that is." The woman who had been
Queen of France to one husband then Queen of England to another, who
had set her children in rebellion against their father, who had defied the
church for a quarter of its wealth for Richard's ransom, sighed theatrically.

"It can be a sweet devil as well as a bitter one," Marion confessed. "I
would have no devil else."

"Is that why you are in Nottingham? To follow your swain to war, as
simple country lasses walk behind their archer into battle and carry his
bow for him?"

"Of course. In the same way as you are here to tuck your son into bed at
night and read him a story."

Eleanor looked more sharply at Marion. "Then why am I here?" she
demanded.

"You know your boy. He can be very brave and inspiring. He can do
things no other can achieve. But sometimes he is reckless, and sometimes
others use that against him. You intend to see that if he's reckless it is in
right cause, and that his valour is not wasted or used foolishly."

"Yes," agreed the Queen Mother. "And so, I think, do you with your man."
She patted a cushion beside her. "Sit for a while, Maid Marion. I think we
would enjoy a talk."

"Hello, Shankshard. How's the constabling going?"

The Sheriff's Chief Constable looked disconcerted to find Robin Hood
amongst those who came to parley at the castle gates. He knew the others,
Huntingdon and Ferrers, but he'd not expected the outlaw he'd hunted for
four bitter years.

"King Richard recruits wolfshead bandits to his ranks now, does he?"
Shankshard sneered. "How desperate is he?"

"My son is a knight full-loved by the Lionheart," the Earl of Huntingdon
replied. "You and your rebels are stripped of all such office and honours,
and worse will befall you if you do not yeild to your soverign's honest will."

"Honest?" snorted Ralph Murdac. "Your so-called king sees England as nothing more than a bank, a tax farm to fund his war-sports in foreign climes. Can he even speak English? Didn't he once say this nation was always cold and raining, and that he'd sell London to pay for his crusades if only he could find a buyer?"

"And your Sheriff and his Prince are better?" sneered Ferrers. "The difference between them is Richard's a man."

"The real difference though," interrupted Robin thoughtfully, "is that Richard's got lots of soldiers surrounding this castle and Lackland hasn't. That Richard's got the church on his side and you're all excommunicated. That London and the cities have roused for Richard and you folks couldn't get the clap given to you for gold by the Goose Gate doxies. Oh, and that Robin Hood and the merry men of Sherwood are here now and if any of you dares lift his head even an inch above your parapets be sure there'll be a shaft in your skull to show for it." He flexed his fingers. "You know what I can do. You know how good my friends are. Maybe it's time to reconsider how much you like the Sheriff?"

"We will not capitulate to a pretender claiming to be Richard," Shankshard proclaimed, loud enough for it to be heard by onlookers.

"Richard's a fake?" Robin mocked. "Marion says it's him. People believe Marion. They like her. Nobody likes you, Constable; former Constable. Queen Eleanor of Aquitaine who birthed the Lionheart says it's him. His nobles and knights who crusaded for God with him say it's him. Even the knights at Tickhill, who surrendered today by the way, say it's him. Tell de Vendenal he'll need a better excuse than that to keep his gates shut."

"Lord William needs no excuse," Murdac replied. "The walls of Nottingham are strong. It has never been taken in war, nor can it be. The lawful Sheriff of this place defies you, and there is naught you can do on it. He spits on your Richard, and all who serve him. He seeks no quarter, and will give none when the tide turns on you. This is his word and our embassage!"

"Well," considered Robin while Huntingdon and Ferrers were finding reply, "that might be de Vendenal's word but you don't have his delivery. Try and be a bit more ominous and doom-y. Get the pauses right. It's far more sinister that way. Like this: when the tide… turns on you!' See? That's far more Sherriff-y."

"You babble like a loon," growled Shankshard.

"But I fight like a man," the outlaw shot back. "If you're not going to surrender, scuttle back to the Sheriff and tell him I'm here. Tell him Richard's listening to me. Tell him not to bother rationing for a long siege, because

I'm going to get him. Tell him it's a shame he's run out of places to run and hide. *Tell him Robin Hood has come for the Sheriff of Nottingham at last!*"

Before the light gave, Richard ordered an assay against the walls of the castle. Men under heavy shields broached the path up to the raised outer drawbridge. Others entered the hunting park on the fortress' north-western side, where Gilbert Whitehand and Much ignited trees so that thick choking smoke would blow up across the battlements.

While the defenders' attention was on the gate to the south and the fire in the gorge, nobody paid much attention to random sniper fire from the river side where the cliffs were tallest and incursion was impractical.

Robin made sure that his shots missed in a haphazard-seeming fashion.

"Steel-headed tips, thick ash shafts, shot into the cliff cracks and mortar-crevices above," Little John observed. "By the time you're done there'll be a chain of shafts sticking from those stones, each one about three feet higher than the last. Rob, tell me you're not making yourself a ladder."

"The highest side is considered the most secure," the outlaw lord replied. "It's watched, but only to prevent engineers trying to set up scaffolding or something. By night a man could haul himself up a series of pegs in the rock and get to the battlements unseen. And that wall goes right into the Inner Bailey you'll note. That's the place to be, John."

"You'll be found and hung."

Robin pinned another shaft into a crevice on the high crag. "Maybe I'd be spotted normally, but I think de Vendenal's added security will actually work for me when I'm inside. There's far more defenders than the usual garrison. Every one of forty wicked lords has brought their retainers with 'em. The numbers in there have doubled, tripled, in the last week. Nobody knows everybody. Maybe after a few weeks cooped up together every face will be known. For now, strangers are the norm."

"You're really going in there?" It was a wildly dangerous stunt even by Robin Hood's standards.

"What's the alternative? A long siege with hostage children slaughtered by our lads every time they loose a flurry? Captive lasses prey to soldiers' lusts as discipline breaks down? Prisoners left to starve as food runs low? We need that gatehouse, Little John. We need to take the Outer Bailey."

"And that's your whole plan?"

Robin shook his head ruefully. "There's something bothering me. Something about the Sheriff. About the way he had Shankshard and that new Castellan speak. It's as if de Vendenal wants to provoke a siege. What does he know that we don't?"

"He's always been tricky, Rob."

"And never more dangerous than when he's in a corner. Just like me. So when I'm inside his castle I'll put him in a corner and see what he does."

"How?"

Robin told him. Little John cringed. "Have you told Marion how she'll become a widow?"

"I told Marion what I plan to do. She offered some helpful refinements to the plan." Robin clapped his big friend's hand. "Whatever happens next, this is our last battle against the Sheriff, John. It's the end. So we toss the dice and see what happens, for good or ill, and we live or die as free men of Sherwood, right?"

"Of the two, I advise the living, Rob."

V

"The twenty-fifth day of March," observed Tuck as the bell of St Nicholas tolled midnight. "The feast of St Dismas, the Good Thief who was crucified beside Christ on Calvary.[81] How appropriate."

"I'll pray to him and Mary and all the saints in Christendom," Marion told the friar, "so long as they return Robin safe to me." She grabbed her forest lord and held him close. "You...remember who you are and remember what you are. Remember who's waiting for you and who's counting on you. Remember what we set out to do." She kissed Robin, hard and long. "Now go and do it."

"Yes, milady," replied the king of Sherwood. "I'll get onto that right now."

He grabbed Marion again and kissed her long and heartily so she'd remember him.

He waved jauntily at his friends, raised his hood over his flaxen hair, and slipped into the night.

The white stone of Castle Rock was dull grey in the moonless night. Robin paddled over the river on a thatched coracle then let the current take the flimsy vessel away so no bankside sentry would discover it. He kept low and moved silently around the castle's water-gate, the fortified tunnel to the vertical shaft up which provisions brought from riverboats could be hauled. The gate was still disputed territory, covered by archers and crossbowmen from both sides.

Further round, the cliff jutted further, actually sloping outward, making the climb even harder. That was the section where Robin had embedded

---

81   *The Gospel of Luke* 23:39-43 offers an account of the thief who was crucified beside Jesus repenting and seeking salvation, and then receiving Christ's remarkable promise, "Truly I tell you, today you will be with me in paradise." It was a popular subject of medieval theology. Apocryphal tradition named the men executed with Jesus as Dismas and Gestas. Elaborate backstories were created for them in later accounts such as the *Gospel of the Innocent*, which has them first encountering the infant Christ as Mary and Joseph flee with him to Egypt. The tale was and is a powerful declaration of a singular distinction of the Christian faith, of a personal saviour offering complete, free, and immediate redemption after true repentance.

He kissed her long and heartily so she'd remember him.

his arrows before the sun had failed. Nobody would expect an incursion on *that* route.

Robin had advantages over other intruders. His long sight and uncanny aim has placed his shafts at strategic points up the cliffside. His powerful draw had hammered the steel points deep, attached to hefty shafts that could bear a light man's weight. Long hours of daily archery had developed the outlaw's arm muscles far beyond those of most people, giving him a powerful grip that let him haul his body up the column of makeshift pitons hand over hand, his feet dangling over the dark drop.

Robin secured his packs carefully, balancing them across his back beside his bow and quiver, making sure they wouldn't shift unexpectedly. He looked back over the water. There was no sign of Marion or the merry men, but he wouldn't have expected to see them even if the moon had not been at its darkest. Nor could they see him.

"Goodbye, Marion," he whispered, just in case.

But it was not Robin Hood's nature to second-guess himself. He had committed to climbing the impossible wall, and now he'd have to do it. He spat on his palms and gripped the first arrow, as near to the stone as he could hold it. The shaft bent as he put his weight on it but the wood held. Robin hauled himself off the ground and reached above him for the next handhold.

It was a hundred and thirty feet to the top of Castle Rock, then another forty to top the ribbon wall that shielded the Inner Bailey's wooden buildings. Sixty arrows, Robin knew. He found himself counting them as he went, trusting to his grip to hold his hanging weight over the lethal drop.

Twice the shafts broke as he pulled on them, causing him to fall back onto the peg below. Once the loose chalk gave way, almost dropping him down to a hard and ignominious end. Where the arrows failed Robin had to rely on his knives to winkle into the rock face and trust to their blades to bear his bulk to the next wooden shaft.

It took over half of an hour to span the cliff. Robin's arm muscles were screaming for rest. His fingers struggled to maintain their grip. He knew he must finish the climb soon or fall to his death. He found himself reciting the names of his friends over and over again, a mantra to force him onwards: "Marion, John, Tuck, Scarlet, Much, David, Stutely, Alan, Arthur, Ros, Gilbert, Riccon, Elaine, George…"

He could hear Little John encouraging him in his head: "C'mon, you big girl's blouse… climb!" and Marion's quiet whisper, "Do not fail us now, Robin in the Hood."

He realised he was drifting. He focussed on his ascent, drowning out the mental commentary from Friar Tuck, "I'll encourage you in a moment, my lad, soon as I've finished this pullet," and Scarlet's "Kill them, Robin. Kill them all!"

Robin lost count of the arrows he'd grasped. The rough cliffs gave way to worked stone, piled high, set deep, the walls of Nottingham Castle. He forced himself on. The route he'd chosen when he was embedding his arrows avoided the arrow slits that lined the curtain. Faint light flickered from some of the link-slots that opened into the Sheriff's hall. Snores and the bodily odours of sleeping men warned that many soldiers were quartered on benches and floors behind those thick walls.

Another arrow snapped. Robin held desperately to the previous one, gasping in agony as he wrenched his shoulder. His muscles burned hot and cold.

He managed to feel out with his toe and find another shaft on which to rest some of his weight. He paused again to try and marshal strength for a final climb. Surely the top could not be much further?

Robin had to rely upon his blades again, worked into the mortar that held the huge castle blocks in place. Looking up he saw an end to the grey monotony of stone wall. The lightless midnight sky was a welcome relief. Still he forced himself to wait for his final climb until a steady sentry paced past whistling something softly, *My Lady's Bower* it might have been, and passed on his patrol.

Steeling himself to a final effort, Robin Hood topped the wall of Nottingham Castle, climbed through a gap in the crenulations, and lost himself in the shadow of the battlements. He allowed himself a moment to massage his screaming shoulders and forearms but knew he needed to move before a guard returned and his abused muscles knotted up.

He strung his bow, straining harder to bend the yew stem than he usually had to for its hundred and twenty pound pull.[82] He drew an arrow from his quiver, tied a white thread around it so it could be found in the dark, and loosed it over the wall to land on the other side of the Leen. If his friends could find the shot it would reassure them of his ascent.

Now Robin could see down to the inner bailey, where he'd been only once before. It was much as Marion had described it, though cluttered now with the provisions of war. To Robin's right the huge brooding bulk of the keep loomed tall and severe. Torches burned to light its three entrance gates and the long approach stair. De Vendenal kept good watch.

Opposite Robin's vantage point was the tower and gate to the middle

---

82   Modern longbows usually take a forty to sixty pound pull, but accounts of professional mediaeval archers suggest that some of them pulled back extraordinary amounts, giving their shafts a range and penetration of astonishing distance and power.

bailey. The way was open but guarded. The other walls of the courtyard were lined with wooden buildings: the Sheriff's hall, the kitchens, guest quarters, a chapel. The more industrial sites, the forge and the armoury, the tanner, the potter and the rest were relegated to the Middle or Outer Baileys with the stables and servants' dormitories.

The narrow wall walkway led to stubby towers at the corners of the site. Robin recognised the Red Tower from which he'd once rescued Marion and her family. The doors from towers to wall were propped open. Brazier-light warned that guards sheltered in each turret, on watch, manning the embrasures in case of attack from the river.

Robin found a ladder leading down to the yard. It would not usually have been there, but a block and tackle was set beside it where stones had been hauled up to stack behind the battlements to drop on any attempts at scaffolding the cliff. The supply work was still only half done; a laden cart of heavy rubble still awaited hauling come the morning. Robin blessed the lazy soldiers and shinned down the rickety ladder to find refuge in the courtyard.

Then he did what every tired soldier who was off-duty had done. He visited the garderobe, relieved himself, slipped into the hall, found himself a spot of floor, and curled up until morning.

"It is only natural to be concerned about your lover," Eleanor of Aquitaine told Marion. The Queen Mother slept little. She was awake despite the hour, sewing on a small quilting hoop, attended by rest-deprived maids. Marion was not going to sleep whilst Robin ventured Nottingham Castle and had somehow gravitated to Eleanor's court.

"I hate not being able to go with him," the lady of Sherwood admitted.

"That is the hardest part of it," the Queen Mother confessed. "Wait until you have children. When your sons are in the field or your daughters in childbed and you cannot be with them, though you so much desire it."

Eleanor had set her sons against her husband in battle, Marion remembered. She had pitted Richard against John, too and yet she also made peace between them when she could. And her daughters were scattered across all of Christendom: the Countesses of Champagne and of Bloix, Duchess of Saxony, Queen of Castille, and Dowager Queen of Sicily. If Richard had succeeded in wedding his sister Joan to Saladin then Eleanor's family reach would have crossed the whole world.

"What do you hope for, Lady Matilda, once this conflict is done?" the Queen Mother wondered. "What is Robin Hood's true goal in aiding my son?"

She is dangerous and clever, Marion recognised. *Perhaps more dangerous and clever than anyone I have ever met.* Yet truth was Marion's best weapon. "Robin and I hope to teach King Richard something important," she confessed. "We want him to see that the people of England matter. That they have rights, by natural law and the grace of God. That feudal power requires in equal measure feudal responsibility."

"And what should Richard do with such understanding?"

"He should limit the power of his barons and churchmen, so that they're subject to the same justice as all others. He should ensure that no man is charged without evidence nor condemned without a fair hearing. He should see his subjects as more than cattle to be milked, but rather as charges to be nurtured. Richard has a greatness in him, your majesty, I see that; but it is a greatness that could be fanned to more."

"You did not see such greatness in my other son when he pursued you?" Eleanor asked.

"I saw a head that needed hitting with my chamber-pot and I did it," Marion admitted defiantly. There could be no retreat in conversation with Eleanor of Aquitaine. "John… he's clever but he's brittle. If ever he gives rights to England it will be with a sword at his throat, I think. Richard would never surrender any part of his authority by force, but if only he could be made to see…"

"And what of you, Matilda? If Robin achieves his goal and returns glorious and triumphant, to be Richard's knight and Lord Forester of England? What will you do then?"

"I'll petition for my father's lands back. The Fitzwarrens have done good service to the Lionheart. My brother's here at this siege, with my sister's husband Greystoke. My other brothers fight for Richard in the south, save for Adam, now Lord Longchamp's brother-in-law, who fights for the king alongside my father in Normandy. If Richard has any gratitude at all he'll restore what's ours. And then I'll settle down with Robin and… live happily ever after. Once we've righted the injustices of the realm and made sure everyone has a future."

Eleanor threaded her needle through her sewing again and again. "What if Robin does not return from Nottingham Castle?" she asked.

The clergy amongst Richard's forces and those new-arrived in the arch-bishop's retinue were up all the night hearing confessions from the soldiers who might die upon the morn. A few of the outlaws found their way to priests too. "I know you bless us, Brother Tuck," Wat o' the Crabstaff apolo-gised to the outlaws' fat friar, "but it does no harm to get shrived twice to be sure!"

"Go ahead," Tuck assured the tinker. "It does no harm to actually amend your ways as well before seeking absolution."

Tuck waited until just before dawn before venturing towards the tent raised for the Archbishop of Canterbury. He paused outside, reluctant to announce himself to the Templar guards. Brother Thomas, once of Foun-tains Abbey, was after all recusant and outcast.

A sparse dark-mantled man finished relieving himself in the gutter and slipped up beside the fat friar. "You're the one called Tuck, then?"

"By those who don't see past my belly, so I am. God knows me as Thom-as, for so I was christened."

"They say you were monk before you turned outlaw."

"I was a friar after I left my abbey, and I served in the small villages."

"They say you tutored Robin Hood as a boy."

"Tutored's too strong a word. Kept him from roguery for the few hours a day I could get his backside on a schoolbench, maybe."

"They say you minister the Host to the men of the forest."

Tuck turned irritably. "*They* say altogether too much sometimes. *They* need a box around the ears. And if I do offer the rites of Christ to those who need 'em, I do it because someone must. It's not the dish the feast comes on that matters but the quality of the meat."

"If you're excommunicate then that meat is poisoned, Brother Thomas."

"So some would say. My hope's in a God who's less Pharisee and more Saviour. And it's His body, broken for even the like of me, and His blood, shed so even I have hope of salvation, that I pass on to my flock. What man who possesses a rope, however tattered and frayed, wouldn't toss it into rough water to try and rescue drowning men?"

The sparse man chuckled. "You argue like a prelate of Rome," he admit-ted. "Or maybe more like one of those saints of the old church, rascals and rogues some of them, but mightily of service to the Lord all the same."

Tuck swallowed hard. "I would it was, but truth is I'm a very poor ser-vant. I drink and eat and swive and swear. I try to do what's right and I fail more than I win. I confess my lads and lasses, its true, but can never take my own sins to a father in Christ."

"Is that why you were hovering by Canterbury's tent? In hopes that a holier than yourself might grant you absolution?"

"I suppose so. I'd never have gone in, though."

"Just as well. Hubert Walter only got the job because he fought beside Richard in the east and helped with his ransom. He's more soldier than saint, and more politician than priest. He's been Lionheart's diplomat and dogsbody and now he's Richard's Chancellor and Justiciar. He's about as holy as you are, maybe less so, and I reckon he's got exactly the same doubts about his place in God's grace as you have, brother."

Tuck snorted. "I don't know why, but I find that vaguely comforting."

"Tell you what," the sparse man offered, "I'll hear your sins. You hear mine. God hears all. A bargain?"

"A bargain," agreed Friar Tuck. "Thank you, your grace."

The two men spent some time in confession and prayer, and then the fat friar headed off to find breakfast and the sparse man returned to the Archbishop's tent to be dressed.

Before dawn Robin was in the fortress kitchens, flirting outrageously with the slatterns, charming the cook, and administering his own special ingredient to the common pot. He left the scullery bearing a bumper of stew to deliver round to the sentries who were just now beginning a cold, wet morning watch.

Robin wasn't sure how effective the poppy juice would be. It made men slow and sleepy but the cauldron was very large and the dose he had to use was limited. Nor would all the men of the castle sup from this round of provisions; certainly the great nobles would expect better than the common fare. Still, if Robin could set guards nodding at their posts and archers snoozing at their watchpoints, it was a step in the right direction.

The outlaw passed the inner and middle gates with a cheery wave to the sentries and a hot bowl of stew. The man who brought the breakfast was always welcome.

The sack on Robin's shoulder began to move. The badger inside had woken from its poppy-sleep and was becoming irritable.

Robin passed round the prisoner-pits that had been hastily cut into the turf of the Outer Bailey. The holding cells were crude but effective, eight foot deep trenches topped with metal grills. There seemed to be no sanitation or shelter for the unfortunate hostages who huddled out of reach of their brutal guards. Robin noted faces of soldiers with whom he'd want to have a word later. For now he contented himself with serving them stew.

The outer wall was harder to get onto. Ralph Murdac commanded here, and as dawn approached he checked the watch and verified the defences. Robin avoided him. Murdac might not recognise the outlaw lord, as Shankshard would have, but the cruel Castellan was clever enough to question whose company the breakfast-deliverer came from and why he was bringing food so early.

Robin identified himself to the watch as being of Roger de Montbegum's company. It amused him to affiliate himself with the man who might once have been matched with Lady Matilda Fitzwarren. When asked by whose say he brought the vittles, Robin answered that it was the Sheriff's orders. As he guessed, no one was about to question de Vendenal's command.

Robin handed the last of the sedative stew to the men on the main gate. He climbed up with his empty bumper to the wheelhouse tower where the chains of the drawbridge were wound in on a huge wooden spool.

He readied his equipment and pounded on the door. "Breakfast!"

A viewing port slid open as the men within checked who was on the stair. Robin held up the soup jug and waggled it. "Get it while it's hot!"

Three bolts and a bar were withdrawn. Security was tight here. Robin untied the neck of his sack. As the door opened he tossed the whole bag inside, furious badger and all.

The brock clawed its way from the canvas, livid at its imprisonment. The animal was large for its species, close to two feet long, weighing two stone, and it was fighting mad. An angry badger will take on a wolf or a bear. This one went straight for the surprised gatehouse guards.

Robin strung his bow and kicked open the door. The four guards were slashing at the fast-moving creature that leapt at them, waving their swords to try and keep the enraged predator at bay.

Robin's arrow took the first soldier through the throat and dropped him dead. A second man fell before he could react. The third knew what was happening but was too fatally distracted by a badger at his groin to avoid an arrow through the eye. The final man rushed in at Robin and took a shaft into his chest that hurled him back across the room into the wheel mechanism.

Robin regretted shooting the badger more than any of the guards.

The gristly assault completed, Robin sealed the door behind him and moved to the gate mechanism. As he'd suspected, the drawbridge was secured with chain, not rope. De Vendenal would not allow any easy sabotage. Likewise, the winding gear was padlocked shut. It would be a long and noisy business to hack it free and send the bridge down for an attack to commence.

Robin pulled out the flask of *aqua fortis*[83] from his belt-pouch. He carefully poured the contents over the padlock and chain and left the acid to do its work. He slipped out of the wheelhouse with his stew-pot and hastened back to the Inner Ward. He needed to be on that side of the gates when the drawbridge crashed down.

"Nothing is happening," breathed Edgar, Lord of Greystoke. "The bridge isn't coming down."

The thin March mist was clearing as the sun filtered up behind the castle, though the day would be dull and wet. Only a couple of weeks to Easter, people were complaining, and still no spring. It's a judgement of God. The seasons no longer process as they did in old King Henry's day.

"The bridge will fall," Little John insisted. "If Rob says he'll do it, he'll do it."

"It was a dangerous mission," Sir Mark Fitzwarren told the big shepherd and his new-arrived brother-in-law. "No man can fault him if he failed." And failure would mean Robin's life, the crusader didn't need to add.

"The bridge will fall," Little John repeated. "Give him time."

There was movement behind the rank of soldiers set as vanguard to charge the breech. Little John, Greystoke, and Fitzwarren turned as Alan a Dale scuttled to cover behind the row of overturned farm carts. "The king and Chester want to know if the bridge is down," the minstrel noted. "I'm thinking it's not."

"It'll come down," John of Hathersage insisted, growling. "Everybody needs patience and a little faith. Tell Chester and Lionheart that, from me, right?"

"I'll let them know."

"What's going on down in the camp?" Sir Mark asked nervously. "Are the battering rams ready? Do the archers stand prepared?"

---

83   *Aqua fortis* (Latin for 'strong water'), dilute Nitric Acid (HNO_3), was - and is - used for etching metals. It was prepared by mixing sand, alum, or vitriol (sulphuric acid) with saltpetre, distilling with fire, then catching the condensate.

"Scarlet's got the lads stood by, with their drawstrings covered to keep the wet out. He's got them so ready that they're terrified of him. There's a bunch of burly volunteers ready to hit the portcullis with a very large oak tree then attach chains so the oxen can haul it away. All we need is…"

"The bloody drawbridge will come down!" Little John insisted. "It'll come down, all right? If our Rob says…"

"What's keeping them?" worried Elaine of Loughborough. She busied herself checking the stacks of linens and thread in the hospital tent. There were dour grey and black monks present to do the chirurgery, to sever limbs and cauterise stumps, but the Sherwood women were present to deal with all lesser hurts.

"They'll start when they start," Ros of Waltham told Alan's wife. "Get me more long bandages, Tad, there's a good boy. Don't worry, Elaine. Men'll start fighting whenever they have the chance. That's their nature and their curse. And we'll patch them up afterwards so they can do it all again. That's ours."

"I don't like it," Malkyn of Woodbarrow confessed. She was painfully young, new-come to Sherwood to avoid marriage to a much older man, blissfully returned to young love with David of Doncaster. "Why can't Richard and John just duel it out and stop dragging everybody else into it?"

"That's not the way of kings," Ros lectured her. "Nor the way of the world, lass. When there's a pack of frothing wolves running mad it's not enough to take down their leader. You have to hunt down every one before there's safety again. That's what Rob and John are about here, aye, and Alan and David and all our bold lads. God bless 'em for it and keep 'em all safe!"

"I hope and pray all this preparation of ours is wasted," Betris of Bradford worried. "May every single salve and dressing go unused here today."

"They'll be needed," Elaine told her team. "Now stand ready. It cannot be long."

In the king's camp, the Lionheart was dressed in simple mail. He stood with Chester, Ferrers, and Huntingdon waiting for the alarum.

"I sent the herald to find out progress," David of Scotland promised his monarch. He was surprised to discover he was tenser about Robin Hood's fate than he had expected. The lad had a way of worming himself into men's affections, even that of his probable father. Huntingdon, late-wed to Chester's sister, a girl half his age, had every reason to distance himself from his old bastards, but Robin was as wild as his mother had been, with his father's courage.

"We're ready, sire," Scarlet promised. "Everything's in order for your word. We can pepper the walls with arrows for ten minutes straight while you take the gate."

"No point if the drawbridge doesn't fall," Ferrers noted sourly. It would take hours, under fire, to construct a makeshift cantilever over the chasm.

"Oh, it'll be down," Scarlet echoed Little John's words. "I know it makes no sense, but Robin Loxley does things nobody else would ever consider, and he makes 'em work. Give him time."

Much the Miller's Son tugged on Scarlet's sleeve. "Will Scathlock," he whispered urgently, "What if Robin doesn't make it work this time? I mean, Rob's plans always work, but what if this one doesn't?"

"Then we'll have to send you into the castle to rescue him," threatened the soldier.

Much paled. He looked up at the formidable wall and swallowed hard. "All right then," he agreed. "But what if I have to fight that Sheriff of Nottingham?"

Scarlet choked back a laugh and clapped Much hard on the back. "If it comes to that, man, then I'll climb the wall beside you and we'll do it together. Agreed?"

"And me," added David of Doncaster. "We wouldn't expect you to fight De Vendenal and all his men on your own, Much. There'd be three of us."

"That would be better, yes," Much answered, relieved. "And maybe we could ask Little John an' all?"

On the curtain wall, Gill o' th' Red Cap pushed the headgear for which he was named far back on his pate and peered through the loop-hole nearest to the royal camp. The King of England and his retinue stood three hundred and fifty yards distant; a mere twenty-five yards off the furthest an arrow from the walls could reasonably be expected to travel.[84]

Gill was the best archer in Nottingham Castle. He shortened his bow-string until the yew creaked. The pull was now two hundred pounds, lethal for the weapon, impossible for any but the strongest of men to draw, near-impossible for all but the finest archers to aim accurately. But Gill estimated he now could send an arrow the whole distance to the Lionheart's chest.

In fact those were his exact orders from the Sheriff of Nottingham.

He took his time, lining his shot. He drew the cord taut, bringing his fingers to his cheek, straining to steady the string. He took a breath. He loosed.

The arrow arced just as Gill wanted it to and fell straight at Richard of England.

---

84   The actual range and accuracy of the mediaeval longbow is still disputed, with estimates from 180 to 250 yards being common. *The Great Warbow: From Hastings to the Mary Rose* by Matthew Strickland and Robert Hardy, Sutton Publishing (2005), ISBN 0-7509-3167-1, reports that no practice range of less than 220 yards was allowed in the time of Henry VIII and a professional archer of Edward III's era could send a missile 399 yards, around a quarter of a mile.

VI

Stressed metal deformed with a metallic scream. The *aqua fortis* had eaten through the inch-thick links enough that the heavy chain could no longer restrain the weight of the hinged bridge. A warning shout went up from the castle. The melted link snapped and the long wooden bridge pivoted down.

It crashed onto the lip of the outer roadway with a shattering crunch. Some of its boards sprang loose in response to the sudden shock. It bounced then settled again, damaged but intact enough to bear attackers across the gorge.

Little John sprang up. "Now!" he boomed in a voice that could not be denied. He hefted both his quarterstaff and a hand-and-a-half bastard sword and pointed to the gate. "*Charge!*"

The lethal arrow flew straight at the king. David of Doncaster cried out warning and shouldered Richard aside. The Lionheart toppled into the dust, aggrieved. David fell back, clutching the shaft that transfixed his chest.

"David!" cried out Much, scrambling forward to his friend.

"Shields!" shouted Scarlet. "Cover the king!"

No more shots reached the royal retinue. Richard rose, wrathful. He looked down at the lad who had saved his life. "Look to him," he commanded. Gilbert Whitehand nodded solemnly.

The Lionheart turned angrily to the wall. He drew his sword and swore. "Judas' balls, I'll have 'em now! Loose at their king, will they? Treacherous scum not fit for hanging!"

David reached out a hand for Much. He tried to speak but only blood welled from his mouth. The light in his eyes failed.

Gilbert of the White Hand closed the young man's eyes. "God take him," he prayed. "May he be in heaven half an hour before the devil knows he's dead."

"And may he pick Lucifer's pocket on the way," added Arthur a Bland. "Now lads, to your bows. They've got an archer amongst 'em up there. So show 'em what the free men of Sherwood can do with their shafts! Draw! Fire!"

King Richard didn't wait for his heralds. He began the charge up the causeway at full pelt, shield raised for cover, sword in hand. "For Lionheart and Saint John!" he shouted. "England! England! England!"[85]

Chester and Huntingdon, caught unawares, hastened to chase after him. His banner-bearer, realising that the royal standard was being left behind, set off after the furious monarch at a pelt, but fell to the defenders' arrow-flights.

"Shoot faster!" Arthur demanded of the merry men. "I don't want 'em to get near an arrow slit without having to pick a shaft from their teeth!"

Scarlet grabbed Much and dragged him after the king. He stopped at the fallen standard bearer and picked up the three golden lions on their blood-red background. "Take this pole," he told Much. "It's important. It's the king's banner, his honour. You take this flag and you follow Richard wherever he goes, and you stay right by him holding it whatever happens, right?"

"Alright," agreed the miller's son.

"You keep with Richard. You hold his standard. While it flies we're not beaten. You got it?"

"I hold it," Much confirmed.

"Then go. After Lionheart." Scarlet smacked Much on the backside and sent him off. He turned, red-faced as he surrendered to his own battle madness. "Right, you whoreson bastards!" he bawled at the castle, "I'm coming to feed you your own guts!"

He went with the men bearing the battering ram, to join Little John and the others at the gate.

---

85   Richard's ordering of the siege and his furious attack are described in Roger de Hovenden's *Itinerarium Regis Ricardi* (c A.D. 1220): "[The king arrived] with such a vast multitude of men, and such a clangour of trumpets and clarions, that those who were in the castle were astonished and confounded and alarmed, and trembling came upon them, but still they did not believe that the king had come and supposed that the whole of this was done by the chiefs of the army for the purpose of deceiving them. The king, however, took up his quarters next to the castle, so that the archers of the castle pierced the kings men at his very feet. The king being incensed with this put on his armour, and commanded his army to make an assault on the castle [...] Clothed in a simple coat of light mail, with a steel cap on his head, he advanced as far as the gate of the castle, preceded by men bearing before them large shields."

Maid Marion was at the hospital tent when David's body was dragged in. "He's dead," Elaine confirmed. "Ros, look to Malkyn."

The lady of Sherwood nodded to Alan's wife to leave her in charge and stalked from the tent. "Tuck!" she called to summon the friar. "It's time. Bring them to me."

"My lady," acknowledged Brother Thomas.

By 'them', Marion meant the people of Nottingham.

Missiles flew from the chink-slits above the outer gate. Outlaw arrows rattled against the stonework in response. Some of the Sherwood shots actually found the six-inch wide loopholes and embedded themselves in the men crouched behind them. Other of the men commanded by Arthur a Bland remained with bows nocked, scanning the battlements for sign of movement. Anyone who appeared from behind one of the crenulations was a target.

A tiny sally port beside the main gate opened, letting a file of Sheriff's guards out to harry the attackers who were trying to burst the portcullis. The soldiers ran straight into Little John.

"Ten of you?" the giant of Hathersage bellowed scornfully. "Are you trying to insult me? Are you?" He lunged in with stave and sword, hacking his way through armoured men as if they were delinquent choirboys; except his blows did not smart until lauds but shattered skulls and severed limbs.

Seeing the counterassault was thwarted, Shankshard hastily ordered the port closed and barred again.

The wooden ram navigated the turn at the top of the approach. Burly men charged forward and crashed the thick stump into the metal gate-bars. On the third attack the portcullis bent, just enough for the engineers to attach two-inch-link chains to the rails. The oxen were already yoked and ready to drive away, dragging the barrier off with them.

"Sheriff!" shouted Little John, "I'm coming for you!"

King Richard arrived, trailed by Much with his standard and an array of winded nobles. The white-faced miller's son called over to Little John, "They killed David!"

The big man of Sherwood ground his teeth together and seized the straining portcullis, adding his strength to the oxen as if he alone might tear down the Sheriff's fortification.

Archers along the ribbon wall tried to shoot the oxen in their traces.

Gilbert and Arthur kept up the rain of arrows to deter them. Whenever a shot did take down one of the twenty-four beasts hauling at the gate, Alan a Dale or Riccon darted in to cut its yoke so the rest could carry on.

A warning horn sounded from the gatehouse, calling for reinforcements. Many of the defenders were falling down, woozy-headed and confused.

"England! England!" yelled Richard Lionheart, deflecting arrows with his huge red and gold shield. "Heave, you hearts, heave!"

The portcullis failed with a scream of tortured metal. The heavy grill clattered down onto the damaged bridge, then fell over the side into the gorge below.

"Rams!" ordered the king. "Break the gate!"

The bravos with the battering log went in again, this time to crash the heavy weight into the metal-bound wooden gates under the first arch. Cunning engineers hurried in too, with chisels and mallets to work at the stone rimming the doorway, seeking vulnerable hinges and bolt-points.

"Ladders!" demanded Will Scarlet. "Get ladders up there. I'm going in!"

When the second alarm blared from the outer gate, Castellan Murdac ordered that the middle and inner gates be sealed. Every able-bodied soldier was called to the walls.

"We're not trying to hold the outer gate?" Ralph de Worcester objected when no reinforcement was detached to the melee.

"Don't be soft," growled Ralph Murdac. "The bridge is down and the portcullis gone. The outer ward's lost." He bellowed commands over the wall to men below. "Kill the hostages!"

"Aye milord!" called back one of the Sheriff's sergeants at arms.

Another cry came from the outer gate. The wooden doors had failed. Mounted knights, led by Huntingdon, Ferrers, and Chester, were now into the forecourt.

"Archers, fire!" screamed Murdac.

Robin Hood, lined beside the Castellan on the keep tower with a dozen other bowmen, drew back his string and obeyed. His fellows were aiming their shots at the distant mounted men who were now fighting into the Outer Bailey; the outlaw could identify the colours of Fitzwarren and Greystoke and a furious knot of fighting where Little John and Scarlet made their stand. Robin took careful aim and brought down the Sheriff's man bearing the order to execute the captives. In the chaotic missile exchange below no-one noted where each shot came from or went.

A couple of the bowmen beside Robin staggered as their breakfast caught up with them. The poppy blurred their vision and dulled their senses.

"What's the matter with you, oafs?" bawled Murdac. "Shoot, damn you, or I'll have your eyes!"

"It's the plague!" gasped Robin, loud enough for the other soldiers to hear him. "There's plague loose in the castle!"

Murdac lashed out and caught him an unexpected buffet. "Silence your tongue or lose it! Back to your job!"

Robin ignored the blood on his face where the Constable's mailed glove had torn it. He redrew his bow and returned to picking off the Sheriff's men below.

Sir Mark Fitzwarren paused to check on Lord Greystoke. "Are you well, Edgar?" he asked his brother-in-law.

"Winded, is all," gasped the knight who Mark had just hauled from under a pile of footmen. "They got me off my horse and I took a bit of a tumble." He felt tenderly at his left arm. "I think this might be broken."

"Get back to Marion at the medicine tent," Sir Mark insisted. "I'm not about to tell Anne that she's a widow so soon after being a mother." Word had reached Greystoke while he rode to war that Sir Richard at the Lee's elder daughter had borne him a child. Lady Aline would now be eleven days old; nobody suspected how she would one day end the story of Robin Hood.

Mark looked around for a horse to commandeer for Greystoke's retreat. The melee had become general, random clashes across the open space beneath the middle wall under a hail of arrows from the keep's defenders.

Then reinforcements arrived. They were not the disciplined reserve kept for emergency under the command of the Archbishop of Canterbury. They were not soldiers at all. The citizenry of Nottingham poured through the sundered gate and swarmed the battlefield.

Mark saw who led them, a slim woman with blazing red hair loosed to her waist, Boadicea in calfskin, equipped with bow and dagger. He blinked and mouthed her name: "Tildy?"

The newcomers moved with determination and discipline. The fat friar hastened them up the slope to the prisoner pits. Men, and even women of the town, swiftly hauled away the bars that contained the hostages. They had brought hammers to strike chains, stretchers for those unable to run for freedom.

"Hold off the guards," Marion told the merry men. Foresters who had been swarming the field in general melee closed ranks upon the surprised warders of the hostages. Scarlet and Little John charged straight into the prison-keepers without mercy.

The biggest of the brutes made for Marion herself. Mark realised what was happening too late to run to his sister's aid. The lady of Sherwood raised her bow and fired. Thugs went down, one, two, three…

Constable Shankshard rode in to prevent the release of the prisoners. His big warhorse was taller than Marion, and directed right at her.

Little John shouted wordlessly and caught the beast by its neck. He hauled it round, off its feet, snapping its spine. Shankshard tumbled to the ground.

"Oi, Constable!" Will Scarlet snarled, rounding on the downed official. "You want to arrest someone, try an' take me!"

Shankshard rolled to his feet, wielding his sword two-handed. He was plate-mailed and could withstand a few blows. Scarlet was in ragged chain links, far more vulnerable to a heavy swipe.

Behind Will, Little John hauled one of the jailers off his feet and swung him like a club to drub the other warders.

Shankshard was an experienced and competent warrior. So was Scarlet. They rounded then clashed, foined, feinted, fell back, and came again. Neither spoke. Both were men of deeds not words.

Shankshard began defensively, allowing his enemy to exhaust his fury and his strength; except that Scarlet seemed to have no end to his fury. The blood-soaked fighter came again and again, always on the attack, heedless of a dozen cuts he'd taken, more eager to kill than to survive. Shankshard gave back.

Will Scathlock pressed close with sword and poignard, even with teeth when he had the chance. Nothing else mattered to him now but the fight before him. He fought again whatever personal battle had first scarred him Scarlet.

Shankshard switched to the offensive, relying on sophisticated techniques of gliding and binding[86] to overcome his adversary's brutal assaults.

---

86   Gliding is a long continuous attack with the arm and sword fully extended, used not to stab but to break past an opponent's weapon and disarm him. Binding is putting continuous pressure on the enemy's blade, pushing it away to a different line.

He sliced through Scarlet's mail-coat at the shoulder. He was surprised when the madman did not shy away but instead shifted attacks, displaying his own knowledge of the traverse and beat,[87] then bringing his sharp needle-dagger up in a perfect volte[88] through the eye-hole of the Constable's helm.

Shankshard staggered back, blinded, dying.

Scarlet rammed his sword into the Constable's gut and kept on twisting it until the entrails spilled loose.

"He's done," Tuck advised Will Scarlet. For a moment the monk thought he might be attacked next.

"There's more Sheriff's men over there," Little John pointed out. "You can go be insane to them, Will."

Mark Fitzwarren hastened over to where Marion was supervising evacuation of the hostages. "Tildy, what are you doing? This is a field of war. You don't belong here."

The Saxon-haired woman gestured to the captives. "And neither do these. So I'm taking them away. You can have de Vendenal and Murdac and Montbegum and all the rest. These are *mine!*"

From the outer curtain wall Gill o' th' Redcap recognised the Maid Marion. He'd seen her before, at the archery contest where Robin had beaten him to win her hand. His face twisted into a cruel smile as he drew back his bow and sighted on her. "Goodbye, people's queen."

The shot that took him came from high up on the fortress keep. It was at extreme range, but true and expert, through the heart, knocking the Sheriff's archer backwards into the battlement wall, scattering his bow and arrow beyond his reach. Gill looked down at the red-fletched shaft in his chest in disbelief.

"Nobody can make that kind of..." he gasped, before all words left him.

Marion belatedly realised the danger she'd been in and how she had been delivered. She courtesyed her thanks to the keep, beaming and blushing to her neck. She was appreciated.

"Hurry up getting those children clear," Tuck harried Master Whatton. "We need to be gone before the Sheriff works out what's happening."

The alderman clutched his Tercie to him and hurried after his retreating neighbours.

---

87   A traverse is a sidestep where the legs do not cross each other. A beat redirects a cut or thrust, pushing the opponent's blade aside, leaving his body vulnerable to a counterattack.

88   A volte combines a sidestep with a thrusting attack from a second short-bladed weapon.

King Richard looked bemused as the onlookers invaded his battle. "What's going on?" he demanded of Maid Marion.

"We're clearing the battlefield for you, majesty," she replied. "Prince John's men are your concern. William de Vendenal's hostages are ours. We have them now, so you can go back to your war."

Richard surveyed the citizens of Nottingham, not plundering the battlefield but reclaiming their own. Much swayed beside him, doggedly clinging to the flag as he'd been instructed, wide-eyed and blood-splattered and determined.

"Did Robin Hood plan this?" Lionheart demanded.

Marion met the king's gaze, and on this battlefield her authority matched his own. "Yes, he did. Now you have your gatehouse and Nottingham has its children. Next: the Sheriff."

Ralph Murdac watched the fall of the Outer Bailey with a mounting fury. He saw Shankshard fall. He saw the captives delivered from their pits. He saw the king's standard carried atop the broken outer gatehouse and raised in victory.

"God's wounds, how did they do that?" he demanded, not of the archers who flanked him on the keep's south-eastern tower but of himself. "Why did the bridge go down? *How* did it go down?"

He checked the middle gate with its raised drawbridge over a turgid moat. It seemed secure, well-manned, ready; yet so had the outer defence. "Harry those men by the pits," he ordered his archers. "Aim for that big fellow in the sheepskin, or the one that killed the Constable."

Robin had finished the supply of arrows in his quiver. He hastened over to the barrel of fresh shafts in the centre of the tower roof. He helped himself to a generous supply. He counted the men on the tower with him. Nine.

He loosed arrows into them. He was up to number four by the time the others realised how their comrades had fallen. Two more went down before they could turn and face him. The pair of remaining bowmen turned their weapons on him, but the poppy juice slowed them.

Robin fired again and again, dodging the two close shots that his enemies were able to loose. "Sorry, lads, but I'd prefer the big fellow in the smelly sheepskin and the madman who tore open Shankshard to remain un-shot."

Only Ralph Murdac remained, but he was the most dangerous of them all. He closed too near for a bow to be useful and sent the weapon clattering from Robin's hand with a sweep of his mace.

"So there's a traitor in our midst!" the cruel Castellan sneered.

Robin kicked him backwards with a foot on the chestplate. "Actually, I've never been loyal to William de Vendenal," he admitted. "I've always preferred that Robin Hood fellow."

The capuchin had fallen from Robin's head. He gave Murdac a cheeky grin.

"Hood!" the Castellan realised.

"Murdac the Murderer," the outlaw tossed back. "Did you think we weren't going to end up facing each other?" Robin drew the sword from his side.

The Castellan snorted. He wasn't a fussy old man like the predecessor he'd executed. He was a warrior knight, armed and armoured, against a peasant bandit in leathers. "I won't kill you now," he promised Robin Hood. "I'll cripple you but keep you alive. The Sheriff will want to devise something very special for you before you're ended."

"Likewise me with him," Robin promised. "I'd bet you my end for him's cleverer than his for me but there's no point in wagering with you since you won't be alive to pay up!"

Murdac slashed his sword in a cross pattern and approached Robin slowly. "I've been trained to kill with this blade since I was six," he warned. "I don't do my killing with a stick and catgut at a distance. I get close, where I can taste the blood and hear the screams."

"Your mother must be very proud," Robin assured him. "Your father too, if he's still in the kennels."

Murdac released a cry of rage and lunged for Robin.

The outlaw danced to the side, letting the Castellan's blade slide past him. He spun round and caught Murdac's arm instead, then dislocated it.

Murdac's sword dropped from a nerveless hand.

"I've been an outlaw since I ran from the foresters when I was thirteen," Robin told him. "I've led a rebellion against the Sheriff of Nottingham and all his cronies for the last four years. I've faced Black Gisbourne and Aelstan the Butcher and everything de Vendenal's thrown at me. Do you think I haven't been *practicing*?"

Murdac scooped up his fallen blade with his off-hand. Robin hooked the Castellan's legs from under him.

"You ordered the murder of children just now," the outlaw lord accused.

"You set your men to kill my friends. You've terrorised the county and served a villain who's done even worse than you. Are you going to beg for mercy?"

Murdac tried to slash at Robin. The rebel stamped down hard on his wrist then kicked his helm until he held quiet.

Robin pulled his hood back up, shadowing his face; like an executioner. "I gave you your chance to surrender at the gate yesterday," the Hooded Man told the stunned murderer. "This time I'll just send you back to the Sheriff."

Murdac tried to regain his wits as he felt Robin hauling him to his feet. His dislocated arm and shattered wrist made it hard to struggle. His armour seemed too heavy to move. "Wait…" he groaned, ready to bargain for ransom.

Robin heaved him over the edge of the tower, aiming him so he would crash through the roof of the Sheriff's hall below.

"Tell de Vendenal I'm coming," Robin called after him.

VII

illiam de Vendenal was in control.

"Shankshard is fallen," Roger de Montbegum warned. "The outer gate is fallen."

"Shankshard is replaceable," the Sheriff of Nottingham replied. "Even with the Outer Bailey taken the castle is secure." *Indeed*, he reflected, *a taste of victory is the more likely to pin Lionheart to his siege and allow my plans to progress.*

"Men are falling sick at their posts."

De Vendenal hauled one of the sleepy soldiers from the trestle where he'd sunk. He pulled up the man's eyelid, smelled his breath, then dropped him disdainfully face-first onto the flagstones. "Poppy juice," he concluded. "Have the scullions flogged for not keeping a proper watch on the vittles and set a guard on the cook-pot hereafter."

"The common soldiers drop into slumber at their very posts."

"Then let the noble lords who huddle here go out and man the watches. Send Wellbuef, Avanel, Camera, Kellam, all those useless bleating fops who mill around getting in the way of the castle's defence. Let them kick the men until we have soldiers who can shoot."

Montbegum nodded. The Sheriff was never a man to cross, and for all the man's poise he seemed more than ever one wrong word away from drawing a knife and slitting a throat. "I'll... set everyone on it."

"Do that. Stir them all. Set those men aside who won't awaken even when burned with brands. They'll rouse once they've pissed out their sedative, in time for the next attack."

"If Richard makes for the middle gate now..."

"He won't. He'll make a feint, discover it too well defended for a quick breach, and draw his men back in good order for another day. He'll make a few more sallies to soothe his ego, possibly send Huntingdon or Derby on a useless assault at the moat, then amuse himself by hanging the prisoners he took at the gatehouse. At last he'll get bored and head back to his tent for a feast."

"You're very sure."

"I'm much cleverer than he is, and all those who guide him. Richard's brave, even cunning in his own thick way, but he's also a creature of habit. Like the lion he's compared with, he's fierce but lazy. When no easy fight presents itself he'll wait for the siege engines he's summoned and for de

Puiset to turn up with reinforcements. He'll resort to his eastern assault tactics, attrition then sudden assault. All the while the hourglass sands will be running out on his reign."

Montbegum was almost convinced. Almost. "Philip de Worcester says… there is no way the drawbridge should have failed."

"Philip should have his mouth sewed shut and might have yet. We have a saboteur amongst us. Of course we do. Who else poisoned the provender and severed the wheel-chain? And yet he's a saboteur who baulked at mass murder. A man who laces a cauldron with poppy juice could as well lace it with deadly nightshade, but he didn't. A bold man then, but principled, disguised amongst us, recklessly, outrageously daring…" The Sheriff of Nottingham frowned. He looked around suddenly, as if expecting an arrow in his back. "Robin Hood is in the castle!"

Montbegum gasped. "Hood? The forest outlaw?"

"Yes. These events have his stink all over them. He was here. Which means… he is *still* here."

"I can hardly believe that…"

"You need not believe anything, Montbegum, except that when I give orders they will be instantly obeyed. Like these commands now." The Sheriff's eyes narrowed as he surveyed the chaotic crowded dining hall. Where was Robin Hood? "Gather every noble in the fortress. Have them rouse every man that will wake. Begin a search, from the lowest dungeon to the highest turret, with groups of no less than three searchers together. Send word to the warders of the middle drawbridge to carry out my contingencies and disconnect the winding mechanisms so that those gates cannot be sabotaged. Man the inner watchpoints I previously designated; none must pass but they are recognised and vouched for by two comrades or an officer known to the guard. Loxley is here, and I shall have him!"

Montbegum had seen nothing else break through the Sheriff's veneer of calm. For the first time de Vendenal's body language betrayed uncertainly; maybe even fear?

"You cannot be certain that the wolfshead is in the castle," Montbegum offered.

Ralph Murdac crashed through the tiles of the hall roof, bounced off a cross-beam, then burst and splattered across the floor.

"He is here," said de Vendenal.

King Richard the Lionheart stood beneath the broken outer gate, where his standard was raised in place of the arms of Nottingham castle. He surveyed his conquest with a visceral satisfaction.

He noticed the young man who'd followed him through the fray, the forest lad who'd taken up the royal banner and drawn the kings' knights on after their monarch. The youngster still hovered beside the fluttering flag. No one had told him to stop. He was weeping.

"You were kin or friend to the lad who hurled himself in front of the arrow that else would have killed me," Richard recognised.

"His name was David. He was champion boxer of Doncaster. He was my best friend," the miller's son blurted. "He were brave and right clever too, and... he was..." Much looked at the king in misery. "I never know the right words to say what I mean."

"He was a great heart and a bold fellow, who saved the King of England and changed the destinies of nations," Richard declared. His brow furrowed. "And yet he was a common forest vagabond, with no breeding or title. He had no reason to be loyal to me."

"He just did it 'cause it was right," Much wept. "You al'us have to do what's right. Even if it kills you."

Lionheart was surprised to find himself a little shamed by an outlaw simpleton. "Who told you that?" he asked,

"Our Robin. And Marion. And Tuck, when he's sober. And... well, everyone knows it, don't they? Right inside, deeper than words even go. You have to do what's right, no matter what. You have to fight for people who can't do it themselves. You have to help folks when they're in trouble. You have to stop bad men doing bad things. What else are we for? What else are you for?"

Other nobles had gathered round their king. Richard looked from Huntingdon to Ferrers, from Chester to the Archbishop of Canterbury. "Only a fool speaks so to a king," he told them, "and it is why kings must attend to their words."

Much looked up, puzzled.

Richard clapped him on the shoulder. "You followed me through the thick of battle and bore my standard bravely, though your friend lay dead for saving me. You shall have a farm of me, with lands and livestock. And your friend shall have a tomb, with masses sung each day for his soul's sake, in the Abbey of Westminster where kings are set to rest."

Much hesitated. "King Lionheart?" he ventured.

"Speak."

"Sir, thank you for David's tomb, but I think if it's all the same he'd like to be buried in Sherwood. There's a little bit of a bank by the river where Stutely lies, and the others who've gone to heaven. I think David would like to lie there, please. Then I can go and talk to him sometimes, and we can watch the little birds diving into the water, and I can tell him how his friends are doing. In Sherwood Forest nothing's forgotten, you see. I'm sure David would want the choirs though. He likes singing."

Richard smiled. "A Sherwood rest for him, then. Let his memorial be that I remember him, and will never forget what you have said."

"And," Much asked urgently, "please King Lionheart, can I not have a farm but a mill? Only I don't know about farming, but I've ground corn between stones since ever I could walk and I can do that. I would take very good care of your mill."

"A forest plot and a new mill, then," Richard agreed, "for the heroes of the Siege of Nottingham."

The outlaws were forming up. The news came before the gory remains of the Castellan had even been scraped from the bloody straw. The men of Sherwood, in their Lincoln green camouflage, were assembling in a single line beside the outer curtain wall. Seven-score of them, the observers said, and they stood with perfect discipline waiting for something.

De Vendenal ventured to the battlements to see for himself. Without Murdac and Shankshard there was no one he trusted to go check for him. He kept Lewis of Newark at his side as bodyguard.

There, sheltered from the castle's arrows behind crude wooden shields, stood the whole strength of Robin Hood's men. The Sheriff could discern the great giant known as Little John and the portly monk they called Friar Tuck. Even Matilda of Leaford was there, organising their ranks. They stood silent, quite separate from King Richard's command that were hauling away captives for the gallows. They were waiting.

The Sheriff noted three covered carts with them, each piled high with contents obscured under canvas. Coils of rope were carefully laid out at intervals along their ranks, ready for some unknown purpose. A few men carried torches though it was only early evening. At the furthest end of the line, a pair of youngsters and an old poacher struggled with a bull.

De Vendenal's eyes darted down to the middle gate. Everything *seemed* in good order there. The Worcesters commanded there now; but could he rely upon the venal knights not to turn their coats? Richard's unexpected capture of the Outer Bailey had shaken the confidence of the Sheriff's allies. Terms offered by Huntingdon and Chester at parlay yesterday might seem fairer now that prisoners were being led to the gibbet beyond the walls.

The Sheriff had ordered the middle drawbridge disabled to preclude more treachery or trickery, but he could not afford to underestimate Robin Hood. A simple trick with a cook-pot had halved the castle's strength for a few hours. How many of the Sheriff's tested brutes remained conscious and loyal? How reliable were the other polyglot companies of soldiers crammed together inside the siege defences?

What was Robin Hood planning?

De Vendenal looked out over the line of forest men. They were waiting for a signal. Waiting to do what?

The Sheriff glanced to Lewis of Newark. The herald was useless. No-one could discern the plans of Robin Hood save William de Vendenal alone. The Sheriff flailed his mind for the answer: what linked a line of waiting outlaws, high shields, rope, torches, carts of hidden equipment, and a bull?

"Find how the search for Robin Hood progresses. Report back quickly," he ordered Lewis.

The Sheriff felt vulnerable on the wall. He descended into the keep once more, seeking comfort in the thick dark walls of the castle's strongest part. He stood on the gallery above the inner hall; darker and more confined than the feasting hall beside the inner courtyard, which was currently splattered with his Castellan. He looked down at the deserted space lit by dusty shafts from the thin arrow-slit windows. The walls were bare now, stripped of banners and tapestries that might catch fire. He snarled when he saw the archers in the window-nooks were dozing, drugged at their posts.

The guards to the upper floors were alert, however. They snapped to attention as their Sheriff approached them. De Vendenal pulled off their helmets so he could check their faces.

Lewis returned. "They haven't found him," he reported briefly. "They're searching again, everywhere, but so far there's no sign. Maybe he left?"

"How?" snarled the Sheriff. "He threw Murdac through the roof! That means he was on one of the south-eastern towers or more likely atop the keep itself! There is exactly one—one!—spiral stairway to the roof of the keep and to the turrets above. One. It's not like he could have taken a different route. So how did he escape? Robin Hood is clever, but he cannot fly."

The herald was at a loss. "I… don't know, my lord."

De Vendenal hissed. "How would I do it? I would… yes, I'd send Murdac down precisely so that guards would rush up to the rooftop. I'd be on

What was Robin Hood planning?

the stairs, halfway down, facing upwards, dressed in a borrowed surcoat. When the soldiers rushed up behind me I'd start scrambling up the spiral too, as if I were another one of them, ahead of the rest, leading those that came after. I'd run up there with the others and join in the general search. No-one would question me, because I arrived with the rest! And then… I'd go back down with the men I'd joined and stay with them, known and accepted, as they continued on their hunt."

Lewis of Newark frowned. "But that means Robin Hood could be anywhere!"

"Go back to the captains," the Sheriff commanded him. "Hood uses even our search against us. Every man, *every man*, is to report to his master. Every wench too, even the meanest kitchen whore. *Everyone* is verified. Then all will be assigned their places, including search parties of three or more who will quarter the fortress again. Every area they search will be sealed off under guard to prevent it being occupied anew. Anyone they do not recognise must be brought to their commander to be identified. Is that clear?"

"It will take some time, Lord William. So many of the men are somnolent…"

"Do it. And seal the keep. Hood is playing us still. What does he intend next?"

Lewis hastened off again. De Vendenal looked around the keep's hall, thinking furiously, trying to second-guess Robin Hood. The soldiers closed and barred the huge reinforced door, locking the bailey off from even the rest of the castle.

"You six men, with me," the Sheriff decided. "*We* shall search this keep from cellar to tower, every inch. Robin of Loxley is arrogant. If he is hiding then it is most likely to be in my most secure stronghold. Let us winkle him out!"

Robin's outlaws were assembled outside, waiting. De Vendenal did not like it. He hastened to find their leader before whatever they were massed for came to pass.

The Sheriff of Nottingham chased Robin Hood!

The search took too long. De Vendenal retreated to his solar. Of all the rooms in the keep it alone faced the inner ward and had proper windows with horn glazing. The Sheriff glanced over at his carved fireplace, his secret exit if things became too difficult, and resisted the urge to use it now. He positioned his guards flanking the only door. He checked under his desk—again—and poured himself a glass of wine. He ensured that his hand did not tremble.

He set the cup aside again. If Robin Hood could pass through the fortress undetected to doctor the common pot then he could penetrate the Sheriff's solar to add opium pulp to a wine pitcher. It would be easy enough for a man of Loxley's talents to enter here with the searchers he'd attached himself to, then lurk behind as they moved on down to chapel and gallery. And then he could…

…*stay right here and wait for my arrival in the one place I am bound to go, sooner or later*, the Sheriff realised.

Robin Hood dropped out of the wide chimney-breast he'd concealed himself inside, the Sheriff's own chimney, which was not lit because firewood was rationed in a siege and because a secret passage lay behind the cunning stonework. The outlaw drew back his bow.

"Guards!" called de Vendenal urgently, swinging round. "*Guards!*"

A precise arrow pinned one of the Sheriff's men to the wall. Another dropped the second sentry dead.

The Sheriff caught up a silver salver on the table before him and spun it at the approaching outlaw like a discus. Robin dodged the metal plate, but by then the Sheriff was at the door and fresh soldiers were pressing in. The wolfshead loosed more shots in rapid succession, taking down the landing guards, but the arrow for de Vendenal slammed into the jamb while the Sheriff dodged away down the stairs.

"Tally-ho,[89] then," the outlaw lord said to himself, and set off in pursuit.

De Vendenal raced down to the second floor landing, where doors led off into the chapel and minstrel gallery. A wider stair descended to the great hall. Surprised guards sprang to alert as their Sheriff clattered past them.

"Robin Hood!" he hissed, pointing. "Perhaps you'd like to kill him?"

The sentries hastened to react. Robin had them at a disadvantage. Fortress stairs were constructed on a tight clockwise spiral, so that the invaders

---

89   This anachronism, first recorded in the sixteenth century as a hunting instruction to charge when the hounds first begin to chase their quarry, and still used by some military pilots when sighting a target, probably came from the French instruction *taille haut*, "size up", used in the battlefield to command a final assault. It's used in our text here along with other out-of-era expressions as the best way of conveying the sense of Robin's dialogue, with his somewhat flippant and colloquial speech patterns. After all, if our cast spoke in accurate Norman French, middle Anglo-Saxon, and mediaeval Latin it might get in the way of some readers' enjoyment – and would be beyond the author's competence.

heading upwards in single file had their right hands, their sword hands, restricted by the narrow central column, while the defenders fighting downward had space to strike freely. Robin sliced down the first charging man then kicked him back into his fellow. The second sentinel was still tangled under his comrade's corpse when the outlaw ended him.

"Sheriff?" Robin called to de Vendenal. "I told you I was coming. Have you worked out my plan yet?"

"Guards!" the Sheriff called to the archers who slumbered in the window-nooks. "You men downstairs, get up here!" He tried to do the mathematics of how many men he had left to put between himself and the Sherwood avenger.

Another pair of soldiers responded, abandoning their watch on the keeps' barricaded inner portals and racing across the hall to join their master. Robin slid onto the gallery and shot them down. "You're running out of minions to hide behind," the outlaw warned the Sheriff.

De Vendenal ducked another arrow and kept to cover as more of his men charged the main stair to the gallery. He calculated that Hood might be able to shoot two, maybe three of them before they were too close. There would still be half a dozen soldiers to hack the intruder down.

"There are *always* more minions, Loxley," the Sheriff crowed.

Robin had done the same calculation. After two lethal shots he shouldered his bow, saluted the inrushing bullies, and launched himself from the balcony over to the wheel of candles that served as the dark hall's chandelier.

"Get more men!" de Vendenal called. "Unbar the keep door. Let reinforcements through!"

Robin dangled upside-down from the swinging chandelier, held on by his folded knees, and shot down the guards that raced for the exit. "This is really meant to be an intimate grudge match, William," he warned the Sheriff as he somersaulted down to the long trestle table below.

Guards rushed down the stairs again to mob Robin. He upended the table-top and used it to push them all back, then abandoned it to leap atop the next trestle for a vantage with his sword.

William de Vendenal bent over a sleeping soldier and borrowed his Genoese crossbow.

Guards tried to scramble onto the table with Robin. The outlaw launched himself again, vaulting over their heads to balance on the staircase balustrade. He retreated up it, fending off soldiers who surged after him three at a time.

At the gallery Robin dropped and rolled, coming up beside a tall iron candelabrum. He seized the sconce and rammed it into the chest of the first man who charged him. The soldier's momentum allowed him to guide the man in a high arc, right over the outlaw's head, then screaming over the gallery rail to a sickening crunch below.

The remaining men hesitated for a mere second. "Catch!" Robin told them, and tossed them the candelabrum. They both grabbed it by instinct; by the time they realised their mistake Robin's blade had scored across their necks. "You've run out of minions after all," the outlaw warned the Sheriff as the melee ended.

"Idiots," de Vendenal eulogised them. "But they served their purpose. I have other tools." The Sheriff raised his crossbow and aimed it right at Robin Hood. "Do not move. I may not be the shot you are but I doubt I'd miss at this range."

Robin held still. "I neutralised your troops but not their weapons," he breathed.

"Indeed." Keeping his crossbow steady, William de Vendenal carefully walked up the stairs to join the outlaw lord on the gallery. "Cast away your sword. That's it. Now step back. Your ploy has failed, Loxley, whatever it was. You are mine!"

"You think I've failed? You still haven't worked out why I came after you alone in your strongest stronghold? Maybe I overestimated your brains."

"*I* am the one holding the bow," the Sheriff pointed out. "You cannot expect to have taken me hostage for the castle's surrender, or even for escape. It would never work. I would not permit it and my fellow defenders are not that loyal. Therefore you wished to have ado with me in a more personal manner. Perhaps you sought vengeance; for your dead comrades, for your oppressed peasants, for your personal reputation. Yes, that's it. I can see the loathing and anger in your eyes. You intended to duel with me, and were arrogant enough to believe you could prevail."

"I'm still planning to fight you, Sheriff," Robin admitted. "You really haven't seen what's happening, have you? Come on! What about that huge brute of an animal out there that Arthur's scarcely restraining?"

De Vendenal paused. "What about it? What's it for? Speak!"

"Or what? You'll shoot me? You're going to do that anyway."

"Oh yes, but only a crippling shot. I intend to take you alive, Loxley. Still, indulge your old enemy. What was the animal's intended purpose?"

Robin grinned. "It's just a load of old bull!" he laughed as he reached for his bow.

De Vendenal fired the crossbow. The wire snapped. The bolt went wild, embedding itself uselessly in the painted frieze at the back of the gallery.

"Oh, did I mention that I got to all the weapons when I was prowling around before?" Robin wondered. "So much for your shaft. Want to bet you can dodge mine?"

De Vendenal didn't hesitate. The Sheriff closed the distance to the outlaw in an instant, drawing his sword as he came. He moved too fast for the surprised wolfshead, getting to melee range before Robin's arrow was set. He swung his sword to slice the yew bow in half.

Robin caught the blow on the horn grip halfway up the weapon's curve. That deflected de Vendenal's blade long enough for Robin to fall back and seize up his own sword.

The two men clashed, Sheriff and outlaw, above the great hall of Nottingham Castle. Beyond the sealed keep were Prince's men and King's men, forest rogues and frightened townies, all waiting for whatever would happen next. The future was decided in the dark confines of the Sheriff's gallery.

"You've no idea what you're trying to thwart, have you?" de Vendenal scorned. "After you're dead, my power will be absolute. Philip of France is coming. Richard will fall. John will be Philip's puppet lackey. I will be rewarded beyond imagination."

"You're in this for the money? That's the whole reason you've done everything you have?"

"Wealth and influence, yes, but also opportunity. John has no legitimate heirs, you know, and his health is variable. For a man of my capacity there are always possibilities."

"Hard to exploit those possibilities, though, when you're dead," Robin pointed out. "Maybe you missed the part where I came to you in the name of all those you're wronged and oppressed, the people's champion to bring you down!"

"Swords, not sanctimony, forge the future, Loxley. I'm actually glad you've accrued such a legend. Imagine what they'll say of the man who killed you."

The Sheriff almost took Robin by surprise with a clever feint. The outlaw ducked just in time; only wisps of his blonde locks fluttered to the gallery floor.

"Not bad, William," Robin laughed. "You should come out from behind your minions and do your own dirty work more often."

De Vendenal avoided the forest lord's thrust with a cunning parry of his own and planted an elbow in Robin's face. "I like my tools," he confessed to his enemy, "but a true villain is more than his minions."

The fight progressed to the staircase. De Vendenal forced Robin down it, seeking advantage in being above his opponent. Robin was too clever to allow it, retreating until they were level in the hall amidst the fallen soldiers. Hood and de Vendenal weaved around each other, now on stairs, now on tables, around the narrow ledge to the window nooks, over to the roasting fireplace, first one ascendant and then the other. No sane man would have wagered even a penny on a certain outcome.

The Sheriff moved the fight towards the alcove where the siege stores were stacked. Everything he needed would be there. Robin was not the only one who could scheme.

"Almost time, William," Robin assured the Sheriff. "You know that plan of yours, keeping the Lionheart busy while King Philip attacked…?"

De Vendenal's heart lurched. If Robin Hood had the same intent, to divert the Sheriff of Nottingham while some other assault assured his fall…

It suddenly made sense: the outlaws' bizarre preparations; the intimidation that had provoked sealing off the keep; Robin's foolhardy solo attack. The Sheriff looked at his enemy in horror.

Robin winked. "Too late, Sheriff!" he cried.

The outlaw had a horn at his belt. He winded it now.

A coal-brazier constantly burned, to light fire arrows and the pitch-buckets over the gate. De Vendenal upturned it over Robin Hood, spilling the blazing coals so they seared the outlaw's cloak, setting it alight. Robin jumped back to cast his hood and mantle aside and roll on the floor to douse himself.

The Sheriff kicked over the jars of oil so they ignited the scattered embers around the wolfshead. A wall of flame blazed up around Robin Hood.

Another horn sounded outside, down in the Outer Bailey; an outlaw's hunting horn, brassy and insolent. The free men of Sherwood raised a mighty cheer.

De Vendenal snarled. He was too late! Whatever Hood had delayed him for was happening… now!

"Burn, Robin Hood!" the Sheriff screamed at his trapped enemy. "Burn now and burn in perdition!" De Vendenal turned and retreated from the conflagration, up the gallery stairs, over the corpses of his guards, back up the tight spiral to his solar. Every schemer must know when to fight and when to flee, and when it was best to return another day.

Somehow Robin Hood had arranged for Nottingham Castle to fall. The shouts of his merry men were deafening even in the fortress keep. De Vendenal knew now… *knew*…that his only hope of survival was escape.

He barricaded his solar door, then turned the hidden carving that opened the fireplace passage. A narrow vertical shaft with hand and foot niches led straight down through the interior of the keep's thickest wall. From there chalk tunnels went to the Nottingham safe-house and beyond the city to the other side of the Leen.

A fortune in bullion and precious gems was concealed in an antechamber below. It would take him far from Nottingham, safe all the way to Normandy and King Philip's side.

"I almost succeeded," the Sheriff hissed, pale and furious. "May Robin Hood rot in hell."

"What's going on?" demanded Roger de Montbegum. "Where's de Vendenal? What's going on in the keep?"

"I'm not sure, milord," Lewis of Newark admitted. "My Lord Sheriff ordered the gates sealed, but now there is no answer from the guards inside. A horn sounded, but not one of ours. And see that smoke rising from within?"

"Break down the doors!" Montbegum commanded. "Bring hammers and axes. Bring a ram!"

"Nottingham Keep is constructed to resist such things," Lewis warned the nobleman. "Gaining entry will take a very long time."

In the burning hall, Robin staggered to his feet. He was cornered by the fire. More oil jars shattered as the heat reached them, turning the alcove into an inferno.

"This isn't quite what I had in mind," the outlaw lord admitted to himself. The hall was of stone construction and would not burn, but the fumes and the temperature would claim him if the blaze did not.

Robin reached for his bow. Beyond the burning oil pots were huge bath jugs[90] set aside for emergency drinking water and for firefighting. He shot

---

90   Bath jugs were named for the Hebrew measurement, wherein a *bath* was 8.3 gallons of fluid (10 U.S. gallons), and from which we probably derive our modern usage of the word.

off the contents of his quiver, shattering a pot each time, flooding the flagstones with water as well as oil.

He curled and jumped into the flames. He landed, burning, in the water he had spilled on the other side. He rolled, quenched himself, and ran off after William de Vendenal.

Robin Hood hunted the Sheriff of Nottingham!

"Alright," Gilbert Whitehand said to Little John. "We've blown horns and cheered and shouted. What now?"

"Now we go get some ale," the giant answered with a shrug. "Rob just said to line up and do all we did. That's it. Let's get a pint."

De Vendenal pulled the chain that caused the counterbalance to close his escape passage. As the stone rumbled into place his supposedly-sealed solar door crashed open.

"You didn't think I'd tamper with your bolts and hinges while I was loose?" Robin Hood demanded. He fired an arrow that pinned the links of the closing chain to the wall, halting the passage before it could fully shut.

The Sheriff dodged away, making for the ladder to the catacombs below.

Robin pressed himself through the narrow gap into the secret tunnel, then paused to unlodge the shaft that prevented its proper closure. "Have you worked it out yet, William?" he called after the Sheriff. "*This* is the plan. You're clever. Too clever. So I had to make that work against you."

De Vendenal reached the narrow tunnel carved through Castle Rock. He chose the route under the river, out of Nottingham.

Robin's voice echoed after him. "I needed you to believe that I could take down your fortress. That's why I sabotaged the main gate, so you'd doubt your other defences. It's why my men lined up as if they had a way in. It's why I faced you down one on one, as if I was distracting you. A confidence trick."

The Sheriff shielded his candle and pressed on. It wasn't far to the deadfall he'd arranged. From there he could collapse the whole tunnel on top of the lord of Sherwood.

Hood kept talking. "You see, I reckoned you'd have one absolutely-secret bolt-hole only you knew about. Something that'd get you clear if all else failed. Probably linked to a treasure-horde so you could take your ill-gotten gains with you and live to scheme another day. That's the people's treasure, though, robbed for and murdered for by you and your thugs, so we want it back."

De Vendenal found the hidden lever. A cunning frame kept the weight of the tunnel ceiling in place. Triggered, the whole passage behind the Sheriff would tumble down, crushing his pursuer.

"Your tunnel was obviously the only way out of the castle, so I needed you scared enough to use it," Robin called. "If you hadn't been ingenious with your fire trap I'd have had to fumble my attack so you could get away. Fortunately you lived up to my expectations. And here we are. You've deserted your post and your allies. They'll certainly throw themselves on the king's mercy in a day or two to save their skins. Your plans with King Philip are in tatters. You're the wolfshead now, William. I don't recommend you fleeing to Sherwood Forest."

"You've done very well, Robin Hood," the Sheriff admitted. "You've gone from nuisance to obstacle to major threat. You've harmed me more than I thought anyone ever could, and you've played me well, I admit it. But you've underestimated me too. Now comes my revenge. Goodbye!"

He pulled the lever and dropped the tunnel.

VIII

The former Sheriff of Nottingham waited until it was fully night, then emerged from the tunnel's concealed exit. He was a full mile across the Leen. Even if it hadn't been dark, Nottingham Castle would have been a mere set of towers over the thick treeline.

De Vendenal shouldered the heavy pack of gold across his shoulders, checked his sword, and framed his lantern to light his way. Two miles into the wood was a hunting lodge he maintained, with men and resources to see him safe away to the coast, and there to the Continent.

My plans are thwarted for now, he confessed to himself, *but Robin Hood is dead.*

Two miles to the lodge. Two miles through Sherwood.

The night folded in. The Sheriff moved quickly while trying to remain as silent as possible. Wild animals rustled in the undergrowth. Owls and bats hunted amongst the branches overhead. Hostile reflective eyes glared at him as he passed.

Sherwood hated him.

He pressed on. When he heard something that might be a voice murmuring ahead he diverted off to the left, hoping he did not lose the path. He had to slash through thick bramble with his blade. A possible footstep turned him right again, along an old streambed.

Time passed. De Vendenal refilled his lamp and hastened on. He began to worry that he had missed the lodge. He began to fret that the trees around him were shifting to block his way.

Some animal cried out, almost like a human in pain, too near for comfort. The Sheriff veered aside again, through a muddy quag, then into a thick stand of ancient oaks.

There was no moon. De Vendenal never knew where the light came from, but the pale glow illuminated Robin in the Hood.

"Hello, Sheriff," said the Lord of Sherwood.

De Vendenal shied away. "You died."

Robin shrugged. "Then I'm a forest ghost. Why not? It's my forest and I'm her champion. Maybe I'll always be here, at need? Or maybe I'm just smart enough to know not to chase a plotting villain down a tunnel he designed when I can wait for him to come to a kingdom that is mine."

The Sheriff backed away, fumbling for his sword.

Another face lit up, like a green man of old. "Hello, Sheriff," the giant greeted him.

And another, tonsured and round, but grave in judgement tonight like the wrath of God. "Sheriff."

One by one they glimmered around him, firefly-lit, like hungry spectres, the dispossessed of Sherwood, the free men of England.

"Sheriff!" called Will Scarlet, still bloody from his day's work.

"Sheriff!" called Much the Miller, his cry an accusation.

"Sheriff!" hissed Ros of Wickham.

"Sheriff!" challenged Alan a Dale.

"William," disdained Elaine his wife.

"Sheriff," cackled Arthur a Bland, "well, well, well!"

Marion burned before him, her beautiful face set like Nemesis. "Lord William de Vendenal, you have oppressed the people of this land. You have betrayed king, country, and office. You have robbed from the poor to give to the rich. How do you plead?"

De Vendenal turned round, staring from outlaw to outlaw, surrounded. He held his sword before him. "Plead? I don't plead to forest scum! I do not tremble like a superstitious peasant. I am William de Vendenal, your superior. I am…"

"Nothing," said Robin in the Hood, and his voice was deeper than the Sheriff had heard before, and older. "You are nothing now. I have taken it from you."

De Vendenal tried to speak, to voice his defiance. He found himself transfixed like prey before a predator, caught in the gaze of the forest king.

Robin moved to him, knocked his weapon aside so it fell lost in the greensward. "Tomorrow we shall take you to Richard," he promised the fallen Sheriff. "Tonight you dine with us in Sherwood. Tonight you'll learn our secrets at last. You will not enjoy it."

On the third day of the siege, after Richard the Lionheart had hung his prisoners, after de Puiset had arrived with reinforcements and captives from Tickhill, after negotiation with the Archbishop of Canterbury, the defenders of Nottingham Castle opened their gates and yielded themselves absolutely to the justice of their king.

Word reached Philip of France as he was loading his ships for England.

At the same time, forces led by the banners of Longchamp, Coutances, Fitz-warren and many other allies of the English king begin reclaiming Normandy for the Lionheart. The armada was quietly dismissed; the French forces were needed elsewhere.

Three days after the surrender of Nottingham Castle, King Richard held there a high feast and a Royal Council. He sat in state, flanked by the Archbishops of Canterbury and York, advised by the Queen Mother Eleanor of Aquitaine, and their deliberations lasted four days. Thereafter he commanded Prince John to appear before him within forty days to answer charges of treason. Lackland did not come, and dared not venture into England again while his brother lived.

The men who had resisted Richard on John's behalf at Tickhill and at Nottingham were feasted as the king's guests, then stripped of rank, office, and lands until they paid heavy fines to renew the Lionheart's war-coffers. Some eventually managed to do this; others vanished into obscurity.

William de Vendenal was present at banquet and judgement but he took no part in either, muttering to himself, playing with his fingers, starting at any noise. He may not even have understood what was happening as he was marched to the gallows and hung over Nottingham's gates. Earl William of Ferrers was appointed Sheriff of Nottingham in his place.

Little John was present at the feasting with all the company of Sherwood. He clapped Ferrers on the shoulder. "Looking forward to doing business with you, Sheriff," he told the earl.

The outlaws were pardoned formally, to the cheers of the Nottingham crowd. Some, like Arthur and Gilbert, were granted life pensions sufficient for their needs. Much was given his mill. Scarlet was offered a commission in the king's army, a charter to assemble his own company and rise as high and far as his soldiery might take him. Only Marion and Robin were unsurprised when he declined, preferring a quiet retirement where his personal demons could sleep.

Tuck was assigned the hermitage of Finnyngley, and a very free and casual order prevailed there in the years when the fat friar ministered; and yet there was grace. Little John returned to Hathersage with money for land, and with Ros of Wickham and her son, and there were other children to come; yet in the end he found his way to Sherwood again.

Sir Robin FitzHuntingdon received estates and office, a King's Forester possessed of the lands once taken from his wife's family and new estates of his own, master of Loxley, with rights to hunt in royal enclosures and duties to maintain the forest law; but the country people knew those rights were his already, by older authority than their Norman overlords. They held their peace and clapped, but they knew. The king of England and the king of Sherwood hunted together at Palm Sunday that year, and perhaps Richard understood something at last of what the outlaw lord was trying to show him.[91]

A brief peace came to England, while foreign wars raged over the Channel, as John stepped lightly to earn his brother's goodwill and Philip suffered a slow attrition of the territory he had seized. The Lionheart never returned to his crusade and to Saladin, but neither, once had had drained the realm of all the coin he could attain, did he ever return to England. The king spent his last years in European battle and died when a wound from an inconsequential siege festered. He passed away in his mother's lap. It was John who returned as king, only to face rebellion again and to yield to the *Magna Carta* that enshrined forever the rights of the free. Something had awoken in England, from the deep woods to the depths of the human heart, an ideal that would never be forgotten.

"Not bad," judged Robin Hood, as he stretched out on the sunny grass by the Major Oak with Marion laid against him, staring up at the coming summer sky. "What shall we do next?"

The lady of Sherwood whispered a suggestion in his ear. He laughed and pulled her towards him.

The forest kept their secrets.

THE END

---

91   Roger of Hovenden records that "Richard King of England did a perambulation of Clipstone [a royal hunting lodge] and Sherwood which of he had never seen before and it pleased him much."

John Manwood wrote in his *Treatise of the Forest Laws* (c1600): "I have seen many ancient records in the tower of Nottingham Castle very badly kept, and scarce legible; in which Castle the Court is usually kept for Peverill-Fee: Amongst which it appears, that in the year 1194, King Richard being hunting in Sherwood Forest, did chase a hart out of the forest into Barnsdale into Yorkshire; and because he could not recover him, he made a proclamation at Tickhill in Yorkshire, and at several other places thereabout, that no person should kill, hurt or chase the said Hart; and this was afterwards called a Hart-Royal Proclaim'd."

On George a Green, the Forgotten Merry Man
I.A. Watson reintroduces a neglected hero

Pinder is a mediaeval northern English word from the root "pound", as in dog-pound. A pinder or pinner was a civic catcher of stray animals, not only of dogs but of wandering cattle, sheep, goats, horses, and poultry. He was called upon by the town or village that employed him to help handle any wild animal or untrained beast that troubled the settlement. A pinder was generally fast, tough, and probably rough.

One of the most obscure of Robin Hood's merry men was George a Green, the Pinner of Wakefield. He's hardly heard of these days (although naturally he shows up in our Robin Hood volume; we aim at completeness). George's media spotlight has long since faded, but the *tale* of his tale is remarkably modern.

George, like Maid Marion and Friar Tuck and perhaps some others of Robin's band, started out life in his own stories. Just as Marvel Comics likes to guest-star Wolverine or Spider-Man in other titles to boost sales, wandering minstrels and tavern tale-tellers seem to have slipped Robin Hood into George's adventure. Eventually George was overshadowed by the more famous outlaw of Sherwood and at last dwindled to a mere background player. But there was a time…

In summer 1599 , theatregoers had a choice of entertainments to spend their money on. At the newly-opened Globe they could see a new play called *Henry V*, a long-awaited sequel to the vastly popular *Henry VI* parts one and two, by fan-favourite Will Shakespeare. Or they could avoid the long queues and instead settle for a rather less popular production entitled *George a Green, the Pinner of Wakefield*. Yes, George's play came out the same week as *Henry V*, with exactly the same success as *Battleship* being released alongside the *Avengers* movie.

The basics of the play are that George is a tough handsome peasant lad who loves the beautiful Betris. Betris' father, the miserly Grime, instead intends to sell his daughter in marriage to the villainous rebel Bonfild, principal henchman of the even-more-villainous Earl of Kendall who seeks to bring Scots raiders down to ravage the realm. Then the usual things happen. George's friend dresses up as a woman and is lusted after by Grime. The English King, Edward in this setting, disguises himself to go amongst the people. The Scots King James disguises himself too. George makes Kendall eat his warrant of authority. There's a bit with a dog.

And then, in act two, for no good reason other than to pull in the crowds as far as I can see, Robin, Marion, Tuck, and Much show up. As is traditional in hero team-ups then as now, at first Robin and George fight, and then join together to take down Kendall and Bonfild. At the end, the various disguises come off and King Edward commands Grime to wed his daughter to the triumphant George a Green. Hurrah!

George's story was elaborated and expanded upon in a volume entitled *The History of George a'Green, Pinder of the Town of Wakefield, His Birth, Calling, Valour and Reputation in the Country*, by "N.W.", printed in 1706. This gives a good deal more information about the hero, including a long assurance that his surname does not, as was often the case, denote that he was a "natural" child (a bastard). This seems very important to the author, as does his assertion that George was properly schooled and did rather well there. After all, we wouldn't want fair Betris married off to just anyone. Yes, the Pinder of Wakefield was rebooted!

The Pinder also appears in Child Ballad 124, which he entitled "The Pinder of Wakefield," collected from an early seventeenth century source. George isn't named in that one, and his story is rather different. A "jolly pinder" boasts that no-one trespasses upon his watch, Robin tests that, and the pinder joins the merry men. It's one of a number of ballads wherein some tradesman or artisan encounters Robin, fights him to a standstill or better, then is invited to join the outlaw band. A similar encounter appears as a part of Child Ballad 123, as a prologue to the actual story of Robin saving three brothers from being hanged by the Sheriff of Nottingham.

George comes from that forgotten breed of "local" hero who must once have been celebrated in taverns and at home hearths all across England. Most have faded without trace. A few echoes remain, of Clym of the Clough, Adam Cloudslee and suchlike, but many of them have probably been absorbed entirely into Robin Hood's legend, their deeds ascribed after to the Sherwood outlaw. George at least managed to carve out a bit part amongst the Merry Men, somewhere at the back behind David of Doncaster, old Will Stutely, Gilbert of the White Hand, and Riccon Hazel of Flintshire, but at least in front of the tinker Wat o'th' Crabstaff and peddler Gamble Gold.

Look for his Hollywood revival any day now.

IW

How History Was Turned
I.A. Watson rambles on the birth of a nation

It's easy to forget a millennium on, but in 1066 England lost a war and was brutally conquered and colonised. The Normans were Viking stock who had descended on Brittany two generations earlier and had stolen the top third of the lands that would one day make the nation of France. Their most dangerous warlord, William the Bastard, led a hungry force of ambitious reavers in an audacious territory-grab to steal a country and it worked!

Leave it to the history books to look at the rights and wrongs of it, how William was gifted England by saintly but ineffective King Edward the Confessor, which made his actions legal under the Norman code but not under the Saxon law of England where a Parliament of the wise elected a new monarch from a list of suitable royal candidates. Focus on what happened after William won the battle of Hastings, that bloody decade when the Norman conquerors stamped their mark on their new land so hard that the imprint of it is with us a thousand years later.

Those short years after the conquest changed every aspect of English life. For many folks it ended it; the population of the north dropped by as much as half, in what we'd nowadays call ethnic cleansing that left villages burned to the ground and farmland destroyed to starve out any survivors. The loose alliance of Celtic churchmen (and women) was replaced by the strict hierarchies and organised codes of the Catholic faith. The first of the great cathedrals and their powerful dioceses were established. Wooden hill-forts and high places primarily intended to defend a local population and their herds from marauders were replaced with stone castles that could project force over a cowed indigenous peasant workforce. Ancient personal freedoms were lost in a feudal system that tied serfs to their master's land as surely as a slave, denying them ownership of property, freedom of travel, and even the right to wed without their overlord's consent.

I'm sure that Saxon England had been far from a perfect place. Norman England was still a shock to those who survived the coming of the conquerors. A science fiction story where aliens take over the Earth with their superior technology and advanced culture and reorder the planet into work-camps and breeding programmes would hardly be any stranger than the impact those elitist, calculating, ambitious Normans had on the country they had won.

Time scabs over anything. A hundred and twenty-five years later the wounds were still there in England but those original grievances had become an inheritance. Men might remember the wrongs done to their forefathers and foremothers, might mourn for a lost age of different freedoms, but mostly they had to survive in their current age, a different world of manors and churches, of religious and state law, of taxes and tithes; an ordered society designed for productivity, each person placed to support, and in theory at least, be protected by, those above him.

This was England by A.D. 1190, the time of our Robin Hood tales.

Another forgotten aspect of that time is that England was an unimportant part of international politics. Given the significance the country and its wider union as the United Kingdom of Great Britain would later have on world history through its navy, empire, industrial revolution, and starring role in two World Wars, it's difficult to recall a time when a king or lord might view England as one of his lesser holdings, a foggy wet and unpleasant territory best avoided for the summer warmth of more prosperous and profitable European lands.

Richard the Lionheart, who ruled England from 1189-99, was also Richard IV of Normandy, Duke of Aquitaine, Gascony, and Cyprus, Count of Anjou, Maine, and Nantes, and Overlord of Brittany. He didn't speak the common language of England and spent less than eleven months of an eleven-year reign in the country. His wife Berengaria of Navarre has the distinction of being the only English queen never to visit England during her husband's rule. Richard was typical of many rulers and lords who held widespread disparate estates that supported their lifestyle but were absentee landlords.

By 1190 this was starting to change. The Norman lords of England were starting to define themselves as English. Marriage and bastardy had mingled Saxon and Norman as it had mingled Saxon, Roman, and Celt before. In the lifetime of Richard and John, war and politics meant that lords really had to decide whether to hold lands and allegiances in England or mainland Europe; it was not practical any more to own both. The English language began to develop, as bastard a hybrid of ancient Celtic, Saxon, Latin, Greek, Norman, French, and Viking as the people who spoke it; we still speak it today.

England was forming. William's grandchildren and great-grandchildren went to civil war with each other to rule. The country was torn apart by the contest of Empress Maud and King Stephen, aunt and nephew, both claiming to be monarch of England. A generation of strife, dividing families and wrecking territories, was the crucible for forging the medieval age as we tend to picture it. When that bloody conflict was finally resolved, after everyone was exhausted or dead, the rulership was passed to Maud's son, Henry II, who managed to maintain the state over thirty-five years of relative stability. On his death his crown passed to his rebellious son Richard I, known for his courage as the Lionheart. When Richard died, Henry II's last surviving son inherited as King John.

England was forming but not as its rulers might have wished or intended. The church was the richest and most powerful faction, an international organisation with its own military as well as spiritual armies. The barons descended from William's rewarded reavers had grown proud, powerful, and independent, jealous of their rights and privileges. Merchants and craftsmen were becoming important too, as cities began to take on authority of their own and trade controlled capital and labour. A new middle-class was gradually growing. And those serfs, the oppressed mass that accounted for eighty percent of the population, they too had their ideas and their dreams.

It turned out that nothing was forgotten. A thousand years before, Julius Caesar had written in his campaign memoirs of wild English natives attacking his legions stark naked save for blue woad paint, terrifying his troops with their reckless bravery. At times of need since, Britons had hidden from their enemies in trackless marshland and dense forest, gathering their rebellions and returning to fight again with relentless force.[92] Now, after a hundred and thirty years of the new regime, the resistance that had forced the Norman conquerors to more than decimate their new subjects bubbled up again.

The English (and Welsh) bowman was a game-changer. With man-high bows that could punch a yew-shaft through the best plate mail, a row of these yeomen could devastate a mounted, armoured column of knights. They proved it again and again, at Crécy and Agincourt and a hundred other places. Those bows, shaped from easy-to-find materials, used by commoners, shifted the balance of power. One man hidden in forest cover could kill a king. A hundred could fight an army.

It all came to a head with the 1215 Baron's Revolt against weak King John – the weaselly John Lackland of our Robin Hood stories. Great men like Bigod, de Clare, FitzWalter, de Lacy, de Manderville, and de Percy assembled against their ruler, challenged his divine right, and eventually forced him to sign the *Magna Carta*, the great charter, which established

---

92   King Alfred the Great, Ethelred the Unready, and Hereward the Wake, for example.

basic principles of human rights and altered the character of England forever. Every great statement of principle since, from the American Declaration of Independence to the U.N.'s Universal Declaration of Human Rights owes a debt to these rebels.

That Charter, though sometimes revoked and often ignored, changed the course of English history. It and the principles it enshrined, of trial by jury, limits to royal power, and basic freedoms,[93] cultivated a slow transformation where Saxon and Norman became English. France and Russia effected radical social change through revolution, Germany and Spain through civil war. England blossomed through a gradual growth of individual liberties which eventually encouraged education, social welfare, political freedoms, and an understanding of natural human rights. Canada, the United States, Australia and other democracies have lifted that same banner and held it high. We celebrate our rebels when they bring us such great gifts.

I.A. Watson
Freeman of Yorkshire, England
February 2014

---

93   Clause 29 is one of three still in force today in British law: "NO freeman shall be taken or imprisoned, to be disseised of his Freehold, or Liberties, or free Customs, to be outlawed, or exiled, or any other wise destroyed; nor will We [the Crown] not pass upon him, nor condemn him, but by lawful judgement of his Peers, or by the Law of the land. We will sell to no man, we will not deny or defer to any man either Justice or Right."

Clause 48 insisted that all "evil customs" associated with forests were abolished.

A Sign of the Times
I.A. Watson reflects upon the forbidden legend of Robin Hood.

Volumes 1-3 of this Robin Hood series were almost planned; by which I mean I set out to write a Robin Hood book at suggestion of publisher Airship 27, then found that the plot I'd sketched out and the things I wanted to include in the story fitted better as three books than one. Fortunately my publishers were helpful, so I got three Best Pulp Novel nominations in three different years.

This volume wasn't planned at all. I was convinced to write a short Robin tale for promotional purposes, for a magazine and then for inclusion on my online Robin Hood site at http://www.chillwater.org.uk/writing/robinhome.htm And then another. We discussed the possibility of collecting them in a compilation prestige edition with the whole trilogy, as special features.

And then I did a word count. The unpublished Robin Hood material on my hard drive exceeded the word count of any of those three published novels. Eighty percent of it had never seen the light of day before. And Robin is the master of escaping into the daylight.

So, volume four! That allowed me to tell some stories that wouldn't fit into the three-part adventure that followed the consequences of Robin and Marion's first meeting and subsequent courtship/rebellion. I could pick up on some plot points it wasn't feasible or appropriate to develop in those books. I could work in most of the other major stories from Robin's pre-19th century canon. I could mesh the cast more into real-world history, placing the merry man at some turning points in Richard's reign; the fall of London and the Lionheart's return to England. And I could revisit some characters I'd had fun writing and see how they were getting on.

So far so good. But books should be more than just more-of-the-same-you-liked-last-time. A fourth volume, and an anthology at that, must have something to say, a theme to develop, a larger purpose. Oh, and it needed a title.

Look at the dedication at the front of this edition. Those are the names of fellow writers and artists who contributed serious or hopefully-not-serious suggestions for what to call this publication. Thanks, guys, for *Robin Hood: Dead on Target*, *Giving Prince John the Shaft*, and the too-on-the-nail *Further Adventures of Robin Hood Part 1*. But also suggested were *Beyond Sherwood*, apposite because much of this volume's content takes Robin outside his traditional haunt and past his main phase as the Sheriff's outlaw enemy, *Four Ballads of Robin Hood*, touching on Robin's legendary nature, and *The Forgotten Adventures of Robin Hood*. This last was especially apt given that when I came to assemble the volume I found another Robin Hood story I'd written, which appears now as the prologue to this volume, that I'd *completely forgotten I'd written!*

Those suggestions got me thinking. Actually, the tales presented here aren't about Robin's adventures being forgotten. They're about them being remembered, and told. And about their telling, and the people they are told about, being forbidden.

Like it says in the frontispiece: "It was forbidden to speak of Robin Hood, yet everyone knew his name."

And there, like a mystical white deer emerging from the depths of Sherwood, was the book's theme. It had secretly woven itself into the stories already; outlaws, by their nature forbidden, and stories about their joyous rebellion for what's right, tales becoming legend. A little tweaking and rewriting and the book might well be about that; and suppressed legends are a worthy topic to write about.

All of which neatly reduced down to *Robin Hood: Forbidden Legend*.

But…

Legendary and *iconic* are much abused word these days, co-opted by the marketing industry in the same way that amazing, stunning, fantastic, marvellous, and brilliant have been before them. As a writer who values words, I don't accept that a video game series that first appeared five years ago can be legendary. I don't think proprietary characters from a modern cartoon series are yet iconic.

Sherlock Holmes and Dracula are probably the most recent icons added to our fictional pantheon if we use icon in the modern sense as person or thing regarded as a symbol.[94] In another fifty years, James Bond and Doctor Who may join them. Each of these possesses the characteristics prerequisite of the appellation: they occupy distinctive epitomising primary niches in their kind of storytelling and their folklore and trappings are familiar to the vast majority of people.

Robin Hood, though. Legendary and forbidden?

It's hard to argue that Robin Hood isn't an icon. For hundreds of years he's been the patron saint of rebels, of breaking-the-law-for-good-reason, of laughing at authority, of doing wrong to do greater right. Someone who

---

94　*The Oxford English Dictionary*'s second definition of icon is "[a] person or thing regarded as a representative symbol of something".

does that today is often described as "a Robin Hood", from the good 'ol Duke boys of Hazzard County to the anonymous do-gooders so beloved of the popular press in the Christmas silly season. Through the century from 1268 onward there are at least eight mentions in the rolls of English Justices to "Robinhoods" or "Rabunhods", referring to felons who behaved like the infamous outlaw.

A similar recorded description appears in a legal petition presented to Parliament in 1439 that cited a felon "who having no liflode [living], ne sufficeante of goodes [or sufficient goods], gadered and assembled unto him many misdoers, beynge of his clothynge, and, in manere of insurrection, wente into the wodes in that countrie, like as it hadde be Robyn Hude and his meyne."[95] Robert Cecil branded Guy Fawkes and the conspirators of the Gunpowder Plot as "Robin Hoods" after their 1605 attempt to blow up the Palace of Westminster and the sitting Parliament along with it. Now *that's* iconic.[96]

Icons who have stories attached to them tend to accrete legends. In English lore the greatest of these are King Arthur and Robin Hood. Most people can name Robin's principal companions, his main exploits, and his greatest adversary. Robin's first riverside encounter with either Little John or Friar Tuck, the archery contest where he disguised himself to win the prize, and his dying final arrow-shot are generally well known.

A couple of hundred years back ballad-listeners would have also cited Robin's encounter with the Poor Knight Sir Richard at the Lee, his rescue of the Widow's Three Sons, his capture of a pirate ship from a humble fishing skiff, his mighty leap from cliff to sea to escape capture, his exploits disguised as a beggar, Little John's undercover time in the Sheriff's guard, vile Gisbourne's outlaw hunt, Prince John's thwarted lust for the Maid Marion, Robin stealing an unwilling bride from her forced wedding, and a dozen other exploits. Many of these less remembered tales have wormed their way back into my retelling of Hood's exploits. How could they not?

Legends have meanings beyond the mere narrative. Even old fairy tales have their messages; "don't talk with strangers in the wood" or "kind deeds done with no thought of reward often have unexpected and wonderful

---

95   The deficiencies of Piers Venables of Ashton, Derbyshire appear in *Rotulae Parliamentariae* volume 16 – that's the official rolls (minutes) of the English Parliament. The government acknowledged Robin Hood – as common knowledge!

96   Every English schoolchild knows the old Guy Fawkes Night / Bonfire Night rhyme: "Remember, remember the 5th of November / Gunpowder treason and plot/ I see no reason why gunpowder treason / should ever be forgot!" There's another forbidden legend

consequences". Legends tend to embody ideals, worldviews, cultural expectations and aspirations. Hercules and Jason tell us much about Greek civilisation. Thor tells us a lot about the Vikings, John Bunyan and John Henry about American pioneers. Robin Hood tells us about medieval England and about our world today.

More than most legends, an outlaw who bucks the system to bring true justice to those who'd use the law for their own ends resonates today as much as he did for those 13th century tavern patrons. We still live in a society where powerful, rich and seemingly-overwhelming interests sometimes seek to regulate, oppress, and exploit. We still enjoy Robin Hood scoffing at such authority and sparking off rebellion wherever he appears; and usually rebelling in such a good-humoured way as to make civil disobedience *fun*.[97]

Legends affect our thinking. They're part of our cultural heritage that in turn shapes our opinions, expectations, loyalties, and ethics. Anyone raised knowing about Robin Hood knows that sometimes 'the Sheriff' has to be defied, that sometimes good men must assemble to stand for what matters, that the poor and defenceless must never be forgotten or abandoned to their misery.

One of the most satisfying parts of writing these Robin Hood stories has been meshing the presumably-fictional Robin into real history. Legends work best when they rub shoulders with real life. Key events in the stories of this book really happened.

William de Longchamp did fall from power and flee London, leaving it and the Tower to a triumphant John. He did have a sister Melisend, whose final fate is unrecorded. Longchamp was senior amongst the people who recovered Richard from captivity and remained a stanch supporter of the Lionheart during his continental wars for the rest of his life.

London did walk a tightrope to retain independence during John's reign and fast-changing fortunes. One of three provisions of the *Magna Carta* that is still in English law-books today in their original form is clause 9: "The City of London shall have all the old liberties and customs which it hath been used to have."

Formidable Queen Eleanor did squeeze church and barons for Richard's ransom. Prince John tried to counter-bid and was roundly reproved. He probably got his face spit-washed by Eleanor's hanky too.

Richard the Lionheart did return to an England under John's control

---

97   A grim, vengeance-filled Sherwood outlaw can be a compelling story, but its not the story of Robin Hood; the Count of Monte Cristo maybe?

in 1194. He had allies in Huntingdon and de Puiset, both of whom played prominent parts in retaking key strategic assets back for the king. Huntingdon's prominence in capturing Nottingham Castle alongside Richard may have been one reason for his association as Robin Hood in Elizabethan literature. The fortress at Nottingham did fall to force for the only time in its history; then again, Richard had with him the same siege experts that had reduced formidable Moor fortresses in the Holy Land.

Lord William de Vendenal vanished from history after the castle's capture. A new sheriff was listed from that year.

Richard returned to England only briefly, as the concluding section of "The Black Monk" describes. Five years later he was dead, having named his younger brother as his heir. King John reigned for seventeen years, during which he lost Normandy and his crown jewels,[98] and was forced by the Baron's Revolt to accede to the provisions of the *Magna Carta*; twice, since he went back on it the first time.

The *Magna Carta* signing is really the natural end of the era of Robin Hood. That landmark declaration of rights directly addressed many of the injustices which Robin was narrated to have fought. Landowners, lords, and kings were still often cruel and unfair after that, of course, but they could no longer do it under cover of the law and pretence of right. After that document, the balance began to inexorably tilt towards representation, democracy, and universal liberty. We're still working through all of its ramifications. I hope we'll one day get there.

And the forbidden aspect of Robin's legend? Well, his tales have variously been considered low tavern fare, low playgoers' fare, seditious anarchy, communist nonsense, vestiges of secret pagan forest worship, remembrances of the fairy green man, political manifesto disguised as ribaldry, social satire, and more things than could be listed if this endpiece was an entire book itself. Labelling something controls it. Robin doesn't like to be controlled. He won't be pinned down. Forbid him and he will never go away. Forbid him and we will never forget him.

I've enjoyed in the course of these stories assembling many of the major players of the Baron's Revolt and associating them with each other and with Robin's ideals. In this version of the legend at least, the Fitzwarren alliance and its unconventional forest adjunct were the glue that first brought those rebel lords together. I intend to some day address that final Robin Hood

---

98   In 1216, during the Baron's Revolt, the royal retinue took a shortcut across the tidal estuaries known as the Wash. Much of John's baggage was lost to "quicksand and whirlpools", including the crown jewels. This has occasioned generations of history classroom laundry humour about Lackland "losing his crown in the wash".

story, surely the crowning achievement of the rebel's remarkable career, an impossible shot that reverberates through history to the free world today; and perhaps echoes to those parts of the world that still yearn to be free.

Legends amuse and exemplify, but legends and their icons also inspire. Let the tyrants and evil Sheriffs beware. Truth can be forbidden but never silenced. There is still a forest, and somewhere in it there is Robin Hood!

Forbidden legends are the most dangerous and powerful of all.

I.A. Watson
On the edge of Sherwood
February 2014

More of I.A. Watson's Robin Hood stories appear in his novels:

ROBIN HOOD: KING OF SHERWOOD,
(soon to be re-issued in a new edition by Airship 27 Productions)

ROBIN HOOD: ARROW OF JUSTICE
(soon to be re-issued in a new edition by Airship 27 Productions)

ROBIN HOOD: FREEDOM'S CHAMPION
ISBN: 0-615852-94-7 ISBN 13: 978-0-615852-94-2

All these books are produced and published by Airship 27 Productions. Links to the Amazon.com, Kindle and PDF versions of these books may be found at Airship27Hangar.com

Sample chapters, links to purchase print or electronic copies, maps and additional information about Robin Hood's cast and world appear at I.A. Watson's **Robin Hood Homepage** at www.chillwater.org.uk/writing/robinhome.htm

A full list of I.A. Watson's fiction works with more free material is available at http://www.chillwater.org.uk/writing/iawatsonhome.htm

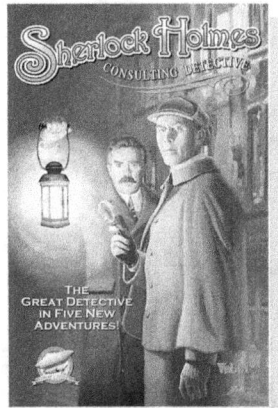

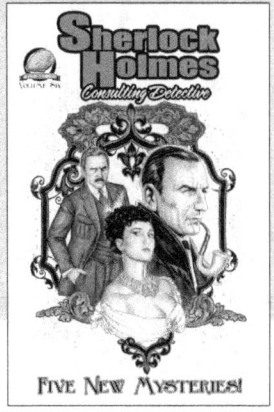

SET SAIL FOR ADVENTURE

The greatest seafaring adventurer of all times returns to the high seas, Sinbad the Sailor!

Born of countless legends and myths, this fearless rogue sets sail across the seven seas aboard his ship, the Blue Nymph, accompanied by an international crew of colorful, larger-than-life characters. Chief among these are the irascible Omar, a veteran seamen and trusted first mate, the blond Viking giant, Ralf Gunarson, the sophisticated archer from Gaul, Henri Delacrois and the mysterious, lovely and deadly female samurai, Tishimi Osara. All of them banded together to follow their famous captain on perilous new voyages across the world's oceans.

So pack up your you traveling bags, bid ado to your loved ones and get ready to sail with the tide as Sinbad El Ari takes the tiller and the Blue Nymph sets sails once more; its destination worlds of wonder, mystery and high adventure.

www.ingramcontent.com/pod-product-compliance
Lightning Source LLC
Chambersburg PA
CBHW071234250626
47163CB00001B/169